I0631674

THE FLOAT

A Novel

by

WF Waldrip

WF Waldrip
The Float

WF Waldrip is an attorney, adventurer and a novelist, who since early childhood dreamed of writing stories that readers would enjoy. He is the author of *The Guards Themselves, Honor Among Thieves* and *The Float*.

BOOKS BY WF WALDRIP

The Float

Honor Among Thieves

The Guards Themselves

The Float

WF Waldrip

FIRST PHARAOH Paperback EDITION

OCTOBER 2016

Copyright © 2016 by WF Waldrip

All rights reserved. Published in the United States by Pharaoh LLC, Phoenix, Arizona.

The Float is a work of fiction. Names, characters, places, and incidents are either the product of the author's imagination or are used fictitiously. Any resemblance to actual persons, living or dead, events, or locales is entirely coincidental.

The Cataloging-in-Publication Data is on file at Library of Congress.

ISBN: 978-0-9978434-1-5

In accordance with the U.S. Copyright Act of 1976, the scanning, uploading, and electronic sharing of any part of this book without the permission of the publisher is unlawful piracy and theft of the author's intellectual property. If you would like to use material from the book (other than for review purposes), prior written permission must be obtained by contacting the author at wwaldrip@gmail.com Thank you for your support of the author's rights.

ACKNOWLEDGEMENTS

The author expresses his sincere gratitude to Maurice Azurdia and Joaquin Chan for their inimitable contributions toward the creation of The Float. Without their steadfast assistance, the entire project would have been stillborn. Thank you, gentlemen.

Thanks are also due Deb for her long-suffering patience in enduring my grouchiness while writing The Float.

For my mother, Barbara Lee Kelley

People have long argued about the location of Hell.
Frankly, we have discovered it.

Comte Louise Antoine de Bouganville, 1768

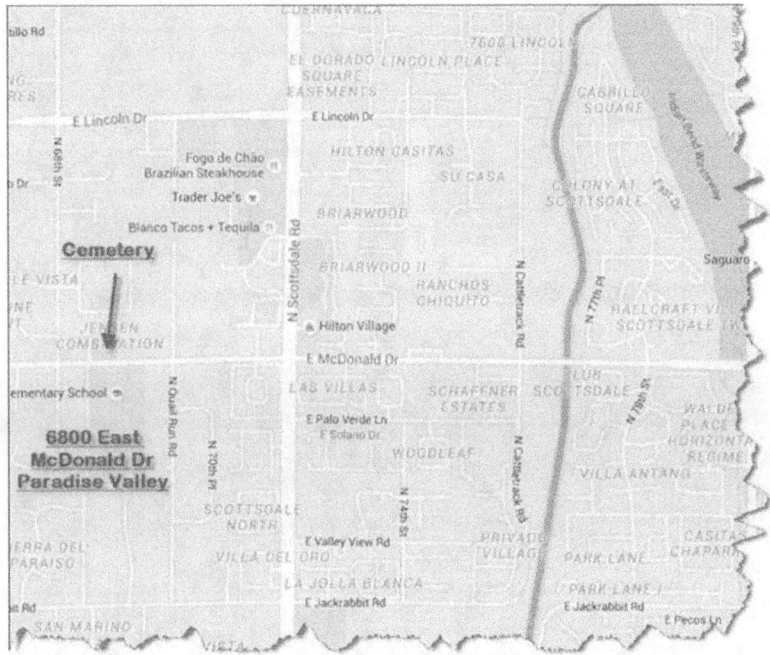

ANNO DOMINI NOSTRI IESU CHRISTO
1813

DON LUIS MARIA CABEZA de Baca eagerly broke the red wax disc bearing the embossed seal of the Spanish Crown and unfolded the crisp bundle of papers. He carefully smoothed them atop the heavy table with the palms of his hands, pressed a jeweled lorgnette, elaborately mounted in chased silver, against the bridge of his nose, and leaned forward to begin reading.

Fernando VII de Borbon, by the grace of God most famous and exalted King of the Castilians, Sovereign and Duke of Aquitaine and Castile, to his devoted and illustrious servant Don Luis de Baca, our kinsman and dearest friend, receive our greetings and our grace.

Don Luis glossed over the document's salutary platitudes, impatient to reach its donative provisions.

The sincere love and esteem in which we enfold you and the due solicitude that befits and is incumbent on our position and incites us to provide for our devotee, and to do our utmost for the benefit of our faithful dependent inasmuch as it is consistent with God.

The nobleman peevishly flipped through the remaining pages. Toward the bottom of the pile he encountered a map of New Spain, which he avidly scrutinized.

Our magnificence rules over the whole of the known world, beyond the seas as far as the rising of the sun and back through the setting sun. Our dominions encompass deserts, plains, and mountains beyond counting, produce and sustain an infinite variety of horses, wild asses, bears, panthers, centaurs, white blackbirds, silent crickets, women with the heads of animals, giants thirty cubits tall, in fact every type of beast living under the firmament. In our possessions may be found in abundance gold and other diverse and sundry objects of incalculable value of every description, carbuncles, moonstones, onyx, rubies, emeralds, and sapphires.

"Yes, yes," de Baca muttered under his breath as he searched the remaining pages for the specific language he sought. "But where is the tangible reward for my longsuffering devotion, you venal *idiota*? If words were *reales* I would already be as rich as a sultan."

The inestimable regard with which we embrace you compels us in our boundless munificence to demonstrate our sincere friendship and warm affection by bestowing on you as a token of our fidelity and esteem certain lands located in our possessions of New Spain. By virtue of these emoluments you may by the grace of God prosper in His name secure in the knowledge that we remain your pious benefactor. May Jesus Christ defend you and yours from all evil and grant you His benediction.

"*Maldita sea!*" de Baca spat, shoving aside the stack of papers. He was disgusted that the Crown had awarded him land in New Spain rather than a position at Court, an estate in Andalusia, or jewels. "Is it not enough that the *idiota* has bankrupted the country; he now presumes to propitiate me with the gift of worthless property on the other side of the earth? His stupidity is matched only by his presumptuousness! Gallio!" he angrily shouted toward the heavy oak door. "Gallio!"

After a delay, the portal creaked slowly open and an elderly, bent man with a fringe of white hair shuffled into the room. "Yes, my lord?"

"Come here and assist me." De Baca pointed to the documents spread across the table. His amanuensis hobbled across the stone-tiled floor, where de Baca handed the old man a reading glass. "You have been to New Spain, have you not?"

"*Si*, my lord," acknowledged the old man. "I was taken by my master to New Spain when I was a boy to work in his fields of sugar cane. I lived there until I could purchase my way back to *España*."

"And what were your impressions of it?"

Gallio shrugged. "I saw little of New Spain except for the cane fields, my lord. I remember only that it was hot and very *húmedo*, with an abundance of malignant insects and other devilish creatures. There is a bird there, *señor*, about the bigness of a man's thumb and of such iridescence that it beggers description. This bird is produced at night by flowers and, though it possesses no wings, yet is capable of flying both forwards and backwards and can also suspend itself in mid-air. It possesses a long, curved beak with which it sucks the blood from sleeping men. There is also a flying mouse there that preys upon sleeping men and cattle, and likewise drains them of blood. I had never seen such a collection of grotesque creatures as abound in New Spain. There is nothing in *España* with which to compare them, my lord."

De Baca scowled. "Fortune has unexpectedly burdened me with domains in New Spain, Gallio. Study this chart and tell me what you know of them." He swept his hand over the map in the general area of the Mexican mainland.

The old man hunched over the map and placed the reading glass scarcely an inch from his rheumy eye. "I do not know this region," he announced after a moment. He lowered the reading glass and looked blankly at the Hildago.

"Do not know it?" de Baca demanded. "Did you not just tell me that you previously lived in New Spain?"

"*Si*," Gallio patiently acknowledged. "But I lived here, my lord," he placed the tip of his bony finger, its nail long and yellow, on the island of Hispaniola. "Your domains are here; many leagues distant across the *mar*." He dragged his wizened finger across the map to what is now the American Southwest. "I know little of this area, my lord," he repeated.

De Baca turned his attention to the *terra incognita* at the end of Gallio's finger. Completely bereft of detail, it was nothing more than a featureless void.

"Can it be so dissimilar to that region of New Spain with which you *are* familiar?" he asked, more-or-less rhetorically. "How much can it possibly differ from the cane fields that you worked in your youth?"

"I freely confess my ignorance, my lord," Gallio admitted, "though I believe it probable that your possessions there are likely to depart substantially from the tropical island where my master's fields were located, as the *Meseta Central* departs from the *Sierra de Guadarrama*." He looked, almost wistfully, at the map again. "I am told that the sun never sets, nor does it ever rain, on the mainland expanses of New Spain, the region where your new demesnes are apparently located. I have also heard of venomous serpents and other horrifying monsters that abound there, with bells on the end of their tails which they shake vigorously before striking and killing you. These bells resemble the sound of castanets. I am sorry to inform my lord that it is reputed to be an area unfit for godly creatures, a primitive, barbaric place. Nothing is said to exist there but misery and death."

The aristocrat stared at the documents spread before him on the table. "In his laudable wisdom," he sardonically began, "the king has bestowed upon me worthless demesnes in New Spain, though I am uncertain what I am expected to do with them. Perhaps they are amenable to cultivation, perhaps to mining. If what you say is true, however, only stones will grow in the absence of rain, though I am neither a farmer nor a miner." He turned to his factotum, who looked on mutely. "You are an old man, Gallio, and the days allotted to you in this vale of tears are few. It is not fitting," he continued, "that I burden you with the disagreeable task of going abroad in order to superintend my unsought acquisitions in New Spain."

The old man remained stoical, silently grateful for his advanced age.

"However, we must manfully bear such misfortunes as may befall us, confident that God, in His infinite wisdom and mercy, does nothing in vain or without purpose."

"The hand of providence may often be seen in the affairs of men that would otherwise remain obscure, my lord," Gallio counseled. De Baca looked at him with forbearance. "While living in New Spain as a boy, I heard many stories of our redoubtable ancestors, the fearsome *conquistadores,* not excepting even the venerated Cortez himself, caching prodigious amounts of gold in New Spain."

The nobleman directed a penetrating gaze at the old man. "Do you suggest that I reduce myself to the role of freebooter in an effort to locate and secure this supposed bonanza half-way around the globe?" he disdainfully inquired.

"No, indeed, my lord," Gallio quickly assured him with a self-conscious bow. "Your esteemed station would render such an absurd proposal unthinkable, an outrage to your exalted person. But the quantities of gold in certain regions of New Spain are reputably so immense, and so pure, that ingots as large as hens' eggs are reputed to litter the ground. One need only bend and pluck them from the soil."

De Baca's skepticism remained unassuaged. "Yet you did not avail yourself of the copious amounts of gold that you saw lying about your master's cane fields, Gallio? You found it preferable to remain in servitude?"

"New Spain is a vast region, my lord, and encompasses a great deal of the entire Western Hemisphere. The gold I speak of is found on the mainland, not on the multitude of islands that lie offshore in the Caribbean Sea, where my master's fields were located."

"I see," de Baca thoughtfully replied. "But by your own account, New Spain is primitive and barbaric, a place of misery and death. Why would *conquistadores,* or anyone else, secret gold there?"

"Just so, my lord. It is said that some of Cortez's men, disaffected by their prevailing wretchedness and incessant wars with the native *indios*, absconded with a quantity of the *general's* own personal treasure. They supposedly conveyed it northward, in the form of a huge wheel, into the vicinity where my lord's new lands are located."

"A fable, Gallio. Cortez was not a man to be trifled with, as Montezuma quickly learned to his infinite sorrow. Why would that worthy gentleman have allowed his men to abscond with *any* quantity of gold? Why did he not simply pursue them and recover it?"

The old man's eyes glittered. "As I said, my lord, the mainland of New Spain is an abominable place. Nothing exists there but suffering and death. That is why Cortez's faithless soldiers fled northward with their booty, confident that not even the valiant *general* would dare follow them into that odious Gehenna. Cortez simply made good his losses on the broad backs of the *indios*."

De Baca reflected before speaking again. "If New Spain is as insalubrious as you have portrayed it, there appears little incentive for me to undertake the protracted, and hazardous, journey necessary to ascertain the truth of your words, rumors of gold notwithstanding."

Gallio smiled craftily. "Your lordship may recall that he already possesses a *finca* in Durango, in New Spain," he reminded him.

"Indeed, I had forgotten that," de Baca conceded. He brightened. "Is it near my new demesnes?"

Gallio shook his head. "I fear not. Even so, it is undoubtedly closer to them than is *España*, and there are on site any number of worthy gentlemen at your lordship's disposal."

"*Excelente!*" de Baca beamed. "Fetch an inkpot and quill! I wish to dictate a letter, ordering my minions in Durango to hasten to my new demesnes in the north. They will thereafter report to me such things as are to be found there."

Gallio bowed and backed away from the table, then turned and scuttled from the room. With luck, his dilettante employer would soon depart for New Spain, leaving him to enjoy the comforts of de Baca's villa in peace and tranquility.

ONE

"HEY, YOU'RE MOVING IT!" complained Chet. He unconsciously frowned at the plastic knob dangling at the end of the slender chain that Cameron held in his right hand.

"No, I'm not." Cameron held his breath in an effort to ensure that he didn't unintentionally contribute to the movement of the cheap pendulum that was suspended above the game board spread on the floor between the two boys.

"Yes, you are," Chet insisted. "I can see it swing a little bit."

Cameron realized the physical effort required to answer his impatient friend would necessarily cause the knob to oscillate, however slightly. He'd only had the 'Kreskin's ESP' game a few days, his mother having bought it for his birthday after weeks of Cameron's unrelenting harping. She had to have searched far and wide for the game because Kreskin's dated from the 60's and, although it was in great condition, the one she gave him had obviously been used. No matter. Cameron was elated to actually own such a rarity.

Cameron's interest in paranormal subjects was initially sparked when he was seven, after his mother took him to a magic show at a local school. Although those magicians were tyros, their acts confined to conventional sleight-of-hand and pedestrian illusions available for purchase at any magic shop, he was riveted. His interest piqued, Cameron began scouring the Internet about all things magic, which led him inevitably to 'Kreskin's ESP,' a once-popular parlor game that purported to allow users to identify and cultivate their inherent powers of Extra Sensory Perception through the use of a pendulum and a deck of special "ESP Cards."

"Well, if it's moving, it's moving by itself because I'm not moving it," Cameron said. His arm was getting tired and he was finding it increasingly difficult to hold it steady above the game board.

"Wait, I think it's trying to spell something out," Chet blurted excitedly as he hunched further over the game board, on which was printed the alphabet and various symbols. "Don't help it," he pleaded. "Let it do it itself."

"I *am* letting it do it itself," Cameron crossly retorted. The act of speaking caused his outstretched arm to waver, involuntarily increasing the arc of the languidly swinging pendulum.

As the two boys watched intently, the plumb dangling from Cameron's hand wobbled over the game board in wide, lazy circles. Its circuit quickly began to tighten, however, and its momentum began to increase. Even though he strained to remain absolutely still, Cameron wondered whether the pendulum was animated only through imperceptible movements of his arm or shoulder. He flicked his eyes from the suspended knob to Chet, who appeared transfixed.

The pendulum slowed. It seemed to momentarily hover above one of the letters imprinted on the game board before resuming its erratic transit. Another letter eventually followed, then a third and a fourth.

"Are you doing that?" Chet whispered without taking his eyes off the pendulum.

"No," Cameron breathed. The pendulum swept a wide arc over the game board without slowing again. After another interminable minute, he finally lowered his tired arm, allowing the pendulum's chain to curl like a serpent atop the game board.

"H-O-P-E," Chet murmured. He looked blankly at Cameron. "It spelled 'hope.' 'Hope' what? What are you hoping for, Cam? You already got what you wanted for your birthday."

"I'm not sure that's what it said."

"That's what it looked like to me," Chet affirmed. "Hope."

"It's kinda hard to tell *what* it was spelling," Cameron said. "The pendulum was sorta all over the place. I think it depends on your angle."

Chet scowled. "What do *you* think it said?"

"Well, I guess it *could've* said 'hope,'" Cameron admitted.

"So are you hoping for something? Is that supposed to mean something?"

Cameron shook his head. "Not to me. The only thing I was hoping for was that this thing would actually do something." He gestured toward the colorful box that previously housed the pendulum and board, as well as the deck of genuine "ESP Cards."

"It *is* doing something," Chet grinned. "Let's keep messing with it. Lemme do it this time." He scooped up the pendulum and held it over the game board. "I'm gonna ask it 'hope,' what?"

Despite the boys' assiduous efforts during the remainder of that afternoon, and periodically over the following weeks, the pendulum stubbornly refused to divulge additional revelations if, indeed, it had ever done so. Despite its obstinacy, Chet remained absolutely convinced that it had spelled out the word 'hope.' Cameron was less sanguine. Aside from the fact that 'hope,' at least deprived of any context, was meaningless, he wasn't even sure the pendulum had actually designated those particular letters. Cameron suspected that, like the Bible and Shakespeare, one could discover in 'Kreskin's ESP' pretty much whatever one was looking for.

As boys are wont to do as weeks turn into months and months into years, Cameron gradually lost interest in the tedium of Kreskin's ESP, as well as its oracular cousin, the Ouija board. Many years later when he reflected on it, Cameron recalled owning a copy of the formerly popular board game, but couldn't remember what ultimately became of it. In all probability his mom ended up selling Kreskin's at a yard sale. And, even though Kreskin's turned out to be rather less electrifying that he'd originally hoped, Cameron's original, boyish interest in simple parlor magic eventually broadened to include hypnotism, UFO's, teratology, alchemy, psychometry, hauntings, Theosophy, the Golden Dawn, and such occult luminaries as Agrippa, Levi, Swedenborg, Cagliostro, Gurdjieff, Mrs. Piper, and D.D. Home. Although the passage of time inevitably eroded Chet's enthusiasm for such subjects, Cameron's curiosity remained undiminished.

ANNO DOMINI NOSTRI IESU CHRISTO
1821

"EXCELLENCY, I REGRET to inform you of the disappearance of five more *campesinos* during the night." The liveried functionary delivered his dolorous message with trepidation while standing at rigid attention. The *alcalde,* a punctilious man with a spade beard and the reputation as a martinet, personally appointed to his post by no less a personage than the illustrious Luis Maria Cabeza de Baca himself, looked up from his desk after an appropriate delay. His face glistened with perspiration. In defiance of the stifling heat, the *alcalde* insisted on wearing a fitted woolen tunic, its scarlet color and gold-plated buttons signifying the dignity of his office.

In a futile effort to combat the incessant heat of New Spain, citizens, not excluding His Excellency the *alcalde*, draped bed sheets soaked in water over open windows, or hung wetted lengths of canvas in exterior doorways, in a vain attempt to cool the interior of buildings through evaporation. It didn't work. Nothing worked. All one could do was attempt to minimize one's physical exertions as much as possible and huddle in the shade. A measure of respite came only when the sun eventually dropped behind the western hills and the earth, itself, finally shuddered with relief. Citizens dutifully hauled their sleeping mats and cots outdoors, into the cooling evening air, where they would sleep fitfully until the sun began its angry upward march the following morning.

"This land is unfit for living!" the *alcalde* muttered. "It is small wonder the authorities in *Sevilla* fobbed it off onto that blockhead Don Luis. That miserable fellow is the only one stupid enough to consider it a weal, though he has never even trod one foot in this pestilential hell-hole."

The functionary remained at uncomfortable attention, sweating profusely.

"What are the names of the latest *campesinos*?" scowled the *alcalde*. The subordinate extended a scrap of rumpled paper, damp with perspiration. The *alcalde* took the list and glanced at it. "At this rate the entire *pueblo* will be depopulated within a year's time." He looked up at the bearer of the unhappy tidings. "And what are your men doing to find these unfortunates?"

"We are searching the surrounding *desierto*, Excellency. However, it is a vast area and the soldiers are fearful."

"Fearful!" spat the *alcalde*. "Your soldiers are more like timorous old women than men. Of what are they fearful?"

"They fear *indios* and the heat, Excellency. But mostly they fear the dead."

The *alcalde* scoffed. "You are prey to childish superstitions, Diego. *Indios* and heat, yes, but it is not the dead they should fear. The dead are powerless to harm anyone."

The functionary's eyes flitted onto his superior's clammy face. "Then where are the *campesinos,* Excellency? Did they simply depart, leaving their children and possessions behind?"

TWO

"WOULD YOU BELIEVE ME IF I told you I saw a ghost?"

She looked at him quizzically. "What?"

"Would you believe me if I told you I saw a ghost?" he repeated.

"You saw a ghost?" She arched her eyebrow.

"I didn't say that. I simply asked whether you'd believe me if I *said* I did."

She replaced her coffee cup on its saucer and looked at him skeptically. "What are you talking about?"

They were sitting on the small patio of their favorite restaurant. It was early spring and, although the sunshine that cascaded onto them through the broken clouds was delightfully warm, a thunderstorm had produced sheets of rain the previous night. The air was cool and fresh.

"No, answer me," he insisted. "If I told you that I saw a ghost, would you believe me?"

She reflected a moment before responding. "It would depend," she finally said.

"On what?"

She took a sip of coffee, watching him over the rim of her cup. "What's this about? Are you telling me that you saw an actual, dyed-in-the-wool ghost?" She couldn't help but smile.

"See! You're already making fun of me! I'm sorry I even brought it up," he playfully sulked as he drained his coffee cup.

"So tell me what you're talking about. What did you see?" She pushed her cup and saucer aside and leaned forward on her elbows, seemingly intrigued.

His eyes flitted over her face as he tried to ascertain whether she was really interested or merely toying with him. "Well," he finally began, "I was driving home last night and, you know that old cemetery on McDonald Drive?"

"The one on the north side of the road, out in the middle of the desert?" She leaned forward slightly more. "I could never figure that place out . . . why's it even there? Who's buried in it?"

"I don't know, but it was lightening like crazy when I drove past it last night. Something caught my eye and, when I glanced over, I saw somebody standing among the graves in a flash of lightning. It was only an instant, but I saw 'em." He paused and looked at her expectantly.

Leaning back in her chair, she folded her arms and looked at him benignly. "That's it? You saw somebody standing in a cemetery while you were driving past it? That's your 'ghost'? How do you know it wasn't just the caretaker?"

"Because there *is* no caretaker and nobody lives out there. Besides, even if there *was* a caretaker, why would he be standing in the cemetery at night, in the middle of a raging rainstorm?" he rhetorically countered, undeterred.

She signaled their waiter and pointed wordlessly to her coffee cup. "I guess he'd have to stand *somewhere*," she suggested.

"In a cemetery, in the middle of a thunderstorm? Really?"

Their waiter glided over and refilled their coffee cups. "Will there be anything else?" he mechanically inquired.

"No, we're good for now," she smiled. Although displeased, their waiter managed to conceal his annoyance. These two tightwads were denying space to other customers who would probably do more than just sit and drink coffee. He turned abruptly and departed, heading toward potentially more profitable tables.

She took a sip of fresh coffee. "You sure it was actually someone, a person, standing there? Not a tombstone?"

He shook his head. "It was too tall to be a tombstone. Besides, that cemetery is really old and most of the tombstones have collapsed. "

"Grave robbers?"

"I thought of that, but do people still *do* that? Grave robbing sounds like something out of Dickens. Besides, what is there to rob? And even if it *was* grave robbers, why would anybody rob a grave in the middle of a downpour?"

She unconsciously frowned as she reflected. "Well, assuming that you really saw someone in the cemetery last night, there *has* to be a rational explanation because ghosts don't exist. It had to be a person but, I'll grant you, why were they standing in a cemetery, at night, in the middle of a thunderstorm, getting drenched?" She grinned wickedly. "It's all very spooky."

"We should drive over there," he suggested. "I've driven past that cemetery a zillion times over the years and it's always intrigued me. This'll give us an excuse to finally check it out."

"Doesn't somebody own it?" she asked, rhetorically. "Will we get in trouble?"

"I have no idea *who* owns it. All I know is that it's old, it's creepy, all the graves are overgrown, and I've never seen anyone there. Except for the ghost last night," he quickly added.

"Well, if he's still there, we can ask him," she suggested with a wink.

"Ghosts don't appear during the day. Everybody knows that."

"Right. Just during rain storms, in old cemeteries," she laughed. "It sounds like a Hollywood cliché." She took a sip of coffee. "So when do you want to go?"

He removed his baseball cap and idly scratched his head before responding. His sandy-colored hair was cropped short because he considered combing one's hair an egregious waste of time. Replacing his cap on his head, he pushed his chair away from their table and luxuriantly stretched his lanky twenty-eight-year-old frame. "Now. It's supposed to rain again this afternoon and, if it does, you'll back out. And if we don't do it while we're talking about it, we probably never will." He stood and looked at her expectantly. As a legal process server, Cameron typically worked odd hours and he was eager to take advantage of their shared day off.

"Can't argue with that," she conceded. Fishing through her purse, she withdrew a five-dollar bill and slipped it beneath her saucer. "Let's blow this pop stand," she said, sliding her chair out and standing.   A year older than Cameron, she looked appreciably younger because of her petite frame, small breasts, and ubiquitous pony tail.   Nancy worked in a local high school cafeteria, where she was the frequent object of lewd invitations from its oversexed male students, a phenomenon she found repugnant as much for its predictability as for its boorishness.   The tradeoff was that she was afforded the luxury of dressing casually most of the time and always had weekends and holidays off.

Together, they headed for the parking lot where his Jeep was parked.

THE DRIVE TO THE CEMETERY took forty-five minutes. The Jeep had no doors but, because of the recent showers, the ambient air was cool and they enjoyed the breeze that swirled around them.   It was ordinarily so hot during the scorching summer that riding in his Jeep was akin to standing in front of a blast furnace, their faces and arms burned by the dusty air.

"Have you ever seen a road leading to that cemetery?" she shouted over the buffeting wind as they drove east on McDonald Drive.

"I never really looked," he yelled in response, shaking his head.   "But there's obviously gotta be a way in and out. How else could they have buried anyone?"

"True," she nodded. "I've just never seen a way in."

"Well, there's gotta be one," he reiterated. He glanced into the rear-view mirror before slowing the Jeep and pulling onto the unpaved shoulder, along which he now drove at a reduced speed.   Although the wind noise abated somewhat, the Jeep's off-road tires rumbled noisily and flipped small stones into the passenger compartment. She was beginning to regret her enthusiastic decision to accompany him to the old cemetery.

"The cemetery's about two clicks up the road on the left," he said, squinting through the bug-splattered windshield. "See if you can spot a road leading to it."

She peered out at their surroundings as they drove along the shoulder, though the only thing that met her eyes was lifeless desert, punctuated here and there with spindly creosote bushes. There weren't even any other cars on the road. About a half-mile away was a small range of hills. "I don't see squat," she said.

"The cemetery is near the base of those hills," he said, pointing. "There's gotta be a way to get to it, other than just driving through the desert."

"I didn't pay attention to any hills," she admitted, "but my recollection is that the cemetery's pretty close to the road."

"Yeah, it's closer to the road than to those hills," he explained. "But I'll bet most people just drive right past it because they don't realize it's here. Ya kinda gotta be lookin' for it."

"Like you," she noted, with some resignation. He appeared not to have heard her.

"There it is," he announced as he applied the brakes. The Jeep slowed to a halt. "There." Her gaze followed his outstretched arm.

Situated on the bench land, probably less than two hundred yards north of the road and completely surrounded by desert, she saw it: a small dusty, abandoned cemetery. Most of the awkward tablets marking the graves had disintegrated long ago; the handful that remained upright threatened to fall over imminently. The rudimentary wire fence that once surrounded the old burial ground had disappeared sometime in the past; ranchers probably appropriated the wire to use around their homesteads. Only a few forlorn, decaying wooden posts still stood as mute sentries around the perimeter of the grave yard.

"So where's the road in?" she asked.

He slipped the transmission into 'P' and switched the ignition off. "Beats the hell outta me." He hopped from the Jeep onto the unpaved shoulder and peered up and down the road. "I don't think there is one," he announced. "Let's just walk out to it."

She wasn't keen on the idea of walking through a desert teeming with rattlesnakes. "Why don't we drive out there?" she hopefully suggested.

He shook his head. "I think this may be private land and they might not want people driving on it."

"So they don't want anyone driving on their private land, but they don't mind if you walk on it?" she skeptically retorted. "If it's private land, whoever owns it probably doesn't want anyone on it, whether they're driving or walking. Besides, look around; we're out in the middle of nowhere. Who's gonna complain? Dead people in a cemetery?"

He hesitated. "I don't know ..."

"Well, I'm not walking. Either you can go by yourself, and I'll wait here, or you can drive out there." In order to emphasize her resolve, she reclined her seat and closed her eyes.

He hesitated then, with a sigh, climbed back into the Jeep. "I guess I'll drive."

She raised her seat and grinned at him. "Good thinking."

Casting her a sour look, he started the engine and cranked the steering wheel to the left. The Jeep slowly climbed over the dirt berm that separated the open desert from the roadway. Driving between scraggly creosote bushes, the Jeep approached the desolate burial ground, which she surveyed through the windshield.

It was apparent that no one had visited the cemetery in a very long time. Its neglected condition rendered it impossible to determine how many graves it contained, though there must have been quite a few judging from the diffusion of broken tombstones that lay scattered about the site. Neither road nor path led from the thoroughfare they'd just quitted. On the far side of the grave yard, however, she discerned the vestige of a path that seemingly led from the cemetery toward the range of hills that loomed in the distance.

The Jeep drew to a halt near one of the rotting wooden fence posts that presumably marked the terminus of the cemetery. "Well, here we are," he announced as he killed the engine. He hopped from the vehicle and looked at her expectantly; she peered apprehensively over the side of the Jeep to insure there were no snakes concealed in the sagebrush. Satisfied the coast was clear, she stepped gingerly from the vehicle, though he was already striding into the cemetery itself.

"I saw it right over here," he called over his shoulder as he skirted a tangle of rusted wire.

Surveying it up close, she immediately realized the cemetery was appreciably larger than it initially appeared. Judging from the handful of tilted fence posts that more-or-less surrounded it like forlorn guardians, the burial ground was at least three hundred feet square. Although difficult to see from afar because they were surrounded by sagebrush, a pair of decaying charnel houses crouched together near the far corner of the cemetery. She thought they resembled ornate, weathered children's playhouses.

"Hey, come on!" he shouted from inside the cemetery. Somewhat reluctantly, she began picking her way toward him.

"See any snakes?" she apprehensively called as she stepped past the fence post, into the confines of the cemetery itself.

"Snakes? Not a one," he assured her. "C'mon, c'mon," he chastened.

She slowly made her way through the burial ground, stepping over collapsed tombstones and around sunken graves. A few of the plots were surrounded by low, filigreed wrought iron fences, their gates long rusted shut and blocked with weeds, though most were unadorned. Dun-colored grasshoppers, disturbed by her footfalls on the damp ground, swarmed around her as she walked. A whiptail lizard used a crumbled tombstone as a platform to sun itself. She paused here and there and tried, unsuccessfully, to decipher some of the eroded inscriptions.

"Hey!" she called. "How old do you think this place is?" Receiving no response, she looked up to see Cameron bent forward, hands on his knees, staring intently at something on the ground. He didn't appear to have heard her. "Hey!" she said again.

He looked up. "Come look at this!" he excitedly urged. She walked toward him.

"What?" she asked as she approached.

He stood to one side of a mound of soil. Straightening, he pointed to the damp earth in front of him. "Check this out." Yawning before him in the ground was an oblong pit about four feet deep. An ancient, fractured tombstone lay face down at one end.

"Whoa." She instinctively drew back. "Is that what I think it is?"

"Yep, it's a grave," he said.

She took a half-step forward and looked cautiously into the pit. "Anybody home?" she asked, apprehensively.

He shook his head. "It's empty."

"Not even a coffin?" The relief in her voice was palpable.

"Nope, nuthin'. They took everything, even the coffin, or there was nothing in here to begin with." He paused. "Either that, or they didn't dig down deep enough to find whatever was in here."

Nancy wrinkled her nose. "God, do you smell that? It smells like something died."

"Well, we are in a cemetery," Cameron laughed.

"No, I'm not kidding. It really smells bad. Can't you smell it?"

The air surrounding the open grave was pungent with the unmistakable tang of decaying flesh.

"Yeah, it's pretty bad," Cameron acknowledged. He glanced into the untenanted pit. "It's not coming from here, though, 'cause it's empty."

Standing so close to the open grave unnerved her, so she inched away. "You think there may be a body buried deeper down?"

He shook his head. "I doubt it. They didn't dig these old graves very deep. They didn't have backhoes like they do today and had to use picks and shovels."

"Well, something stinks to high heaven," she reaffirmed.

"Sometimes old, musty ground just smells bad," Cameron shrugged.

"Yeah, maybe," she muttered, unconvinced.

"Either that, or some animal died out in the desert," he added.

Nancy didn't reply. She looked toward the vacant hole. "What do you mean they 'took everything'?" she asked, changing the subject. "Who's 'they'?"

"Whoever opened this grave."

She was skeptical. "How do you know somebody opened it?"

"Well, it didn't dig itself." He pointed to the grave. "It rained last night, yet the edges of the hole are sharp. That means somebody dug it up after it stopped raining, either late last night or early this morning." He gestured toward the adjacent mound of earth. "There's where they piled the dirt. It's not compacted and there's no little rivulets where rain water flowed off of it, so it had to have been shoveled there after it stopped raining...like I said, either late last night or this morning, probably before dawn to keep anybody driving on McDonald from spotting them." He paused, waiting for her reaction. What he said made sense, but she didn't know how to respond. She simply nodded. "And check this out." He pointed to the ground next to the mound of dirt. "See, some sort of animal *was* here."

Sunk into the damp earth between the pile of dirt and the pit were several cloven hoof prints. Too small for a cow, they were only about three inches long. Like the open grave, their edges were sharp, so whatever creature left them had done so after it ceased raining the previous night. "Well, there goes your ghost theory," she said. "As far as I know, ghosts don't have hooves." She wryly smiled. "I don't even know whether they have feet!" Nancy paused. "How come some animal's hoof prints are still here, but not the footprints of whoever dug up the grave? What happened to *his* footprints? If he dug the grave after it stopped raining, his footprints would still be here, too, wouldn't they? But the only prints are those." She pointed to the hoof marks.

"The animal must've come by after the grave was already open."

Nancy appeared perplexed. "Apparently, but, like I said, what happened to the footprints of whoever dug up the grave? If he dug the grave after it stopped raining, his footprints would still be here. But, if they got washed away by the rain, the edges of the grave would have been eroded at the same time, and they're not." She looked at Cameron. "So somebody dug this grave up last night when the rain was apparently strong enough to wash away their footprints, but not strong enough to erode the edges of the grave or pool in the bottom. Then some sort of animal happened to wander by, and conveniently died, after the rain ended? Does that really make sense to you?"

Cameron made a helpless gesture. "If something happens it must be possible. Unless the animal dug the grave after it stopped raining," he grinned.

An involuntary chill passed down Nancy's spine and she cast a nervous glance around the cemetery. "Wait a minute. If this is a grave, where's the coffin? Even if somebody dug it up, why would they haul the coffin out? Wouldn't they just rob the body, or whatever grave robbers do, and split?"

"In a lot of old homesteaders' cemeteries, like this one, they dispensed with coffins because lumber was too scarce and expensive to waste on coffins. They'd just wrap the body in something like canvas, or an old blanket, and bury it. They probably chose this particular grave to rob because there was probably no coffin to screw with."

"But how did whoever it was know that? And how did they know there was anything worth stealing?"

"I don't know," he admitted. "I'm just guessing. What I *do* know is that I wasn't hallucinating last night. There *was* somebody out here in the middle of the by-God rainstorm. And whoever it was dug this grave up after the rain stopped."

"I think we should call the police."

"No way. They'll probably think we're just pranksters, or that we had something to do with it. Cops get paid to arrest people."

Nancy looked unconvinced. "So, assuming that somebody really *did* dig up an old grave, why is that *our* problem?" she asked.

"It isn't our problem, but don't you find it strange? Aren't you even a little bit interested in finding out what happened out here last night?" He was becoming enthusiastic.

She was not enthusiastic about the prospect of blundering into a bunch of Charles Manson grave-robbing crazies out in the middle of a deserted cemetery. "Let's look around some more," she deflected.

She averted her eyes as they stepped around the open grave and began angling toward the crumbling charnel houses at the rear of the grave yard. For the first time that morning, they heard the sound of a lone automobile on McDonald Drive, 200 yards to the south. The audible swish of its tires on the paved roadway was unmistakable, though they were only able to discern the momentary flash of its roofline above the intervening sagebrush as it sped down McDonald Drive. Like Cameron said earlier that morning, people drive past this place a zillion times and don't even know it's here.

"You think there's anybody in them?" he speculated aloud as they neared the collapsing structures.

"If there are, I don't want to see them," she asserted. The air was still very humid from last night's rainstorm and it was starting to get hot and muggy. Clouds were beginning to form on the horizon, promising more thunderstorms that evening. Grasshoppers flew angrily from beneath their shoes as they kicked their way through the thick weeds. But he was already far in advance and didn't hear her.

"Oh, wow!" he exclaimed from the far side of one of the structures.

"What is it?" she called with some apprehension. She stopped walking, uncertain whether she wanted to proceed.

"Come look at this!" he shouted.

"Yeah, okay," she muttered without enthusiasm. She stepped over a broken fragment of tombstone and headed toward the charnel houses.

He was hunkered down between the structures when she approached, trying to avail himself of a small patch of shade. "Check this out." He stood and turned.

"What is it?" she asked, uneasily.

"No, come look," is all he would say as he disappeared around the building.

Nancy momentarily hesitated, but followed.

He was leaning casually against the rear wall of the crypt. "Look," he said, pointing.

Part of the structure had collapsed inward, leaving a gaping hole in the masonry wall. "Can you see anything inside?" she gulped. She didn't look through the hole and didn't really want to know what may have been inside the tomb.

"Yeah, a bunch of old bones. No kidding," he grinned.

She couldn't help herself. She peered inside.

Scattered about the packed earthen floor was an assemblage of moldering, yellow bones. Although they were, at first blush, impossible to identify as human remains, the upper half of a muddy skull lying on its side in one corner betrayed their provenance. "Oh my God!" she murmured. "This is incredible."

"Yeah, I know," he concurred. "Like something out of a horror movie."

"Animals must've come through the hole and scattered them," she speculated.

He pointed to the range of hills that loomed beyond the cemetery. "I'll bet those hills are loaded with coyotes and bobcats. They probably come down here and help themselves to the smorgasbord. See that path?" He pointed to the trail she'd previously noticed when they initially drove up, leading from the cemetery into the hills.

"Ewwwwwwww ... you're gross," she protested. "But even if that's what happened, it must've been a long time ago because there's nothing here for them to eat except old bones." An idea struck her. "Hey, maybe that's what happened to that grave...an animal came down from the hills and dug it up."

"Not unless animals use shovels," he replied. "When animals dig things up, they don't place the dirt in a neat pile. They fling it all over the place. And, if it had been an animal, they'd have made a mess of whatever was in the grave. Even if they packed whatever it was off, there'd be drag marks and fragments of it layin' around.

And what I saw last night was no animal. No, a human uncovered that grave."

She was silent. "I think that's really sad," she finally said, indicating the ruined charnel house. "People placed their loved ones in here because they wanted to honor and protect them. But they've been abandoned, forgotten, and reduced to being food for animals. It makes me really sad and I think somebody should do something."

He looked at her thoughtfully. "Who? We don't even know who owns this place, if anybody."

"Well, *somebody* buried all these people here. Somebody apparently owned it at one time, anyway. But I wanna get out of here ... it's depressing me and creeping me out." She turned and began making her way back to their Jeep. He trailed behind her.

"Sometimes the old homesteaders who originally settled around here in the 19th century just arbitrarily staked out a community 'burying ground.' I'm guessing that's what happened here. Maybe a bunch of 'em died in the 1918 flu epidemic. I don't know. But, whatever killed 'em, they had to bury 'em right away. They didn't have air conditioning back then and would have had to plant 'em in a hurry." She listened in silence, eager to leave the cemetery. "We're right on the border between Phoenix and Scottsdale," he continued as they walked. "I'll try to check the public records one day next week to see who actually owns this place. But I don't even know where it's technically located, Phoenix or Scottsdale. There may or may not be any records at all, especially since it's obviously really old."

She felt sorry for the people buried there and was sorry they'd come. But she said nothing as they climbed into the Jeep and drove slowly through the desert, back to McDonald Drive.

THREE

CAMERON STARTED HIS INVESTIGATION at the City of Phoenix Office of Records. A young receptionist led him down a harshly-lit hallway to a stark room filled with rows of beige metal filing cabinets, where she showed him how to operate the microfiche. He had no idea where to even begin.

"I'm looking for information on an old cemetery," he revealed before she departed.

"Where is it?"

"It's pretty much right on the Phoenix-Scottsdale border," he replied.

"Well, if it's in Scottsdale, you'll have to ask them," she replied, stating the obvious. "If it's in Phoenix, all Phoenix cemeteries have to have special permits and comply with zoning laws. Otherwise, they're considered a public nuisance. What's the name of it?"

"I don't think it has a name," he conceded. "It's really old and basically abandoned."

"If it doesn't have a name you're probably gonna have a hard time finding any information on it. Do you know its legal description?"

"No. It's basically just out in the middle of the desert."

"Hmm . . .where is it exactly?" Cameron described the location as accurately as possible. "It sounds like it's more likely to be in Scottsdale than in Phoenix," she opined when he'd finished. "You should probably check with them." Were he cynically inclined, Cameron might suspect that she was simply trying to get rid of him so she could go to lunch.

With dismay he surveyed the forest of steel filing cabinets that filled the room. "Is there a list of all the cemeteries located in the City of Phoenix?"

"Just the newer ones," she told him. "If the one you're looking for is really old, though, there's probably not gonna be a record of it. The old property records, before zoning laws, are pretty spotty. But if it's not located within the boundaries of the city there won't be any record of it, anyway."

"Can you show me where the existing cemetery records are?" he asked, hopefully.

"This way," she headed toward the back of the room. "We don't get too many questions about cemeteries," she called over her shoulder. "You trying to find a dead relative or something?"

"Something like that," Cameron responded, his confidence already fading.

CAMERON FARED NO BETTER WITH the City of Scottsdale. The assistant record's clerk, a young woman with ear gauges, an ankh tattoo on the back of one hand and the yin-yang symbol on the back of the other, lectured him that, although cemeteries were historically considered public nuisances, of the same ilk as slaughter houses, feed lots, houses of prostitution, and landfills, they were now scrupulously regulated. *Of course* they had records of mortuaries and cemeteries located in the City of Scottsdale, at least those licensed within the last 50 years. The cemetery you're inquiring about is more than 50 years old? Well, well, she tut-tutted, as far as she knew, and she'd worked there nearly three years, the City of Scottsdale doesn't maintain records for cemeteries that old. Are you sure the cemetery is actually located in Scottsdale? Based on Cameron's recitation of its location, she could almost guarantee that it's in Phoenix, not Scottsdale. Had he tried looking for information about it at the City of Phoenix records office? They're really helpful over there, she authoritatively assured him. She was certain they'd have whatever information he wanted.

"The City of Phoenix doesn't have any record of the cemetery. I was just there," Cameron patiently told her. "They told me the cemetery was located in Scottsdale and sent me over here."

"Well, I can pretty much guarantee that it's not in the City of Scottsdale," she sniffed. "Even if it is, we wouldn't have any information on it if it's as old as you say it is."

Cameron rubbed his forehead, tiredly. "I really don't know *how* old it is. That's why I'm trying to find some information about it.

"Well, I doubt whether we have anything on it, especially since I'm pretty sure it's in Phoenix."

It was clear she was ceding no ground with respect to the cemetery's location.

"Can you just show me where the records are for cemeteries located within Scottsdale? You have those, right?"

"We only have records on cemeteries that are actually located within the corporate boundaries of the City of Scottsdale," she repeated.

"Yeah, fine," Cameron sighed. "Where are those?"

"You can do a search on any of the public computer terminals," the clerk indicated with a wave of her hand. She apparently didn't intend to budge from her seat behind the 'Information' desk.

"Thanks," Cameron muttered as he turned away, though he wasn't certain why he was thanking her.

"That's why we're here," she said, turning her attention back to her *Essentials of Dietary Nutrition, Concepts, Modalities, and Analysis* textbook.

ACCORDING TO THE CITY OF PHOENIX, the old cemetery was located within the City of Scottsdale. According to the City of Scottsdale, it unquestionably lay within the City of Phoenix. Aside from that paradox, Cameron had learned absolutely zero. The resulting lacuna compelled his visit to the office of the Maricopa County Recorder, on Jefferson Street, in downtown Phoenix.

The oldest documents in the Recorder's office date from the 1870's, when explorers, miners, fortune hunters, misanthropes, self-promoters, sociopaths, ranchers, hucksters, grifters, gamblers, con men, debtors, criminals, the socially dispossessed, and the merely curious braved the quarrelsome Apaches and drifted westward into the *terra incognita* of Arizona Territory in the aftermath of the Civil War. Some of these rootless vagabonds, particularly Confederate sympathizers and veterans of the Lost Cause who fancied themselves to have lost everything in that conflict, continued farther south, across the Mexican border, as porous then as now, where they established scattered English-speaking colonies intended to duplicate, sans slaves, the society of the antebellum South, at least as they perceived it. Remnants of these isolated anachronistic Mexican microcosms of Dixie exist to the present day.

The clerk at the county recorder's office was initially as helpful, or as unhelpful, as his counterparts at the city level. "Unless the cemetery you're interested in was surveyed, platted, and the deed recorded when it was originally established, we're unlikely to have anything on it," he informed Cameron. "I wouldn't even know where to tell you to begin to look for the property records. Based on where you said it's located; it sounds like it's in either Phoenix or Scottsdale. You may want to check with their Planning and Zoning offices for information, 'cause I don't think you're gonna find anything here."

Cameron didn't bother to tell him that he'd already been there, done that. "Yeah, I'll do that," he said. "Can you think of any place else that might have information about this particular cemetery?"

The clerk pursed his lips in thought. "Maybe somebody in the history department at Arizona State University or the Arizona Historical Society."

"I hadn't thought of either of those places," Cameron admitted, genuinely impressed by the suggestions.

"I don't know whether you know, but the Arizona Historical Society is actually pretty close by. You know where the capital is? The Historical Society is there, on the second floor, I think. Somebody there is *bound* to know something about your cemetery...that's their business, right?" The clerk smiled.

Arizona's copper-domed capital building was located on 19th Avenue, a few blocks west of the county recorder's office. "You'd think so," Cameron agreed. "Since I'm pretty much already in the neighborhood, I'll head over there to see if I can find somebody's brain to pick. I really appreciate your help." Cameron turned for the door, enroute to the parking lot.

"I hope you find what you're looking for," the clerk called after him.

"THERE ARE QUITE A FEW OLD burial grounds scattered throughout Arizona. They're usually quite small and were basically created on an *ad hoc* basis," confirmed the white-haired docent in the musty, cramped headquarters of the Arizona Historical Society. His name badge identified him as 'Mr. Williamson.' "Most of them are located in the rural counties, adjacent to 19th-century silver and copper mining towns that ultimately went bust when the mines finally played out. But there are a surprising number of 'wildcat' cemeteries around Phoenix, too. Given the circumstances of their creation, almost none of them have any records or documentation unless, say, they've been associated with a particular family over multiple generations. And there are, no doubt, additional isolated graves and entire cemeteries that we know nothing about. It's a bit like blundering into the undiscovered pyramid of an ancient pharaoh," he smiled.

"I already checked the records of Phoenix and Scottsdale, and the Maricopa County Recorder, too," Cameron told the docent. "None of them had any information about this particular cemetery."

"No, they wouldn't," the docent responded. "Virtually none of them have any land records associated with them. Like I said, they were established out of simple necessity." The old man paused. "People die."

"So do you think the cemetery on McDonald may be a wildcat cemetery?" Cameron asked.

"Originally, it's certainly possible," Mr. Williamson affirmed, "but that particular cemetery is pretty well known."

"Pretty well known? You're familiar with it?" Cameron was surprised by the docent's nonchalance.

"Yes, of course. Because of its proximity to the metropolitan area, that cemetery has long been the subject of speculation. People have been poking around it for years; one of the universities even sent an archeological team out there years ago that I was involved with. Although it looks positively ancient, the cemetery was probably established early in the 19th century, when Mexico and Arizona were still part of Spain. It's likely to have originally contained the remains of Spanish settlers, though subsequent burials certainly took place there. For example, the two tombs that look like small houses were constructed long after the original cemetery was created, but we have no idea who they were built for or whose bodies they once contained. But, given the nature of such impromptu cemeteries, that's hardly surprising."

"Yeah, we weren't able to find any carvings or anything, either," Cameron said. "And both tombs were empty . . . except for a few old bones," he quickly added.

"In an effort to learn more about the origin of the cemetery, we even opened what we thought were probably some of the oldest graves there," Williamson resumed. He paused and gazed over the top of his bifocals at Cameron. "And what do you think was in them?"

Cameron was taken aback. "Skeletons, I guess," he responded, nonplused.

"Nothing," the old man said with a wry smile.

"Nothing? They were empty?" Cameron couldn't mask his surprise.

"Every grave we opened, and we opened five or six, was empty. In fact, they'd apparently never contained any bodies at all."

"I thought you said that Spanish settlers were buried there."

The old man nodded. "Given the provenance of the cemetery, that seems most likely," he acknowledged. "But, for whatever reason, the graves we opened were bereft of any remains. That's one of the curiosities of the place."

"I don't understand," Cameron confessed. "Why go to the trouble of digging graves if you're not gonna actually bury somebody in 'em?"

The docent smiled. "People create graves for many reasons, not always to bury someone. They're called 'cenotaphs': funeral monuments to people who are actually buried someplace else. Napoleon's grave on St. Helena, for example. Napoleon's actual body is interred at *L'Hotel des Invalides,* in Paris, yet there's a grave for him on St. Helena. If you didn't know better you'd think

Napoleon's body was there, not thousands of miles away in France. Custer is another example. Although most of the soldiers who died at the Little Big Horn are buried in a mass grave on the battlefield, and there's a cross marking where Custer supposedly fell, he's actually buried at West Point. You can't always rely on the fact that there's an actual body in a grave."

"So you think all the graves are probably empty?"

"It's impossible to say. The cemetery is in such poor condition that we don't even know how many graves are actually there. The absence of any formal records just exacerbates things." Williamson paused. "I have my own theory, though."

"Oh?"

Delighted to have such a complaisant listener, a smile illuminated the old man's face. "Like I said, and as you undoubtedly already know, Mexico and most of the Southwest, including Arizona, used to be part of Spain. Back then, the Spanish Crown sometimes gave sections of land, called 'Floats,' to favored individuals. A Float was basically chunk of land, usually around 100,000 acres, that the Spanish government awarded to somebody. Although the exact boundaries of Floats were usually pretty vague, the idea was that they would eventually be surveyed and their borders definitively established. Sometimes, though, that didn't happen and the Floats remained a sort of 'no-man's land,' surrounded, like islands, by the ordinary counties and cities that eventually grew up around them. While I don't have any specific proof, I've always suspected that cemetery could be part of an old Spanish Float. If it was established on a heretofore *unidentified* Float, that would explain why neither Phoenix nor Scottsdale has any record of it . . . for all practical purposes, it might as well be located on another planet!"

Cameron was becoming excited. This was turning into something far more interesting than he'd originally suspected. "Is there a way to find out?"

"The historical record speaks of a total of five separate Floats that Spain granted to a Spanish nobleman named Luis Maria Cabeza de Baca in what are now the United States: two in New Mexico, two in Arizona, and one in Colorado. There are several references in the surviving documents to a town named 'Esperanza' located on one of the Floats, but nobody's ever been able to figure out which one because no remains of Esperanza have ever been found. But that may be because Esperanza, and the cemetery we've been discussing, were both located on an unknown sixth Float." The docent smiled mysteriously. "If you're interested, we can pull some of the old Spanish property records and see what we can find."

"I'd like that very much," Cameron responded with genuine enthusiasm. "But I'm curious: why were Floats created in the first place? I mean, what was their original function? And why were they called 'Floats'?"

"It's unknown where the term 'Float' came from; that's just what the Spanish called them. Floats were created centuries after the Conquest in the sixteenth century, but awarding land to its subjects was a longstanding practice of the Spanish Crown that lasted well into the eighteenth and nineteenth centuries. After the Conquest, Spain imported hordes of bureaucrats, priests, and soldiers into the New World to explore and civilize the Indians. By 'civilize' they meant kill and enslave them, of course," he ruefully smiled. "Anyway, Catholic friars and Spanish armies crisscrossed the West in the decades after the Conquest. General Sebastian Vizcaino was the first European to explore much of what is now southern California in the 1600's and at least one Spaniard, Coronado, made it all the way to what is now Kansas. Spanish priests also established a string of missions throughout the West, some of which are still in operation, like San Xavier, south of Tucson. Floats, specifically, were awarded as tokens of esteem and for various services rendered the Crown by notable Spaniards...it was much cheaper to fob surplus real estate onto them than deplete the strained finances of the Empire by giving them cash."

"Do you have any idea why Spain gave what's-his-name the particular land it gave him? Or why?"

"De Baca?"

"Yeah. Why'd Spain give it to him in the first place? Why *that* land?"

The old man looked thoughtful. "Frankly, I suspect the Crown probably gave de Baca whatever land it considered to be the least productive or desirable. At that time, the Spanish government didn't have any cash to spare because generations of profligate spending had emptied the Crown's treasury. On top of that, Spain's Central American gold and silver mines had basically dried up. But, because of its previous conquest of the New World, Spain had plenty of real estate, some of which it happily gave de Baca. It's known that de Baca subsequently traveled to New Spain to take physical possession of his Floats. A sworn document from 1860, long after de Baca's death in 1827, says that, in 1816 or 1817, de Baca was finally forced to abandon the Floats 'on account of the hostility of the Navajos.' Following his death, de Baca's heirs tried to live on the various Floats until they, too, were finally driven off by the continuing predations of the Indians. After that, the family evidently fragmented until they basically disappear from the historical record."

"If de Baca was, like you said, a nobleman, he must've been pretty rich."

Williamson smiled. "Based on the surviving documents, it appears that de Baca was something of a scoundrel. That notwithstanding, de Baca was, at one point, at least, fairly well-heeled. We shouldn't find that particularly surprising, since he was a member of the Spanish elite and recognized as such at Court. Even in the absence of other, definitive evidence, we can surmise that de Baca was comparatively rich because he was able to leave Spain in order to take possession of the land given him by the Crown, half-way around the world. Although we don't know the exact year that he departed Spain, a transatlantic voyage in the nineteenth century was a costly undertaking. Ironically, though, after the Navajos finally ran him off the Floats, de Baca died after being shot for smuggling and embezzlement. Rich people typically don't engage in smuggling and embezzlement or, if they do, are generally sufficiently well-connected to bribe the right people to avoid being shot." The docent paused. "Basically, it would seem that, sometime after arriving in the New World, de Baca suffered some sort of economic reversal that required him to engage in 'white collar crime' in order to recoup at least some of his losses. It's even possible that de Baca had amassed his previous fortune in Spain by participating in some sort of illegal activity over there, and had basically worn out his welcome. *That* may have provided the Crown the incentive for giving him the Floats in the first place...they just wanted to get rid of de Baca and giving him land on the other side of the world was a face-saving way to make that happen. It's not the first time such a stratagem had been employed. For example, in 1095, when Pope Urban II called the First Crusade, Europe was overrun with landless knights. These knights were what we'd call today 'bully boys,' basically freebooters who rode around the countryside taking whatever they wanted from the peasants, who were powerless to defend themselves...basically Hells Angels on horseback. The knights' predations created serious economic and social problems and there's substantial evidence that the Pope ordered the Crusade, not so much to free the Holy Land from the Muslims, as is commonly believed, but simply to rid Europe of its out-of-control knights. In order to induce them to pack up and leave, the Pope offered the knights absolution and all the booty and land they were able to seize from the Muslims. The Pope realized that, once the knights departed Europe on Crusade, few of them would ever return because most of them would die either in battle or from disease." The old man smiled. "Problem solved."

Cameron furrowed his brow. "You think that's what happened to de Baca?"

Mr. Williamson shrugged. "Who knows? One theory is as good as the next. However, if we step back and look at the big picture, it makes as much sense as anything else."

"So what happened to de Baca's money?"

"Although the records are spotty, it appears that Cabeza de Baca died penniless. It's unclear what became of all his ambulatory assets, to the extent he still had any."

"'Ambulatory assets?'"

"Moveable, like money and jewels," Williamson explained. "You see, banks and safety deposit boxes are by-in-large products of the Industrial Revolution. In pre-industrial Europe, wealthy people typically carried their valuables on their persons, where they could keep an eye on them. That's why, in old portraits of nobility that you see in museums, the subjects are often wearing a great deal of jewelry: gold rings, various gems, and whatnot. Aside from displaying their social status, wearing jewelry kept it within arm's length and, theoretically anyway, safe. And, although it sounds like a cliché today, wealthy people frequently buried their chattels...think of *Treasure Island* or Oak Island, off the coast of Nova Scotia. But it wasn't only pirates who tried to safeguard valuables by burying them. God knows how much money ordinary people have hidden over the centuries that still remains undiscovered."

"So you think de Baca may have buried his money? Maybe his heirs inherited it?"

"He was married three times and had nearly two dozen children. It's likely that he also had a number of illegitimate children by several mistresses. If de Baca had a will it's never been found so, under the laws of primogeniture that existed at that time, his oldest surviving son probably inherited everything." Williamson looked curiously at Cameron. "There's nothing in the historical record that shows one way or the other, however. But, since de Baca undoubtedly made a lot of enemies, I guess it's conceivable that he may have hoarded whatever he had and concealed it somewhere, though I think that improbable. Like I said, all indications are that de Baca died penniless."

"Where do you think he would have stashed it?" Cameron pressed.

The old man's lips curved into a knowing smile. "If he had anything, perhaps he buried it in the McDonald Drive cemetery?" Cameron was startled by the docent's perspicacity, though Williamson chose to ignore the surprised expression that crossed Cameron's face. He smoothly continued. "Seriously, I don't have the slightest idea. If I knew where de Baca concealed his money, assuming he even did so, it could hardly be said to be hidden! Since de Baca lived in Spain before taking up residence in the New World, he could have concealed what remained of his wealth *anywhere*." He fixed a penetrating gaze on Cameron. "It seems you've taking quite a liking to our friend, de Baca."

"I just find it interesting, that's all," Cameron stammered. He decided to pursue a different tack. "Since you brought it up, if the old cemetery on McDonald was part of a Float, how come there's no town near it? Wouldn't it have made more sense to have a cemetery actually close to a town?"

"Maybe there *was* a town at some point and all traces of it simply disappeared over the years. But people locate cemeteries where they do for any number of reasons. For example, the victims of epidemics were historically burned in the hope of preventing the spread of infection. If that wasn't possible, they were rapidly buried as far away from human habitation as possible."

"What if they *didn't* die in an epidemic?"

Williamson rubbed his chin in thought before responding. "Western societies generally either feared, or revered, their dead...sometimes simultaneously, but with fear predominating, at least until the ascendency of Christianity. The

Romans, for example, imported their ideas of an afterlife from the Etruscans, and both feared and respected the dead. Although the dead were not considered inherently malevolent, the Romans believed they possessed the ability to return to the realm of the living and engage in various mischievous activities, including luring people back with them into the nether world. The only way to insure that the dead didn't come back to harass the living, or to limit their return to certain days, was to appease the dead through certain prescribed rituals. In Book I of his history of Rome, for example, Livy relates that the first thing one of the earliest kings of Rome, Numa Pompilius, did was specifically instruct the people how to conduct funerals to appease the spirits of the dead." He paused. "Christianity changed all that. Because the physical resurrection of the flesh was fundamental to Christian doctrine, safeguarding the dead was essential. Over time, miraculous powers were attributed to the corpses of prominent Christians...they blessed and protected the living. But for pagans, even casual contact with a corpse was considered polluting and it was bad luck to even look at a corpse, as the mere sight of it contaminated the viewer and even daytime funerals were forbidden. The dead were either cremated or consigned to *nekropoloi*, cities of the dead. The reason Roman tombs line the Appian Way is because the Senate passed laws requiring that *sepulchrum* be located outside the city walls. For pagans, the dead were to be avoided at all costs but, if that wasn't possible, they had to be propitiated and mollified. It was only after the death of the Emperor Julian and the consequent domination of Christianity, with its cult of sacred relics and a potentially blissful afterlife, that death began to be looked at somewhat more benignly. Only then were burial grounds allowed within the walls of a city but, even then, only on sanctified ground."

"So what are you saying? That they put the cemetery so far away because they weren't Christians?"

"It could have been that...religious beliefs are remarkably durable," the docent replied. "In only slightly modified form, classical pagan motifs underpin fundamental Christian beliefs. The earliest Christians, for example, believed fully in the existence of the pagan gods and were convinced that they regularly interceded in the lives of humans. In order to establish that *their* god was superior to the hodgepodge of gods worshipped by the pagans, however, Augustine and his Christian successors ultimately subordinated the classical gods to the role of devils or fallen angles. But even the demonization of their traditional gods couldn't shake the pagans from their religious lethargy. Roman society, particularly, was extremely conservative in matters of faith. The pagans were perfectly happy with their panoply of gods, which had defined their culture for centuries, and were in no hurry to embrace Christian monotheism. In order to compete with paganism, the early church fathers *had* to incorporate pagan concepts into Christianity, which remains unabashedly polytheistic to this day: God the Father, God the Son, God the Holy Spirit, and all that. It's no coincidence that even the most 'Christian' holiday, Christmas, falls on December twenty-fifth. That date was deliberately appropriated by the early Christians in order to appeal to the followers of Mithra, an ancient Persian sky god, who, like Jesus, was supposedly born on December twenty-fifth. December twenty-fifth was also the *deis*

Solis, the birthday of the sun, whom the ancient Romans deified as *"Sol Invictus."* Williamson smiled. "I guess it wouldn't be entirely inaccurate to say that Christianity is 'paganism-light'. Christianity's pagan antecedents would probably horrify most contemporary Christians but what is, is," he shrugged as his voice trailed off.

The docent looked directly at Cameron. "If the cemetery was associated with a previously unknown sixth Float, I suspect they placed it far from town because, like the ancient Romans, they didn't want to be defiled by being in proximity to the dead."

Cameron was silent as he reflected on the docent's revelations. "You said there are records of the Floats here?" he finally asked.

"Well, not the originals. The originals are in museums in Seville and Mexico City, but we have copies of them."

"If you have time I'd like to look at them," Cameron told him. "You're the first person I've talked to that actually seems to know anything."

"I have time," the old man assured him. "I don't get to see too many people," he said, wistfully. "Just occasional school field trips, but the only things kids want to hear about are Geronimo and Wyatt Earp. The fact is, not very many people even know the Historical Society exits!" Cameron thought it prudent not to inform Mr. Williamson that, until the clerk at the county recorder's office told him about it, he, too, was unaware of the existence of the Arizona Historical Society. "It's not too often that I get the opportunity to search for old Spanish land grants," the docent continued. He gestured for Cameron to follow as he shuffled into an adjacent room and flipped on the harsh neon light. Three massive filing cabinets, as tall as a man and nearly as wide, with numerous narrow drawers, occupied the far wall. A large metal table occupied the center of the floor. "This is our map and documents room. All our land grant stuff," Mr. Williamson explained.

Mr. Williamson ambled over and removed a stack of microfiche cards from a manila envelope taped to one side of a filing cabinet. Idly flipping through them, he removed a single card from the stack. Seating himself before a microfiche viewer, he flicked it on and slid the card into the machine. Cameron watched with interest over the docent's shoulder, although Mr. Williamson scanned the card so rapidly that the columns of printing on it were reduced to a blur.

"Those are the records?" Cameron ventured.

"This? No, this just tells me which drawer to look in," murmured the docent. He switched the viewer off and stood. "I think we may have something," he smiled.

"WHO?"

"Luis Maria Cabeza de Baca. The Spanish government gave him a bunch of land in New Mexico in the early 1800's and, in the mid-1800's, Baca's heirs swapped *that* land with the U.S. government for some land in Arizona. I'm kind of unclear on what exactly happened, but that's the long and short of it. The land they got in Arizona was called a 'Float.'"

Nancy arched her eyebrow. "Like a root beer float?"

"Yeah, real funny," Cameron said. "Anyway, until I talked to the guy at the Historical Society, they only knew of two Floats in Arizona. Thanks to me, now they know another one. Thank you very much." He bowed ceremoniously. "Please, no autographs."

She arched her eyebrow again. "So that cemetery is located on land that belonged to some Spaniard? Who owns it now?"

"Nobody. That's the weird part. According to the guy at the Historical Society, Baca's heirs died a long time ago and everybody evidently just forgot about the Float. Phoenix thought Scottsdale owned it, Scottsdale thought Phoenix owned it, so nobody did anything. It's also adjacent to the Indian rez, so maybe the Indians figure they have some claim to it. Who knows? But because nobody knows who owns it, if anybody, it's just been sitting there."

Nancy was surprised, and not a little impressed, that Cameron had managed to discover so much about the cemetery, though the particulars remained somewhat hazy. "So the cemetery's the Float?"

"The cemetery is only *part* of the Float. According to the Historical Society guy, the Float is around 100,000 acres. It must go from McDonald all the way back into those hills behind it."

"So who's buried in the cemetery?"

Cameron shrugged. "Nobody really knows. The Historical Society guy confirmed what I said. People used to establish cemeteries wherever they happened to settle, so I guess it could be anybody, especially since nobody really owns the Float. He said that one of the universities dug up a few of the graves a while back, though, and they were empty."

"Empty? That's weird."

Cameron nodded. "What's weird is that nobody in Phoenix or Scottsdale seems to give a crap about it. They acted like they were doing me a favor just by talking to me. That cemetery is like the 800-pound gorilla in the room that everybody ignores."

"Okay, so you know that the land the cemetery's on isn't really owned by anybody and that anybody could be buried there. Right?"

"Based on what the guy at the Historical Society said, that's about the size of it," he acknowledged. "But you haven't heard the best part."

Nancy took a sip of coffee. "There's a 'best part'?" she dryly asked.

Cameron leaned forward and lowered his voice. "Yeah, get this. De Baca was a Spanish nobleman. But when he croaked, he apparently died without a pot to pee in or a window to throw it out of. According to the guy at the Historical Society, nobody even knows where he was buried. They probably just ended up dumping him in a pauper's grave somewhere."

"So?"

"So what happened to his money?"

"How do you know he even *had* any money?" Nancy skeptically retorted.

"The guy at the Historical Society said he did, only something happened to it."

Nancy placed her cup on its saucer. "Like what?"

"That's the point," Cameron said, triumphantly. "Maybe it's buried in that cemetery." It was only a slight bending of the truth.

"So that's why somebody was out there, digging?"

"Maybe," he said. "Or maybe it was just some dumbass kid on a prank."

"How would a dumbass kid even know any of what you've been telling me?" Nancy resumed sipping coffee, staring off into space. "Besides, the hoof print we saw was from an animal, not a kid." Her eyes slid back onto Cameron. "Why else would anybody be out there, digging up a grave? Whatever they were looking for they must've found, because the grave was completely empty when we saw it."

"Maybe, but maybe it was empty to begin with." Cameron reminded her.

She replaced her coffee cup on its saucer and shook her head. "If it was empty to begin with, why were they digging it up? What would be the point?"

"Pretty cool, huh? So what do you want to do?" Cameron eagerly asked her.

Nancy looked perplexed. "Me? What do I want to do? I want to sit here and drink coffee. You're the one who saw the 'ghost'."

"I want to hike back into those hills behind the cemetery," Cameron announced. "There was supposed to be a town called 'Esperanza' on one of the Floats, and I'm thinking it may be somewhere in those hills. Who knows what could be back there!"

Nancy signaled their waiter for a coffee refill. "Scorpions," she replied. "There's scorpions out there. Oh yeah, and rattlesnakes."

Their waiter drifted over with a decanter of coffee and wordlessly refilled their cups before drifting away again. "Quit being such a weenie," Cameron chided her after the waiter departed.

"I'm not being a weenie. I'm just not the outdoorsy type. You know that," she shrugged.

"Aren't you just a little bit intrigued?" Cameron needled her. "Like you said, why would anybody dig up an old grave in an abandoned cemetery?"

"Why do people do *anything*?" she asked, rhetorically, as she sipped her coffee. "The world is full of crazy people. I sure as heck don't need to hike through the desert in order to track 'em down because they're everywhere. Just go to a bus station at two a.m. Or the DMV anytime. And anybody who digs up a grave is obviously crazy."

"Maybe. But maybe they're crazy like a fox. Besides, we might find something really interesting back in those hills," he challenged.

"Yeah, like I said: scorpions and rattlesnakes. Really interesting, all right. Don't you think that if there was anything worth finding, somebody would have found it by now?"

Cameron leaned back in his chair and folded his arms. "Let me ask you something," he began. "How many mountains are there around Phoenix, do you think?"

"Mountains? I don't know...a bunch." Nancy wrinkled her face as she thought. "North Mountain, South Mountain, Mummy Mountain, Piestewa Peak, Camelback . . ." her voice trailed off.

"The McDowell's, the White Tanks, Thompson Peak, the Estrellas, Black Mountain, Papago Park, Shaw Butte, Lookout Mountain, the Superstitions," Cameron added. "And those are just off the top of our heads. There's also a bunch that I don't even know the names of!"

"What's your point?" Nancy asked, dubiously.

"Cameron leaned forward and looked at her intently. "The point is that there's a boat-load of mountains around here, most of which have loads of established hiking trails. *That's* where people go to hike, Nancy, because you can drive right up to 'em and there's tons of parking spaces, hiking trails, covered rest areas, drinking fountains, dog runs, and whatnot. *Nobody* goes hiking where there's none of that stuff...why would they?"

"So?"

"So I'll bet that maybe nobody even hikes in those hills behind the cemetery," he triumphantly concluded. "*That's* why we've probably never heard anything about 'em. It wouldn't surprise me if nobody's been back there since de Baca's time!"

Nancy looked at Cameron skeptically. "How would *you* know?"

"Well, I don't *know*," he admitted. "But have *you* ever been back in those hills?"

"Why would I hike back there?" she laughed. "I don't hike *anywhere*."

"I guess that's fair enough," Cameron conceded. "But do you know *anyone* who has?" He looked at her expectantly.

Nancy drained her coffee cup before answering. "No, but that doesn't mean anything because nobody I know hikes. They're smart enough to stay inside, where it's air conditioned," she grinned.

"Well, I'm gonna go look back into those hills," Cameron asserted. "I can't believe you're not interested...you're the one who just said that whoever was digging out there the other night must've found what he was looking for."

"And?" Nancy looked around for their waiter.

"Well, what was it? And what happened to it?"

Their waiter seemed to have vaporized. "Who cares? You think whatever, or whoever, it was, he carted it off into those hills? Why would he do that?"

"I don't know, but the whole thing is damned intriguing," Cameron said. "Spanish land grants, an old cemetery, Spanish *reales*, a ghost..."

Nancy spotted their waiter and waved at him. She turned back toward Cameron as the waiter ambled over to their table. "If you say so. Only it wasn't a ghost. Like I said, ghosts don't have hooves."

"Whatever," he sighed. "I'm still hiking back in there before it gets too hot."

"Hey, a man's gotta do what a man's gotta do," she said. "We'll take a refill and the check," she informed their taciturn waiter as he approached. "Let me know when you decide to go," she continued to Cameron. "If I'm just sitting around, and it's not too hot, I might be persuaded to accompany you on your wild goose chase. Not promising anything—"

Cameron smiled. "I know."

FOUR

THEY PARKED CAMERON'S JEEP on the far, northern, edge of the cemetery, where they had previously observed the faint outline of a path leading toward the range of hills that reared in the distance.

"Why can't we just drive out to the hills and save a ton of walking?" Nancy asked. "Why are we parking so far away?"

"I still don't know exactly where we are," Cameron explained, "Phoenix or Scottsdale. Maybe neither. But if those hills are part of the Phoenix Mountain Preserve, or some 'citizen for good' *thinks* they are, they're liable to call the cops if they see us drivin' out here." He smiled cynically. "The only ones allowed to drive motorized vehicles in the Mountain Preserve are developers who level the mountains so they can build houses on top of them. And, aside from not wanting to get hassled, I just don't want to draw any attention to ourselves. Nobody'll pay any attention to two hikers."

"I don't like parking so close to that gross charnel house," Nancy said.

"Are you afraid one of the skeletons will reanimate itself and drive the Jeep away?" he teased.

"Real funny, Cameron," she said, sarcastically. "That was a real knee-slapper. I didn't realize we were still in the fourth grade."

Cameron stepped from the Jeep onto the parched earth and Daisy, his golden retriever, excitedly bounced after him. Although it had rained as recently as a week ago, the ground had already soaked up what little precipitation had fallen. It was as though it had never rained at all. "I tried finding those hills on Google Earth," he said, ignoring her derision. "I couldn't go right to 'em because I don't know their name, but I managed to locate 'em by scanning the general area." He shouldered a day pack onto his back and looked at Nancy. "You got water?"

She sighed as she stepped from the Jeep. "Yeah, in my pack." Nancy reached behind her seat and withdrew it. Both of them wore long pants, hiking boots, and hats. "So what did you see?"

"On Google?"

"Yeah."

"You can see this trail," he nodded toward the path at their feet. "It curves around into those hills and just sorta disappears. But it looked like there may be some buildings back in there—hard to tell because of the shadows and they blended in with the ground, but it looked like it."

"Buildings? Like houses?"

"I don't think so. Looked more like old foundations," Cameron said. "Like I said, it was hard to tell." He grinned at Nancy. "We'll soon find out."

"Yeah, I guess," she sighed. "Speaking of which, we'd better get going, before it gets any hotter. I'm already sweating and we haven't even started walking." Nancy shouldered her back pack and stepped onto the faint path.

THE GROUND BEGAN TO RISE almost imperceptibly as they leisurely walked toward the range of hills. Daisy zig-zagged through the desert in front of them, her tongue lolling from her mouth. The rocky terrain was slightly undulating and covered with creosote bushes, barrel cactus, and clumps of stunted *palo verde* trees. Almost immediately after they stepped away from the Jeep a cottontail rabbit exploded from the base of a greasewood bush and darted helter-skelter into the cemetery. Nancy jumped and uttered an involuntary yelp of surprise, though Cameron apparently didn't notice because he was already yards ahead. Although she had no fear of becoming lost, Nancy periodically stopped walking and looked around, just to get a feel for the lay of the surrounding land.

From their slightly elevated position, she could see the old cemetery was bigger than it appeared when standing adjacent to it. In the distance beyond the burial ground she could see a few cars proceeding along McDonald Drive, oblivious to both the cemetery and their presence. She squinted because of the sunlight that reflected off the windshield of Cameron's Jeep.

Turning back toward the range of hills, Nancy yelled at Cameron, "Hey! Wait up!"

He paused and looked back at her. "C'mon, slow poke. What are you looking at?"

"Nuthin'," Nancy replied, more to herself than to Cameron. "Just lookin' around."

"Well, come on. I figure it'll take a little better than an hour to reach the base of the hills." He resumed walking as Nancy adjusted her pack and began trudging in his direction.

IT TOOK CLOSER TO TWO HOURS.

"Damn! It's already blazing out here!" Cameron exclaimed. He slung his pack to the ground and removed a bottle of water. Twisting the cap off, he gulped its tepid contents. Daisy sat next to him, panting, looking up at him expectantly. Cameron fished through his pack and removed a collapsible dog bowl. He squatted, placed it on the ground, and filled it with water. Daisy noisily began drinking, slopping water from the bowl onto the ground. When she'd finished, she plopped down onto the earth.

Nancy unshouldered her pack and placed it on the ground between her feet. She scratched Daisy's ears, who responded by enthusiastically wagging her tail. "The trouble with the damned desert is that there's never any place to sit down," she grumbled, looking around. "If you sit directly on the ground you'll fry your butt off. That is if you don't get stung by a scorpion first." She removed her hat and used it to wipe the perspiration from her face. Her hair was plastered to her head with sweat and the air on her scalp felt good.

"Well, we're almost there," Cameron consoled her.

"'There' where? We barely reached the base." Nancy bent to remove a water bottle from her pack. She stood upright and looked intently south as she slowly unscrewed the cap. "You can't even see the cemetery from here," she said, absently, before taking a drink. "It just blends in with the desert."

Cameron followed her gaze. Far to the south he could see occasional flashes of sunlight glinting off cars traveling along McDonald Drive, though they were much too far away to actually hear them. The two were surrounded by empty, motionless desert. The silence was almost oppressive.

"Well, we're still on the path," he said, pointing to the faint trail that disappeared into the range of hills before them. "We're obviously still headed in the right direction."

Nancy replaced her hat on her head and drained her water bottle. "It's obvious that nobody's been out here in forever: no Coke cans, no spent cartridge cases, no trash, no nuthin'. I wonder why somebody made this trail in the first place? What the heck is out there?" She frowned toward the looming hills that stretched before them.

"I *knew* you were intrigued!" Cameron chortled. "But *somebody* was out here a long time ago." Nancy looked at him expectantly. "When I was at the Arizona Historical Society Mr. Williamson showed me the remains of an old, rusted lever-action rifle that somebody found out here a long time ago. The wooden stock had rotted away and the metal was trashed, but he was still able to date it to the 1800's. So *somebody* must've lost it out here way back when."

"That's pretty cool," Nancy conceded. "We might as well see if we can find another one," she winked, shouldering her pack.

Cameron slung his pack onto his back. "We should be able to see some of the buildings I saw on Google Earth once we hike to the far side of that closest hill." He pointed at one of the smaller foothills that rose from the desert floor that gently sloped upward before them. "C'mon, Daisy!" he whistled. Daisy leapt to her feet and began trotting toward the hill.

"I thought you said you couldn't be sure *what* you saw on Google," she responded, shouldering her pack and trudging forward.

Cameron strode onto the path in front of her. "I said I couldn't be sure because of all the shadows, but it looked like there were buildings back there."

"Even if there *are* buildings, it doesn't look like anybody's been back here in a long time," Nancy remarked. "Maybe that's where your ghost lives," she teased.

"Ghosts don't have hooves and don't live in houses," Cameron called over his shoulder. "I thought we already established that."

"Well, *somebody* had to live in 'em, assuming they're there," she concluded, as she aimed her hiking boot at a pebble and kicked it off the trail.

"We'll soon find out," Cameron promised without breaking stride.

THEY WERE INDEED THERE.

After another 45 minutes of hiking, Nancy and Cameron finally clambered to the summit of the small foothill, enabling them to see at least a portion of what lay beyond. A panorama of unsullied desert stretched before them, through which undulated the trail leading back toward the cemetery.   Nancy promptly deposited her pack onto the ground and bent forward at her waist to rest, placing her hands on her knees.

"It looks like a whole lotta nuthin'," she announced between breaths.

Cameron unscrewed the cap from a bottle of water and absently handed it to her.   "Not exactly," he said.   "Look," he pointed.

Nancy stood erect and took the water from his outstretched hand.   She took a swallow of its warm contents and squinted against the haze.   "I don't see anything but miles and miles of stinkin' desert.   What are you looking at?"

"Look down into that valley," Cameron urged her.

Nancy tried to focus on whatever it was he was pointing at.   "I have no idea what you're lookin' at," she finally said.

"Buildings," he murmured.

"Really? Where?" She couldn't restrain the excitement in her voice.

Cameron stepped behind Nancy and grasped her head in his hands. Slowly rotating her head, he swiveled it to the direction he was indicating. "Right there, near that one hill, you can see some walls...see?"

Nancy squinted again, harder this time. "I think so," she finally said, without conviction. "It's really hard to see 'cause of the glare and it's so far away."

Cameron placed his pack on the ground and, after a moment of rummaging, withdrew a pair of binoculars. "Try these."

She pressed the binoculars to her eyes and fiddled with them until they were adjusted. Turning the focusing wheel finally brought the structures into view, although it was difficult to hold the binoculars steady because she was still breathing heavily from their hike up the hill. "I see 'em," Nancy finally murmured.

"Pretty cool, huh?" Cameron excitedly responded.

"Actually, yeah," she conceded. "You can see really well with these things." Nancy was silent as she scanned the seemingly lifeless desert through Cameron's binoculars. Heat waves shimmered in the distant air, distorting the view. "It looks like there's a bunch of buildings down there," Nancy finally concluded, handing the binoculars back to Cameron.

He quickly readjusted the binoculars to fit his face and directed them toward the structures. "Yep, sure it looks like it," he said after a moment. "Like you said, it's hard to tell, but there's definitely something down there. How long do you think it'll take us to hike down there?" Cameron excitedly asked, more to himself than to Nancy.

"You've gotta be kidding. I'm not hiking all the way down there!" she exclaimed. "I'm pooped. Besides, it's not even noon and it's already too hot."

"So you're gonna make me hike down there by myself?" Cameron pouted.

Nancy arched an eyebrow. "I'm not making you do anything. I'm just telling you that I'm not hiking to those buildings, or whatever they are. You can do whatever you want and I'll wait for you back at the Jeep. Just give me the keys so I can listen to the radio, or drive for help in the event you don't show up by nightfall."

He couldn't tell whether she was being serious about not returning. "They're not very far, Nancy. You can see 'em right there," he insisted.

She looked at him dubiously. "Yeah, 'right there' by using binoculars. Even then, they're hard to see. No, I think I'll pass." She took another drink of water and watched Cameron out of the corner of her eye. He looked utterly deflated and Nancy couldn't help but feel sorry for him. She touched his arm tenderly. "Look, why don't we try lookin' on Google Earth again?" she suggested. "Maybe we'll be able to tell exactly what they are, now that we sorta know what we're lookin' for."

Cameron shook his head. "I told you, I already tried that. When I tried to zoom in, the image got so pixilated that I couldn't see anything. And when I tried zooming out, everything just blended together. I couldn't distinguish a heap of rocks from a building. The only way to see exactly what's there is to actually hike down to it."

Although Nancy knew that Cameron was probably right, she really didn't feel like continuing the hike. Her boots chafed her feet, she was hot, and it would probably be mid-afternoon before they even reached the structures they saw through the binoculars. By then the heat would be unbearable besides which, even when they reached them, they'd probably turn out to be nothing more than abandoned corrals or, worse, boulders. And they'd *still* have to hike back to Cameron's Jeep. No thanks.

"I'm sorry, Sweetie, but I can't go on," she said, apologetically. "I'm tired and hot. And don't forget that we've still gotta hike back to the Jeep." She attempted to put a positive spin on it. "Now that we know something's actually out here, we can plan better for our next hike!" she optimistically assured him.

Despite Nancy's attempt to mollify him, Cameron couldn't conceal his disappointment. "Yeah, okay, I guess." He looked wistfully toward the distant structures, shimmering in the increasing heat.   He squatted and stuffed his binoculars back into his pack, then stood. "We might as well head back," he sighed as he shouldered his pack. Cameron brightened. "Like you said, at least we know there's something out there."

Nancy picked up her pack and slung it onto her back. "Yep.   Not sure *what* it is, but it's definitely something," she acknowledged. "But all I know right now is that I'm hot and my feet are starting to hurt."

Cameron turned and headed back down the hill, toward the Jeep. "I wonder if anybody's ever actually hiked down to those places?" he mused.

"Why would they?" she responded, trailing after him. "Like you said, there's a zillion parks around here with established hiking trails. Why would anyone bother to hike out here, in the middle of nowhere? For what?" Nancy stepped on some loose rocks and twisted her ankle. "Dammit!" she exclaimed.

Cameron stopped and turned toward her. "You okay?"

"Yeah, just not paying attention to where I'm walking," she muttered, scattering the offending rocks with a well-placed kick.

"Well, be careful," Cameron cautioned as he turned away.

After about a half-hour of walking, they stopped to rest and share a drink of tepid water from Nancy's canteen.   "Ever heard of 'voice phenomena'?" Cameron asked, wiping his perspiring forehead with his sleeve.

"Voice phenomena? Nope. What is it?" Nancy took another swig of water before handing the canteen back to Cameron.   A rivulet of perspiration coursed down her spine, causing her to shiver despite the heat.

"In the late '50's, some Swedish guy went into the woods to record bird songs on a tape recorder. When he got back to his house and played the tape, he heard a voice on the background of the tape, talking to him."

Nancy looked at him uncomprehendingly. "Huh? What are you talking about? Who was talking to him?"

"That's the point," Cameron said. He took a sip from the canteen. "He had no idea whose voice was on the tape. It was just some guy talking about nocturnal bird songs."

Nancy still didn't understand. "So this guy went out to record bird songs but, instead of bird songs, he recorded somebody's voice? And he had no idea who it was?"

"That's pretty much the size of it."

She was skeptical. "How did he know that he didn't just intercept a stray radio broadcast?"

"For one thing, the guy was trying to record birds and a voice on the tape recorder was talking about nocturnal bird songs. What are the odds of that? Besides that, since then, many people, including scientists, have recorded voices. And a lot of the recordings were done under controlled conditions, in sound-proof rooms, so there was no chance of picking up freak radio signals. There's a ton of information about voice phenomena on the Net," he concluded.

"So what are the voices supposed to be? Dead people?" Nancy asked, dubiously.

Cameron shrugged. "Nobody knows, but I'll bet you didn't know that Thomas Edison spent much of his career working on an invention that he could use to communicate with the dead. That's how he ended up inventing the phonograph."

"You're right, I didn't know that," Nancy admitted.

"Edison was a genius and *he* believed it possible to communicate with the dead, so why not?"

They resumed their plodding trek back to the Jeep. "It sounds pretty creepy," Nancy opined. "So do the voices talk about anything besides bird songs?"

"They've used all kinds of sophisticated electronic equipment to make sure they filter out all possible electromagnetic interference: oscilloscopes, voice printers, videotape recorders, sound spectrographs, speech diagrams. The voices are still there and fall within the human frequency range, so they're real human voices."

"So what do they say?" Nancy persisted.

"They've recorded the voices of men, women, and children. They often identify themselves and give their names and hometowns. Sometimes they claim to be dead relatives and will address the people in the recording rooms by name. They'll respond to specific questions and comment on who is present in the room and what they're wearing. Other times, the words are nonsensical, either because they're spoken in a foreign language or because they're just plain incomprehensible. But even some apparently meaningless communications end up making sense years later, so they're apparently prescient. Sometimes, anyway."

Nancy shook her head in wonderment. "I've never heard of any of this stuff, but it sounds kinda like spiritualism...you know, disembodied voices, table lifting, and trumpets floating around the room."

"Yeah, a lot of people have criticized voice phenomena for that reason: the corniness of the messages," Cameron agreed. "But it's like everything else; you can't throw the baby out with the bathwater. There's enough legitimate recordings to warrant taking it seriously. And even if *all* the voices that have been recorded talked gibberish, the fact remains that they're still voices that had to have come from *somewhere*."

"Wait, I gotta rest a second," Nancy panted. She stopped, unscrewed the cap of her canteen, and took another swig of water. "Did I ever tell you one reason I hate the damned desert is because there's no place to sit down?" she asked as she passed the canteen to Cameron.

"Yeah, once or twice," he smiled, taking a drink. "I can see the sun shining off the windshield of the Jeep," he told her, pointing toward the lowlands that stretched southward.

Nancy squinted in the direction Cameron indicated, then gestured for the canteen. "Yeah, I see it, too." She took another sip of water when he handed it back to her. "But what's this voice phenomena business got to do with anything?"

"I'm gonna try it," Cameron said.

"Where? Out here? All you'll pick up is wind noise."

"Not here, out in the open. Down there," he responded, pointing.

"The cemetery?"

"Yeah." He grinned.

"Either way, you'll have the same problem. Too much background noise."

"Not inside one of the charnel houses."

Nancy was stunned. "Are you kidding, Cameron? You really intend to try to communicate with dead people inside one of those tombs? I guess you didn't see what I saw: bones scattered everywhere."

"No, I saw them," Cameron acknowledged. "But we don't know whether they were human or animal bones. Besides, where better to attempt communication with dead people than a tomb?"

"The skull we saw was no animal. It was human." Nancy couldn't believe the words she heard coming from Cameron. "Why do you even *want* to communicate with whoever it is? What do you intend to ask them?"

He shrugged. "Just general stuff about the Baca Float. Who was digging in the cemetery the other night. What's with those buildings we saw back there in the hills." Cameron shrugged. "It probably won't work, anyway."

Nancy resumed walking in the direction of the Jeep, quickening her step. "Well, just don't ask me to join you. The whole thing creeps me out."

Cameron followed behind her. "Yeah, I know," he sighed. "I'll bring Daisy. Some people think that, because their hearing range is greater than ours, dogs can hear voice phenomena better than humans. One guy had a Great Dane that would growl whenever he heard somebody talking on a voice phenomena recording, although the dog otherwise paid no attention to ordinary recorded voices." Hearing her name, Daisy looked quizzically at Cameron and wagged her tail.

"You should bring someone else with you besides Daisy, Cameron. Just as long as it isn't me."

"Yeah, I know," he acknowledged as he gingerly stepped over a barrel cactus.

Nancy shook her head. "I can't imagine spending time in one of those charnel houses. They're full of old bones and you don't know what kind of diseases you'll catch. Besides that, it's gonna be as hot as blazes inside, and isn't there some kind of law against desecrating a grave?"

"I won't be desecrating anything," Cameron protested. "I'm just gonna see if voice phenomena really works."

Nancy stopped and turned to face him. "So what are you gonna say? 'Yoo hoo, is anybody home?' Rap three times if you can hear me.'"

Cameron ignored her teasing. "According to what I've read on the Net, people develop their own methods for communicating. Some people suggest starting off with something like, 'Good evening, friends. It's such-and-such a date and the time is such-and-such. I wonder if there is anyone here who knows me and who can speak to me using this tape recorder.'"

"If you ask me, the whole thing sounds like a joke," Nancy opined before turning back toward the Jeep.

He shrugged. "Maybe it is. I just figure it can't hurt to try."

"What about the heat?" She called over her shoulder. "Or are you gonna be like the Polacks, who send their rocket ship to the sun at night?"

"I'll probably wait until the weather cools off a bit," Cameron conceded. "By that time we'll be able to hike all the way back to those buildings, too."

"Well, I want to look at 'em on Google Earth before we try hiking back there again. I wanna make sure there actually *are* buildings back in those hills. You, yourself, said that you couldn't be sure."

Cameron didn't respond. They trudged the rest of the way back to his Jeep in silence without stopping to rest.

FIVE

MAN, HAVE YOU BEEN EATING MUD PIES?" Chet cracked.

"If you don't wanna do it, just say so," Cameron sighed.

Chet chuckled. "I never said I didn't want to do it. I just asked if you've been eating mud pies." He paused and looked askance at Cameron. "Nancy won't let you do it by yourself, right?"

"She thought it was a good idea to have someone with me, but so do I. Daisy'll be there, too."

"Well, I'm ordinarily not too big on things that go bump in the night, but it actually sounds like a hoot. Have you ever actually tried it before, like at your house?"

They were having a beer at a neighborhood bar around the corner from Chet's apartment. "Yeah, I made a few recordings," Cameron admitted.

Chet leaned forward and focused intently on Cameron. "So what did you hear?"

Cameron took a drink of beer. "Some stuff," he said, noncommittally.

Chet made a face. "'Some stuff?' Like what kind of stuff?"

"Well, it's actually kinda hard to hear," Cameron conceded. "The voices are real faint and the messages are only a few seconds long. You have to listen real close to hear them."

Chet leaned back and looked dubious. "How do you know you're hearing voices, rather than the blood flowing through your head? Or traffic noise? Or your own imagination?"

Cameron could see that Chet was going to be as difficult to convince as Nancy. "No, you can definitely hear voices. I use headphones to minimize background noise, which sorta sounds like wind rushing. It's basically like trying to hear someone over a real bad phone connection and the voices almost sound like they're chanting."

"Wind rushing? Like I said, how do you know it's just not the sound of the blood flowing in your own head that you're hearing in the headphones?"

"You just have to hear them for yourself," Cameron adduced, not knowing what else to say.

Chet drained his beer. "Yeah, I'd like that. Did any of the voices actually talk to you?"

Cameron shook his head. "I tried to get them to, but could only pick up some isolated words."

"Like what?"

"'Yesterday.' 'Hard' or 'harp.' 'Music,' I think. Some other words that I couldn't make out." Cameron's voice trailed off.

Chet couldn't hide his amusement. "I don't know, man. It sounds like you may have channeled the ghost of Jerry Garcia! Was the voice a man or a woman, or what?"

Cameron shrugged. "It's so faint that it's hard to tell."

"You still got the tape at your house?" Chet asked.

"Yeah."

"How many ya got?"

"A few," Cameron acknowledged, guardedly.

"Well, let's go listen to 'em!" Chet excitedly suggested.

"It's not quite that easy," Cameron equivocated. "They're *really* hard to hear."

"So? I still wanna hear 'em. Remember, Cam, this is the first time I've ever heard of this stuff and I want to know what I'm getting myself into." Chet sat back and focused a skeptical gaze on Cameron.

"Fair enough," Cameron conceded. "I just want you to understand that it's not as easy as I may have made it sound."

"I didn't think you did. Maybe I'll be able to hear something that you missed," Chet suggested.

Cameron hadn't considered that possibility. "Yeah, that's actually a good idea," he conceded.

"So let's go!" Chet tossed some money onto their table and slid from the booth. "Besides, I wanna ask Jerry Garcia about the lottery numbers."

"That's real original, Chet." Cameron stood. "But just don't bitch when you have a hard time hearing what's on the tapes, because I warned you."

"Yeah, yeah," Chet responded with a wave of his hand. "Blah, blah, blah, blah. Let's go see what you're talking about. I promise not to laugh if it turns out that you've been listening to barking dogs the whole time." He headed for the parking lot. "I'll meet you at your house," he called over his shoulder as Cameron trailed after him.

CAMERON LIVED NEAR 43RD Avenue and Cactus Road. When he unlocked the front door of his apartment Daisy joyfully hopped about the living room, overjoyed to see him. He sat down on the edge of the couch, where she promptly rolled onto her back at his feet. "Hey, Butthead," he smiled as he scratched her stomach.

"Hi, ya, Daisy," Chet greeted Daisy, shutting the door and plopping into a recliner.

"I'm gonna take Daisy out to pee," Cameron told Chet. "She's been cooped up in here all day." He stood and walked to his small kitchen where he removed a leash from a hook, Daisy excitedly following him. "Be back in a few."

"Where's your spook tapes?" Chet asked, looking around. "Maybe I'll listen to 'cm while you're gone."

Cameron snapped Daisy's leash onto her collar and she eagerly dragged him to the front door. "Everything's in my bedroom, but it's not that simple. I've gotta set it up for you...just hang on. I'll only be gone a few minutes. Don't touch anything." He and Daisy exited the apartment. Chet rose from the recliner and went into Cameron's bedroom.

Along with Cameron's neatly-made bed and a chest of drawers, the room contained a large TEAC reel-to-reel tape recorder on a small desk in one corner. At one time it was an expensive, state of the art machine, but was now obsolete. A pair of headphones, equally outdated, rested on the table next to the TEAC. No Ouija boards, no candles, no skulls, no pendulums, no incense. Mildly disappointed, Chet returned to the living room to await Cameron's return.

CAMERON AND DAISY WERE GONE less than fifteen minutes. "That didn't take long," Chet observed.

"She *really* had to pee," Cameron replied as he unsnapped Daily's leash. "Besides, I didn't want you to start screwing with stuff." He looped Daisy's leash over the kitchen hook and returned to the living room.

"Where'd you get that tape recorder? I've only seen 'em in photographs and old movies."

"Craiglist," Cameron told him. "It's a dinosaur, but good for recording voice phenomena. I got it for a song. The headphones, too."

"Well, it looks pretty cool," Chet affirmed. "Like something out of those '50's atomic movies."

"Glad it meets with your approval, Professor," Cameron chuckled. "You ready?"

Chet stood. "Lead the way, Maestro."

In Cameron's bedroom, Daisy curled up on the floor at the foot of the bed, placed her head on her paws, and watched the proceedings with interest. Cameron pulled the chair from the desk and gestured for Chet to sit. "Has Nancy listened to your tapes?" Chet inquired as he complied.

"Nope," said Cameron. "I never told her that I was actually doing it, so it's only been me until now. I've pretty much just been trying to get the hang of it."

"So how does it work? What do I have to do?" Chet asked, looking quizzically at the TEAC.

"Hang on a sec." Cameron leaned over the desk and placed the headphones on his own head. He turned the tape recorder on and adjusted the volume. The tape recorder's reels whirred as Cameron zipped back and forth through the tape, its analogue tape counter slowly rotating. Cameron stopped periodically to listen intently through the headphones. "There," he announced after what seemed a couple of minutes. "See if you can hear it." Cameron straightened, removed the headphones, and handed them to Chet.

Chet clamped the headphones on his ears. Cameron watched him with a slight smile as he pushed the TEAC's 'play' button.

Immediately, the only sound Chet heard was a low rushing noise, almost like he was listening to a windstorm outside. Listening intently, Chet discerned what sounded like a rhythmic hum in the background, almost like faint chanting, though it was nearly inaudible. He looked up at Cameron and shrugged.

"Wait," Cameron mouthed.

Then he heard it. It was extremely subdued, so muffled that he couldn't be certain it wasn't just an element of the underlying rushing noise. A voice on the tape said, "Hello." It was so unexpected that it actually startled Chet.

"Stop!" he blurted. "Go back." He instinctively reached for the TEAC's rewind button.

Cameron pushed Chet's hands away, punched the 'stop' button, and rewound the tape a few feet. "It's at about 218," he said, indicating the tape counter. He pressed the 'play' button again.

Chet closed his eyes and concentrated as rushing noises again filled the headphones. Then, as if someone was speaking from far, far, away, struggling to be heard above the roar of a waterfall, a faint voice emerged from the background: "hello." Then it was gone.

"Stop it and play it again," Chet directed. Cameron complied. "Jesus Christ," Chet murmured after listening to the tape a third time. He looked at Cameron, who was grinning. Chet slowly removed his headphones.

"What did you hear?" Cameron innocently asked as he pushed the TEAC's 'stop' button and sat on the edge of his bed.

"I heard somebody say 'hello.'"

"See what I mean about it being hard to actually hear anything because of the background noise?"

Chet nodded. "Yeah, it was really hard to make out, but it sure sounded like a human voice...it just kinda popped out of nowhere. You got more?"

"Yeah, a bunch more," Cameron assured him. "I began with that one because it was the easiest to hear. You've really gotta strain to hear anything on the other tapes."

"Nancy hasn't heard that?" Chet pointed to the tape.

Cameron shook his head. "No, just you and me." He smiled. "And Daisy." Hearing her name, she lazily wagged her tail.

"What else ya got?" Chet excitedly asked.

"Like I told you earlier, I'm only able to pick out a few isolated words."

"So how do you actually make the recordings?" Chet inquired. "How'd you learn to do it?"

"I found a book on it from the '70's in a used book store," Cameron said, "and there's lots of information on the Net."

"There's books on this stuff?" Chet marveled.

Cameron laughed. "There's books on all kinds of stuff. You'd be amazed, Chet. Anyway, you set the microphone as far away from the tape recorder as possible to minimize the hum of the motor. I even bought electrically-shielded cables to eliminate any electrical interference. The room has to be totally quiet, so I usually do the recordings at one or two in the morning. That way, there's less traffic noise and people walking around outside. I push the 'record' button, turn the volume up all the way, and sit across the room. After inviting anyone who may be present to speak, I keep perfectly still and just wait."

Chet frowned and glanced around uneasily. "So you think there are people, or spirits, or whatever, here right now?"

Cameron shrugged. "Well, I doubt whether they only come here at 2:00 in the morning so I can record them."

"You invite them to talk?" Chet skeptically asked. "How do you do that?"

"I say something like, 'Greetings, friends. It's March second and it's 2:00 a.m. I wonder if there's anyone here who knows me and who will speak to me using the microphone?"

"It's a good thing you live alone, Cameron," Chet observed. "Otherwise, people would think you're crazy. What's Daisy do while all this is going on?"

"She just lays on the floor by me. When I first started recording voice phenomena, Daisy would sometimes growl and stare at particular locations in the room. Other times, she'd swivel her head like she was following movements that I couldn't see. She doesn't do that so much now, though...I guess she's used to it." Cameron reached down and scratched Daisy's ears.

"So you just sit there and let the tape recorder run for an hour, or what?"

"No, only for a couple of minutes or so at a time," Cameron told him. "For every minute of recording, I spend at least ten minutes playing the tape back, trying to hear the voices."

"This is some really weird stuff, man," Chet muttered. "Doesn't it freak you out?"

"It did at first," Cameron admitted. "Now I'm pretty much used to it."

"Do you think the voices you're hearing aren't just static, or sunspots, or something?"

Cameron fixed a penetrating gaze on Chet. "I don't know, Chet, you tell me. You just heard someone on that tape tell you 'hello.' Did it sound like sunspots to you?"

"Not really," he sheepishly admitted. "But lemme hear what else you have."

Cameron stood, stepped over Daisy, and opened the top drawer of the desk where the tape recorder sat. He removed two round tape canisters and a yellow legal pad. "I keep a log of all my sessions," he informed Chet. "Otherwise, I'll just end up with a bunch of tapes full of meaningless noise. Move."

Chet switched places and sat on the edge of the bed. Cameron took Chet's place at the desk and began flipping through the legal pad. "There's one voice in particular that sorta controls everybody else. He basically organizes the other voices and sometimes even announces them."

"Like a ringmaster?"

Cameron chuckled as he continued to scan the recording log. "Yeah, I guess that's as good a description as any."

"Do you know who he is?   I mean, did he give his name? Do you know who he is?"

"He's never specifically identified himself," Cameron said, "but I recognize his voice. I have no idea why he's apparently the main guy."

Chet thoughtfully shook his head. "Maybe you're just picking up fragments of scattered cell phone conversations. The atmosphere is full of electromagnetic waves and whatnot."

Cameron removed the tape from the TEAC and replaced it with a different tape from one of the round canisters.   He double-checked his recording log then zipped through the new tape, carefully watching the tape counter as the reels spun.   When he reached the desired spot, Cameron donned the headphones and pushed the TEAC's 'play' button.

Chet watched from the bed as Cameron listened intently as the reels slowly rotated. After a moment, Cameron pushed the 'stop' button, rewound the tape, removed the headphones, and stood. "Listen to this," he said.

Chet slid from the bed and resumed his seat at the desk before clamping the headphones to his ears. Cameron leaned down and pushed the 'play' button.

As before, a loud rushing noise filled the headphones. Chet could also hear, or thought he could hear, distant rhythmic chanting in the background.   He closed his eyes and concentrated.

"Moloch," said a voice, suddenly.   "It is Moloch." Startled, Chet looked up at Cameron, his eyes wide.   Then, abruptly, there was only white noise.

Chet listened to the rushing sounds for about twenty seconds longer before slowly removing the headphones.

Cameron leaned down and switched the TEAC off. "Well?" He asked.

"Well, I heard *something*," Chet admitted.

"And?"   A slight smile played about Cameron's lips.

Chet looked at him, somberly. "It was either 'Moloch' or 'My Luck.' I couldn't really tell."

SIX

THE BROILING SUMMER YIELDED INEXORABLY to autumn. With Nancy frequently in tow, Cameron continued to research the Baca Float at the Arizona Historical Society and the Hayden Library at Arizona State University, but was unable to locate much additional information about it. It was clear the Baca Float was a historical anomaly, bypassed by history and largely ignored by academia. As Mr. Williamson at the Historical Society dryly remarked, people only want to know about Geronimo and Wyatt Earp and couldn't care less about an obscure 19th century Spanish land grant. Land grants are boring.

They *did* confirm, however, that Luis Maria Cabeza de Baca actually established a formal town on one of his Floats, naming it "Esperanza" and populating it with immigrants from Mexico. Although a handful of historical records made specific reference to it, Esperanza's exact location wasn't identified, its existence and precise whereabouts seemingly taken for granted by contemporary chroniclers.

Cameron continued recording voice phenomena, occasionally with Chet present. Like wreckage from some ancient, long-forgotten vessel that drifts slowly from the featureless depths of an ocean to its glimmering surface, voices periodically emerged from the chaos of background noise. Some of them were reasonably clear, though that was always the exception. Most of the voices were unintelligible, leaving Cameron to secretly wonder whether he was listening to a coherent intelligence or simply the fancies of his own imagination. In one recording, though, a voice that was clearly female spoke with a pronounced accent and repeatedly importuned, "Is it over?" In another, two children sounded as though they were squabbling, though it was impossible to understand exactly what they were saying; after a few seconds, their shrill voices faded before being completely absorbed into the background noise. Cameron never heard them again. Other voices sounded like they were chanting in an unknown language. Nothing he heard on the tapes made much sense.

Moloch appeared only once more during the recording sessions that Chet participated in. Chet was listening to a thirty-second segment that Cameron recorded the previous night, straining to hear something, anything, when Moloch's voice abruptly materialized from the void. "It is Moloch.

We are the dead. We are dead. Don't you see?"
Chet jumped. He rewound the tape to listen
again.

"Do you see them? The dead are there with
you now, Chet."

"Jesus Christ!" Chet yanked the
headphones off and stopped the recorder, his
hands trembling. Startled, Daisy looked up at
Chet from where she was dozing on the floor near
the foot of the bed.

How could Moloch have changed his
message in the few seconds the tape was
rewinding? How did he know Chet's name? What
else did Moloch know?

Chet glanced at his watch. Cameron
wouldn't be home from work for another two
hours, but there was no way he was going to hang
around until then.

'C'mon, Daisy," he said, pushing his chair
away from the desk and standing. "Let's go for a
walk."

Daisy sprang to her feet and trotted to the
kitchen, where her leash was hanging.

"YOU SURE THAT'S WHAT HE SAID?"
Cameron asked.

Chet, who was sitting on the edge of
Cameron's bed, nodded. "It was clear as gin.
Listen for yourself." He gestured toward the tape
recorder.

"Did you log it?"

"Log it? Are you kidding? I was freaking
out!" Chet exclaimed. "But it's still right there.
You can log it after you listen to it. I left the tape
at the exact spot where Moloch spoke to me."

Cameron pulled the chair from the desk and
sat. He put the headphones on and pushed the
TEAC's 'play' button as Chet watched intently

over his shoulder. The tape recorder's reels rotated silently as Cameron closed his eyes and began to listen.

After a few moments he stopped the tape and glanced curiously at Chet. "I didn't hear anything except noise," he said. He rewound the tape and pushed the 'play' button again, listening intently.

Once again Cameron stopped and rewound the tape. Depressing the 'play' button, he strained to hear anything. He shook his head unconsciously

"Seriously, you can't hear it?" Chet marveled, though Cameron was unable to hear him through the headphones.

For a fourth time, Cameron listened to the tape after rewinding it. Finally, he removed the headphones and placed them on the desk top. "See if you can hear anything. All I hear is white noise."

Chet was perplexed. Daisy reluctantly moved to a spot farther from the bed to avoid being stepped on as Chet stood and switched places with Cameron. He plopped into the chair in front of the TEAC. "What are you talking about?" Chet muttered as he clamped the headphones over his ears. He rewound the tape then pushed the 'play' button. It occurred to him that he was trembling slightly.

Chet expected to be confronted immediately with Moloch's voice, but all that met his ears were the customary rushing sounds. He listened momentarily, then rewound the tape and tried again. The same. Frustrated, Chet pulled the earphones from his head.

Observing Chet's consternation from his seat on the edge of the bed, Cameron remarked, "You must've accidently lost it on the tape."

"No, I didn't," Chet crossly responded. "I wanted you to hear it, so I stopped the tape exactly at the point where Moloch started talking."

"So where is he?" Cameron rejoined. "He's obviously not there. If you'd logged it, we could have found it instantly."

"I don't know what could have happened to it," Chet groused. "Like I said, I made a point to stop it at the right place." He placed the earphones back on his head, rewound the tape, and pushed the 'play' button again.

"Well, I don't see how Moloch could have known your name," Cameron said, more to himself than to Chet. "And I don't see how he could have changed his message while you were rewinding it."

Chet strained to discern Moloch's voice on the tape as it snaked its way through the machine, but heard only ordinary background noise. He rewound the tape and tried again: nothing. Cameron watched silently from the corner of the bed. After a third attempt Chet finally gave up in frustration. "I don't know where it went, but it was there," he said as he removed the headphones. "Maybe it got erased somehow."

"Tell me again exactly what Moloch said," Cameron urged.

"I was listening to a tape you recorded the night before and, about half-way into it, a man's voice started talking. It was perfectly clear. He said something like, 'this is Moloch speaking.' Then he called me by name and said that 'the dead' were with me in the room."

"Did you look at Daisy? How did she react?"

"I was so freaked out that I never even looked at her," Chet confessed. "But if she'd done anything unusual I'd have noticed, so I guess she must've not done anything."

"Well, she couldn't have actually heard Moloch's voice because you were wearing headphones. I'm just wondering if she picked up on whatever else was in the room."

Chet looked genuinely shocked. "You mean you think there *were* other things in the room?"

"I don't know," Cameron said. "Maybe Moloch was just messing with you." He paused. "Or maybe you just thought you heard him and really didn't."

Chet shook his head. "No, I heard him, Cam. You'd have heard him, too. It was really freaky, especially when he said my name. I just wish I knew what happened to the tape, why we can't hear Moloch now."

Cameron didn't immediately reply, but looked thoughtful. "I'm thinking that, if Moloch can alter a recording while you're rewinding it, he can also make it disappear completely," he finally said.

"So you think there really is a 'Moloch'?" Chet softly asked.

"I think there's someone, or something, out there who calls himself 'Moloch'," Cameron replied. "*Somebody* talked to you on the tape, right?"

"'Out there' where?" Chet wondered. "Where's 'out there'"?

DAISY LEAPED EXCITEDLY FROM the Jeep and began gamboling around the cemetery, as Cameron and Chet pulled their day packs from the floor behind the seats. "So this is it?" Chet said, looking around. "This is where you want to record?"

Cameron pointed to the decaying charnel house at the far edge of the cemetery. "In there."

Chet donned his pack and drew Cameron's attention to his new hiking boots. "Hey, check these out," he said, pointing to his feet. "They were on sale."

Cameron glanced at Chet's boots. "Yeah nice, but you probably shouldn't have worn a brand new pair of boots on a hike. They're liable to rub the hell out of your feet."

"You're just jealous," Chet replied as he ambled over to the collapsing ruin. Daisy raced over to join him. He gingerly poked his head through the gaping crack in the wall. "Christ, Cam, it's full of bones!" he yelped.

Cameron sighed, shouldered his pack, and headed toward Chet. "I think they're mostly animal bones," he ventured, stepping around an overgrown, partially sunken, grave.

"Animal bones my fanny!" Chet snorted. "Stick your head in and look!" He stepped aside and gestured toward the crack.

In order to mollify Chet, Cameron removed his hat and stuck his head inside the old building. "Yep, animal bones," he announced after a moment, withdrawing his head.

"Yeah, right," Chet sniffed. "Since when do they put dead animals inside tombs?"

"Nobody put 'em in there, Chet," Cameron explained, stepping away from the charnel house. "Coyotes and stuff just drag their kills in there to keep other animals from eating 'em."

"They must've been some bad-ass coyotes," Chet replied, jamming his hat on his head, "because there's a human skull in there." He followed Cameron to the faint trail leading from the cemetery. "This leads to the buildings?" Cameron nodded. "Well, it ain't getting' any cooler. Let's go check 'em out." Chet stepped around Cameron, onto the path, and began striding up the slope toward the distant hills with Cameron behind.

Daisy watched them depart but continued to linger near the charnel house. She trotted around it several times, testing the air, and paused once to dig in the earth. Cameron looked back from the trail and whistled for her, but Daisy ignored his entreaty and continued to explore the vicinity of the tomb.

"Hey, Daisy, c'mon!" Cameron yelled from the path.

Daisy approached its cracked wall, her head lowered and a low growl ebbing deep in her throat. Her ears were laid back against her head. She hesitatingly peered into its dim interior, her growl becoming more intense and the hair on her back standing upright. Daisy continued to stare into the interior of the structure, seemingly transfixed. She snarled, exposing her formidable canine teeth, then slowly began to back away from the charnel house, her body rigid and her eyes unmoving from the crack in its crumbling wall.

Cameron and Chet stopped on the trail and looked back at the cemetery. "What's with Daisy?" Chet asked, mopping copious amounts of sweat from his face with a bandana.

"I don't know, but she apparently saw something she doesn't like," Cameron murmured. "C'mon, Daisy," he shouted. The tension in his voice was palpable.

Daisy didn't acknowledge Cameron's call, but remained rigid, continuing to stare unflinchingly at the charnel house. It was as though she feared averting her eyes, feared turning away.

"I'm gonna go see what's wrong with Daisy," Cameron told Chet. "Go ahead and we'll catch up. Just stay on the trail. You can't get lost."

"Okay, I'll see you two up ahead." Chet stuffed his bandana into a hip pocket and adjusted his pack before striking off for the hills. Cameron turned back toward the cemetery.

"Hey, Daisy, what the heck's wrong with you?" he called as he walked. Daisy had retreated toward a low, rusted wrought iron fence that surrounded a sunken grave, pressing into it, without taking her eyes off the charnel house. She continued to growl, seemingly oblivious to Cameron's approach. He glanced rearward; Chet's figure receded into the colorless desert as he trudged along the trail in the direction of the hills.

The path took Cameron directly past the charnel house that continued to frighten Daisy and he drew near it with a mixture of curiosity and mild apprehension. "Hey, girl, you okay?" he said, softly. Daisy snarled toward the moldering structure, completely ignoring him.

Cameron paused at the charnel house and peered inside through the crack in its crumbling wall. Along the far wall he noted the partial human skull that Nancy and Chet had both remarked on.

"Nuthin' here, Daisy," he assured her, turning away. "C'mon, girl."

Daisy slunk against the wrought iron fence and began to softly whine as Cameron approached her. She lowered her head and wagged her tail uncertainly.

"What the heck's gotten into you?" Cameron cooed as he squatted next to her and scratched her ears. "There's nothing scary in there, you big baby." Daisy responded by enthusiastically wagging her tail and licking Cameron's face. "C'mon, we've gotta catch up with Chet," he smiled.

Cameron stood and began walking toward the charnel house and the trail leading to the hills beyond. Daisy didn't budge, but watched him quizzically while slowly wagging her tail.

"C'mon, Daisy," Cameron urged, turning toward her.

Daisy took a tentative step forward, then abruptly stopped, her front paw suspended in mid-air. Her ears flicked forward and she resumed growling as she stared at the decaying structure.

"Daisy, come on," Cameron repeated, this time with an edge in his voice.

Daisy began to advance, but promptly backed up and pressed against the wrought iron fence again. She whined and began to paw the dirt with her feet.

Cameron strode to Daisy and kneeled in front of her. She was trembling and her terrified eyes were rimmed with white. When he extended his hand to pet her, Daisy meekly lowered her head.

"What's up with you, Silly?" She resumed a low growl deep in her throat as Cameron gently stroked her head. Daisy stared intently beyond Cameron, her gaze fixed on the charnel house behind him. "What are you so afraid of?" He rubbed Daisy's throat and scratched her ears. "Look, you can't stay here all day," he lectured. "Chet's way ahead of us now and he's probably wondering what happened to us. Do you want him to know what a doofus you've been? Now quit being such a baby and come on." Cameron stood, grasped Daisy's collar, and gently tugged it upward, urging her to her feet. She refused to budge, but slumped further against the low wrought iron fence. The low growl in her throat intensified, her attention still focused on the charnel house.   She looked imploringly at Cameron.

"Daisy, dammit, you *can't* just sit here," Cameron scolded her in exasperation. "We've gotta go!" He pulled more firmly on her collar, lifting her front quarters more-or-less upright, though she obstinately refused to cooperate. "We've gotta go. Now!"

Cameron half dragged Daisy into a standing position. She reluctantly yielded and, though she was trembling, Daisy continued to growl. Her gaze remained fixed on the nearby charnel house as she curled her lips to expose her long carnassial teeth. Daisy pressed her body firmly against Cameron's legs.

Cameron took a half-step forward and gently tugged on Daisy's collar, urging her to follow. She resisted and strained rearward, her claws digging into the earth and her head nearly slipping from her collar beneath Cameron's grasp.

"Daisy, what the hell's the matter with you?" Cameron reprimanded her. "There's absolutely nothing over there," he continued, nodding toward the charnel house. "I've never seen you act this way." He released his grip on her collar and Daisy plopped onto the dusty ground. He looked at her in puzzlement while she continued to stare at the structure and softly growl. "Okay, here's what we're gonna do," he finally said. "We're gonna get in the Jeep and drive away from the cemetery, then catch up with Chet from there. Okay?" Discerning the change in the tone of Cameron's voice, Daisy glanced up at him. "Okay, then, let's go!" Cameron excitedly clapped his hands and began to stride away from the charnel house, toward his Jeep parked near the perimeter of the graveyard. After ten steps he turned to insure that Daisy was behind him.

Daisy was on her feet, still staring at the charnel house. When she heard Cameron stop walking, she turned in his direction.

Cameron whistled. "C'mon, Daisy," he called. "Let's go to the Jeep." She immediately trotted to him, wagging her tail. "Good girl!" he smiled, scratching her ears. "Now, let's go find Chet."

Together, they made their way back to Cameron's Jeep. Neither of them looked back at the charnel house as Cameron started the vehicle and pulled into the desert, away from the cemetery.

Because of the flatness of the surrounding table land, Cameron could have easily driven to the base of the hills to which Chet was presumably now hiking. However, Cameron's attitude toward the Float had become increasingly paternalistic over the past several weeks; he viewed it as something of his own personal fief, ignored by society and forgotten by history. Besides, if there really *was* treasure hidden somewhere on the Float, he was loath to crisscross it with Jeep tracks, impliedly inviting hordes of urban hikers and off-roaders to venture onto the Float. The Float had managed to remain hidden in plain sight for over a century, and Cameron intended to keep it that way. He figured he'd drive a short distance from the cemetery, toward the hills, before parking. From that point he and Daisy could rapidly catch up with Chet simply by following the trail leading into the nearby hills.

Cameron scanned the surrounding landscape as the Jeep bumped over the scorched, rock-strewn ground. Because the desert was dotted only here and there with stunted greasewood bushes and sloped slightly upward, he was able to see a great distance ahead. The faint path leading from the grave yard into the hills was easily discernible, though Chet was nowhere to be seen.

"Where's Chet?" he idly asked Daisy. She braced herself against the seat as the swaying Jeep slowly eased its way across a narrow arroyo.

Cameron braked to a stop, put the Jeep in 'P,' and switched the engine off. He squinted through his sunglasses and the bug-spattered windshield in an effort to spot any movement in a desert seemingly devoid of life. Had he stuck to the trail as Cameron suggested, it would have been easy to spot Chet as he trudged toward the hills. But, although Cameron could see in all directions, there was no sign of Chet. He tried to recall what Chet was wearing, but drew a blank. Dammit!" he swore under his breath.

Cameron stepped from the Jeep as Daisy hopped to the ground from the passenger's side. He reached across and honked the horn three times while continuing to scan the area. Daisy wandered around the vicinity of the Jeep, her nose to the ground.

"Hey, Chet!" Cameron hollered. "Where are you?" He honked the horn again. Nothing. "Chet!" Although a warm breeze wafted over him, Cameron was inexplicably cold. "Chet! Chet!" Cameron hadn't spent *that* much time with Daisy at the cemetery; it seemed improbable that Chet could have gotten so far ahead of them.

Cameron was at a loss. He and Daisy could simply hike to the hills, where they would undoubtedly find Chet waiting for them. But what if, for whatever reason, Chet wasn't there? What then? What if Chet was bitten by a rattlesnake and was lying out in the desert somewhere? Or what if he'd simply gotten lost, as improbable as that was? A round trip hike to the hills would take at least two hours, during which time Chet could easily die if bitten by a venomous snake. Alternatively, if Cameron abandoned the original plan, he could drive back to town right now and report to the cops that he and Chet had been separated while hiking. A formal search could then be mobilized.

But what if Chet *wasn't* in any danger? What if he simply made it to the hills more rapidly than Cameron anticipated and was patiently awaiting his imminent arrival? It was possible that Chet was just too far away to hear Cameron honking the Jeep's horn, especially given the breezy conditions. And the fact that Cameron was unable to spot Chet meant absolutely nothing; the heat waves that shimmered from the desert floor distorted everything, rendering it impossible to definitively identify objects. Cameron would look like an utter fool if he organized a full-blown search while Chet was sitting on his butt in the nearby hills, eating energy bars and patiently waiting for them. That aside, Cameron would be responsible for paying the costs of such a potentially unnecessary search, which could be substantial.

After a short period of frustrated reflection, Cameron decided on a compromise: he and Daisy would hike up the trail for a distance with the expectation of rendezvousing with Chet en route. Should they fail to encounter him, they would return to the Jeep and drive into town, where they would notify the authorities that they'd become separated.

"Dammit," Cameron muttered under his breath. He whistled for Daisy, who was exploring the desert on the far side of the Jeep. She romped over to him. "C'mon, Daisy," he smiled, "you wanna drink?" He pulled the collapsible dog bowl from the back of the Jeep and, placing it on the ground, filled it halfway with water from a gallon jug. "It's warm but at least it's wet," he said as Daisy drank noisily, slopping water from the bowl onto the dry earth. When Daisy finished drinking, she looked at Cameron expectantly, water dripping from her muzzle.

Cameron picked up Daisy's empty bowl and placed it back in the Jeep. He shouldered his day pack, adjusted his hat and sunglasses, and took a sip of tepid water from his canteen. "Well, shall we go find Chet?" he asked Daisy, who responded by enthusiastically wagging her tail. Cameron stepped onto the trail leading to the hills, Daisy at his heels. Although he hoped Chet was waiting for them ahead, Cameron had a funny feeling in his stomach.

"SO YOU AND YOUR BUDDY GOT lost hiking." It was the third time the cop made the same statement.

"No, we didn't get lost," Cameron peevishly corrected him, struggling to conceal his annoyance. "We got separated and I never found him. I don't know whether he got bit by a snake, or fell down an abandoned mine shaft, or what."

"Are you sure he just didn't go home? My guess is that he's playin' a prank on you."

"We were in my Jeep so I don't know how he'd get home unless he hitchhiked. And, no, Chet's not playing a prank on me; he wouldn't just go home without telling me. I tried calling his cell phone but couldn't get a signal."

"When's the last time you saw your friend?" the cop asked.

Cameron glanced at his watch. "A little over three hours ago."

The cop sighed as he closed his note book. "He'll show up. He's probably home right now, drinking a beer and wondering why you drove off and left him out in the desert."

"Then why doesn't he answer his cell phone?" Cameron pointedly asked. "When I finally managed to get a signal he still didn't pick up."

"Look, I'm not sure where you guys were hiking is even within our jurisdiction, but I'll turn it over to one of our detectives," the cop said, ignoring the question. He removed a white business card from his uniform pocket, flipped it over, and scrawled something on the back. "Here's my card. The incident number's on the back. Don't expect to hear anything from my end for a few days. Nine times out of ten the person alleged to be missing wasn't missing to begin with, or just shows up." He handed the card to Cameron and returned his pen to his breast pocket. "My advice is to drive to your buddy's apartment and see if he's there. Like I said, he's probably been home for a couple of hours. He's drinkin' a beer, wondering why you abandoned his ass out in the middle of the desert. You guys'll probably get a few laughs out of it."

Cameron took the officer's card without glancing at it. "Yeah, I'll do that," he said without conviction. "So what if Chet's not there?"

The cop shrugged. "If your buddy's not there and doesn't return home in the next day or two, give us a call. Just be sure to refer to the incident number on the back. If the area where you were is within our jurisdiction, you can talk to a detective." The cop nodded toward the business card in Cameron's hand.

"The area is called the 'Baca Float'," Cameron said. "But what if it's not in your jurisdiction?"

"Yeah, whatever," the cop shrugged again. "If it's not in our jurisdiction, you'll have to talk to whoever's jurisdiction it *is* in."

"You've been a big help," Cameron said, icily.

"No problem. That's why we get paid," the cop responded. Cameron couldn't tell whether he was mocking him or being serious.

NANCY WAS INCREDULOUS. "You lost Chet out in the desert?" she blurted when Cameron called her on his cell phone.

"No, I didn't lose him," Cameron crossly responded. "We got separated when Daisy started acting weird and I had to go back and retrieve her. It was no big deal; Chet kept on hiking and I figured we'd just catch up with him. But we never did."

"'Retrieve her' from where?" Nancy was perplexed.

Cameron really didn't feel like getting into it at that moment. "Daisy got sidetracked at the cemetery and I didn't want to leave her behind while she farted around, so I told Chet to go on hiking while I went back to get Daisy. Like I said, it was no big deal. The only problem was that, after I rounded-up Daisy, I couldn't find Chet."

"Did you actually *look* for him?" Nancy asked, dubiously.

Cameron didn't appreciate Nancy's interrogation and was becoming aggravated by her imperious tone.

"*Of course* I looked for him. Daisy and I hiked almost as far as the hill you and I hiked to this summer. From where we were, I could see the entire desert floor below, but there was no sign of Chet. Because I didn't know what else to do, I hiked back to the Jeep and drove to the police."

"So as far as you know, Chet may still be out there?"

"I don't know, Nancy!" Cameron snapped. "That's what I'm trying to tell you. I don't know where Chet is!"

"So are you going back out there to look for him?"

"Daisy and I are headed back out there now," Cameron assured her. "In the meantime, will you drive by Chet's apartment, just to see if he's there? I don't know why he would be, but it won't hurt to check."

"I'll head there as soon as we hang up. I'll call you when I'm there."

"It's kinda weird on the Float, so there may not be any cell reception," Cameron told her. "If I don't answer, leave a message. I'll keep checking my phone."

There was a pause at the other end. "What are you gonna do if you can't find him, Cam?" Nancy finally asked, softly.

"How could I *not* find Chet, Nancy? Chet didn't just vaporize." Cameron spoke as he walked to his Jeep after filing his report with the cop. Daisy waged her tail excitedly as he approached.

"No, I mean what if he fell into a hole or something. What if Chet's lying out there, hurt?"

Cameron was also worried about that, but preferred not to dwell on it. Hopefully, his, and Nancy's, anxieties were groundless. "I'm sure Chet's okay," he assured her, though his absence of conviction was apparent. "We just got our wires crossed and got separated. Chet's probably back where we parked the Jeep, hopping mad because I drove off without him." Cameron wished that were true. He slid into the driver's seat, snapped his seatbelt on, and twisted the key. The Jeep roared to life. "I'm gonna go now, Nancy. Call me as soon as you get to Chet's apartment."

"I'm on my way out the door," Nancy said. "Call me as soon as you find Chet." She paused. "Call me even if you *don't* find Chet...either way, call me."

"I will. Don't worry, Nance. Like the cop said, I'm sure Chet's fine. We'll be back later today and you guys can beat up on me about how I screwed everything up."

"Well, don't *you* fall into a hole or get stung by a scorpion," Nancy scolded him. "I wouldn't know where to start looking for you out there, Cam."

Cameron pulled from the police department parking lot. "It's not me I'm worried about, Nancy. It's Chet."

CAMERON DROVE DIRECTLY BACK to the Float. He sped past the cemetery and bumped his way across the open desert directly to the base of the hills. Because Chet was supposed to have stuck to the path leading from the cemetery, Cameron tried to follow it in the Jeep. Once he passed the spot where he left Chet to return to the cemetery to retrieve Daisy, Cameron slowed the Jeep and proceeded at a crawl. He poked his head out the open door and scanned the faint trial, hoping to spot something that would indicate the direction Chet was headed. Dust boiled into the Jeep's open cab and rocks, dislodged by the Jeep's off-road tires, bounced off its sides.

"You okay, Daisy?" Cameron glanced over as the vehicle swayed over a bump. Daisy wagged her tail. Although she was beginning to pant because of the rising temperature, Daisy was clearly excited to be outdoors, driving around.

The land gradually increased in elevation as they drew nearer the hills. Cameron periodically stopped the Jeep, switched the ignition off, and honked its horn repeatedly. While engrossed in listening for any response, Daisy hopped out and nosed along the trail in front of the vehicle. Hearing nothing but the melancholy sigh of the parched breeze, Cameron started the Jeep and waited for Daisy to race back to the vehicle before resuming their laborious ascent. Cameron was becoming fearful. It had been nearly five hours since he and Chet had parted, yet there was no trace of him. It was as though he'd simply vanished. Cameron's palms were sweaty, though not from the ambient temperature. He was close to panic. "Chet! Chet!" he cried as he frantically honked the Jeep's horn.

Then Cameron saw it. Lying in the center of the trail was one of Chet's new hiking boots. Cameron recognized it immediately.

Even though they were proceeding at a snail's pace, he slammed the brakes on, shoved the transmission lever into 'P,' and leapt out. Daisy jumped from the Jeep excitedly.

Cameron was stunned that he apparently failed to spot Chet's boot earlier that day, when he and Daisy hiked along this exact area of the path. How could they possibly have overlooked it? He reached down to retrieve it.

Although slightly dusty, the boot was essentially pristine and was undoubtedly Chet's; Cameron recognized it from earlier that morning. Curiously, the laces were still tied, as though the boot had been wrenched from Chet's foot. Cameron couldn't imagine why Chet would otherwise remove his boot without untying it. He had a sick feeling in the pit of his stomach.

He carried the boot to the Jeep and placed it carefully on the rear floor board. Cameron honked the Jeep's horn repeatedly, straining his ears for any response. Silence. Frustrated, he stepped from the vehicle and began examining the area around the Jeep, looking for the mate to Chet's boot. Nothing. Daisy wandered about, sniffing the ground and periodically stopping to watch Cameron.

Cameron's frantic search yielded nothing. Although Chet had disappeared only a few hours ago, it seemed like he'd been missing for an eternity. Cameron's discovery of Chet's boot had unnerved him and he wasn't sure what to do next. He looked at his watch: it was approaching 6:00 p.m.; dusk was approaching and the shadows from the stunted desert vegetation were already growing longer. The temperature was also starting to decline, albeit almost imperceptibly. He fished his cell phone from his pants pocket, intending to call Nancy. As before, it was immediately apparent there was no coverage on the Float. Cameron angrily jammed his phone back into his pocket.

"C'mon, Daisy," he called, striding back to the Jeep. Daisy sprang into the passenger's seat as Cameron twisted the ignition key. With daylight fading, he decided to drive to the top of the hill he and Nancy reached during their hike earlier that summer. From that eminence he'd be able to survey the surrounding bench land before it became completely dark. Cameron tried to convince himself that he'd certainly be able to spot *something* from the crest of the hill.

The Jeep slowly rumbled up the trail. Although Cameron had not eaten since picking

Chet up at his apartment earlier that morning, his roiling stomach was so unsettled that he doubted he'd be able to keep any food down, even if he was hungry. He glanced over at Daisy, who *had* to be starving. "You hungry, Daisy?" he smiled. Without taking his eyes from the path, Cameron reached into the back of the Jeep and withdrew a bag of Milk Bones from his pack. He placed the bag on his lap, removed two Milk Bones, and placed them next to Daisy on the passenger's seat. She eagerly scarfed them down and Cameron patted her head. "Atta girl," he praised her. He'd give Daisy another dish of water once they crested the hill.

The effulgent sun had by now dropped behind the surrounding hills and, although there remained ample ambient light, dusk was rapidly descending. Cameron reached down to flick on the Jeep's headlights and periodically honked the Jeep's horn as they climbed. Notwithstanding their ascent, the gradient was slight and rendered it unnecessary for Cameron to utilize the Jeep's four-wheel drive. Below them, far in the distance, Cameron could see cars driving along McDonald Drive.

Cameron didn't want to think about what he should do if, when he reached the top of the hill, Chet was nowhere to be seen. Worse, what if Chet had gotten injured and was, even now, lying helpless somewhere out in the desert? Cameron tried to banish such thoughts from his mind. The likelihood is that Chet had previously concluded that Cameron had, for whatever reason, abandoned him, and had simply walked back to the highway and hitched a ride back to his apartment. Chet certainly couldn't have hiked very far wearing only one boot. Even now, there was probably a message on Cameron's cell phone from Nancy, informing him that Chet was already at his apartment when she arrived there. He would easily be able to retrieve Nancy's voice mail once he got off the Float and back to civilization.

SEVEN

IT WAS NEARLY DARK BY THE TIME the Jeep crested the hill. Although Cameron hoped to find Chet sitting there, drinking a bottle of water and patiently awaiting Cameron's arrival, he knew that such a scenario was probably a fantasy. Still, his heart sank when the Jeep finally reached the hill top and he found it deserted.

Cameron pulled to a halt and switched the ignition off. He sighed and Daisy looked at him expectantly from the passenger's seat, though it was becoming difficult to discern more than her general outline because of the increasing darkness.

Cameron stepped from the Jeep then reached in the back and retrieved Daisy's collapsible dish and a jug of water. Daisy jumped across to the driver's seat and watched with interest. Placing Daisy's dish on the ground, Cameron filled it with water. "C'mon girl," he smiled. Daisy hopped from the Jeep and gratefully began lapping up the warm water as Cameron tipped the jug and took a drink from it. He then refilled Daisy's dish and, walking to the edge of the hill top, peered into the darkness toward the surrounding bottomland. A cool breeze kicked up some dust, causing him to shiver.

Far to the south, the rush hour traffic along McDonald Drive had increased. Glittering headlights created the illusion of a sinuous creature wending its way through the desert. Cameron strained to see any sign of Chet when Daisy trotted up and sat quietly beside him. Cameron reached down and scratched her ears. "Where's Chet, Daisy?" he murmured as he searched the enveloping darkness.

Seeing nothing, Cameron walked back to the Jeep and began honking the horn. In the distance, coyotes began to yip and wail, an eerie, unearthly, lament.

Cameron started hollering Chet's name, listening intently every few seconds. Nothing. Only the coyotes seemed to acknowledge his agitated summons by increasing the intensity of their crying.

Cameron walked to the opposite edge of the hill and looked in the direction of the structures he'd previously located on Google earth and that he and Nancy actually saw on their previous hike. Daisy followed and lay on the cooling ground at his feet. Cameron reached down to pet her then did an abrupt double-take. He strained his eyes into the encompassing void.

A light twinkled far down the valley, a pale cynosure emanating from the ostensibly abandoned structures. It was unmistakable.

Because it was a new moon, the blanket of darkness rendered it impossible for Cameron to identify individual buildings. Yet the tiny light wasn't the freak reflection of a distant headlight or the moon; there was no moon and McDonald Drive was too far away for the lights from passing cars to travel. Moreover, the hills that ringed the valley would have completely blocked any stray external light.

The light flickered like a flame and, as Cameron watched in fascination, was momentarily blotted out, as if someone had stepped in front of it.

Could Chet have actually have made it all the way down to the buildings? Had he lit a fire in an effort to attract attention, or to keep the coyotes at bay? Though it seemed impossible that Chet could have hiked so far in the short period of time that Cameron had returned to the cemetery in order to retrieve Daisy, the light was indisputably real and certainly hadn't lit itself. Someone was definitely down there, among the buildings, and whoever it was had lit a fire. Who could it be other than Chet?

Cameron placed his hands around his mouth like a megaphone. "Chet, Chet!" he shrieked into the valley. The coyotes responded by increasing their mournful cacophony.

Cameron raced back to the Jeep, tripping and sliding in the darkness, where he frantically resumed honking the horn. Daisy ignored his excited exertions, but slowly got to her feet and peered intently into the valley. A growl began to rumble deep in her throat and the hair on her hackles stood upright.

Cameron paused and listened intently. The sigh of the wind carried the lugubrious chorus of coyotes to his ears, but nothing more. He glanced toward the edge of the hill. Daisy appeared as a ghostly form, her body rigid, her head lowered as she continued to stare at the flickering light.

He wasn't sure what to do. Chet was evidently too far away to hear the Jeep's horn, much less Cameron's shouts. He could immediately attempt to drive to Chet, though he was apprehensive about attempting to negotiate in the darkness the broken, rocky, trail leading farther into the valley. If he had a flat, or worse, rolled the Jeep in the darkness and was injured, he would be marooned out here for God knows how long. And what if the guy down there wasn't even Chet? For all Cameron knew, Nancy was over at Chet's apartment at this moment, where they were waiting for Cameron to call. What would be the point in undertaking a hazardous rescue attempt at night if whoever it was down there in the buildings didn't want or need to be rescued? Despite the fact that he knew they were harmless, Cameron was becoming unnerved by the eerie howl of the coyotes, which seemed to surround them.

He stepped from the Jeep and returned to Daisy at the edge of the hill. She took no notice of his arrival, but continued to stare fixedly toward the faint light far below. It was when he reached down to pet her that he discerned how tense Daisy was; only then could Cameron feel Daisy's inaudible growl rumble deep in her throat. "What's wrong, girl?" he softly asked, stroking her head. Daisy began to tremble.

Cameron tried to follow her gaze into the valley, but all that was visible was the tiny point of light in the darkness far below. "What should we do, girl?" he asked as he continued to stroke Daisy's head. She whimpered and backed in the direction of the Jeep. Cameron grasped her collar to restrain her, but she continued to pull away. "It's okay, girl," he soothed her. "It's just dumb ole Chet down there. What are you scared of?" A gust of wind rushed past them, rattling a couple of pebbles over the precipice. Cameron jumped, releasing Daisy's collar. She promptly retreated to the Jeep and leapt into the passenger's seat.

Cameron stood at the edge of the hill and peered once more into the blackness, where the enigmatic light continued to flicker. He turned and walked back to the Jeep. Twisting the ignition key, he flicked the headlights on and swung a wide U-turn in the direction he'd arrived from earlier that evening. Even if it *was* Chet down there, the weather was mild and, although it might be uncomfortable spending a night outdoors, he certainly wouldn't freeze. Cameron was confident that Chet also had enough energy bars and water to last him until tomorrow, a Sunday, when he would be able to drive down and retrieve him in the daylight. Besides, he'd call Nancy as soon as he got off the Float, who would no doubt assure him that Chet was safe and sound back at his apartment.

Hopefully.

Cameron reached over and patted a trembling Daisy, who gratefully licked his hand.

"WHAT'S THIS?" CITY OF SCOTTSDALE Detective Bullard took the file containing the missing person's report on Chet from the clerk's outstretched hand.

"Some guy disappeared hiking," the clerk indifferently responded before turning on his heel and departing.

Bullard plopped down at his desk, took a sip of day-old microwaved coffee, and flipped open the file. He rapidly scanned its abbreviated contents. "Who the hell took this report?" he groused to no one in particular.

At the bottom of the second page, the cop who took the report had sketched a rough map of the area where the two guys were hiking. It resembled a traffic diagram. Based on the drawing, the guy disappeared into the desert north of McDonald Drive and west of Scottsdale Road. This isn't even in the city, Bullard thought. The Indians have jurisdiction over that area.

He stood and, carrying his cup of coffee in one hand and the police report in the other, made his way across the room where an enormous multi-colored, laminated map of the city hung on the wall. Bullard studied it for a moment, sipping coffee.

In order to differentiate them, the city's various "districts" or "neighborhoods" were highlighted in different colors. Bullard placed his cup and the report on a nearby desk and reached up to trace a section of undifferentiated desert, which was outlined in brown, with a fingertip. He nodded unconsciously to himself. As he suspected, Chet disappeared in an area that was outside the city limits and, thus, beyond its jurisdiction. He retrieved his coffee and returned to his desk, glad that he'd managed to eliminate so easily a potential pain-in-the-butt. Let the Indians, or whoever, deal with it.

At his desk, the detective buzzed a clerk.

"Mortimer," grunted a human at the other end.

"This is Bullard. I've got a report on my desk that doesn't belong here. The incident occurred outside the city limits. Come get it and forward it to whoever has jurisdiction."

"Will do," Mortimer assured him.

Bullard tossed the document into his "out" box and finished his coffee before turning his attention to the next missing person file atop the stack. It would be nice if he could dispose of this one so readily.

CAMERON WAS ABLE TO SNAG a signal as soon as he was off the Float. He slowed, pulled the Jeep to the side of the road, and slipped transmission into 'P'. Reaching into the back, he grabbed another Milk Bone for Daisy. She happily crunched as he scrolled down his cell phone's menu to find Nancy's number. His hands were shaking.

"Hi, it's me," Cameron blurted the instant she picked up. "Did you find Chet?"

"He wasn't there," Nancy responded, her voice flat.

Cameron's heart sank. "You drove to his apartment?"

"I drove to Chet's apartment," Nancy confirmed, "right after we spoke earlier. Chet's car was in his parking space, and I banged on the door and yelled but he never answered." She paused. "You didn't find him?" She already knew the answer.

"It was already getting dark by the time I got back out there," Cameron explained. "I drove all the way to the top of that hill where you and I hiked, but never saw him." He decided not to mention finding Chet's boot.

"Dammit, Cam! What are we gonna do?"

"Well, I already reported it to the cops," Cameron lamely responded.

"Yeah, I know. So what are they gonna do to find Chet?"

"I don't know. They said they'd give it to a detective." Cameron was sick at heart but hoped his voice didn't betray his dejection.

"Yeah, but are they actually gonna *do* anything? Have they even started looking for him?"

Cameron sighed. "They told me to wait a couple of days then call them."

"Wait a couple of days!" Nancy blurted. "Cam, you've gotta be kidding! What if Chet's out there right now, at the bottom of some mine shaft with both legs broken? The cops are gonna wait two days before they actually do anything? You can't be serious."

"That's what they told me, Nancy. What do you want from me?"

"I'll tell you want I *don't* want. I don't want you to lose Chet," she declared.

Cameron ignored her reproachful tone. "According to the cop, most people who are reported missing aren't really missing and show up after a day or two. That's why they wait a couple of days before doing anything."

There was silence for a few moments. "Cam, I think something bad happened to Chet," Nancy finally said, very softly.

DETECTIVE WOODY MOE WAS A FULL-BLOODED Native American, a member of the Tohono O'odham Nation, and had worked for the Salt River Tribal PD for fifteen years. He wasn't sure why he got saddled with this particular missing person file, but suspected that it ended up on his desk largely by default: nobody else in the small tribal police department wanted to mess with it. He had no way of knowing the file had already bounced around other local police departments for the previous week before landing with the tribal police. None of those departments thought they had jurisdiction over the Float, so they simply passed the file on to the next agency which *might* have jurisdiction. Out of sight, out of mind.

Moe was aware of the contents of the pasteboard folder even without opening it because somebody had scrawled "Missing Person" on a florescent pink Post-It note and stuck it on the outside. He sat at his desk and opened the file.

Because missing persons reports were routine on the rez they generated little excitement. Typically, a tribal member on a bender was reported missing by his anxious wife, only to sheepishly return home, after sobering up, a few days later. But Moe immediately saw this was no tribal member. According to the perfunctory report in the file, the missing guy was from Phoenix, was out hiking with a friend, and got separated. The friend apparently made it back to the car without the missing guy. Moe flipped back to the first page of the report; it was dated a week ago. In all probability, the missing guy had shown up in the interim.

Moe was puzzled, however. Although the rez was contiguous to the cities of Scottsdale, Mesa, Tempe and Fountain Hills, he was unsure whether the area where the two were hiking was actually located on the rez. It looked to him like it was in Scottsdale. So how'd the guy's file end up with the tribal police?

Moe stood and walked into an adjoining room, brandishing the report. "Hey," he addressed a uniformed Salt River cop sitting at a desk, drinking a can of Coke and smoking a cigarette, "is this on the rez?" He placed the report on the desk and pointed to the sketch at the bottom of the page.

The cop took another drag off his cigarette, then hunched over and stared at the diagram. "Hard to say," he announced after a moment.

"Gee, really?" Moe marveled. "If it wasn't 'hard to say' I'd already know the answer and wouldn't have asked you in the first place."

The cop looked at him sourly. He drained his Coke, tossed the empty can into the trash, adjusted his position in his chair, and frowned at the drawing again. "It looks like it," he finally said. He had no idea what his anticipated response was supposed to be, but was eager to get rid of the bothersome detective.

"It looks like what?" Moe probed.

"Uh, it looks like this," he swirled his fingertip around the sketch, "is part of the reservation."

"You ever been on patrol out there?" Moe skeptically asked.

"Well, not personally because there's nuthin' out there but stinkin' desert. What's to patrol? Rabbits?"

Moe gathered the missing person's report from the cop's desk. "I thought it looked more like it's in Scottsdale," he said.

"Yeah, that could be, too," the cop amiably conceded, pleased that Moe was departing. "You may want to shoot it their way," he suggested, then frowned unconsciously as he reflected. "But if it's in Scottsdale, why do you have the file?"

Moe ignored the question and returned to his desk. Irrespective of whether the incident occurred in Scottsdale or on the reservation, it would only take a few minutes to call the missing guy's friend to confirm that he'd returned home. Having done so, the detective could file the entire matter away and move on to more important things.

"WHAT ARE WE GONNA TELL Chet's family?"

"Chet didn't have any sibs and his parents divorced when he was a kid," Cameron replied. "His dad remarried and moved to California and I don't think Chet saw much of him after that; he never talked about his dad, anyway. Chet lived with his mom until she moved somewhere in the mid-west, I think Wisconsin, about ten years ago. I wouldn't have the slightest idea how to get in touch with either of Chet's parents." Cameron and Nancy were sitting on the couch in his apartment, Daisy dozing on the floor at their feet. A week had passed since Chet's disappearance.

"You called his work?"

"Yeah, I called and talked to the manager and told him what happened. I told him that I'd let him know whenever I heard something. I think some people in Chet's office are organizing a search, too."

Nancy took a sip of coffee. "That's really nice." She shook her head in disbelief. "I'm sorry, Cam, but all of this seems impossible. Stuff like this only happens to *other* people. I keep half-expecting to wake up and find out it was all a bad dream." Given the passage of time since his disappearance, both of them realized, but didn't want to admit, that Chet probably perished in the desert from thirst. A lonely, melancholic death.

Cameron reached over, took her cup from her, and placed it on an end table. He put his arm around her. "I know, Nance. I keep going over in my head what could have happened to him, what I could maybe have done differently."

She hugged him. "It's not your fault, Cam" she sniffled. "It's just one of those things. You just went back to get Daisy. How could you have known that something would happen to Chet?" Hearing her name, Daisy lazily wagged the tip of her tail without opening her eyes.

Cameron sighed. "I know. That's what I keep telling myself. But I should have told Chet to just stay put, rather than tell him that we'd catch up to him. I had no idea, Nance..." his voice trailed off.

"Cam, it's *not* your fault," she said, emphatically. "No matter what happened to Chet, it's not your fault. It's nobody's fault."

Cameron nodded wordlessly. He wished he actually believed her.

"Did you ever hear from the police?" Nancy straightened and wiped her eyes on the sleeve of her blouse.

"I called the number on the card the cop gave me a bunch of times and left a ton of messages, including that I found Chet's boot, but nobody returns my calls," Cameron sighed. "I guess that, because we're nobodies, the cops have better stuff to do. I'll bet that if Chet was related to the mayor or the police chief they'd move heaven and earth to find him," he bitterly concluded.

Nancy nodded wordlessly. She'd returned to the Float with Cameron the day after Chet's disappearance, at which time he'd sheepishly confessed finding Chet's boot. He'd earlier informed Nancy about encountering the light emanating from the structures on the far side of the hill.

"It couldn't have been Chet," she opined. "There's no way Chet could have hiked that far in the few minutes it took you to return to the cemetery to get Daisy. It would have been physically impossible. It was just some hikers or campers down there."

They spent that entire day driving Cameron's Jeep around the Float, honking the horn and calling Chet's name. Several times, Cameron stopped the Jeep, presented Chet's boot to Daisy, and allowed her to roam the immediate area in the hope she would pick up his scent. Nothing.

Tired, hot, and disappointed, they were reluctantly forced to suspend their search only when the sun dropped behind the hills and the light began to fade.

"Dammit, Cam, what could have happened to him?" Nancy asked in frustration as they bounced through the desert back toward McDonald Drive. "I didn't see a single mine shaft Chet could have tumbled into, and people don't just disappear! And why would he have gone *anywhere* with just one boot?"

Cameron swerved around a boulder and shook his head without responding. He'd said little during their abortive search of the Float.

Cameron's cell phone began chiming to announce an incoming call. He reached over and retrieved it from the end table, its screen revealing only "unknown number." Cameron took the call. "Hello," he mechanically answered.

"Mr. Wylie?"

He didn't recognize the voice at the other end. Besides, no one he knew addressed him as "Mr. Wylie." How did the damned telemarketers get his cell number? "Speaking," he warily responded.

"Mr. Wylie, this is Detective Woody Moe of the Salt River Tribal Police Department. I'm calling about your friend, Mr. Marion."

"Chet?" Cameron blurted. Nancy bolted upright on the couch and looked at him intently.

"Yes, Chet Marion. Did he return home?"

"No," Cameron tensely replied, "we've not heard anything from Chet or, until now, from the police. We've been waiting a week for someone to call us."

"The cops?" Nancy mouthed. Cameron nodded.

"I only just now got Mr. Marion's file," Moe said. "Otherwise, I'd have contacted you sooner."

"Yeah, I understand," Cameron replied, puzzled that the file had apparently only now been assigned to a detective despite the fact that he reported Chet's disappearance over a week ago. "Have you found Chet?" He was starting to feel sick to his stomach.

There was a discernible pause at the other end. "Like I said, Mr. Wylie, I only just now got Mr. Marion's file. I wanted to call first because, if Mr. Marion is already home, there's no need to go forward with an investigation."

"Wait a minute. You're telling me that you haven't even started an investigation, even though I reported Chet's disappearance over a week ago?" Cameron blurted. "Is this a joke? What have you been doing for the past week?" He glanced at Nancy and frowned.

"Mr. Wylie, I understand your frustration but, like I said, I only received Mr. Marion's file earlier today. I don't know where the file was prior to my getting it. If I knew I'd tell you, but I don't. All I can do is try to locate your friend and the first step is to call and find out if he already made it home." As he spoke, trying to reassure Cameron, Moe already knew two things: (1) the area where Chet disappeared might not even be on the rez. Moe honestly wasn't sure *which* jurisdiction it actually fell within, or whether it was simply an unincorporated section of the county, under the jurisdiction of the county sheriff rather than a particular municipality or the Indian police, and (2) it was entirely possible that Cameron had a hand in whatever had befallen Chet Marion. If Chet had already found his way home, however, both considerations would automatically be mooted.

"I imagine that if Chet was the friend of someone in the police department or the government, you'd be all over it," Cameron bitterly remarked. His observation, borne of anger and frustration, stung Detective Moe.

"Mr. Wylie, your attitude is not helpful. I understand your resentment, but I'm trying to help you. If you don't want my help, that's okay, too."

Cameron hesitated, silently measuring his response before speaking. "Look, I'm sorry if I offended you. I just don't know why nothing has been done to find Chet, even though I reported it over a week ago and the cop said it would be assigned to a detective immediately."

"I don't know what the officer told you, Mr. Wylie. "All I know is that I now have Mr. Marion's file and that's why I'm calling."

"Well, Chet hasn't come home," Cameron informed him. "So now what?"

There was a distinct pause at the other end of the line. "Well, Mr. Wylie, to be perfectly honest, I'm not sure that the area where Mr. Marion disappeared is even within the jurisdiction of the Salt River Tribal Authority."

Although it sounded like bureaucratic doublespeak, Cameron understood what the detective was telling him. "So you're saying that the Baca Float isn't on the reservation?"

"I don't know what you mean by the 'Baca Float,' Moe confessed.   "I'm talking about the area where you and Mr. Marion went hiking."

"I am, too," Cameron responded. "It's called the 'Baca Float.'"

"I didn't know that it had a special name. Where did you hear that?"

"The Arizona Historical Society." Cameron was distressed because he found himself in the position of having to educate the cops despite the fact they displayed little apparent interest in finding Chet. "Let's be honest," he finally offered out of desperation, "I know what you're thinking. You're thinking that I may have done something to Chet." Nancy was startled by Cameron's abrupt, matter-of-fact assertion and her eyes widened. "Let me drive to your office right now. I'll explain everything to you. Despite what you think, I had nothing to do with Chet's disappearance. "

Moe was taken aback by Cameron's unexpected directness. "Mr. Wylie, as far as I know there's no indication that Mr. Marion met with foul play.   At this point, your friend's disappearance appears to be nothing more than an unfortunate accident."

"Look," Cameron continued, "I've been calling the cops repeatedly, every day, since this happened and you're the only one who's called me back. If somebody doesn't step up, Chet's file is just gonna get handed off to somebody else and it'll just be more runaround.   Just like you, nobody even knows what the Baca Float is! I need to talk to *somebody* who's willing to help figure out what happened to Chet!"   Although he struggled to maintain his composure, Cameron was becoming agitated. Nancy reached over and patted his knee.

"I understand, Mr. Wylie," Moe said, softly. "It sometimes gets a little overwhelming when you don't think anybody cares. Well, I *do* care and I'm willing to talk to you about Mr. Marion. When can you be here?"

"You tell me how soon you want me there and I'll be there."

"Well," Moe glanced at his watch, "it's 3:30. How long will it take you to get here?"

"Where's 'here'?" Moe recited the directions to the tribal police department. "I'll be there in 45 minutes," Cameron said. "Less if I hit all the lights."

"No matter. I'll wait until you get here," Moe assured him. "Don't speed."

"On my way," Cameron said. He closed his phone. "C'mon," he said, standing. He pulled Nancy to her feet. "This guy may actually help us."

"Who is he?" Nancy asked as she followed him out the door.

"Some Indian cop, I think." Cameron locked the door and they walked briskly toward the apartment parking lot.

"An Indian cop? How'd *they* get involved?" Nancy marveled.

They ducked into Cameron's Jeep and he cranked the engine. "Beats me, but he's the only one who's called me back. I guess the other cops can't be bothered," he scornfully concluded as they pulled from the parking lot onto Cactus Road.

DETECTIVE MOE RETURNED HIS TELEPHONE to its cradle then signed onto the Internet. He'd never heard of the 'Baca Float,' but intended to research it while he awaited Cameron's arrival.

He began with a Google search. Although there was no lack of basic historical information about the Baca Float, Moe found it largely confusing, raising more questions than it answered. More intriguing was the information *not* addressed online.

Virtually every website he consulted unequivocally affirmed that, although there once apparently existed multiple Floats in three southwestern states, the only Float in Arizona that's still largely intact is located near Prescott. According to the Internet, it's now privately owned, kept under lock and key, and strictly off-limits to visitors. The other quondam Arizona Float, located near the Mexican border, currently lies, for whatever reason, beneath a retirement community called "Rio Rico."

Moe was puzzled. Although he was an Arizona native and had lived in the state all his life, he'd never even *heard* of the Baca Floats. Why all the secrecy? Moreover, why were the Floats, spanning thousands of acres across multiple states, created in the first place? Those questions aside, the Internet was silent with respect to a Float ever having been established in the vicinity of the metropolitan Phoenix area, where the missing guy was hiking when he vaporized. Despite this lacuna, the guy's friend had specifically referenced the Baca Float. What did an old Spanish land grant have to do with anything?

He signed off the Internet and glanced at his watch; the guy should be here any moment. He stood and walked out of his office to the front desk of the modest headquarters building.

"Hey, Gloria," Moe said to the woman with frizzy red hair behind the intake counter. "A guy named 'Cameron Wylie' is coming in to see me in a few minutes."

Gloria looked up from her 'Us' magazine. "Conference room's open. Want him in there?" she indifferently suggested. Her metallic florescent green eye shadow had become smeared around one eye, giving her the bizarre appearance of a circus clown with a black eye. Moe had to struggle to keep from laughing out loud.

"Yeah, that'll work. Put him in there then buzz me," he replied with as much decorum as he could manage. Gloria refocused her attention on her magazine without responding. "Let me ask you something." She looked up from her magazine again, clearly annoyed at being unable to finish the article on 'Marc's Love Child'. "You ever heard of the 'Baca Float'?"

"Is that some kind of dessert?" Gloria asked.

"No, it's a place," Moe said.

"A place? It sounds like a dessert. Or a mixed drink."

He smiled. "No, it's an old Spanish land grant. You've never heard of it?"

"No," Gloria shrugged. "But, hey, I'm from Cleveland. What the heck do I know about Spaniards? It sounds like it could be an iceberg, too." She paused. "Do they have icebergs in Spain?"

"Well I *am* from here and I've never heard of it, either," Moe told her, ignoring her question.

"So where is it?" Gloria asked. "Spain?"

Moe shook his head. "There were apparently a bunch of 'em. The closest one's up by Prescott."

Gloria looked pensive. "Me and my old man like to drive up there sometimes. He likes the buffet at the casino."

"Prescott?" Moe asked, unsure whether they were still talking about the same thing.

"Yeah, Prescott. They have an Indian casino up there. All you can eat crab legs on Sundays. We like the Friday night fish fry, too, but the traffic's so bad that, by the time we get there after work, they quit serving." Gloria looked at Moe reproachfully, as though he were personally responsible for denying them the pleasures of the Friday night fish fry.

"Don't they have fish fries around here?" Moe helpfully suggested.

"Not the same," Gloria sniffed. "They use trash fish, like Pollock, instead of cod. I can tell the difference," she assured him. "Besides, we like to gamble in the casino after the fish fry." She was about to make additional observations about Indian casinos and fish frys, but was interrupted when the glass entrance door abruptly swung open, admitting Cameron and Nancy to the police station lobby. Gloria stood and approached the window. "Help you?" Moe, who could see newcomers over the counter, surmised the male was Cameron Wylie.

"We're here to see Detective Moe," Cameron said, approaching the counter. Gloria glanced at the detective.

"You found him," he said, stepping forward. "Please call me 'Woody.' You must be Mr. Wylie." Moe opened the door that communicated between the lobby and the offices at the rear of the building, and extended his hand. "Please come in."

Cameron warily shook the detective's outstretched hand as he stepped across the threshold. Because he was dressed in worn blue jeans and a denim shirt, the detective looked more like a cowboy than a police officer. "This is my friend, Nancy," Cameron said as Moe closed the door behind them. Nancy extended her hand, guardedly, and the detective shook it warmly. "And you can call me 'Cam.'"

"Hi, Nancy," Moe smiled. "Follow me, please."

Although Cameron wasn't exceptionally tall, he was none-the-less at least a head taller than the figure who escorted them down the hall toward the conference room. Notwithstanding his modest height, however, their host was broad-shouldered with conspicuously powerful arms. An unruly shock of glossy black hair covered his head.

"We're a very small department," he continued over his shoulder. "Only four officers and one detective." He opened the door, flipped on the overhead florescent light, and gestured them in. "Me," he smiled.

The department's conference room was tiny, only about twenty feet square. A small, square conference table occupied the center of the floor, surrounded by four unadorned wooden chairs. "Please, please," Moe gestured, indicating the chairs.

Cameron and Nancy slid chairs out and sat. "You guys want some coffee?" Cameron nodded, but Nancy shook her head. "Be right back."

When Moe returned he held two Styrofoam cups of coffee and had Chet's file tucked beneath one arm. "I'm glad you were able to meet me today," he said, sliding Cameron's coffee in front of him. He placed his coffee and Chet's file on the table, then pulled a chair out and sat opposite Cameron.

"We're glad you're willing to meet with us," Nancy spoke for the first time.

"We didn't think we'd ever hear from anyone," Cameron added, sipping his coffee.

Moe nodded sympathetically. "I understand. I would have called earlier but, like I said when we spoke over the phone, I only received Mr. Marion's file today." He opened Chet's file, which contained only the original police report, and slid it across to Cameron. Nancy leaned over and peered at it with interest.

"I went back to look for Chet, but found nothing except his boot," Cameron confided.

"His boot?"

Cameron nodded ruefully. "Yeah, Chet's boot. I don't know how he could have lost it because it was still laced."

"Where is it?" Moe asked, his interest immediately piqued.

"In my Jeep," Cameron said.

"Please bring it in," Moe directed him. Cameron rose and exited the room, heading for the parking lot in front of the building. Awkward silence filled the small room. "Did you know Mr. Marion, too?" Moe finally asked.

"Chet was mostly Cam's friend," she replied, "but I knew him, too. He's a nice guy."

"What do you suppose could have happened to him?" Moe adopted a deliberately conversational tone.

Nancy surveyed the detective guardedly before responding. The cramped room made her feel claustrophobic. "Chet and Cam were out hiking and got separated. Cam searched for Chet but couldn't find him," she finally said.

Moe nodded. "That's basically what the report says." He indicated the thin file on the table. "Had they known one another for a long time?"

"Yeah, a while," Nancy replied.

"Had they been hiking before?"

"A few times, I think." She didn't like the way the conversation was going. "Look, if you think Cam did anything to Chet, you're wrong. Cam and Chet were friends and Chet just took a wrong turn and got lost...why would Cam do anything to hurt him?" Nancy's eyes flashed defiantly.

Moe remained unperturbed. "There's nothing to indicate that Mr. Wylie had anything to do with Mr. Marion's disappearance. I'm just trying to fill in some of the gaps." He nodded toward the file. "That doesn't contain much, as you can see."

The door swung open as Cameron reentered the conference room, carrying Chet's hiking boot. He handed it to the detective wordlessly.

As Cameron indicated, the boot was still tightly laced to the top and appeared to be virtually brand new. "You didn't relace it?" Moe asked, slowly turning the boot over in his hands.

"That's exactly the way I found it," Cameron told him, resuming his seat.

Moe examined the boot without speaking, looking for blood or other evidence of trauma or violence, but found nothing. Cameron and Nancy glanced at one another. "How is it you found this?" the detective finally asked, looking up.

"I went back to look for Chet," Cameron explained. "That," he pointed at the boot, "was on the trail, but he was nowhere to be found."

"How do you know it's your friend's boot?" Moe asked.

"Chet had just bought new boots and he made a big deal about showing them to me that morning, before we started hiking," Cameron informed him. "I told him it was dumb to go hiking in brand new boots, and that he should have broken them in first."

Moe placed Chet's boot on the tabletop next to him. "Speaking of that, I was trying to figure out the exact area where Mr. Marion disappeared. What did you call it?"

"The 'Baca Float,'" replied Cameron.

"Yeah, the 'Baca Float.' Well, I looked on the Net after we spoke and, although there's a 'Baca Float' up by Prescott, there was no mention of one where Mr. Marion and you were."

"I know," Cameron acknowledged. "I didn't know anything about it until I researched it at the Arizona Historical Society. They think it may be a Float that, for whatever reason, was never recorded. That's why Chet and I were hiking there."

"I don't understand," Moe said. "What's the allure of a Float?"

Cameron glanced at Nancy, who raised her eyebrows in a 'well?' gesture.

"There are stories about treasure being buried on some of the Floats," Cameron sheepishly admitted. He realized how naïve' he must have sounded.

Moe looked dubious. "So you and Mr. Marion were looking for buried treasure?"

"Well, not really. Nancy and I had previously seen some old buildings off in the hills, and me and Chet intended to hike back there to explore them."

"That's when he disappeared?"

"Yeah. My dog was giving me problems, so I went back to mess with her while Chet continued hiking. I told him that I'd catch up with him but, by the time I got back on the trail, he'd disappeared."

"How long do you think it was between the time you parted company, and the time you resumed hiking?" Moe asked.

"Fifteen minutes?" Cameron speculated. "Maybe a little more."

Moe looked thoughtful. "How far do you think Mr. Marion could have hiked in that time?"

"Not very far, Chet wasn't the outdoorsy type and he walked pretty slow." Cameron shook his head sadly. "It's like he just vaporized."

Moe was stumped. He turned his attention to Nancy. "Were you there, too?"

She shook her head. "No, just Cam and Chet. Like Cam said, he and I hiked the area a few weeks earlier, but I wasn't with them when Chet disappeared."

Although it was certainly possible that Cameron, for whatever reason, had murdered his friend and dumped his body out in the desert, Moe tended to believe his story. If Cameron had killed Chet, what was the purpose of hanging onto his boot or volunteering that he had it?

"Do you own a gun?" Mr. Wylie.

"Yeah, a .22 pistol," Cameron said.

"Did you have it with you that day?"

"No. I usually take it with me when I go hiking out in the desert, but where we were is basically in the middle of town, so I didn't bring it. I didn't want the hassle of people calling the cops in a panic if someone saw me walking around with a pistol, even if it was in a holster."

Moe nodded. Assuming what Cameron said was true, if he killed his friend while they were hiking, he'd had to have done so by running over him, hitting him in the head with something, stabbing him, or pushing him over a cliff, none of which sounded easy or efficient. Besides, there wasn't a hint of motive. He gathered up Chet's file and boot and rose from the table. "I'd like you to show me exactly where Mr. Marion disappeared."

The detective led them back down the hall, to a larger room containing four long conference tables arranged in two rows. The overhead neon light buzzed audibly when he flipped it on. Moe placed Chet's file and boot on one of the tables and walked across the room to the far wall, where an enormous multi-colored map was tacked. "Here's the reservation," he said, indicating a red area on the right-hand side of the map, about half-way up. "According to the report in the file, you and Mr. Marion were somewhere around here." He pointed to another area of the map, slightly northwest of the reservation. Cameron and Nancy stepped to the map, trying to orient themselves to its various features and landmarks.

"Here's where we were," Cameron said, placing his index finger on the map. Nancy nodded. Although the range of unnamed hills was clearly diagrammed, the cemetery near their base wasn't indicated.

Moe scrutinized the area Cameron indicated. As he suspected, the expanse didn't appear to be part of the rez. Yet neither did it appear to be part of any other body politic or municipality. Rather, the area where Chet disappeared was apparently an expansive tract of raw, unclaimed desert, surrounded on all sides by an urban metropolis. Given the skyrocketing prices of local real estate over the past three decades, how was it possible that some municipality hadn't long ago incorporated the Float into its geographic boundaries? It was as though the Float had simply escaped everyone's notice. Its puzzling invisibility aside, the detective now understood how Chet's file ended up on his desk: after being bounced around for more than a week, somebody in the last municipality to have it made the decision to fob it off onto the Salt River Tribal PD, the last-resort depository for problematical cases. Let the Indians deal with it. Although it wasn't the first time Moe had encountered the phenomenon, it made him sick this time because the delay occasioned by all the bureaucratic finger-pointing probably cost a man his life.

"You were hiking to those hills?" The detective tapped the map with his finger.

"Yeah, there's some buildings back behind them," Cameron answered. "You can't see them from the front and we wanted to check them out."

"What kind of buildings?" Moe asked.

"I don't know," Cameron explained. "That's what we wanted to find out. You can see them on Google Earth." He reached forward and touched the map. "There's an old cemetery right here, too, but it's not shown on this map. We parked by it and hiked from there. There's no way Chet could have made it all the way to the hills in the few minutes we were apart. Although it's not that far, it's uphill and Chet wasn't walking very fast."

Moe examined the area that Cameron indicated. The map was drawn to scale and the hills appeared to be a couple of miles beyond the unmarked cemetery. "Is there a trail or something that leads from the cemetery to the hills north of it?" he asked, still staring at the map.

"Yeah, but not much of one. It's hard to see because it's pretty overgrown. I told Chet to stay on the trail while I went back to get Daisy."

"Daisy?" the detective looked quizzically at Cameron.

"My dog," he explained.

Moe turned his attention back to the map. "Do you know whether there were any vertical mine shafts or holes along the trail that Mr. Marion could have accidentally slipped and fallen into?"

"Cam and I hiked the trail a few weeks earlier and there was nothing that Chet could have stumbled into," Nancy interjected. "Had there been, we would have seen it."

"Where on the trail did you find the boot?" Moe asked. "Closer to the cemetery or closer to the hills?"

"The hills. It was right in the middle of the trail," Cameron replied. "Look, Detective ...," he added.

"Woody," said Moe, still looking at the map.

"Detective Woody...," Cameron continued.

"No, just 'Woody,'" Moe responded, still looking at the map. "Please call me 'Woody.'"

Cameron was becoming somewhat exasperated. "Okay, Woody, I know you mean well and are just doing your job, but Chet's been missing for a week! Can't *somebody* just organize a search for him?"

Moe finally turned away from the map. "Here, please sit." He gestured to the chairs at the nearest conference table. Cameron and Nancy exchanged glances before sliding chairs out and sitting. The detective sat across the table, facing them.

"First off, I want to personally apologize for the lack of meaningful response to your friend's disappearance by law enforcement," Moe began. "I know that Mr. Marion has been missing for over a week now, yet you've evidently not been provided any information about efforts to locate him." Cameron and Nancy listened intently. "I don't know where your friend's file's been for the past week but, now that I have it, I intend to find him." He thought it best not to mention his suspicion that Chet's file had languished in various other police departments before being sent to his office.

"How?" Nancy asked. "You know as well as we do that nobody can survive in the desert a whole week without food or water." She looked at Cameron apologetically as she spoke, who remained stoical.

The American Southwest, a region stretching northward from Mexico is a killing field. Inaccessible and rugged, the number of migrants who perish annually in this lethal environment while attempting to trek to the United States from Mexico and Central America is unknowable. Their chalky bones lie scattered and forgotten in the desolation, baking in the sun.

In 1541, Spanish explorer Melchior Diaz led a *compañía* of the finest troops of His Very Fortunate, Most Excellent, Esteemed, Sanctified, Honored, Blessed, August, Serene, Celestial, Omniscient, Sublime, Noble, Compassionate, Generous, and Catholic Majesty, Carlos I of Spain. This gallant assemblage was charged with reaching the *Golfo de California*, the isolated expanse of water wedged between the Mexican mainland and the bony finger of Baja California to the west. En route, Diaz fell victim to a ghastly accident, impaling himself on his own lance. The luckless *Capitán* finally succumbed to his wounds, and the ferocious heat, twenty agonizing days later, after apologizing to his men for taking so long to die. The dreary town of Sonoita, in Sonora, Mexico, now marks the terminus of that ill-fated expedition, broiling beneath an unrelenting sun. Countless others subsequently followed *Don* Melchior down that same mournful *via dolorosa.* The end of the world.

The City of Phoenix was established at the northern extremity of this great Sonoran Desert, on the banks of the Salt River, and remains its captive. Most people, if they are aware of it at all, know of this region only though wildlife documentaries on television, or through alluring photographs in travel magazines of lush golf courses and beautiful, tanned people reclining on chaise lounges next to sparkling swimming pools. The reality is that the desert remains a murderous host, even to sophisticated urbanites.

In July 2002, a young couple, Joe and Laura Popiela, decided to hike Picacho Peak, a curious saddle-shaped imminence north of Tucson immediately adjacent to Interstate 10, the primary thoroughfare between Phoenix and Tucson. A Dairy Queen directly across the interstate from the peak invites travelers to stop for a frozen Dilly Bar, while an adjacent enterprise sells Indian blankets, scorpion paperweights, and cowboy hats to motoring tourists. Why anyone would want a blanket when the ambient outdoor temperature commonly exceeds 115 degrees defies explanation. Myriad other businesses and dwellings cluster around Picacho Peak on both sides of the interstate. The hike to the top of the peak is a mere six-mile roundtrip from the parking lot at its base; busy, noisy Interstate 10 is almost always within sight from anywhere on the trail.

Laura was found dead on the trail by another hiker. Her husband's body was found not far away. He'd left the trail, evidently in an effort to find a short cut down to the parking lot, dying within sight of the couple's car. It was surmised they'd failed to bring enough water with them on their short hike and had perished from heat exhaustion. A local deputy sheriff later remarked with admirable understatement, "The heat out here is nothing to play with."

Death in the Arizona desert remains a commonplace.

In the summer of 2015, a visitor from Great Britain decided to trek to the top of Camelback Mountain, a massif in central Phoenix, so named because of its purported resemblance to that eponymous creature and a popular hiking destination for local residents. When her body was later discovered, it was surmised the unlucky tourist had failed to carry sufficient water, wandered from the trail in a delirium, and perished. Later that year, a 64-year-old grandfather and his 12-year-old grandson hiking near Gila Bend, a small community 70 miles southwest of Phoenix, became disoriented in the desert vastness. Both died. In July of 2016, six people died of hyperthermia while hiking in the Santa Catalina Mountains outside Tucson. Although the bodies of all the foregoing unfortunates were ultimately recovered, the bones of countless others, scattered by wild animals, lie abandoned and unidentified beneath a pitiless sun.

Moe nodded thoughtfully. "It's possible that Mr. Marion is still alive, but..."

"He's dead," Cameron said, his voice cracking. "Chet's dead because of my stupidity."

"We don't know that Mr. Marion's dead," the detective interjected. "It's possible he's still alive." Even as he spoke the words, he didn't believe them.

"How do you intend to find Chet?" Nancy repeated.

Moe stood and walked back to the map on the wall. Cameron and Nancy remained seated at the conference table. "Like I said, we're a very small police department. We don't have all the resources and gadgets, like helicopters and such, that departments like Phoenix and Scottsdale have. Those guys spend more on their Christmas parties than our entire annual budget! But what we *do* have is a commitment to find your friend." He pointed to the map. "What complicates Mr. Marion's case is *where* he got lost. You see, that area doesn't fall within the boundaries of any political subdivision."

"I don't understand," said Cameron.

"The area where you guys were hiking doesn't belong to anybody, to any city. It just *is*," Moe tried to explain. "Look." He traced the perimeter of the Float with his finger. "Here's where you were. But the county line stops here, right at the edge. The Float, as you call it, is apparently under nobody's jurisdiction, basically a no-man's land." He turned away from the map and looked at Cameron. "I'm not saying it's right, but that could be why nobody's done anything...they didn't know *what* to do."

"But you're willing to do something?" Nancy skeptically retorted. "Even though it's not in your jurisdiction, either?"

Moe returned to the table and resumed his seat. "Yeah, I am. Even if it *isn't* in my jurisdiction, who's going to complain? It isn't like I'll be stepping on somebody else's toes. That's the whole point. It isn't in *anybody's* jurisdiction."

"Why would you do that?" Cameron quietly asked.

"Because it's the right thing to do and your friend deserves a proper burial," Moe responded, softly. "If I don't help you, who will?"

EIGHT

CAMERON PULLED TO A STOP in the identical spot he'd previously parked near the cemetery and switched the Jeep's engine off. Moe surveyed the surrounding desert from the passenger's seat. "How'd you even find this place?" he marveled.

Cameron wasn't convinced he should mention that he saw someone standing in the cemetery at night, in the middle of a rainstorm, earlier that year. "Just driving around," he casually replied. "You can see it from McDonald Drive if you look."

"I guess I never looked," Moe said, stepping from the vehicle. Daisy jumped out after him and hung near the Jeep instead of exploring.

"The trailhead starts over in that far corner," Cameron said, pointing.

"You know," Moe volunteered, looking around, "cemeteries are taboo in my culture. "My grandparents, even my parents, wouldn't be caught dead here." He smiled self-consciously at the unintended irony of his observation. "Too many evil spirits."

"In that case, I'm guessing the *only* way your grandparents or parents would be caught here is if they *were* dead." Cameron remarked.

Moe crossed into the overgrown cemetery, kicking through weeds as he walked. "You know anyone buried here?" he called over his shoulder.

"Nope, nobody."

"These graves are in really bad shape," the detective remarked as he continued to explore. He stopped and looked back at Cameron. "Nobody's tended them in a long time. I think that's very sad."

Cameron remained near the vehicle while Moe continued to poke about the abandoned graveyard. Rather than romp around the area, Daisy uncharacteristically lay on the ground near him, her eyes fixed on the detective.

"Hey!" Moe called. "It looks like somebody was digging out here. Do you know anything about that?" He stood looking down at the uncovered grave Cameron and Nancy found during their original visit.

"Yeah, I saw it," Cameron responded. "Let me show you where Chet and me separated."

Moe looked up. "Yeah, okay." He began cutting his way back toward the Jeep. Cameron climbed into the driver's seat and Daisy eagerly jumped into the back.

"The buildings you guys wanted to check out are behind those hills?" the detective asked when he returned to Cameron's Jeep and snapped his seat belt on.

"Yeah," Cameron said.   He cranked the engine to life and pulled away from the cemetery, the Jeep swaying from side to side over the uneven ground.   "The trail leads to an overlook, but you've gotta hike from there down to the buildings themselves," he explained as he skirted the burial ground, heading toward the hills. "Nancy and I hiked back there earlier this summer, but it was pretty late in the day by the time we finally got to the overlook and we were both miserably hot. We didn't feel like hiking all the way down to the buildings, although we could see them in the distance." Cameron jerked the Jeep's steering wheel to the left to avoid a large rock in the center of the trail. "And I'd looked at them on Google Earth, too. That's why I invited Chet, to check out the buildings."

Moe nodded and grabbed the handhold on the Jeep's dashboard to prevent being thrown from the vehicle. Dust boiled into the open cabin. "Where was Chet when you went back to get Daisy?" he yelled over the engine noise.

"Here," Cameron abruptly responded, braking. He switched the engine off.

Through the bug-smeared windshield, Moe could see the trail continue to ascend toward the hills. He turned in his seat and looked behind to see how far they'd driven from the cemetery: scarcely a quarter-mile. Daisy leapt to the ground and busily began to explore the desert in the immediate vicinity of the Jeep. Cameron and the detective stepped from the vehicle.

"This is the last place you saw Chet?" Moe asked again.

"Yeah, right about here," Cameron confirmed, looking around to corroborate his recollection.

"Where'd you find his boot?"

Cameron pointed further up the trail. "Up there, a mile from here."

"And you saw no sign of him between here and there?"

"Nothing." Cameron shook his head, sadly. "Chet's boot was just laying on the trail, almost like somebody'd put it there so I'd be sure to see it."

It was immediately apparent to Moe that Cameron was right: nobody could have hiked a mile, uphill, from where they were, to the spot where he'd found Chet's boot, in the roughly fifteen minutes it had taken Cameron to retrieve Daisy from the cemetery at the base of the trail. Such a feat would have been physically impossible.

"I told Chet to stay on the trail," Cameron reminded Moe, "and that I'd catch up with him as soon as I retrieved Daisy. He'd have had no reason to leave the trail and just take off through the desert on his own."

Moe scanned the horizon. Vultures wheeling in the distance might indicate they'd spotted Chet's body, but the cloudless sky was as lifeless as the surrounding desert. He turned his attention to the area around the Jeep.

The detective wasn't sure what to look for that might suggest what had happened to the luckless hiker. The desert was characteristically riddled with abandoned mine shafts and it wasn't inconceivable that Chet had spotted one, left the trail to investigate, and tumbled down it. It happened with depressing regularity and Moe had personally investigated several such accidents in the past. Problem was, he saw no mine shafts in the vicinity; the desert appeared pristine and undisturbed

"What are we looking for?" Cameron called to Moe where he was searching on the opposite side of the Jeep.

"I don't know," the detective confessed, "but I'll know it when I see it. Anything that doesn't look right, something that might give us an idea of what happened to Chet. Something that just doesn't look right," he repeated, scanning the ground before him. It was barren of footprints, litter, or any other evidence that Chet may have tread there. Had Chet simply collapsed from heat stroke his body should be laying on the trail, where Cameron would presumably have already found it. Even if coyotes had encountered Chet's body, they typically wouldn't drag it far before feasting on it.

The men repeatedly crisscrossed the area without result. Daisy wandered about, never straying far. Ultimately, Cameron looked up and said aloud what both were already thinking. "There's nothing here."

Moe couldn't conceal his dismay. "Yeah, you're right," he conceded. "I guess we should check out the place where you found Chet's boot." He began trudging back toward Cameron's Jeep. "Maybe we can go to that overlook you talked about, too."

Cameron returned to the Jeep as Daisy leapt into the back and settled down onto the rear seat. When Moe slid into the passenger's seat, Cameron turned to him before starting the engine. "I think I may know a way to find Chet," he said.

The detective looked at him with mild curiosity. "How?"

"I've been interested in voice phenomenon for a while and Chet and I were doing some stuff with it," Cameron began.   Moe looked at him blankly, so he continued. "It's where you can hear voices from other places," he explained.

"'Other places?" Moe asked, dubiously.

"Well, it's kind of hard to explain," Cameron conceded.   "I've been doing voice phenomenon recordings at my house, and Chet and I were going to try it out here, down at that cemetery."

"Why?"   the   detective   asked,   clearly skeptical. "Cemeteries are not good places. You shouldn't go there. You don't want to talk to the dead." He gravely shook his head.

"Well, I'm not sure it's the dead we're talking to," Cameron rapidly backtracked.   "They're just voices on tape...not sure where they come from."

Moe looked directly at Cameron.   "They come from the dead," he quietly said. "You don't want to talk to Chet from there."

Cameron once knew a guy who graduated from Northern Arizona University, located just south of the vast Navajo Indian Reservation, who insisted that Navajo students often refused to enter science buildings where human skeletons were   on   display   because   skeletons   were considered taboo in traditional Navajo culture. Although   not   entirely   unexpected,   Cameron likewise considered Moe's attitude a quaint, if naïve, atavistic relic of ancestral religious beliefs. He twisted the ignition key without comment, eased the transmission lever into 'D,' and the Jeep resumed trundling up the trail.

"THERE," CAMERON DREW TO A HALT, shoved the transmission lever into 'P', and killed the engine. "Chet's boot was right there." He pointed over the hood, to a spot about twenty feet in front of the Jeep.

"You sure?" Moe asked.

"Yeah, I'm sure," Cameron said. "I made a point to remember that it was directly across from that big saguaro over there." He tilted his head toward the massive cactus that has become the leitmotif of the West in general and Arizona in particular.

The detective stepped from the Jeep onto the trail. Daisy didn't budge from the back seat, but watched Cameron with palpable apprehension. When he finally exited the vehicle, she reluctantly followed.

Because of the gradual inclination of the trail, the corresponding increase in elevation was initially almost imperceptible. It was only when Moe gazed downward, toward the desert floor, that he realized they'd probably already climbed 1,000 feet. Even the air temperature was noticeably less oppressive. Far to the south, sunlight glinted off cars traveling along McDonald Drive, though the distance rendered them silent.

"Wow," is all he said.

"Yeah, it's beautiful," Cameron agreed. "It's amazing that nobody apparently hikes up here."

The detective walked up the trail to the spot where Cameron found Chet's boot. He squatted and examined the surrounding soil, seeing nothing. Moe stood and strode into the adjacent desert, pungent creosote bushes slapping his trouser legs, where he began to search the vicinity. Cameron watched him from beside the Jeep for a moment before following, though he had no idea what he was supposed to be doing. Daisy remained near the vehicle and nervously trotted back and forth as she intently watched Cameron, the whites of her eyes showing.

"Find anything?" he called to Moe after a few minutes.

"No, nothing," the detective responded without looking up.

"What is it we should to be looking for?"

The detective didn't answer.

They combed the area for more than ninety minutes, finding nothing. Although it was somewhat cooler at their present elevation, both men were drenched with sweat. Cameron made his way back to the Jeep, where he unscrewed the cap of his canteen and guzzled the vapid water. He leaned down and began plucking cactus thorns from his cuffs when Daisy approached him and began licking his hands. "You thirsty?" he asked, scratching Daisy's ears.

Moe returned to the Jeep while Cameron was pouring water from his canteen into Daisy's canvas dog bowl. Cameron looked up as the detective removed his baseball cap and mopped his head with a bandana. "Nothing?" he asked again.

The detective shook his head. "It doesn't look like anybody's ever been up here." Cameron handed him the canteen and Moe took a long draught. "Except you and Nancy, I mean," he corrected himself. Water slopped onto the lacerated earth as Daisy noisily drank from her collapsible dish.

"Well," Cameron responded, taking the canteen from Moe's outstretched hand and replacing the cap, "I know that's not true because there's buildings on the other side of these hills." He nodded toward the top of the trail. "*Somebody* had to build 'em. Besides that, somebody had to make this trail." He folded Daisy's dish and jammed it and the canteen behind the driver's seat.

"Yeah, I know," Moe acknowledged. "I didn't mean that, *literally*, no one has ever been here."

They clambered back into the Jeep and the engine roared to life. Daisy jumped onto the rear seat, eager to start moving again.

"How far up the trail are the buildings?" Moe asked.

"The overlook is less than a mile," Cameron replied. "But the trail ends there and you've gotta hike from there to the buildings. The night I went back to look for Chet, I could see a light in one of them."

"People live there?" Moe marveled. "How do they get in and out? Not on this crappy trail!"

"I don't think anyone actually lives back there," Cameron responded as the Jeep labored over a boulder, one rear wheel spinning over the rough surface and the smell of burning rubber filling the air. "I think it was probably just some hikers. It couldn't have been Chet because there's no way he could've have hiked all the way back there in such a short amount of time."

"He was only wearing one boot, too," the detective added.

It took them another half-hour to reach the flat-topped turnaround on the crest of the hill. Cameron swung the Jeep in a wide circle and pointed it back down the trail before switching the engine off. Daisy peered out, over the back seat, and began to whine softly.

Cameron turned in his seat to look at her. "What's wrong with you?"

Moe hopped out of the Jeep, ambled over to the edge, and gazed into the steep valley that receded into the distance. Cameron joined him a few minutes later, though he couldn't coax Daisy out of the Jeep.

"That's where the buildings are?" the detective asked.

"Yeah," Cameron nodded. "They're hard to see in the haze, but they're down there. Like I said, you can see them on Google Earth and Nancy and I could see them when we hiked up here earlier this summer. It almost looks like a little town. That's where I saw the light, too." A breeze sighed past, cooling them, and Cameron shivered slightly.

"As far as you know, the trail we took is the only way up here?"

"As far as I know," Cameron acknowledged. "It's the only one you can see on Google Earth."

"There weren't any other cars parked up here when you were here before?"

"Nope," Cameron responded. "Just me."

Moe turned to face him. "Unless there's a way in from the other side, how did whoever was down there *get* down there? Since you didn't see any cars parked here, they'd have to have hiked across the desert, up the trail, then down from this point to whatever buildings are down there. How long would that take, do you think?"

Cameron shrugged. "I don't know...hours, anyway, and they'd have to carry a lot of water."

"Fresh water weighs eight and one-half pounds per gallon," Moe told him. "How many gallons do you think they'd need in this heat?"

Cameron reflected a moment before responding. "I'd guess at least three gallons for the hike in and as many for the hike out, plus whatever water they needed while they were down there." He indicated the general direction of the distant buildings.

"So, by your reckoning, they'd need, say, about eight gallons of water?"

"Yeah, probably about that," Cameron agreed. "Maybe more, depending on the heat and the number of hikers."

"But it would be a minimum of eight gallons each, irrespective of the number of hikers, right?"

"Yeah, I guess," Cameron conceded.

"That would be 68 pounds, just for water," the detective said, "and that's not counting anything else, like food or a sleeping bag." He paused. "Who would go on a hike carrying 68 pounds of water? Why would anyone do that?"

Cameron reflected before responding. "Maybe somebody drove them up the trail and just dropped them off. They hiked to the buildings from here.   That would cut their water consumption by half."

Moe shook his head. "I checked the trail all the way up. There aren't any tracks except yours. Since it hasn't rained since you drove up here last time, other tire tracks couldn't have been washed away, either." He frowned unconsciously. "No, nobody dropped them off."

Cameron was puzzled. "I don't understand where you're going. What's any of this got to do with Chet?"

Moe walked back to the Jeep and sat in the passenger's seat, staring silently out at the desert floor that flowed outward from the hills, far below. Daisy lay panting on the back seat. Uncertain of what to do, Cameron trailed Moe back to the vehicle.

"Assuming that you actually saw a light down there," the detective began, unprompted, "somebody had to have been down there among those buildings." As he spoke, he continued to stare, distantly, out the Jeep's windshield. "Now, I don't know exactly how it relates to Chet's disappearance, but what I *do* know is that you found Chet's boot just down the trail, in relative proximity. On top of that, Chet's boot was fully laced, which makes no sense. It's too coincidental not to be connected in some way..." Moe's voice trailed off. He turned and looked intently at Cameron. "I've been a cop long enough to know that there *are* no coincidences."

Cameron was incredulous. "You think Chet was *kidnapped*? Why would anyone kidnap Chet?"

"I didn't say Chet was kidnapped," Moe corrected him. "I said they were connected."

"Connected how?"

The detective turned and stared vacantly out the windshield. "I don't know," he said, "but I think we need to hike down to those buildings."

NINE

MOE, CAMERON AND NANCY PILED out of Cameron's Jeep atop the turnaround. Initially reluctant, Daisy finally jumped from the backseat onto the desiccated ground. She yawned and stretched before proceeding to investigate the area in the immediate vicinity of the Jeep. Although it was still dark when they left Cameron's apartment earlier that morning, the eastern horizon was already beginning to lighten and the temperature had begun its ineluctable upward march.

"How long do you think it'll take to hike down there?" Nancy asked as she shouldered her backpack. "I want to get back here before it gets too hot."

"Depends on how rough the trail is," Cameron replied. "I don't think it's probably more than a couple of miles as the crow flies, but the trail may be a bear." He whistled for Daisy and she promptly trotted over to him. Cameron slipped two water bottles into the pockets of the nylon harness she wore. "You ready for an adventure?" he asked, scratching her ears.

"I don't care how far it is 'as the crow flies'," the detective scoffed. "What if the crow is walking, carrying a twenty-pound pack?" He squared his shoulders and allowed his pack to slip into place. In a holster on his right hip he carried a .357 Magnum Colt Python revolver with a four-inch barrel. Cameron's Walther .22 pistol was in his backpack.

"That would be one bad-ass crow," Nancy observed. She walked to the edge of the plateau and looked down into the valley, still cloaked in darkness. Cameron donned his pack and adjusted the straps, then wandered over to join her. "I still don't think Chet could have made it all the way down there," she softly remarked.

Cameron lowered his voice. "Between you and me, I don't think so, either. But Woody thinks whoever was down there may know something about Chet." He paused contemplatively. "Besides, we've nowhere else to look." Cameron confided to neither Nancy nor the detective that, since the disappearance, he'd repeatedly, if unsuccessfully, attempted to establish contact with Chet using the TEAC tape recorder in his bedroom. Even the faint voices that he and Chet previously heard had grown silent.

"Well, shall we see what's down there?" Moe asked as he approached them. "I don't think it's going to get any cooler." It was growing brighter by the minute and, beneath their packs, their shirts were already damp from perspiration.

Cameron jammed his boonie hat on his head. "Might as well." He glanced around, looking for Daisy. "C'mon, Daisy!" he called and she bounded over to him.

"Think the Jeep will be safe?" Nancy asked.

"I checked the ground. The only tire tracks are from when Cam and I were up here last weekend. I don't think anybody's around to mess with the vehicle," Moe said.

Cameron shrugged. "Even if they did, there's nothing in it for them to steal. Besides, there's not much I can do to stop them." He stepped over the rim of the plateau, onto the trail leading to the valley below.

CAMERON TOOK THE LEAD, NANCY TOOK the middle, and Moe brought up the rear. Daisy clung near Cameron and, although he initially feared tripping over her, she was careful not to impede his gait. The packs each of them wore contained multiple bottles of water, a sandwich and packets of granola, Band Aids, and small pocket comb and tweezers for removing cactus thorns. The detective also placed a pair of binoculars in his pack, as well as a small cassette tape recorder. In her nylon harness, Daisy carried additional bottles of water and her collapsible dog bowl. Although all of them had cell phones, Cameron had previously advised them there was no signal.

For the first three-quarters of a mile, the faint trail descended gradually in a series of switchbacks. Although periodically wide enough to accommodate a vehicle, for most of its length the trail obligated them to hike in single file. They proceeded cautiously in the half-light because the dawn had not yet penetrated the gloom of the valley and the track was strewn with loose rocks. It was still far too dark to discern the structures they knew lay in the distance. The ambient temperature grew noticeably cooler as they dropped further into the valley.

Following a sharp turn, the trail abruptly dead-ended into an enormous pile of brush and boulders. On one side of the path reared a dizzying palisade of shale; on the other, a precipitous twenty-five-foot drop into a tangled arroyo. They drew to a halt.

"What the heck?" Nancy blurted.

Moe gazed upward, along the contiguous wall of rock. "Looks like a collapse," he observed. "You can see a big indentation in the cliff face where it used to be."

Daisy lay on the stony ground at Cameron's feet, quietly panting, as Cameron and Nancy peered upward. The shale escarpment loomed over them in the gloom.

"I don't see anything," Nancy said after a moment, though the semi-darkness rendered it difficult to specifically identify anything.

"I see what he's talking about," Cameron murmured. "You can see the place it fell from."

"Earthquake?" Nancy ventured.

"Probably, or some sort of tremor. Other than dynamite, that's about the only thing that could have caused a collapse this big," Moe observed.

"Why would anyone use dynamite?" Nancy puzzled.

"Maybe a miner," Cameron speculated. "They may have found a vein of silver or something in the cliff face and used dynamite to expose it."

"Yeah, maybe," the detective said. "There's lots of mines around here and that's quite possible."

"Didn't they realize they were blocking the path?" Nancy mused. "There's a ton of crap piled up here!"

"Multiple tons," Moe corrected her.

"Whatever," Nancy continued. "But it seems like painting yourself into a corner. You blow up a cliff in order to access some ore but, in the process, block your only way in or out. Miners must not be too bright," she chuckled.

Maybe they did it to keep people out," Cameron suggested.

"*Or to keep them in,*" the detective quietly added, more to himself than to his companions.

Moe approached the obstruction, which completely covered the trail, and began to examine it more closely. More than fifteen feet in height, a portion of the mound opposite the shale wall, near the edge of the trail, had tumbled into the arroyo below. He grasped a tree limb protruding from the mass and tugged on it, but it was firmly wedged. "We're gonna have to go over it," he announced. "Let me go first to see what's on the other side."

"Fair enough," Cameron said. "Do you have enough light to see?"

"Yeah, I think so," the detective replied, unshouldering his pack and dumping it on the ground. "It's getting lighter by the minute, anyway." He placed his foot on the limb and heaved himself upward. Moe carefully tested each foot and handhold before trusting either with his entire weight. In scarcely five minutes he stood atop the mound. "Wow!" he said, looking farther into the valley beyond.

"What is it?" Cameron and Nancy both anxiously called from the base.

"The trail drops off quite a bit on the other side," the detective responded, looking down at them. "It's a lot steeper."

"Can Daisy make it?" Cameron asked. Before Moe could respond, they heard the distant sound of an automotive horn. All three of them listened intently as the horn continued to blare.

"The Jeep." Nancy finally said.

"Crap!" Cameron spat. "Who's up there screwing with it?"

"Maybe it's Chet?" Moe suggested, although he knew how unlikely it was that Chet was even still alive.

"I don't know," Cameron responded with disgust. He looked at Nancy. "Well, what do you think we should do? I can head back to the Jeep to see what's up while you two go on, and I'll catch up with you." The horn continued to blare in the distance, unabated.

"No, that's a bad idea," Moe interjected from atop the mound. "I don't think we should split up. That's what happened to you and Chet. Either we all go back to the Jeep, or we all go on."

"You, yourself, said there's nothing in the Jeep to steal," Nancy said, looking at Cameron. "And if it *is* Chet, he'll know that we'll return to the Jeep sooner or later. All he has to do is wait there."

Cameron reflected for a moment. "Look, either somebody's just messing with the Jeep or they're trying to signal us. I don't know why they'd mess with it, but they'll probably be gone by the time I get back up there. If that's the case, I'll hurry back and rejoin you. But, if by some miracle it's Chet, he obviously needs help, bad, I just can't justify going on if there's any chance that it may be him up there. We've already come this far; I think you guys should keep going and I'll catch up."

"I guess," the detective uneasily responded.

Suddenly, the horn stopped.   Silence prevailed.

"Battery dead?" Nancy ventured.

Cameron shook his head.   "No, that wouldn't have drained it that fast.   If it's Chet maybe he just figured no one's coming, which is all the more reason I should go back." He gestured toward the pile. "You guys go on.   I'll be right behind you, I promise."

"You got your pistol?" the detective asked from the top of the mound.

"Yeah, my .22's in my pack," Cameron told him.

"I'd keep it right where you can get to it," Moe advised. Cameron nodded.

"You won't be able to call us on your cell phone," Nancy reminded him.   "There's no service out here."   She approached the mound and gingerly began its ascent. Moe reached down from his perch at the top and hauled her up as she approached the summit.

"What about Daisy?" Cameron called from the base.

"I think she'll be able to scramble up, but you may have to help her," Moe replied. "Toss my pack up first, though."

Cameron retrieved the detective's pack and heaved it to Moe, who snatched it from the air as it sailed upward. Cameron then turned to Daisy, who'd been observing them with undisguised apprehension.   "Can you climb, girl?" he cajoled her.   Daisy halfheartedly wagged her tail.   "Call her, Nance," he directed.   "I'll boost her up."

Nancy whistled, clapped her hands, and called Daisy's name. The dog walked slowly to the mound and warily began to sniff it. Cameron spoke soothingly to her. "It's okay, Daisy," he reassured her. "There's nothing to worry about." He clambered up the pile a few feet and looked down at her. "See? Nuthin' to it!" Cameron hopped to the ground and placed Daisy's front paws on the mound, then gently pushed her rump.

"C'mon, Daisy!" Nancy urged from atop the pile. She squatted and reached toward the dog.

Daisy stiffened her legs, declining to scale the heap. Cameron urged her more forcefully, but still she resisted.

"C'mon, Daisy," Nancy continued to importune.

TEN MINUTES LATER, by half-pushing, half-lifting her, they managed to wrestle Daisy to the top of the mound. Cameron stood at the bottom, looking up at Nancy and Moe, trembling from exertion, his shirt plastered to his body with sweat.

"Damn," he grumbled, mopping his face. "I'm gonna have to put Daisy on a diet!"

"The slope on the other side isn't as steep," Moe observed. "It should be a lot easier to get her over on the way back." The detective reached down and rubbed Daisy's head while Cameron sipped water from his canteen. Nancy removed Daisy's collapsible dish from her halter, half-filled it with water, and placed it on the ground. Daisy happily began lapping from it. Moe removed his binoculars from his pack then turned to face the valley that extended beyond, hoping to spot something noteworthy from his elevated vantage.

He was right. The trail on the opposite side of the mound immediately became fainter, steeper, and rockier.

The sun had now partially emerged above the hills behind them, casting long shadows across the landscape. The air temperature was beginning to rise uncomfortably. Through his binoculars, far down in the valley, the detective could clearly discern a motley collection of structures in the growing light. "Hey, check it out," he said, passing the binoculars to Nancy.

She peered through them. "Yep," she confirmed after a moment, "I can see them."

Nancy handed the binoculars back to Moe, then scooped Daisy's bowl up and crammed it into her harness. "We'd better get movin'. The longer we tarry, the hotter it's gonna get." She turned and looked down at Cameron, who watched them anxiously from the base of the earthen pile. "If you're gonna head back to the Jeep, you'd better get crackin', mister. We'll hook up with you on our way back."

"Yeah, okay," Cam responded with a distinct lack of enthusiasm. "You guys just watch your step and don't do anything dumb." He turned and began to ascend the trail down which they'd just come.

Moe half-slid, half-scrambled down the far side of the mound. Nancy grasped Daisy's collar and, together, they descended to the ground.

"How long do you think it'll take us to reach the valley?" Nancy asked Moe as they resumed their downward trek.

"An hour, maybe more. If the light Cam saw the other night was from Chet, he had to have hiked a long way." He stepped around a bristling cholla growing adjacent to the trail. "But I doubt if it was Chet. It wouldn't have made sense for him to hike down here."

"Yeah, but it was *somebody*," Nancy affirmed, "and they may have seen Chet."

They hiked the narrow, rocky trail in silence, stopping only for periodic drinks of water. The desert flora consisted of rangy palo verde trees and stunted cacti, neither of which afforded any shade. Daisy trotted easily in front, turning her head frequently to insure her companions remained in close proximity, her tongue lolling from her mouth in the increasing heat.

Ninety minutes later they reached the valley floor where the trail finally flattened out. Moe wearily drew to a halt and deposited his backpack onto the stony ground. Nancy followed suit; Daisy headed for the semi-shade of a nearby greasewood bush. The collapsed wooden ribs of an old corral moldered fifty yards in front of them.

Although scarcely 10:00 a.m. it was already oppressively hot. The detective removed his baseball cap, already soaked with sweat, and mopped his head with a bandana. He withdrew a bottle of water from his pack and drank deeply as he gazed around.

"I wonder if Cam's okay," Nancy said, uneasily, looking back to the trail they'd just descended.

"I'm sure he's right behind us," the detective assured her without conviction.

The valley was ringed on all sides by steep hills, including the one they'd just descended. Aside from the abandoned corral, Moe saw no other signs of purposeful enterprise. The trail that debouched into the broad valley could have been created as readily by wildlife as by humans.

"Well, we know that *somebody* was here," Nancy remarked, indicating the corral. Moe jammed his cap back on his head, lifted his pack from the ground, and wandered toward it. Nancy trailed behind. Daisy watched them from the greasewood bush.

As he drew near, Moe could see a dead animal, a horse, lying on its side close to a splintered wooden trough on the near side of the corral. Half-buried in dirt, its chalky bones protruded through its stiff, brittle hide. The empty sockets of its sightless eyes faced them as they approached. On the ground next to one of the corral's log posts a small heap of rotting leather, nearly buried in blown dust, suggested the remains of a saddle.

"Ugh!" Nancy grimaced. "How long do you think *that's* been here?"

Moe walked up to the corral and looked down at the desiccated form. "A long time," the detective said, sadly. He glanced into the trough; the bottom was filled with dirt. "He must have either starved or died of thirst a long time ago."

"That's sad," Nancy murmured.

Moe looked up. "It's more than sad. It's evil."

"So where's the ranch house?" Nancy inquired, looking around. "Nobody would just build a corral out in the middle of nowhere."

Moe turned away from the corral. "There's apparently an entire *town* up ahead."

"I hope we don't run into more stuff like this," Nancy said in disgust, turning away from the corral.

Moe whistled for Daisy, who hadn't stirred from beneath the spindly bush several yards away. He leaned down and slapped his thigh. "C'mon, girl!" She didn't budge. He sighed and walked back to her. "C'mon, Daisy, are you going to stay there all day?" Daisy pressed closer to the shrubbery. He bent down, grasped her collar, and gently tugged. Still she resisted.

Nancy walked over and joined him. "She must be freaked out by the dead horse."

"All animals, especially dogs, hear and see things that people don't," the detective remarked. "But I don't think it's the horse. It's something else." He could see that Daisy was trembling.

"Well, whatever it is, she doesn't want to budge," Nancy observed as he tried to drag the uncooperative dog from beneath the sheltering greasewood. "Here, let me try." She bent down and gently stroked beneath Daisy's chin. "C'mon, knothead," she cajoled. "You don't want to stay here all day, do you?" Daisy nervously licked her lips but refused to budge.

"Leave her," the detective finally urged. "She'll follow us."

Nancy straightened. "How do you know?"

"Because she's afraid to stay here alone." Moe turned and walked back to the vicinity of the corral. Nancy reluctantly followed, repeatedly glancing behind to see whether Daisy abandoned the sanctuary of her greasewood bush.

"Well, Daisy doesn't look like she's gonna budge," she sighed.

Moe stopped. "No, she will. She's just scared. But she'll be more scared if she thinks we're going to leave her here." He looked back at Daisy, who continued to sit forlornly in the brush. "We'd better go. Otherwise, we'll be standing here all day." The detective turned and began to walk beyond the corral; after a moment of hesitation, Nancy called to Daisy once more then followed.

Watching them depart, Daisy pawed the ground and began to whine softly. "We're going," Nancy called over her shoulder. "You better come, too." Before disappearing behind the corral, she glanced rearward and saw Daisy, still crouched beneath the greasewood bush. For reasons she couldn't articulate, Nancy didn't relish lagging behind and hastened to catch up with the detective.

The valley floor was rocky and, although Moe continually scanned it as they proceeded, devoid of discernible tracks. He glanced rearward to insure that Nancy was still trailing him. "How far ahead do you think the buildings are?" she called.

"Google Earth made it look like they should be right along here," the detective replied, "though I don't remember it showing that corral. Or, if it did, I couldn't see it." He looked back, anxiously searching for Daisy, and was relieved to see her slinking along the trail behind them. Thank God.

The detective abruptly stopped. "We're here," he announced, quietly.

CAMERON SAW THEM UPON reaching the trail head.

Three figures wearing battered cuirasses and peculiar, blousy trousers caked with filth huddled around the Jeep, dented morions on their heads. Chipped swords dangled from their hips, glinting in the sun. Distorted by the heat waves that flared through the scorching air, the silent, numinous figures seemed oblivious to Cameron's approach. The air suddenly reeked with the stench of rotting meat.

Cameron abruptly stopped about thirty feet from the startling figures because he didn't know what else to do. "Hey!" he yelled, apprehensively. While taking a brief rest on his hike back to the Jeep, he'd transferred his .22 pistol from his pack to the pocket of his jeans. He instinctively grasped it without removing it from his pocket, though he had no idea how effective the diminutive weapon would be against three potentially hostile assailants. "That's my car!" he angrily shouted.

The figures dumbly turned in Cameron's direction, their feral beards tangled and matted. Shaggy black eyebrows overhung pink sockets devoid of eyes.

"Holy shit!" Cameron gulped, instinctively backing away. Even from where he stood, he could see that the Jeep's canvas top, seats, and tires had all been slashed. The vehicle's hood was propped open and the Jeep rested on the rocky ground on its rims. "Get the hell away from my car!" he warned.

The figures appeared not to comprehend but stood unmoving, wordless. Cameron reluctantly displayed the Walther pistol. "Get the hell out of here," he repeated. He was trembling.

The figures stood facing Cameron for a few moments, weaving almost imperceptibly in the shimmering heat, before turning away. Mutely, they began to shamble away from the Jeep, their disintegrating leather boots making no sound as the figures shuffled like mechanical automata across the stony earth. Cameron watched, dumbfounded.

"Hey! What did you do to my car!" He shouted at the retreating figures as they drifted into the open desert. Emboldened, he stepped after them. "Hey!"

They ignored him but, like sleepwalkers, ambled down the hill, away from the Jeep. A massive patch of cholla cactus, waist high and bristling with angry thorns, grew immediately in front of them. Called "jumping cactus" because of the facility with which the cholla's thorns become dislodged and buried in the flesh of careless passersby, human or animal, the figures seemed unaware of the perilous cactus. Unknowing or uncaring, they made no effort to skirt it, but plunged into the thicket, their methodical pace unaltered.

Cameron cautiously approached the Jeep, from whence he witnessed the preternatural retreat. It astonished him when the three figures passed completely through the forest of cholla without injury, indeed, apparently without even disturbing the fragile cactus. Then they were gone.

"Holy crap," Cameron murmured to himself. Sweat poured down his sides and, notwithstanding the searing heat, he shivered. He rapidly glanced around to confirm that no additional intruders were in the vicinity.

Although he feared following the apparitions, Cameron had to satisfy himself that he hadn't simply imagined the three figures. He looked at dismay at his vandalized Jeep; the damage done to it was certainly real enough.

Cameron held the Walther .22 pistol in his right hand and stepped cautiously into the desert after the ghostly beings.

MOE'S PULSE QUICKENED. He and Nancy rapidly closed the distance in order to finally see the object of their quest. Before them stretched an amalgam of collapsed structures, the trail on which they trod widening into more-or-less the simulacrum of a street. Daisy trotted up to them.

"Wow," breathed Nancy.

There was seemingly no order to the construction. Crumbling adobe buildings were juxtaposed beside piles of rock; adjacent to empty lots, clapboard hovels rotted in the sun; undifferentiated heaps of lumber disintegrated by holes yawning in the earth. A decaying wooden sidewalk ran in front of a few of the buildings, leading nowhere.

"It looks like a set from an old western movie," Nancy remarked as she surveyed the place. "I wonder when it was built. Do you think it has a name?"

Moe looked at her. "I think it's the town Cam's been talking about," he said. "I think it's Esperanza." He squatted and examined the ground. "No footprints," he announced before standing. "I wonder where the light Cameron saw came from."

"It could have come from anywhere. Cam told me that it didn't look like an electric light because it flickered like a lantern," Nancy said.

The detective looked around. "There's no power lines coming in so, unless somebody had a gas generator, it had to have been either a lantern or a campfire."

"Let's look around," Nancy urged.

"These buildings look like they're about ready to fall down," Moe cautioned. "And if something happens, we're a long way from help. So stay close."

Nancy removed her cell phone from her shirt pocket and checked to see whether there was any reception. There wasn't.

"Which way you wanna go?" Moe asked. He patted his pocket to confirm that the cassette recorder was still there.

"Let's just walk up the street to begin with," she replied. "If we see something interesting, we'll check it out."

"I wish I'd brought a metal detector," Moe groused. "There's probably some pretty cool old stuff scattered around here."

Nancy laughed. "You'd really like to cart a metal detector all the way down here?"

As they slowly proceeded down the thoroughfare, they were confronted with increasing squalor and decay. It was impossible to ascertain whether a particular structure had been a home, a commercial enterprise, or something else entirely. Walls leaned crazily outward, roofs collapsed onto splintered floors, shapeless mounds of adobe melted under the sun, marking the site of forgotten habitations. Twisted wheels writhed in overgrown clearings and rusted scraps of iron littered the ground. Most of the structures appeared, at least originally, to have been single story, though a sprinkling of clearly taller buildings had been erected among them. Generally staying nearby, Daisy parted from them once or twice in order to investigate a particular patch of ground, which she repeatedly circled, growling almost imperceptibly.

"What happened to this place?" Nancy marveled as they walked. "It looks like a bomb went off." Moe simply shook his head.

The dirt street bifurcating the lugubrious settlement doglegged around a small hillock after little more than a block. At the dogleg they bore left, around the hillock, and were immediately confronted by a startling apparition: an intact, pristine building reared before them. Two, perhaps three stories tall, the edifice appeared to be constructed of lumber; its balustraded, whitewashed exterior sparkled in the sunlight. Astonished by its unexpectedness, they spontaneously halted and stared in disbelief.

"Now there's something you don't see every day," the unflappable detective remarked.

"Yeah, I'll say," Nancy concurred. "What *is* it?" she asked. "It looks like a hotel!"

"Well, let's find out," Moe proposed. "I wonder if we need reservations?" he joked, walking toward the building. Nancy quickly followed, though Daisy lingered behind.

"Not *this* again," Nancy complained to Moe. She walked back to Daisy. "C'mon, dammit! Nancy grasped Daisy's harness and attempted to drag the reluctant dog along. "Next time we're gonna leave you at home!" Although the obstinate animal stiffened her legs and strained against her, Nancy inexorably tugged Daisy forward as Moe clumped up the steps leading to the structure's elevated portico.

"Why don't you just leave Daisy out here?" the detective suggested from the porch. "She won't go anywhere without us and she'll stay right here. Nothing will happen to her. It beats trying to drag her where she obviously doesn't want to go."

Nancy released Daisy's collar and the dog slumped to the ground. "I can't figure out what's wrong with her," she grumbled.

"She's scared," Moe shrugged. He looked about inquisitively as he waited for Nancy to join him.

Daisy lay on the ground at Nancy's feet, panting. "Wait right here," she instructed her. Daisy wagged her tail. Nancy removed Daisy's collapsible bowl from her harness and filled it with water. She scratched Daisy's ears and the dog gratefully licked her hand. "I'll be right back, okay?" Nancy assured her. She turned to rejoin the detective as Daisy enthusiastically drank. Nancy glanced back at Daisy before clumping up the short flight of steps to the elevated porch.

The porch was one of those wide, wrap-around verandas frequently associated with the antebellum South. Though begrimed, the porch appeared to be in relative repair, doubtlessly because its expansive roof largely shielded it from the destructive rays of the sun. Feeling somewhat like trespassers, they instinctively tread very lightly on its weathered boards. Nancy pointed to a pair of carved double doors that opened onto the veranda. "Should we knock, or what?"

The detective stopped to listen. Hearing nothing, he abruptly hollered, "Hello! Is anyone here?" His voice sounded harsh, incongruous in the stillness. "Hello!" he again yelled. Silence. "Maybe the light Cam saw could've come from here?" he speculated.

"I don't know," Nancy replied. "All Cam said is that it was far away."

They approached the double doors and Moe rapped smartly on one of them. Eliciting no response, he tested the knob. The door was unlocked. He knocked a second time. "Hello!" he shouted. "Is anyone here?" Leaving the door, he strode down the porch to one of the windows that lined it and attempted to peer inside through the dirty pane. Diaphanous interior curtains frustrated his gaze.

Moe returned to Nancy, where he gently rotated the one of the oblong doorknobs and gingerly pushed against one of the double doors. Nancy glanced back at Daisy, who watched them with curiosity. The door swung open with a raspy scrape and the detective stepped across the threshold, into the structure. "Hello!" he again yelled. Nancy crowded in behind him.

The large room they entered was stifling and brightly lit by sunlight streaming through the yellowed curtains. Though barren of furniture, an antique candelabrum was suspended from an ornate ceiling medallion. Long strings of solidified candle wax hung from the chandelier and spatters of dried wax marred the wooden floor beneath it. The interior smelled musty and old.

"Look," Moe pointed toward the floor, where a path through the accumulated dust led to a closed door at the far end of the room.

"Do you think someone's here," Nancy whispered.

Rather than respond directly to her question, the detective abruptly shouted. "Hello!" His voice echoed in the emptiness. Intentionally leaving the door ajar, Moe stepped further inside, Nancy behind him.

"It's hot as hell in here," the detective grunted. They still wore their backpacks and their shirts were soaked with sweat. "I want to try something. Stay here. Don't say anything." He walked to the far corner of the room as Nancy watched nervously. Moe removed from his breast pocket the cassette recorder and punched the 'record' button. He gently placed it upright on the floor and moved several feet away. Glancing over at Nancy, he placed a finger to his lips.

"Hello, anybody," Moe began to speak in an even, modulated tone. "It's September twenty-ninth. If anyone is here and would like to speak, please do so now." He paused. "If Chet Marion is present, please identify yourself." He stood motionless and watched as the tiny spindles of the recorder slowly rotated.

"Chet, if you're here, please communicate." Moe repeated. His voice was even, unemotional.

Nancy wondered how much longer she'd be able to tolerate the stifling heat in the room. Moe seemed unaffected by it.

The cassette recorder abruptly tipped forward and fell onto the floor. Moe quickly stepped forward to right it but it skittered away from him and slid across the dusty floor until it banged into the far wall. Nancy jumped.

"What the hell was *that*?" Nancy blurted.

Moe looked at her with astonishment. He was about to speak when the cassette recorder rose from the floor and flew across the room directly at him. The detective sidestepped it as it sailed past and thudded into the opposite wall.

Moe raced forward and snatched the recorder from the floor. "Let's get out of here!" he shouted. Nancy spun and darted out the door, Moe at her heels. The detective clasped the recorder in one hand as they tumbled from the house. Seeing them frantically spill off the porch, Daisy jumped to her feet, raced back and forth, and barked excitedly. Racing away from the structure, they didn't slow until they'd distanced themselves from it, the detective still holding the cassette recorder. They finally stumbled to a breathless halt.

"If I hadn't seen it myself, I wouldn't have believed it," Nancy gasped. "And I'm not even sure that I saw it!"

"I think it's called poltergeist phenomena. I've read about it," Moe responded.

"I saw that movie," she said. "I thought it was just bullshit."

Trembling from exertion, they collapsed onto the tilted porch in front of what may once have been a small dwelling. Moe placed the cassette recorder on the decayed wood between them. Daisy lay on the ground near them, panting.

"The 'Drummer of Tedworth', in England, was the first reliably recorded poltergeist disturbance," Moe informed her while he caught his breath. "That was in the 1600s, so it's been around a long time."

Nancy looked at the detective in amazement "You know about this stuff?" she asked, incredulously.

Moe smiled cryptically. "I started reading up on it a little after Cam told me about voice phenomena," he explained. "Before that, I probably knew less about it than you do. Based on what I've read, voice phenomena and poltergeists are related because they're both manifestations of seemingly disembodied entities. Nobody knows what causes either of 'em but, with respect to poltergeists, they sometimes break things and set fires but seldom cause physical injury."

"I thought it was just Hollywood baloney," Nancy said.

"Maybe it is. You can't believe everything you read," Moe conceded.

"I'm not talking about just reading stuff," Nancy affirmed. "I'm talking about what happened back at that house." She paused. "So now what? You can go back there if you want, but I think me and Daisy will stay right here."

Moe picked the cassette recorder up from the porch and looked idly at it. "It's a long hike back to the Jeep and it'll be late afternoon before we get there. We'll probably run into Cam on our way back up the hill. I don't know about you, but I don't want to be stuck down here after dark."

"Yep," Nancy concurred. "I don't want to be here when the sun goes down. You don't have to ask me twice." She stood. "Right, Daisy?" The dog wagged her tail and leapt to her feet, eager to depart.

Nancy refilled Daisy's canvas bowl before finishing off the water remaining in the bottle. The dog eagerly drank while Moe and Nancy adjusted their packs. Still unnerved, they began retracing their steps back through the town, toward the distant hills. Nancy continually glanced around as they walked, unable to shake the feeling that they were being watched.

THE PHOSPHORECENT SUN WAS suspended above the western horizon when they finally got back to the Jeep.   Notwithstanding their fatigue, Moe and Nancy hastened toward it, where they saw Cameron sitting in the passenger's seat.

"Damn! What happened to the Jeep?" Moe marveled as they approached.

Cameron jumped to the ground and eagerly raced to them.   "You guys won't believe what happened!" he blurted as Daisy joyously licked his hands.

"Yeah, tell me about it," Nancy dryly responded. Her eyes flitted to the vehicle. "Who did *that*?"

Aside from having its roof, seats, and tires slashed, the Jeep's wiring had been ripped from beneath the dash board, its windshield broken, and the glass on all its gauges smashed.

"Well, whoever it was, I'm guessing it probably wasn't Chet," Moe remarked.

"They tore the cables out and took the battery, too," Cameron sighed. "They really did a number on it."

Moe squatted and scrutinized the soil leading to the Jeep.   "No tire tracks," he announced after a moment. He stood. "Whoever did this didn't drive up here."

"Somebody *hiked* all the way up here just to trash Cam's Jeep?" Nancy asked, incredulously.

"I *saw* who did it," Cameron said, the strain in his voice palpable. "And, no, they didn't drive up here. But I doubt you'll believe me when I tell you."

"Try us," Nancy responded, raising an eyebrow. "We'll have a contest."

Cameron walked to the rim of the plateau and pointed downward. "There's the battery," he said, looking back at Nancy and the detective. They walked over and peered downward.

The Jeep's battery was lodged, upside down, at the base of a stunted mesquite tree about thirty feet below the rim of the plateau. It appeared that, after removing it from the vehicle, someone simply heaved the battery over the edge, where it tumbled downward until coming to rest beneath the tree.

"So who did this?" Nancy asked as they walked back to the Jeep.

"Three guys," Cameron said. "At least I think they were guys." He proceeded to describe what happened without embellishment.

"And they just disappeared into a hole in the ground?" Nancy dubiously asked when Cameron concluded his narrative.

"There's an old mine shaft about 75 yards that way," he pointed beyond the disabled Jeep. "All I can figure is that they must've ducked down it. I don't know where else they could have gone. There was nowhere else for them to go. . . they were there one minute, then just disappeared. I sure as hell wasn't gonna follow 'em!"

"I agree," Moe softly pronounced after listening to Cameron. "Whoever, or whatever, wrecked your Jeep didn't have to come up here to do it because they were already here."

Nancy frowned. "Already here? *Where?*" She gestured toward the empty desert. "We haven't seen anyone all day!"

"We didn't see anyone in that house, either, but *something* caused my cassette recorder to sail across the room," Moe reminded her. "Besides,

Cam saw them and Jeeps don't vandalize themselves."

Cameron was puzzled. "What happened to you guys?"

Nancy rapidly brought him up to speed about the abandoned town lying on the other side of the hills, and the incident involving the flying tape recorder.

"I knew it!" Cameron exclaimed. "It's gotta be Esperanza!"

The detective shook his head. "Maybe originally, but that big house was built fairly recently, certainly within the last fifty years."

"You sure nobody was living in it?" Cameron asked.

"There was no furniture, at least where we were, there was dust everywhere, and it looked like nobody'd been there in forever," Nancy replied.

"Cam, who do you think would have built something like that down there?" Moe interjected. "They would have to have hauled a lot of building material and equipment all the way down the trail, which would have been a huge pain in the butt. Why would anyone do that and then just walk away and leave it?"

Cameron shrugged. "Maybe because they had an experience like what you had: stuff flying around the place."

"Woody said it was poltergeist phenomena," Nancy suggested.

Cameron looked pensive. "Based on how you just described it, I don't know what else it *could* have been. Although I've never actually seen poltergeist phenomena, I've read a lot about it. Poltergeists are normally associated with churches, cemeteries, and old houses and a common characteristic of poltergeist phenomena is playing tricks or damaging stuff. In fact, it's sometimes even called 'trickster phenomena.'"

"The Drummer of Tedworth." Nancy winked at Moe.

"How'd you know about the Drummer of Tedworth?" Cameron asked in surprise.

"Woody told me," Nancy informed him, matter-of-factly.

Cameron looked at the detective. "How'd *you* know?"

Moe smiled. "I've been doing some homework, too."

"So poltergeists destroyed your Jeep? And you actually watched them go down a hole afterward?" Nancy looked skeptical and turned to the detective. "I guess you were right when you said that poltergeists sometimes break things."

Cameron looked at her, gravely. "I don't know what destroyed the Jeep, but I know what didn't: people, because there's no people out here." He turned to Moe. "I'll show you the shaft where they disappeared."

They tramped through the desert, past the spiny thicket of cholla, to the last spot Cameron saw the three figures. Cameron was glad to have reinforcements and still held his .22 pistol.

"There," he announced as they approached the site. "Be careful."

Yawning in the earth before them was a vertical shaft, the apparent remnant of an old mine. Invisible from a distance, it plunged downward about 40 feet before making an abrupt 90-degree turn and disappearing into darkness. The detective crept to the edge of the aperture and peered into the gloom. The surrounding air was thick with the smell of rotting meat.

Because the sun was low on the horizon, the shaft was cloaked in shadow. Despite this,

Moe could discern the vestiges of timbers shoring up the walls and, heaped at the bottom, rusted fragments of old mining equipment. Emboldened, Cameron and Nancy joined Moe at the lip of the vertical pit.

"The desert around Phoenix is riddled with abandoned gold and silver mines like this," the detective said, still intently studying the shaft in the fading light. "The department gets regular calls to rescue hikers and dirt-bikers who fall into them; they typically don't even see them until it's too late and they tumble in. A couple of years ago, a girl died when the quad she was riding fell into one."

"Why don't they just dynamite 'em, or fill 'em in, or something?" Nancy asked. She glanced around nervously as the sun started to slip inexorably behind the western horizon and the shadows began to lengthen.

"Too many of 'em," Moe shrugged, carefully stepping away from the shaft. "On top of that, there's no central registry so nobody even knows where all of 'em are located...they're everywhere. The first we generally learn of them is when somebody falls into one. Besides, the mines were abandoned years ago ... who's gonna pay to fill 'em in?" He turned and began walking back toward the Jeep. "It's gonna be dark before you know it, there's no cell phone service, and it's a long way back to town."

"Yeah, we'd better start hiking out of here," Cameron said. "I'll call a wrecker as soon as we get cell coverage."

As they headed for the trailhead, Nancy turned to Moe. "So you think whoever Cam saw disappeared down that mine shaft? How is that even possible?"

"If something happens, it must be possible," the detective replied without emotion. "The Jeep was obviously trashed and Cam followed the perps. He saw them disappear and there's nowhere else they could have disappeared to. I don't pretend to understand it, but I don't understand a lot of what happened today." He turned to Cameron. "I don't know how much your deductible is, but whatever it is I'm paying it. It's not right that you should get saddled with it."

Cameron looked at him with a wistful smile. "I don't expect that. Chet was my friend and it was my idea to come here."

"We'll talk about it," Moe said as they began their descent to the cemetery.

TEN

AS MOE AND NANCY WATCHED, Cameron rotated the volume dial to maximum then placed the cassette recorder on his coffee table. "I tried listening on the other cassette recorder, but it must have jarred something loose when it hit the wall," he said. "Hopefully, we'll be able to hear something on this one." He sat on the couch and reached forward to push the 'play' button. The spindles began to slowly rotate.

A slight rustling noise emanated from the tiny speaker, the sound of the cassette recorder shifting in Moe's hands, followed by a clunk when he placed the recorder on the house's wooden floor. Then silence. Nancy and Moe glanced at one another. Cameron's gaze remained fixed on the tape recorder.

"Hello?" A voice abruptly emerged from the tape. More silence ensued, followed by indistinct whispering noises. Then, "It's Chet." All three of them involuntarily jumped. Although Daisy had been dozing at the foot of the couch, her head immediately snapped up when she heard the familiar voice on the tape.

"Jesus Christ," the detective murmured under his breath. They unconsciously held their collective breath as they stared at the tape recorder, straining to discern more words. Although its spindles continued to slowly turn, no additional sounds emerged from the cassette recorder until a thud when it fell over, followed by a harsh scraping sound, reflective of it sliding across the floor. A bang evidenced its collision with the wall. Thereafter, only silence.

After listening several more seconds, Cameron reached forward and clicked the recorder off. He looked wordlessly at Nancy and Moe.

"Do you think that was really Chet?" Nancy finally asked.

Cameron sighed. "It sounded like Chet, but I can't be certain."

"If it was Chet, how could he have...?" Nancy's voice trailed off. She looked plaintively at Moe.

"Let's hear it again," the detective suggested.

Cameron rewound the tape and they listened to it a second time, then a third, then a fourth. The entire recording lasted perhaps five seconds. He clicked the 'stop' button.

"Well, it sure sounds like Chet," Nancy said after hearing the tape repeated. "But I don't know how that's possible."

Unnerved, Cameron looked at Moe. "What do you think?"

The detective slowly shook his head. "Well, I never talked to Chet and don't know what his voice sounds like. But you guys are familiar with his voice so you're in the best position to know." He paused and looked gravely at Cameron. "Native American culture is replete with traditions about unseen forces...spirit guides, ancestors, guardians, whatever you want to call them. Certain tribe members often go off by themselves into the wilderness, sometimes for weeks at a time, and try to communicate with the spirits. Sitting Bull and Crazy Horse were probably the most famous among the plains tribes, but there were lots of others from every tribe I've ever heard of. They'd fast and pray, hoping for visions of the spirit world. That was the purpose of sweat lodges and peyote, too. I don't know what we just heard was Chet, but I have no other explanation, rational or otherwise." Moe smiled, wryly. "I guess the biggest difference is that traditional Native Americans didn't have tape recorders."

"But we weren't fasting or praying," Nancy said.

Cameron nodded thoughtfully. "True. So if it was Chet, he must *really* have wanted to get through to us."

CAMERON SLID THE CHAIR OUT from the desk in his bedroom and plopped down in front of the TEAC recorder. Adjusting the cumbersome earphones on his head, he carefully noted the date, time, and numerical display on the analogue tape-counter on a yellow legal pad before switching the recorder on. He depressed the machine's 'record' button and watched as the reels made a single revolution before beginning to speak into the microphone before him on the desk.

"Greetings, friends. It's October twenty-fifth and I would like to speak with Chet Marion, if he is present." He paused a moment and glanced at his watch, where its second hand silently marked time. "Chet, or anyone here, tell me what you know of the disposition and whereabouts of Maria Luis de Baca's *reales,* or any of de Baca's tangible assets in his possession at the time of his death. Inform me what became of them."

Cameron leaned back in his chair as the TEAC's tape-counter slowly rotated. He checked his watch again and, when two minutes had elapsed, reached forward and depressed the TEAC's 'record' button a second time. Noting on his legal pad the elapsed time, as well as the numbers now displayed on its analogue tape-counter, Cameron then switched the TEAC off. He'd listen to resulting recording later. Hopefully, it would confirm what he'd already been able to determine about the vanished treasure of Maria Luis de Baca.

"AS WE PREVIOUSLY DISCUSSED," Mr. Williamson resumed, "de Baca was purportedly broke when he died in 1827. We shouldn't find that particularly surprising, since he undoubtedly had to spend a lot of money to settle his various Floats and to pay the army of mercenaries he needed to protect them from marauding Indians."

They were sitting in the docent's cluttered Historical Society office. Because of its flattened tires, Cameron's insurance company was forced to send a flatbed truck to retrieve his Jeep from the desert and haul it back into town. He didn't even want to think what that was going to cost, to say nothing of the actual cost of repairing the Jeep.

In the meantime, he returned to the Arizona Historical Society in the red Mustang convertible provided by his insurance company, where he sat with Mr. Williamson. After driving a Jeep for so long, Cameron had forgotten how close to the ground ordinary cars are and he struggled to climb out of the Mustang. He felt as though he was riding in a bath tub. Cameron was eager to ask the docent more questions about the Baca Float and Esperanza.

Mr. Williamson emerged from a back room when he heard Cameron enter. "Hello, again," he warmly smiled.

"Remember me?"

"Of course. You're the only person who didn't come in to ask about Wyatt Earp. Did you find out anything more about your cemetery?"

Cameron shook the old man's outstretched hand, which felt like dried parchment. "That's why I'm here," he explained. "I have some more questions about Spanish Floats."

Mr. Williamson motioned him toward a metal desk. "Well, let's see if we can figure out the answers. If I don't know them, I'll certainly make something up!" he chuckled.

Cameron slid a chair out and sat at the desk. "Some friends and I found Esperanza, I think. It's in the hills behind the cemetery."

"Indeed?" Williamson responded. "The five known Floats contain the vestiges of a number of settlements. The buildings were small and usually constructed of waddle and daub or *adobe* because there were no trees in the desert big enough to use as building material. After they were abandoned, virtually all of the structures eventually melted back into the earth, leaving no visible traces. Because none of them had cement foundations their outlines can generally be seen only from the air.   With respect to Esperanza, although it's known that Cabeza de Baca created a pueblo by that name, there's no record of its exact location. The other settlements established on his Floats are well known, however."

"Well, I think we found it," Cameron reiterated.   "It's pretty much in ruins, like you said, but one big building looks to be in excellent condition." Because he'd never actually set foot in the settlement, Cameron merely conveyed to the docent the description provided him by Nancy and the detective. He intentionally omitted mention of Chet's disappearance and any mention of the cassette recorder incident.

"I suppose it's not impossible that you may have located Esperanza," the docent conceded after listening to Cameron. "Since nobody knows where it was located, your opinion is probably as valid   as   anyone's."   Notwithstanding   his assurances, Mr. Williamson was unable to mask the skepticism in his voice.   "Did you take photographs?"

Cameron's   face   assumed   a   pained expression. "My friends tried taking pictures with their cell phones but none of them came out. They were all black. They thought maybe the lack of cell service out there may have somehow interfered with the camera function but, thinking about it later, I don't know what that would have to do with anything. Anyway, they weren't able to take any pictures."

The old man looked genuinely pained. "I was hoping we might have been able to determine the approximate age of the buildings, based on their architectural style and the materials used in their construction. Oh, well," he sighed, "how can I help you today?"

Cameron leaned forward in his chair. "This is gonna sound weird, but are there any records of people disappearing from the Floats?"

Mr. Williamson looked perplexed. "Disappearing? I don't understand."

Cameron smiled sheepishly. "I'm not sure I completely understand, either. What I'm asking is whether you're aware of any records of people just disappearing off the Floats."

The docent unconsciously frowned and looked off into space. "Like all large bureaucracies throughout history, the Spanish Empire kept extensive records," he finally began. "*Peones*, peasants of mixed Spanish and Indian blood, or *mestizos,* and, before them, Indians, were vital to the Spanish economy, which needed them to work its gold and silver mines and settle what is now the American Southwest. *Peones* were used for everything, even to harvest cochineal beetles, the cactus-eating insects that they dried and crushed to produce a red powder, which wealthy Europeans used as a natural dye. Even the British 'red coats' used cochineal powder to dye their uniforms. Until the Germans invented chemical dyes in the 1800's everybody had to use cochineal powder, which the Spanish basically had a monopoly on. Quite simply, the Spanish economy would have completely collapsed without peón labor."

Cameron was perplexed by the docent's apparent digression. "I don't understand what cochineal beetles, or whatever they were, have to do with the Floats," he said.

Williamson held a hand up, urging patience. "The Spanish didn't technically enslave *peones* like they did the Indians they encountered in the New World, but that's basically how they treated them. The closest modern analogue is probably

France, which remained a feudal society until the 1789 revolution. Prior to that, Bourbon France was divided into a patchwork of provinces ruled by wealthy aristocrats who owned not just the land, but the people on it. Pre-revolution Russia is another example, where the czar owned everything in the country, including its inhabitants. The Russian peasantry was considered a commodity, no different from timber or minerals. The Spanish Crown exhibited exactly the same attitude toward its *peones*."

"Beginning with the Conquest, the Spanish government created a semi-feudal system under which conquistadors were awarded large swathes of land, called *encomiendas,* along with the Indians who occupied them. Because there were never enough *encomiendas* to go around, the largest and most lucrative ones went to the most successful *conquistadores.* In addition to extorting the Indians' labor, *encomenderos,* the Spanish landowners, also had the right to impose taxes on things like meat, cloth, salt, and honey. Under the *encomienda* system, the Indians were basically reduced to a state of vassalage to the *encomenderos* and, although the *encomenderos* were legally obligated to treat the indigenous peoples humanely, they rarely did so. As a result, the *encomiendas* promptly wiped out most of the Indians through overwork, disease, starvation, or simply by absorbing them though inter-marriage. Although the "New Law of the Indies" officially abolished the *encomienda* system in 1542, Spanish landowners in the New World basically just looked the other way, allowing *encomiendas* to flourish for another two centuries. But instead of using Indians for labor, most of whom were by that time dead, the *encomenderos* simply substituted *peones*."

Because he found the docent's history lecture to be interesting, if irrelevant, Cameron listened politely.

"It was the Catholic Church's responsibility to maintain accurate records of the *peones* because, if too many of them died, the labor shortage would have proven catastrophic to Spain's imperial ambitions: the gold Spain needed to finance its Continental wars couldn't be mined and the expansion of its empire across the globe would have abruptly terminated. As a consequence, the Catholic Church was diligent about recording births, deaths, and christenings. But to address your question directly," the docent finally summarized, "although I've never specifically looked, I suppose the church probably also kept records of instances where people simply 'disappeared'. People vanished all the time back then: their haciendas were attacked by Indians and they were carried off as trophies of war, spirited off to Mexico, or simply sold into slavery. Entire families travelling from one place to another were never heard from again; people disappeared for all sorts of reasons. As I said, however, it was vital for the various officials in Spain to keep an accurate head-count of the peón population and they utilized the Catholic Church for that purpose. They didn't do so out of sense of altruism, but to insure a constant labor supply. The Society probably has some of those records."

"Why did the Spanish need so many laborers? For what?"

The docent smiled. "For complex religious, commercial, and social reasons, cultures throughout history have always coveted gold, and the Sixteenth Century Spanish were no exception. Prior to the discovery of the New World, Spain obtained most of its gold by laboriously dredging the auriferous Volta, Senegal, and Niger rivers in West Africa. Columbus turned the *status quo* on its head, though. After 1492, *the* overriding reason for the exploration and colonization of the New World was simply the pursuit of gold. As Cortez is famously said to have informed the Aztec emperor, Moctezuma, 'We Spanish suffer from a disease for which gold is the only cure.' In order to fully exploit the New World's vast gold deposits, the Spanish needed an endless supply of human capital." Cameron manifested his understanding by nodding.

Williamson continued. "The conquistadors were not soldiers in the conventional sense because they weren't members of the regular armed forces of the Spanish Crown. The closest things to conquistadors that we have today are probably professional mercenaries and, even then, that's not an exact comparison. Most became *conquistadores*, not in the expectation of receiving regular compensation, but because they hoped to acquire an *encomienda*. If, for whatever reason, they weren't rewarded with an *encomienda*, they appropriated whatever they could get their hands on: land, gold, livestock, even Indians. From an economic perspective, the conquistadors were basically investors in a commercial enterprise that carried enormous risks but also promised great rewards. That's why, as I mentioned, the campaigns of conquest in the New World focused on places that were already wealthy and well-populated by indigenous Americans. An isolated, empty *encomienda* that had neither gold, nor a native labor force to exploit, would have no economic value. Why waste the blood and effort to conquer such a place?"

"Were the *conquistadores* entitled to keep whatever gold they found?"

The old man shook his head. "No. Technically, all the gold remained the property of the Spanish Crown. It was supposed to have been refined on the individual *encomiendas* then shipped back to Spain. Even today, we read in the papers about the discovery of some old Spanish galleon, carrying tons of gold from Mexico or Guatemala, which foundered in a storm and sank offshore. It was to discourage the *conquistadores* from hoarding the gold they discovered that the entire *encomienda* system was created in the first place. But, of course, smuggling and outright theft remained rampant."

"Are there any records of conquistadors getting an *encomienda* here?" Cameron asked out of curiosity.

"In Arizona?"

Cameron nodded.

"Most of the *encomiendas* for which there are surviving records were located in what are now Mexico, Guatemala, and El Salvador. Hernan Cortez, who conquered the Aztecs, and his lieutenant, Bernal Diaz, both received large *encomiendas in* Guatemala, for example. There were others in Nicaragua, Belize, and Cuba. Pizarro, who conquered the Incas, introduced the *encomienda* system as far south as Peru. The thing to remember is that *encomiendas* were established only where two things existed: large deposits of gold and substantial populations of indigenous Indians. The combination of those two things provided the *raison d'etre* for the entire *encomienda* system. The absence of either would have deprived the Spanish of any reason to settle the New World." Mr. Williamson paused. "I'm not aware of any *encomiendas* north of Mexico's Central Highlands, where Mexico City is presently located. With specific regard to Arizona, the harsh climate of the American Southwest discouraged the agglutination of large, stationary populations of Indians. On top of that, there's comparatively little easily-accessible gold here, at least compared to Central America. As a consequence, there was little to entice the *conquistadores* to Arizona. That's not to say it didn't happen; I'm just not aware of it if it did. The Society has no record of it, anyway." A mischievous smile traced the old man's lips. "But rumors have abounded for centuries that some gold from Mexico may have found its way north."

Cameron's interest was instantly piqued. "North? You mean Arizona?"

The docent nodded. "Perhaps. A handful of sixteenth and seventeenth century documents, admittedly of questionable provenance, say that some of Cortez's men melted a large quantify of gold the general had pilfered for himself, along with an unknown amount of gold dust, and cast it into a wheel ten feet in diameter and several inches thick. They knew that once the theft came to light, their lives wouldn't have been worth a tinker's damn," if you'll pardon the expression, he smiled, "because Cortez was a brutal man; it was said that he was capable of thrusting his index finger completely through an apple. In order to spirit the gold away as quickly as possible, Cortez's men supposedly recruited some Indians, slipped an axel through a hole in the center of the wheel, and just rolled it away. The logical direction for them to flee would have been north because everywhere south, all the way to Peru, was teeming with *conquistadores*. By contrast, the north was barren of both Spaniards and *encomiendas*. Additionally, the terrain to the north was relatively flat and free of the thick jungle that characterized most of Central America to the south, which would have made it difficult for them to roll their gold wheel. Whether the story is true or not, if you want my personal opinion, I suspect that some of the conquistadors *did* end up settling in the Southwest, including Arizona, and marrying native women, even though the Spanish Crown may not have awarded them an *encomienda* here...they just appropriated whatever they wanted because land was plentiful and there was no organized opposition to them."

Cameron listened intently. "Do you think the story is true?"

"About the gold wheel?" Cameron nodded. "Like I said, the *encomienda* system all but guaranteed wholesale corruption. Not just the theft of gold that belonged to the Crown, but with respect to virtually every aspect and level of society. But, since the Spanish valued gold over all other commodities, gold would be the one thing landless *conquistadores* would actually have risked their lives for, even if it meant stealing it. So, yes, I think it's possible there's some truth to it."

"Why didn't Cortez just go after them and recover the gold his men stole?" Cameron asked. "Didn't he notice that it and his men were missing? How far could they possibly have rolled a wheel that must've weighed a ton?"

"Multiple tons," Mr. Williamson corrected him. "You have to remember that all the gold from the New World belonged to the king of Spain, not to Cortez personally. Like all *encomenderos*, Cortez simply skimmed as much as he thought he could get away with. If the incident actually occurred and Cortez had made too much of it, one of his ambitious political rivals like the governor of Cuba, Diego Velasquez de Cuellar, would have gotten wind of the incident and reported it back to

Spain. If that happened, Cortez would certainly have been shipped back to Europe in chains. No, I suspect that once he discovered the theft, Cortez probably did his best to quietly sweep the whole thing under the rug. There's no doubt he must've been angry, but what could he realistically do? Today, it would be like somebody operating an illicit methamphetamine lab calling the police to report the theft of some of his product."

"So let me get this straight," Cameron slowly began, trying to put into context everything he'd learned from the docent since his first visit. "In the 17th century, the king of Spain gave de Baca some land in what are now Arizona and Colorado, but even before that happened..."

"Centuries before," the old man clarified.

"*Centuries* before, *conquistadores* may also have come here with a huge amount of gold they'd stolen from Cortez?" Mr. Williamson merely smiled. "Do you think de Baca took up residence on his floats specifically to look for Cortez's gold? Maybe that's where all his money went!"

"We have no evidence that Cabeza de Baca was even *aware* of the tradition that Cortez's men had spirited some of his gold northward," the docent replied. "All one can do is speculate."

Cameron was silent as he tried to digest the information. "With respect to the records you talked about a moment ago, do they indicate whether people were killed by Indians, died of diseases, or what?" Cameron probed.

"Usually," Mr. Williamson confirmed, "except for infants. Infant mortality was so high that the Church seldom bothered to note it. Also, given the limits of their medical knowledge, they generally attributed death to things like 'grippe,' 'ague,' 'bilious fever,' 'catarrh,' or 'scrofula.' It's anybody's guess what people actually died of."

"You have those records here?" Cameron figured that, notwithstanding their apparent imprecision, the historical archives might provide additional information about Esperanza, perhaps even about Cortez's mysterious golden wheel. Besides, he had nowhere else to look.

"Let's see exactly what we have," Mr. Williamson replied, standing. "All the records are on microfiche and in Spanish, though. Can you read Spanish?" He was gratified with the interest Cameron displayed in such a recondite feature of Arizona history.

"I can try," Cameron smiled.

CAMERON SWUNG OPEN THE DOOR to the pawn shop, his arrival announced by a jarring electronic buzzer. The stifling interior was musty and dim, illuminated by a stuttering neon light overhead. Every square foot appeared to be occupied by merchandise. Here, heaps of inoperative VCR's. There, piles of corroding tools. Elsewhere, a thicket of rusted bicycles. A mélange of guitars hung along its walls, joined by broken cuckoo clocks, chipped beer signs, and glassy-eyed deer heads caked with dust. A waist-high showcase, its cracked glass panels indifferently repaired more than once in the past with lengths of strapping tape, contained tarnished costume jewelry and Rolex knock-offs. To Cameron's right an alcove was haphazardly stacked with furniture. The smell of boiled cabbage permeated the room.

"No toilet! No toilet!" screeched a short, hirsute human wearing sandals and a soiled turban who materialized from some dark recess at the rear of the store. His beard was surmounted by an elaborately coiffed mustache and sweat stains ringed the armpits of his Hawaiian shirt.

He had a revolver strapped to his hip and he waved his hands excitedly as he spoke.

"I don't need the toilet," Cameron said, annoyed by the man's abrupt manner.

"What you want?" he asked with suspicion. "No toilet," he again warned.

"You buy gold?"

"Sure, sure, I buy. Everybody buy. Show me," the man impatiently demanded. There was food detritus in his beard and he reeked of body odor.

"Well, I'm still in the process of getting it," Cameron conceded. "I was just wondering if there's a limit to how much you'd be willing to buy."

"No limit, no limit," the man yawped. "You have, I buy. No problem." He looked warily at Cameron. "When you have?"

"I'm not sure..."

"No problem," the man interrupted with a dismissive wave of his hand. "You bring here first. I give you best price. You ask for 'Jay,' only for 'Jay.' No problem. You need ring? Come, I show you nice ring." He began threading his way toward the battered jewelry showcase.

"I don't need a ring," Cameron said, backing toward the door.

"I have very nice ring." The man continued to speak over his shoulder as he walked. "You have wife?"

The jolting buzzer proclaimed Cameron's departure from the store.

ANNO DOMINI NOSTRI IESU CHRISTO
1821

HE BEGAN, AS HE ALWAYS DID, by talking to the people who were probably the last to see them.

"No, *Capitán,* I did not notice anything unusual last night. Iñez and his wife placed their sleeping mats where they customarily do, out of the roadway, about two or three *varas* from my own. Iñez and I chatted for a while until I heard him begin to snore. I then turned on my side, facing away from him, and went to sleep. I do not know what happened after that. When I awoke just before dawn today and saw that their sleeping mats were empty, I merely thought they had gone to relieve themselves. Other than that, I do not know."

In its essential details, the foregoing narrative was repeated by everyone to whom Capitán Diego spoke: the *zapatero,* the *herrero,* the *carnicero.*

"No, *Capitán,* we saw nothing."

"*Si, Capitán,* Luz was in perfect spirits when last I talked to her."

"No, *Capitán,* I neither saw nor heard anything during the night."

"It can only be devils, or the Evil One, himself, who is to blame." Invariably, they would cross themselves before scurrying away.

It was the same for the forty or so people who had already vanished from Esperanza during the previous months. The disappearances started immediately after the first settlers began to arrive from Mexico, riding in rickety wagons, pulling handcarts, or simply walking. At first it was thought that stealthy, marauding Apaches had crept into the ramshackle settlement during the night, murdering people as they slept. But where was the evidence? There were no bodies, no blood. Then someone remembered that no one could ever recall even *seeing* an Apache anywhere in the vicinity of Esperanza, notwithstanding that the country positively teemed with murderous *Indios* throughout the northward trek. Indeed, it was the rare caravan that didn't lose at least one of its members to the predatory savages. It was as though even the fearless Apaches shunned the Baca Float.

Capitán Diego sighed. He would, as he had previously done, organize a mounted patrol to search for the five missing *campesinos.* The patrol would, as it had previously done, ride around aimlessly for half a day, for he had no idea where to begin the search. Beyond half a day, the horses, and the men riding them, would simply collapse from heat exhaustion. But the *alcalde* demanded a search, so a search he would have. Afterward, the *Capitán* would submit a token report to the *alcalde,* who would duly forward it to his superiors in Durango, along with his own personal addendum expressing his deepest regret at this latest unfortunate vicissitude. Esperanza's remaining denizens would cross themselves, mutter a prayer of thanks to the Blessed Virgin, and put their trust in God, or the gods, that the hand of death would once again pass them by.

Over all, the merciless sun remorselessly seared the molten earth.

ELEVEN

"I WANT NOTHING TO DO WITH IT," Nancy peremptorily sniffed. "It's completely harebrained. You weren't there when Moe's tape recorder flew across the room. And, after Chet's disappearance and your Jeep getting destroyed, I can't believe you want to go back there."

Cameron had just informed her of his desire to conduct a séance in the house at Esperanza. "Nance, that's exactly the point. You can't tell me that you're not the slightest bit intrigued by what happened." He sounded more pleading than assertive.

Nancy arched her brow as she responded. "Sure I can: I'm not the slightest bit intrigued." She placed her coffee cup on its saucer and leaned back in her chair. "Cam, I don't know whether Chet fell into a hole, was kidnapped by Oompa Loompas, or what. But what I *do* know is that this whole thing stinks to high heaven. It was kind of fun at first, discovering that old town and stuff, but now it's just getting too weird. You need to let Woody deal with everything from here on."

"Nance, I *am* letting Woody deal with it. In fact, he's the *only* one who even bothered to help us! But that doesn't mean that we can't help, too. I haven't talked to him about the séance yet because I wanted to run it past you first. What harm can it do? At worst, nothing will happen and we'll just have wasted a little time. But you, yourself, said that it sounded like Chet on the cassette tape and we might actually be able to communicate with him."

"You're wrong, Cam. The worst thing is that something *could* happen. Do I need to remind you again about the guys who trashed your Jeep and the flying tape recorder?"

Cameron shook his head dismissively. "You heard Woody say that poltergeists, assuming that's what they are, seldom actually cause injury. You know, like I said, they're tricksters."

"Yeah, 'tricksters' heaving tape recorders at my head and wrecking your car. I'd forgotten what an expert on the subject Woody is," Nancy dryly remarked. She signaled to their waiter by pointing to her empty cup.

Cameron steered the conversation to a different topic. "I went back to the Arizona Historical Society this week. I wanted to see if they had any more information on Esperanza."

Their waiter glided over with a carafe of hot coffee. "Did they?" Nancy asked as he refilled their cups.

"As a matter of fact they did," Cameron replied after the waiter departed.

She took a sip of fresh coffee. "And?"

"Well, all the records are in Spanish and all the Spanish I know I learned in high school..."

"Yeah, yeah, blah, blah, blah," Nancy scoffed. "Get to the point."

Cameron scowled at her. "Well, as far as I can tell, a boat-load of people in Esperanza either died or just disappeared. They had to keep shipping replacements in from Mexico."

"They disappeared all at once or one at a time?" she asked with feigned innocence.

Cameron refused to be baited. "As far as I could understand the records, people started disappearing right after Esperanza was established. Some were lost to Indian predation and accidents, but others just basically vaporized. At least that's what the records say."

Nancy sipped her coffee before responding. "Cam, I honestly don't understand what any of this has to do with Chet. I mean, you don't even know if that old town back in the hills *is* Esperanza. For all you know, Esperanza could have been located *anywhere.*"

"That's exactly why I want to have a séance there!" he exclaimed. "How else are we gonna find out? Even though the historical record is clear that Esperanza was established on one of the Floats, up 'till now, nobody's been able to locate it. Maybe that's because, until we found it, nobody knew that a sixth Float even existed. Nobody could find Esperanza until now because they weren't looking in the right place." He leaned back and folded his arms triumphantly.

"Cam, even if everything you say is true, I still don't see what any of it has to do with Chet,"

Nancy responded in exasperation. "I mean, isn't Chet the whole point?"

Cameron leaned and looked at her intently. "Nance, you, yourself, heard Chet's voice on the tape. I don't pretend to know how it got there, or what that town has to do with his disappearance, but it is what it is. The common denominator is Esperanza."

She sighed and took another sip of coffee. "That town creeps me out, Cam. I don't think you should go back there."

"If not me, who? If not now, when?" Cam pressed.

"I don't know," she conceded. "But there's gotta be something you can do other than a stupid séance. When are you gonna talk to Woody?"

"Like I said, I wanted to run it past you first, Nance. I'm sure Woody won't be opposed to the idea. I don't know what else I *can* do, Nance."

"What about trying to record Chet's voice again?" she suggested. "You could do that without going back to that town."

Cameron shook his head. "I already tried that with the big tape deck in my bedroom. Nothing." He drained his coffee cup, placed it back on its saucer, and looked contemplatively into the distance. "You know," he resumed after a moment, "now that I think about it, there may be a middle ground. Literally." Nancy listened with interest. "I'm thinking that if I went back out to the cemetery with a cassette recorder, I could maybe pick Chet up there. I mean, the cemetery is relatively close to Esperanza...closer than here, anyway."

"You're talking about recording inside one of those charnel houses, aren't you? I was hoping you'd forgotten about that," Nancy responded.

"I don't know what to tell you," Cameron shrugged. "It's either that, or go back to Esperanza."

IT'S SURPRISING HOW QUICKLY THE temperature in the desert plummets on a November night.

"Damn, it's colder than a well digger's butt out here!" Moe chuckled. "Brrrrrrrrrrr!" He'd just exited the Jeep by unzipping its canvas top and climbing over the tail gate after Cameron drew to a stop at the perimeter of the cemetery. It was 7:00 p.m. and already dark.

The swish of automobile traffic on McDonald Drive, a quarter-mile to the south, was clearly audible in the crisp air. Although their headlights were visible, darkness and the intervening scrub brush concealed the cemetery from the uncaring occupants of the distant vehicles. Daisy promptly followed the detective over the tail gate, where she stretched luxuriantly in the cold air.

"You're right," Nancy acknowledged as she stepped from the passenger's seat. She zipped up her jacket and slipped on a pair of deer skin gloves. "I'm glad they repaired the top to your Jeep, Cam." The body shop returned Cameron's Jeep to his apartment the previous month. Aside from still smelling like paint, it was otherwise impossible to guess the vehicle had been vandalized.

"Yep. Thank God the heater's working, too. When the temperature's like this, it's hard to believe how damned hot it gets during the summer. I don't understand why everyone wants to move to Arizona; it's too hot in the summer and too cold in the winter." Cameron flicked his flashlight on and flashed it about the ancient cemetery, its beam of light ultimately dissipating in the emptiness. They began picking their way across the broken ground, toward the charnel houses. Cameron led, followed by Nancy. Moe brought up the rear. Daisy clung close to Cameron who, along with the detective, had a cassette recorder tucked in his jacket pocket. All three carried flash lights. As usual, the detective was armed with his Colt Python revolver. Their warm breath formed clouds of condensation in the night air.

"I don't know how I always let you talk me into stuff like this," Nancy grumbled to no one in particular as they walked. "I must be on drugs. My feet are already cold."

"I'm glad you're here, Nance," Cameron said over his shoulder. "Nothing bad's gonna happen and three sets of eyes, and ears, are better than two. I promise we'll only be here a few minutes."

"I still don't see why you couldn't come during the day," she continued. "This place creeps me out." She stumbled over a chunk of broken headstone protruding from a scraggly bush, her fall prevented only because the detective darted forward and caught her arm. "Dammit!" she muttered under her breath. Nancy looked at the detective. "Thank you," she smiled in the darkness.

"It's darker than the inside of a black cat around here," Moe asserted, releasing his grasp.

Cameron paused and turned toward them. "There's too much electromagnetic interference in the atmosphere during the day. You know how, when you're driving around at night, you can sometimes pick up radio stations from hundreds of miles away? It's the same with voice phenomena. It's a lot easier to record it at night than during the day. Believe me, if I thought I could do it during the day, I wouldn't be here now."

"Whatever," Nancy groused. She cautiously resumed picking her way through the overgrown burial ground, stiff brambles slapping against her legs.

Cameron beamed his flashlight around. "Wait. Where's Daisy?"

Nancy and Moe stopped abruptly and probed the darkness with their flashlights. "She was with you, wasn't she?" the detective responded.

"Yeah, she was until just a minute ago...where'd she go?" They scanned the area with their flashlights, the beams of light creating grotesque shadows as they rapidly swept across the moldering tombstones. "Daisy! Daisy! C'mon, girl," Cameron shouted into the frigid night air.

Moe whistled shrilly. "Daisy!" he and Nancy called in unison.

"Oh, no!" Cameron groaned. He frantically stumbled forward. "C'mon, Daisy! C'mon!"

She had vanished.

"Oh, my God, no!" Cameron cried. "Daisy! Daisy!" He rushed back to Nancy and Moe, tripping over the stump of a splintered cross jutting from a patch of weeds. "Did you see where she went?" he entreated them. "Where could she have gone?" He was hyperventilating and nearly incoherent.

Moe instantly reached out and placed his hand on Cameron's shoulder. "Cam, look at me!" Cameron ignored him and continued to look frantically about. "Cam!" repeated the detective, more firmly, gently shaking him.

Cameron finally yielded. "Where's Daisy?" he choked.

"She was just here," Nancy affirmed. "I'm sure she's not far. Maybe she just got cold and went back to the Jeep." Nancy was beginning to feel sick and afraid. She shivered because the air temperature seemed to be dropping by the second.

Cameron pointed his flashlight in the direction of the Jeep. The beam reflected off the windshield of the empty vehicle. "Daisy?" Cameron called, hopefully.

"What do we do now?" Nancy softly asked.

"You guys go back to the Jeep and drive around and use the headlights to find Daisy," Moe said. "I'll keep walking to look for her. She can't have gone very far; she was just here."

Cameron nodded dully and wordlessly began trudging back to the Jeep. He was struggling not to panic.

Nancy turned to follow him when, seemingly only a few yards distant, a dog began a long, mournful howl. Moe whirled and whipped his flashlight toward the sound. Its beam splashed against only sunken graves and crumbling tombstones. Nancy and Cameron contributed their flashlights, too, but they revealed nothing.

"Daisy!" Cameron shouted. He began to hasten toward the sound.

Moe stepped in front of him. "Don't!" he commanded. The detective's abruptness startled Cameron. "Wait," Moe cautioned, holding his hand up. All three listened intently.

The forlorn howl terminated. Quietude returned. Nancy was shivering uncontrollably.

Then an abrupt, painful yelp followed by silence.

NANCY SLID INTO THE PASSENGER'S SEAT and slammed the flimsy door as Cameron cranked the engine and flipped the heater on. "It should start blowing hot air right away," he said. "We weren't out there long enough for the engine to completely cool off." He flicked on the Jeep's head lights, as well as its piercing driving lights, instantly transforming the area into day.

Detective Moe strode through the weeds at the far edge of the cemetery, shining his flashlight about. The vapor from his breath hovered in the cold air as he repeatedly called Daisy's name. Cameron slipped the transmission into 'D' and pulled slowly forward as Nancy unzipped the Jeep's thick plastic window. A blast of frosty air assaulted her.

"I'm gonna drive around the perimeter first," Cameron said. Nancy nodded and pointed her flashlight out the open window, seeing nothing but dirt and sage brush.

"Daisy! Daisy!" she shouted into the bleak night.

Cameron slowly drove along the graveyard's crumpled fence line, peering anxiously though the windshield. Like Nancy, he unzipped his window and repeatedly called for Daisy as the Jeep crept forward. Cameron regularly braked, honked the Jeep's horn, and yelled Daisy's name through the open window. Moe had meanwhile left the confines of the cemetery and was scouring the contiguous area. Though the detective was beyond the reach of their headlights, they could see the periodic flash of his light as he made his way through the desert.

Nancy's face was numb from cold. Despite the roaring blast of the Jeep's heater, her feet were cold, too. She knew that nothing good could have resulted from tonight's excursion and was sorry they had come. Nancy wanted to cry but her face was simply too cold and stiff. She couldn't do anything except ride around in a search for Daisy that, in her heart, she knew was hopeless. Nancy shouted Daisy's name into the night once again, but the frigid air was already causing her to become hoarse. She shivered again, not entirely from the cold, as Cameron continued his lugubrious circuit of the graveyard.

ANNO DOMINI NOSTRI IESU CHRISTO
1822

"*SI, SI,*" SAID THE *ALCALDE* with a dismissive wave of his hand. The oily flicker from the nearby lamp glinted off his gold signet ring. The ring prominently displayed the coat-of-arms of the *alcalde's* distinguished ancestors who had fought alongside *El Cid* during the *Reconquista*, when the *tierra madre* finally managed to rid itself of the pestilential Moors. With such noble blood coursing through his veins, the *alcalde* had little patience for the scraping piety of the docile, shabby clergy. "I am mindful of my responsibilities toward the *peones* whose welfare I have been charged to safeguard. I do not require your carping reminders."

"Of course, Excellency. Your benevolent concern for the *peones* is as a father for his own children. In my humble capacity as their shepherd, I merely convey to you my concern over the continuing diminution of my tiny flock." The priest reclined on a sofa in the *alcalde's* quarters, having just consumed two glasses of the *alcalde's* excellent Port. He mopped his sweaty face with a rag.

The *alcalde* eyed him coolly. "You are rightfully alarmed, *monje*. Without the strong backs of my 'children,' whose labor will provide you with the necessities of life? It would be unthinkable to expect a shepherd to work in this heat...much wiser to trust in the ministrations of his devoted flock."

The priest thoughtfully nodded, scratched his tonsured skull then scrutinized his grimy fingernails in the half light. "It is gratifying to God and His Blessed Mother that we are in agreement, Excellency," he finally said. The *alcalde* took a sip of Port and watched the monk over the rim of his glass without responding. "What measures is your *Capitán* taking to locate our lost sheep?" the prelate inquired.

"*Capitán* Diego and his men have scoured the countryside without success in search of them. It is as though they were simply swallowed up by the earth itself," the *alcalde* replied with a shrug. He drained his delicate wine glass and placed it on the silver tray at his elbow. "I have instructed the *Capitán* to establish all-night watches in order to apprehend the wolves responsible for abducting our sheep."

The priest nodded his approval. "The *peones* are a primitive race, Excellency," he opined.   "They worship all manner of fiendish devils and it is all I can do to pray for their benighted souls.   Whatever evils have been visited upon the pueblo, they are entirely attributable to the ignorance and superstitions of the *peones*."

The *alcalde* was struck by the prelate's matter-of-factness.   "But are the *campesinos* not adherents to our Most Sanctified Catholic faith?"

"They   are,"   the   priest   indifferently acknowledged.   "But I fear their allegiance to the Holy Mother Church is rather tepid.   They have overlaid   our   faith   with   a   veneer   of   their abominable paganism and, in secret, remain devoted to their damnable, wicked superstitions. More   appalling,   Excellency,   their   devotion   to Satan, the perpetual foe of God and the Church, is beyond question.   The *peones* renounce God and His sacraments to make loathsome compacts with the devil. These contemptible pacts are written in the *campesinos'* own blood and, by them, they bind themselves to Satan to deny and scorn Christ and the Most Holy Trinity.   In exchange for their monstrous allegiance, the devil grants the *peones* powers to help them in this world, at the expense of their souls in the next.   Many are even rebaptised in the name of the devil, at which time they renounce their Christian names and take another. By so doing, their names are unwittingly struck from the book of life and inscribed in the book of death."

"How do you know these things?" inquired the skeptical *alcalde*.

"Even the prophets recognized, Excellency, 'a league with death' and a 'covenant with hell,'" the priest responded easily, quoting Isaiah 28:15. "Our Fathers Origen and Augustine also cautioned against *pacta cum daemonibus*.   Despite these warnings, the *peones* remain easily seduced by

Satan's wily tongue and his promise of earthly rewards."

"The devil appears to have gotten the better end of the bargain," the *alcalde* drily remarked, "for such 'earthly rewards' as the peasants may have bargained for seem to me rather thin."

The priest smiled craftily. "The offense does not lie in the reward, but in the agreement to work in league with the devil to oppose and deny God. Although the *peones* are naïve and easily duped by the devil, they are astute enough to understand that, were they to openly display the gifts that Satan bestows on them, their infamous bond with him would be exposed. Accordingly, they deliberately conceal their fealty to him."

"The *campesinos* are beyond salvation?"

The monk smiled indulgently. "The *Apostol Pedro* assures us that all who believe in our *Salvador Jesucristo* shall be saved, Excellency." He gazed at the decanter of Port with undisguised cupidity, prompting the *alcalde* to reach over and refill the prelate's cup. He drained it in a single, noisy swallow. Wiping his mouth on the sleeve of his soiled cassock, he continued. "We may be sure that our present ills were precipitated by the iniquities of the *peones*. But, like a loving father, our Blessed Savior gently chides his children, reminding the *peones* that it is only through faithful adherence to His infallible word that they may acquire the keys to celestial bliss."

The *alcalde* reflected a moment before responding. "So nothing is to be done?"

"I fear the predations will continue until the *campesinos* abandon their follies and return to the bosom of The Holy Mother Church, Catholic and Apostolic," responded the priest. "But all is not as grim as it may appear, *don alcalde*. With your Excellency's indulgence, those *peones* whom it pleases God to cleanse from our midst may be readily replaced with others whose faith is above reproach.   And, as to the former, Our Savior is certain to recognize His own.   *Bien está, lo que bien acaba,"* he smiled again, displaying a jumble of mahogany-colored teeth.

TWELVE

THE JEEP WAS ON THE FAR SIDE of the cemetery, trundling away from the detective.

"Cam!" Moe suddenly shouted, and began frantically waving his arms.

Hearing his cry, Nancy swiveled in her seat and craned her neck around in order to spot the detective through the Jeep's rear window. Cameron heard him, too, and immediately swung the vehicle in a wide arc in order to head back toward Moe. The detective was standing in the desert, about fifty yards beyond the cemetery, shining his flashlight onto the ground.

"I don't like the looks of that," Cameron muttered as the Jeep bounced toward the detective. Nancy didn't respond, though a feeling of dread gripped her.

The uneven ground and intervening scrub brush rendered it impossible to see the object that excited Moe's attention. Cameron drew to a stop, the Jeep pointing in the direction where the detective's flashlight was aimed. Because the vehicle's tires rested on a slight incline, its headlights were canted slightly upward, dissipating into the night air. Cameron and Nancy sat wordlessly in the Jeep, unmoving, letting the heater blow over them. They feared what was about to reveal itself. Moe began walking toward them. With a painful sigh, Cameron switched the ignition off, leaving the headlights blazing. Nancy shivered uncontrollably.

"What is it?" Cameron spiritlessly asked when Moe drew near the vehicle. He already knew the answer.

The detective grasped Cameron's shoulder through the open window. "It's Daisy," he said. "Do you have your gun with you?"

"My gun?" Cameron responded, not comprehending. "Is Daisy okay?"

"I'm sorry, my friend," Moe softly responded. Cameron felt tears surge to his eyes and he unsuccessfully attempted blink them away. Her dread confirmed, Nancy silently began to cry in the adjacent seat. "Where is she?" Cameron quietly asked.

The detective directed his flashlight to an area about 100 feet in front of the Jeep. "There."

Cameron swung open the door and stepped from the vehicle. Nancy wiped her eyes on the cuff of her coat before following. "Get your gun, Cam," Moe advised. "There's something out here." Cameron rummaged beneath the driver's seat and withdrew his holstered Walther P22 pistol, which he strapped to his belt with trembling hands. They flicked on their flashlights and, with Moe leading, trudged slowly into the murky desert. The Jeep's brilliant headlights formed monstrous shadows on the uneven ground.

Daisy lay on her side at the bottom of a small arroyo. Although her body was unmarked, her head had been crushed, as though a massive weight and fallen on it. There was no blood and the soil around Daisy appeared undisturbed.

Cameron and Nancy kneeled; he gently stroked Daisy's lifeless fur. Moe stood beside them, directing his flashlight into the darkness, listening intently.

"I love you Daisy," Cameron whispered as tears coursed down his face. "I'm sorry I got you into this, girl. I hope you'll forgive me." Though she tried not to, Nancy began sobbing. "Her collar's gone," Cameron suddenly noted, looking up. "What happened to her collar?" He didn't expect an answer.

Cameron stayed beside Daisy's body for a few minutes then he finally stood. "I don't want the coyotes eating her," he said, without emotion. He walked back to the Jeep while the detective and Nancy waited by the arroyo. Cameron drove to them, making sure the area where Daisy lay was illuminated by the headlights. When he climbed out of the vehicle he left its engine running. In his right hand Cameron carried a folded wool blanket that he kept in the Jeep. "It's cold, Nance. Why don't you get inside the Jeep?" he said, spiritlessly.

Nancy glanced at Moe, who remained silent. "No, Cam, I'm okay. What do you want us to do?"

Cameron looked down at Daisy's body. Using the sleeve of his jacket, he wiped the tears from his eyes. "Just aim your flashlight on Daisy, I guess." He walked to her body and placed the blanket on the soil next to her. The detective assisted him as Cameron began to unfold and smooth the blanket to the extent the rough ground would permit. Gently lifting Daisy, they placed her body in its center then folded each side of the blanket over her. Grasping its corners, they carried the makeshift catafalque to the Jeep, where they gently laid it on the floorboard behind the front seat. Nancy put her arms around Cameron.

"Daisy knew you loved her," she said.

"I'll take her out to the desert to bury her, but not here," he sobbed. "That's what she'd want."

"We need to get back to the vehicle. Now," Moe tersely interjected. "Whatever killed Daisy is probably still hanging around and we'll be safer in the Jeep than standing out here in the open. We can drive around and try to see what did this."

"*What* did this?" Nancy puzzled aloud. The detective didn't respond but walked to the rear of the Jeep. He lifted the back flap and climbed into the back, Daisy's body at his feet, as Cameron and Nancy slid into their seats. Because Cameron had left the heater blasting while burying Daisy, the interior was gratifyingly warm.

"What do we do now?" Cameron asked as he slipped the transmission into 'D.' He struggled to regain his composure.

Moe placed a reassuring hand on Cameron's shoulder. "Drive on the trail toward the hills," he urged. "Maybe we'll see something."

"What are we looking for?" Nancy asked as the Jeep bumped in a wide arc back toward the cemetery.

The detective leaned forward, between the front seats, and peered anxiously through the windshield. "I wish I knew," he softly responded as the Jeep slowly headed up the faint path.

Cameron's Jeep was a tiny speck of light in illimitable darkness as it laboriously ascended the trail. Nancy glanced uneasily out her side window, half-expecting something to crash through it from the featureless void that stretched beyond the range of their headlights. Looking out Cameron's window she could see in the distance below them a glittering stream of headlights from vehicles on McDonald Drive. Cameron focused on driving while Moe keenly surveyed the contiguous desert as they slowly proceeded, his revolver grasped in his hand.

Cameron slammed on the brakes. Notwithstanding that they were proceeding slowly, the abruptness startled Nancy and Moe. "Look," Cameron quietly said, nodding toward the trail in front of the vehicle.

Dangling from a scrawny creosote bush adjacent to the trail was Daisy's pink leather collar. It swung gently to and fro in the slight breeze, the Jeep's headlights flashing off the rhinestones that adorned it.

Cameron heaved his door open and jumped from the vehicle. "Cam, wait!" the detective shouted, flinging open the rear flap and leaping over the tailgate. Together they hastened to the startling discovery, which Cameron snatched from the bush. He turned toward the vehicle and scrutinized in its headlights the brass plate sewn onto the collar: Daisy.

"Let's get back to the Jeep and get the hell out of here," Moe bluntly advised, looking anxiously about. Cameron stuffed Daisy's collar into his jacket pocket and they swiftly returned to the vehicle.

"Was it hers?" Nancy asked as Cameron executed a hard U-turn and headed back to the bench land below.

He nodded. He glanced into the rear-view mirror. "It's like they're taunting us," he said. From the back seat, Moe nodded.

Later, as the Jeep rumbled along the pavement on the way back to his apartment, Cameron sighed painfully. "I don't know what to do now."

From the back seat the detective shook his head. "I don't know either, Cam. I guess something must have piqued Daisy's interest and she went to explore. Whatever she saw, or sensed, just didn't want her there." He paused. "But whatever it was, Daisy didn't suffer, Cam. That much I know."

"But I thought you said that poltergeists or 'tricksters' or whatever they are never actually hurt anyone...or anything," Nancy interjected. Her shivering refused to subside notwithstanding the warm air blasting into the cab from the Jeep's heater.

"I guess we were wrong," Cam softly conceded.

"But what could have done *that*?" Nancy persisted. The detective didn't respond. They drove the rest of the way in silence.

CAMERON DECIDED TO ATTEMPT ANOTHER voice recording at the cemetery during the daylight hours. Knowing that Nancy would refuse to accompany him, he hoped to induce Moe.

"Chet, then Daisy," Cameron said, sadly. "I can walk away, or I can try to find out what happened to them," he appealed to the detective.

Moe nodded. "I know, Cam." They were eating lunch at a pizza restaurant in a strip mall not far from the tribal police building, three days after their calamitous foray to the cemetery. The following morning, Cameron had driven Daisy's body out to a remote spot in the desert, where he buried her with her favorite toy, a stuffed penguin with a squeaker inside, and her collapsible water dish.

"I've been doing more research on the Baca Float," Cameron continued. "Although there's quite a bit of information about the five Floats that appear in the historical record, there's virtually nothing on *this* Float because, until we found it, nobody even knew it existed. What *is* known is that people kept croaking or disappearing from the other Floats and constantly had to be replaced. In fact, the reason there even *were* multiple Floats is because the Spanish kept having to establish new ones after people refused to settle on the old ones. It didn't do any good, though, because, no matter where the Spanish started a new Float, people still disappeared. I think the reason there's no record of this particular Float is because it was probably the last one created and, after everybody ultimately disappeared or moved away, there was no one left to write about it. The Spanish finally just said 'to hell with it' and gave up on the whole Float idea, and the historical record went blank."

The detective listened intently to Cameron's recitation. He took a bite of pizza before responding. "What was the purpose of the Floats? Why were they created in the first place?"

Cameron looked thoughtful. "According to the guy at the Historical Society, the Spanish Crown awarded large tracts of deserted land, called 'Floats,' to favored individuals because giving them land was cheaper than paying them. The vestiges of the five *known* Floats are still around."

"Yeah, but *why*?" Moe pressed. "Why *those* particular tracts of land?" He took another bite of pizza. "I've been doing a little research, too," he smiled, wiping his mouth on a napkin. "I was surprised by the amount of original source material on the subject."

"How do you mean?"

"Did you know that several Spanish conquistadors actually wrote contemporary accounts of the Conquest of New Spain and its aftermath? Paulo Givio, Francisco Lopez de Gomara, Gonzalo de Illescas, and Bernal Diaz all left first-hand accounts of the Conquest," the detective continued.

"Where did you learn that?" Cameron asked, genuinely impressed.

"The Internet is a wonderful thing."

"I've never heard of those guys," Cameron confessed.

"Well, Diaz's 'Conquest of New Spain' is relatively famous but the others are pretty obscure. I was just showing off," the detective grinned.

"So have you read them?"

"Diaz and Lopez, yes. Also, Diego de Landa, who wrote about the Mayans. Not the others, though."

Intrigued, Cameron leaned forward in his chair and laced his fingers together. "Learn anything interesting?"

"As a matter of fact, yeah. Here's what I think happened," Moe expounded. "Cortes arrived in the New World in 1519 and conquered the Aztecs by about 1521. He enslaved the Indians and started sending gold and silver back to Spain. The conventional wisdom is that the Spanish Crown didn't trust the *conquistadores* and suspected them of skimming. So, instead of splitting the profits with them, the king catered to the *conquistadores'* vanity by making them 'Viceroys' and whatnot, and by doling out huge tracts of land to them."

"*Encomiendas,*" Cameron interjected.

The detective smiled in surprise. "Exactly. Where did you learn about *encomiendas?*"

It was Cameron's turn to smile. "The guy at the Historical Society told me about 'em."

Moe nodded and resumed. "Most of the *encomiendas* were located in what's now Central America, but some of them were in Mexico. It's funny, because it occurred to me that modern banks and corporations still do pretty much the same thing the Spanish Crown did back then. Banks give everybody the title of 'vice-president,' because making 'em a 'vice-president' is cheaper than giving 'em a raise." The detective smiled to himself and took a sip of Coke. "Ever notice how many 'vice-presidents' banks have? Even the guy who sweeps the place out at night is a vice-president of something. Anyway," he continued, resuming his narrative, "the king hoped that making the *conquistadores* land barons would keep them happy and discourage them from skimming any of the gold they were sending back to Spain."

"Wait a minute. Are you saying the *conquistadores* were given Floats? My understanding is that Floats weren't created until the 1800's."

Moe nodded. "You're right; the Floats came along long after the *conquistadores*. But hear me out. Although the *conquistadores* initially thought that getting a bunch of land was a good deal, it didn't take 'em long to figure out that they were soldiers, not farmers, and that the king had basically duped them. The land was worthless and they had no idea what to do with it. But the good news, for the *conquistadores*, anyway, is that they were also given the Indians as part of the deal, relative to whom they could do whatever they pleased. The Spanish used the Indians to clear the land and build haciendas where they hoped to live like sultans, at least until all their Indians died from disease, starvation, and overwork. Once all their slaves were gone, the *conquistadores* were too lazy to fend for themselves, so they simply abandoned their properties and moved back to Spain... those that hadn't already died, that is. The Spanish empire eventually collapsed and that was that." Moe triumphantly concluded. "There will be a quiz at the end of the hour."

Cameron was confused. "But what's any of this got to do with the Floats?"

"Spain didn't technically create the various Floats until the 19th century, long after the Conquest. But I'm guessing the Floats were nothing more than palimpsests of the land that was originally given to the *conquistadores*, centuries before. Spain undoubtedly still had *some* property records from the Conquest and figured, 'What the hell, why reinvent the wheel? We'll just recycle the original land grants.' Voilà! Instant Float!"

"So the Floats are actually a lot older than the 1800's?"

The detective nodded. "That's what I'm thinking. I think the Spaniards originally established them in the 1500's, even though the formal records only date from the 1800's. Whatever structures the *conquistadores* originally built on them had completely collapsed in the intervening 300 years so, when the king gave Cabeza de Baca a bunch of Floats, he accepted them in good grace, probably assuming that no European before him had ever set foot on them. Why would he? De Baca was a Spanish nobleman and the Floats were all located in the primitive, unsettled New World. He neither knew, nor cared, that the property had probably been gifted to some nameless conquistador hundreds of years before."

Cam remained puzzled. "Woody, what has any of this got to do with anything?"

The detective smiled mysteriously. "It wasn't by accident that the *conquistadores* were given land by the Crown. "

"I know. You just said the king gave 'em land just to keep 'em happy and to keep 'em from stealing all the gold they were mining."

"That's the conventional explanation," Moe agreed. "But I think there's more to it than that. Remember, the *conquistadores* were *soldiers*. And what do soldiers do? They fight."

"Indians?" Cameron ventured.

"At first, yeah, but it didn't take the conquistadors long to tame most of the native populations. The Spanish had steel weapons and gun powder and the indigenous people didn't. It was kind of like when Mussolini invaded Ethiopia before the Second World War: airplanes against wooden clubs. The fiercest bunch was the Aztecs, and once they collapsed, everybody else basically fell into line. It was only *after* the *conquistadores* conquered the native peoples that the Spanish Crown started divvying up land to them. In other words, the Crown didn't give land to the *conquistadores* in order to clear it of Indians because, by that time, all the Indians had already been killed or enslaved."

"So it's like you just said," Cameron replied. "Spain threw the *conquistadores* a bone as a reward and to keep them honest."

"Partially. But remember, the *conquistadores* were professional soldiers. The Spanish Crown also wanted to exploit their fighting ability."

"Ok, I'll bite," Cameron responded. "If there were no Indians left to kill, who were they supposed to be fighting?"

"The *conquistadores* had only recently emerged from a horrific war against the Muslims that lasted for generations and were considered the most formidable soldiers in Europe," Moe answered. "Because of that, I think the Spanish Crown gave them specific tracts of land in the New World so they could eliminate whatever remained on it."

Cameron sighed. "I still have no idea what you're talking about, Woody."

"Cam, philosophers tell us that the world is a duality, what some have called 'the dialectic of opposites': yin and yang, light and dark, male and female, good and evil. This basic polarity isn't just some empty academic exercise, either, because entire social and economic paradigms have been based on it. Marxism, for example. Take places like Jerusalem or Bodh Gaya, where Buddha was enlightened; they're monuments to spirituality. Among Native Americans, several sites in the U.S. are considered sacred and holy. But there are also places that are considered ill-omened, cursed, whatever. We think of haunted houses and such, but there are vast areas with unwholesome reputations: the Bermuda Triangle, Nazi concentration camps, Soviet gulags, battlefields..."

"The Float?" Cameron interjected.

Moe nodded. "Exactly. I suspect the cemetery and Esperanza both sit on land that was originally granted to some conquistador with the expectation that he'd kick the ass of whatever was living on it."

"And that was?" Cameron probed, expectantly.

The detective looked at him gravely. "I don't honestly know, Cam. But there's some weird shit goin' on out there ... those three guys that trashed your Jeep, for instance."

"Yeah, they were pretty weird all right," Cameron agreed. "Who *were* those fuckers?"

"Damned if I know," Moe admitted with chagrin. "Hell, from the way you described 'em, maybe *they* were conquistadors. Who the hell knows? All I know is that something ain't right in River City."

Cameron looked incredulous. "That doesn't even make sense, Woody. How could they be *conquistadores*? Conquistador look-alikes, maybe. But *conquistadors*? Gimme a break!"

"Ever read Sherlock Holmes, Cam?" Without waiting for a response, Woody continued. "In *The Adventure of the Beryl Coronet*," Holmes said that, once you've excluded the impossible, whatever remains, no matter how improbable, must be the truth."

"So now we're reduced to relying on fictional detectives?" Cameron retorted.

The detective shrugged. "If something happens, it must be possible."

"Yeah, well, if they're conquistadors and were supposed to kill whatever's out there, they sure as hell did a lousy job," Cameron scoffed.

Moe couldn't help but smile. "I'm just speculating, Cam. I don't know what else to tell you. But think about it: you said that people kept dying or just disappearing from the Floats. What happened to them? Did they just decide to abandon everything they owned and head out into the desert? Why would they do that? One or two, here and there, maybe. But so many people that, like you said, Spain had to keep creating new Floats just because nobody would live on the old ones?" He leaned back in his chair and massaged his forehead. "No, my friend, something either killed them or took them." The detective looked intently at Cameron. "And whatever that was is still out there."

"Woody, I'm not even gonna ask how dead conquistadors can still be out walking around," Cam said. "But all of this is just conjecture, right?"

The detective nodded. "Obviously, just conjecture," he conceded. "But when I put everything together, it makes about as much sense as anything else."

Cameron gazed pensively out the restaurant's window, into the parking lot. "Nothing makes sense, Woody." His gaze returned to the detective. "So what's out there? What took Chet and killed Daisy?"

"I think that's what Chet was going to tell us on the tape," Moe replied.

THIRTEEN

"WHAT THE HELL IS THAT?" Ham squinted in the intense sunlight. Although only thirty-five, he appeared far older, his pockmarked face deeply furrowed from a decade, beginning in 1871, of hazing cattle and knocking around through Kansas, Texas, New Mexico, and now, Arizona Territory. He spit a long stream of brown tobacco juice from the gap created by his missing front teeth.

Bill drew his sweaty horse up next to Ham's mount and followed his gaze down into the valley. "Looks like a town," he laconically announced after a moment. "Not much o' one, though. Probably just a passel o' Messicans." He leaned over and spit a glob of tobacco onto the stony, parched earth.

Ham nodded, absently. "I figured there must be a town around here someplace 'cause o' that bone orchard we rode past back there a ways. Even if it's full o' Messicans, it's the first damned place we seed in days." He swiveled in his saddle to face Bill. "My cayuse is pretty much played out, and me, too. Why don't we head down there and see what it's about?"

"Fine by me," shrugged his companion. "I just want to get out of the heat...maybe they got some shade down there," he grinned.

The two cowboys had recently collected their accumulated wages and left the employ of the Bar-T-outfit, in the southeastern part of the territory. They thereafter headed northwest, toward California. Bill had a niece who lived somewhere around there. They were eager to rapidly put as much distance as possible between themselves and the Mexican border, where the greatest amount of Apache predation occurred. The Apaches raided haciendas and settlements across southern Arizona Territory before racing across the border into Mexico with their booty: horses, cattle, guns, and women. There, in the fastness of the Sierra Madre, they were beyond the reach of a vengeful American government.

"The place is kinda tucked away, ain't it?" Bill mused as their weary horses plodded downward into the valley. Because of the steepness of the descent, they were periodically forced to lean back in their saddles. "Ya reckon it's got a name?"

"Ever'place has name," Ham replied. "It's prob'ly somethin' in Messican."

"I got enough trouble with the King's English," Bill joked, expelling another glob of tobacco. This time most of it landed on his boot. "Dammit!" A tendril of brown spittle snaked down his stubbled chin. "You s'pose they got anything to drink?" he speculated.

"Ever'place has something to drink," Ham assured him. "Even Messicans gotta drink sometime, even if it's only mescal." He looked over at his companion. "Tell ya what. You kin get a big glass o' water when we get down there."

"*Water?*" Bill responded with alarm. "I'm thirsty, not dirty."

"Well, I reckon you're half right," Ham laughed, "'cause you're sure as hell dirty, too." His horse abruptly began to slide on some loose rocks, prompting him to vigorously yank the reins to regain control. Bill's mount snorted and reared backward in alarm, nearly dumping him onto the ground.

"Hey, Bill, how many dead people you figure they got back there in that bone yard?" Ham asked when they resumed their descent.

"I reckon all of 'em," Bill retorted. Ham guffawed and they continued to banter back and forth as they rode toward Esperanza.

For the first three-quarters of a mile, the narrow trail was comprised of a series of steep switchbacks. On one side of the trail reared a dizzying palisade of shale; on the other, a precipitous twenty-five-foot drop into a tangled arroyo. Because their mounts continually balked during the descent, the cowboys were forced to spur the animals forward as they plodded to the floor of the valley below.

"Hello, what's this about?" Ham exclaimed, urging his horse downward. "Hut, hut! Goddammit, What the devil's got into you, Brigham?" he scolded as he tugged on the reins and slapped the animal smartly across the withers with them. The struggling horse's hoofs dislodged rocks from the trail, which tumbled into the contiguous arroyo.

"What the hell's wrong with these damned hosses?" Bill complained as he grappled with his own intransigent mount.

"Guess they jist don't like Messicans," Ham guffawed as Brigham reared beneath him. "Damn you, Brig!" he spat as he again slapped the reins across the animal's sweaty neck.

"Don't go a-knockin' me and Mouse over that damned cliff," Bill warned, finally managing to subdue his lunging horse, though the animal continued to whinny and prance about on the narrow trail. He pulled a tattered bandana from the hip pocket of his stained canvas trousers and mopped his face with it, then jammed it back. "Me and Mouse is goin' on ahead o' you, so's you don't dump our asses onto the ground if'n Brig gets away from you." In a single motion, Bill clucked his tongue, jerked his horse's reins, and deftly spurred the animal down the path. "You two kin stay here all day if ya like," he yelled over his shoulder, "We'll bring you a cup o' water after a spell."

Ham laughed, though he continued to wrestle with his obstreperous mount. "Naw, I reckon we might as well tag along. Although the weather's mighty fine, it's hotter than a two-dollar whore out here and me and Brig wanna git into some shade."

After about a half-hour the trail finally flattened out and Bill reached the valley floor. Once he reached level ground, Bill drew Mouse to a stop and turned in the saddle to wait for Ham to catch up.

He could hear Ham's colorful cursing as the cowboy and Brigham approached from behind.

Aside from the wooden ribs of an old corral a hundred yards away, there was no evidence of the town the cowboys had seen earlier from afar.

"We're lucky these damned hosses didn't break an ankle tryin' to get down here," Bill remarked once Ham drew abreast. Brigham's glossy coat was flecked with foam and the animal's eyes rolled in its head, exposing the stark white sclera.

"Yer damned sure right about that," Ham assented. "I weren't sure Mouse was gonna make it!"

Bill scowled at him. "You ain't gotta worry 'bout ol' Mousie," he retorted. He reached forward and reassuringly patted the sweaty, muscular neck of his horse.

Bill trotted up to the deteriorating corral and reined Mouse to a stop. "I reckon this has seen better days," he dryly remarked. When Ham didn't respond, he looked up the trail and saw him struggling with Brigham. "What's the matter with that damned cayuse?" he called.

Brigham was twisting and rearing, refusing to advance. Ham clung to the saddle, trying to avoid being pitched onto the ground by the horse's gyrations. Brigham's eyes were wide with fear, rimmed with white.

"Damned if I know'd," Ham grimly responded through gritted teeth. "He's actin' like he's snake bit."

"Hell, maybe he is," Bill suggested. He tugged on Mouse's reins and they trotted back to the struggling animal. The approach of the unflappable Mouse had a calming effect on Brigham and he immediately became more tractable and began nuzzling the other horse.

Ham stroked Brigham's neck and noticed he was trembling. "This hoss got the jim-jams," he said, perplexed.

"Why don't you put him in the corral yonder?" Bill suggested. "It's pretty near fallin' down, but I don't figure Brigham's likely to go too far. He needs to get rid o' what's ailing him and you kin ride into town with me and Mouse...just keep your paws to yourself," he grinned. He turned Mouse and headed back to the corral at a walk; Brigham began plodding after them, his head low.

When they neared the corral, Ham swung to ground and led his mount by the reins into the enclosure. While Brigham stood patiently, he reached beneath the horse, uncinched the saddle, and lugged it and the saddle blanket to the edge of the corral, where he heaved them over one of the wooden railings. Bill leaned forward in his saddle and watched the ritual from outside the corral.

"If ya got any oats I'd give him some," Bill amiably suggested. "I reckon it may settle him down some." Ham nodded and retrieved a handful of oats and a cloth feed bag from one of his saddle bags. He placed the oats in the bag and affixed it to Brigham's head. "I wonder if they's any water around here?" Ham wondered aloud.

"It don't look like it," Bill said, straightening up and looking around. "That trough don't look like it's had any water in it for a spell. Mouse could use a drink, too, couldn't ya, Mousie," he continued, leaning forward and solicitously patting his horse's neck. "When we get to town we'll round up somebody to ride out and bring Brigham some water. He'll be okay 'till then."

Ham exited the corral, making certain the gate was secure behind him. "I'll be back in jig time," he promised Brigham before climbing onto Mouse behind Bill. "You jest stay put 'till then." They could hear the hollow, comforting sound of Brigham contentedly eating oats through the fabric of the feed bag. "Les go," Ham urged once he was firmly seated behind the cantle of Bill's saddle, just forward of Mouse's rump. "I sure hope to hell that nobody sees me ridin' like a damned squaw."

"What do you care if a Messican sees you?" Bill responded as Mouse began trudging away from the corral with the two men on his back. "Who's he gonna tell? Another Messican? Hell, Ham, Messicans don't even speak English!" Ham nodded thoughtfully, his anxieties somewhat assuaged, and they rode in silence.

THE TRAIL ON WHICH THEY RODE quickly broadened into more-or-less the semblance of a main thoroughfare, lined with a hodge-podge of lifeless structures.

Where is ever'body?" Ham asked, swiveling his head around as they rode. "It's quieter than a ant fart."

There was seemingly no order to the construction surrounding them. Adobe buildings were juxtaposed beside piles of rock; clapboard buildings rotted in the sun adjacent to empty lots; undifferentiated heaps of lumber disintegrated by holes yawning in the earth. A decaying wooden sidewalk ran in front of a few of the buildings, leading nowhere. The settlement appeared utterly destitute of life, devoid even of the slinking, emaciated dogs that populated every other frontier community either of them had ever passed through.

"Ghost town," Bill speculated as Mouse plodded along. He grinned. "I don't reckon you gotta worry about nobody seein' ya ride like a squaw!"

"Hello, what's this!" Ham abruptly exclaimed from behind Bill.

Bill reined Mouse to a halt.   Casually watching them from the opposite side of the abandoned street, in the fleeting shadow of a narrow passageway between two deteriorating hovels, was a person. Bill squinted in the intense sunlight at the slouching figure.

"*Hola!*" Ham called to the enigmatic form, which didn't stir.

"He a mute?" Bill wondered aloud after a moment.

"Dunno. Maybe he ain't right in the head or don't speak English," Ham suggested. "*Hola!*" he again greeted.   "*Habla Inglis?*"   Still the figure failed to respond.

Mouse suddenly began to grow restive, stamping his hooves, tossing his head about, and snorting. As Bill tugged on the reins to regain control of the animal the smell of decaying flesh began to waft over them.

"What in hell is *that?*" Bill asked, wrinkling his nose.

"Damn!" Ham blurted. "No wonder nobody's around...it smells like somethin' died."

"Don't seem to bother that feller none," Bill affirmed, nodding toward the impassive figure, which remained motionless. He continued to struggle with Mouse, who twisted and squirmed beneath the men with increasing urgency.

"I'm gettin' the hell off this cayuse afore he heaves me plumb off!" Ham said. "I want to talk to that feller, anyway." He awkwardly slid off the squirming horse onto the dusty ground and scampered away from the struggling animal. Ham watched from a distance as Mouse slowly yielded to Bill's exertions to restrain him. Satisfied that the horse was finally under control, he turned toward his attention back to the personage whom they spotted earlier.

The air still reeked of dead meat and both men could scarcely keep from gagging. Bill swung from Mouse's saddle and secured the animal to a railing that ran parallel to a collapsed wooden sidewalk. Ham peered into the alley where the figure previously stood, but it now appeared vacant.

"Where'd he go?" Bill inquired as he ambled over.

"Damned if I know'd. Mebbe that damned hoss spooked him and he lit out," Ham absently replied.

Bill shook his head. "Mousie wouldn't hurt a fly," he affirmed, looking around. "I don't know 'bout you, but I can't stand the stench o' this place much longer. Maybe that feller decided he couldn't, too." Across the street, Mouse began nickering and stamping his hoofs.

Ham frowned in the direction of the alley. "Best go retrieve your Winchester, Bill."

"Huh?"

"Go git your Winchester off Mouse," Ham repeated.

"What fer?" Bill asked, perplexed. "T'ain't nuthin' here to shoot!"

"Goddamit, go git it!"

Bill walked back to Mouse and slid his '73 Winchester from its scabbard. He returned to Ham, where he followed his gaze into the empty alley. "Whatcha lookin' at?"

"Somethin' ain't right," Ham muttered as he took the '73 from Bill. "C'mon." The two men cautiously approached the passageway where they'd previously seen the standing figure, the overwhelming stench of rotting flesh increasing with each step. Bill's skin tingled and he felt the hair on the back of his neck stand up.

"Goddamn, it stinks around here," he murmured.

"There ain't no way that feller coulda got outta here without my seein' it," Ham said. "They's somethin' afoot here, Bill." His palm where he gripped the Winchester was slick with sweat.

"Greetings, gentlemen." A peculiar, rasping voice addressed them from behind. Startled, the two cowboys whipped their heads around.

Standing beneath a sagging porch stood a diminutive figure, scarcely five feet tall. Notwithstanding its small stature, the figure's waxy face revealed the features of an adult. What appeared to be a pair of wooly leggings were visible beneath the coarse outer garment that hung below its waist. Its peculiar twisted feet resembled the hooves of an animal more than any human appendages. A fetid miasma clung to the figure and corrupted the surrounding air. Hatless despite the blistering sun, a thin layer of reddish hair covered its scabrous, misshapen head.

"Who are you?" Bill asked, suspiciously.

"Who, hell! *What* are you," Ham added, leveling the Winchester. "I seen some ugly sons o' bitches in my time, but you sure as hell take the cake!"

"Hang on!" Bill interrupted. "I heered o' some critter that the Messicans are skeert of. I can't think o' what they call it, but the Messicans is skeert shitless o' it. They say it ets goats and young'uns and such."

Ham looked around. "I reckon this 'un must already have et all the goats and young'uns around here 'bouts."

"I don't often have the pleasure of company," the being said in its curious, rasping voice, seemingly unperturbed by Ham's overt hostility. "I can only surmise that you've lost your way." He smiled enigmatically, revealing a row of gleaming, pointed teeth. "No one comes to Esperanza willingly." As he spoke, the man, if man it was, casually slouched against one of the wooden posts that supported what remained of the porch.

"I'm Bill and the feller with the Winchester pointed at you is Ham, and we ain't lost," Bill asserted. "You got a name?"

The figure straightened. "I have many names," he said.

"We ain't fussy," Ham growled. "We'll settle for just one."

"Indeed," the being acknowledged, nodding. "My name is Moloch."

"That the name o' the critter you was talkin' about?" Ham inquired.

"It was somethin' like that, but that ain't but half a name," Bill responded. Ham continued to level the rifle at the singular figure. "That sounds like a Injun name...you a Injun?"

"I am all and everything, whatever you wish. Names are, however, unimportant and the catalogue of my names would require a great deal of time, a luxury you do not possess."

"We got time enough for you to tell us where ever'body in this town is," Ham informed him.

"And how come you stink so much," added Bill.

A half-smile crossed over the being's face. He silently gazed into the void for a moment before responding. "We pass through this vale of tears convinced our days are without number," he finally spoke, looking directly at the befuddled

men. "That belief, like life itself, is an illusion. I
suspect Villon, said it best, don't you? 'Life but a
day lasteth, and death knows no relent.'" He
picked at his blotchy scalp before continuing,
waves of putrefying effluvium washing over the
men as he moved his scaly arm. "Take you
gentlemen, for example," the figured continued.
"You blundered your way here in the expectation
of finding ease, liquor, and women. But your
hopes will go unrequited, for there is nothing in
Esperanza but suffering and death."

"We plan on livin' a good long time," Bill
interjected.

"I'm sure you do," replied the being,
indulgently. "Though the same obviously cannot
be said for your unfortunate animal. The heat has
clearly gotten the better of it. I fear that, if you try
to leave, your animal will simply collapse, leaving
you at the mercy of the Apaches."

"We aim to go when we please," Ham said as
Bill turned to look at Mouse.

The horse still stood resignedly at the railing
where Bill previously secured him, his listless
head hung low. Mouse's sides undulated visibly
as he labored to breathe the scorching air. Bill
could see sweaty froth along the animal's heaving
sides.

"Mousie!" Bill cried as he hastened to the
distressed animal.

"What the hell's wrong with Mouse?" Ham
growled as he chambered a .44-40 cartridge in the
Winchester.

"I think he's dyin'!" Bill wailed from beside
the horse. "That fuckin' bastard kilt Mouse!"

"Animals find Esperanza's atmosphere to be
particularly insalubrious," the figure said with
detachment. "Perhaps you'll grow accustomed to
it."

"Shoot that ugly son of a bitch!" Bill roared. He turned from the faltering horse and pointed at Moloch. "He done kilt Mouse!"

The being made no effort to flee, but continued to stand directly in front of Ham, a half-smile on his lips. Ham pointed the Winchester at the center the figure's scrawny chest and pulled the trigger.

NANCY HAVING DECLINED TO participate, Cameron and Moe stood inside the decaying charnel house. Notwithstanding that it was mid-day, the interior was cool and dim. Cameron gingerly stepped over a small mound of indeterminate rubbish, to the far corner of the structure.

"I want to try to minimize any outside interference," he explained to the detective.

Moe examined the interior of the tomb with interest. It was small, less than twenty feet long and fifteen feet wide. The low ceiling was comprised of nothing more than slabs of rough, undressed stone; he could easily touch it with his outstretched fingertips. If the building ever possessed a conventional floor, no trace of it remained; they trod on dirt. Contrary to Moe's expectations, there were no ledges to accommodate coffins or the other trappings of death. The structure was nothing more than a modest, decaying building littered with dry brush, stones, and a scattering of desiccated bones.

Cameron kicked at the packed earth to create a level area on which to place the cassette recorder. "With any luck we'll be able to pick something up, hopefully Chet," he said as he withdrew the tape recorder from his pocket.

"Where do you want me?" Moe asked.

Cameron glanced briefly about the interior. "One place is as good as the next, I guess. Wherever you're comfortable, Woody. We won't be here long."

The detective nodded and moved to the opposite corner. He gingerly stepped over some chalky bones, half-covered in dirt and, using the edge of his boot, gently nudged aside the partial human skull that Nancy had previously spotted. He leaned against the cold stone wall. "Ready when you are," he said.

Cameron took a deep breath to steady his voice, paused, then depressed the recorder's 'record' buttons. "Good afternoon, friends," he began. "This is Cameron Wylie speaking. If anyone present wishes to communicate, please do so now." He carefully bent down and placed the tape recorder on the earthen floor. Slowly straightening, he looked over at Moe, who silently nodded.

Cameron timed the recording using his wrist watch. After two minutes he stooped and clicked the recorder off. "I'm gonna move to a different part of the room and try again. Sometimes you get better results just a few feet away. After that, we'll move to the other charnel house and try."

"Do what you have to do, Cam," Moe said.

They switched places and Cameron conducted the procedure from the opposite corner of the chamber. Afterward, they crossed to the adjacent tomb, the size and configuration of which was identical to the first. Although they entered the first structure by squeezing through a large fissure in an exterior wall, the bricks that previously blocked the entrance to the second charnel house had been removed sometime in the past, if they ever existed at all. Accordingly, they stepped into its interior through a gaping portal. Like its neighbor, the Spartan, dirt-floored tomb was littered with debris, though untenanted. Cameron was gratified that no scattered bones were immediately apparent. They repeated the process two more times in the second crypt and both men shivered when they stepped from the charnel house into the gratifying sunlight.

"I'm not exactly fainthearted, but I'm glad you decided to do this during the daytime," Moe remarked as they headed for Cameron's Jeep, parked adjacent to the structures.

Cameron climbed into the driver's seat. "There's no way I'm coming out here again after dark. I don't even like coming here during the day anymore and don't begrudge Nancy for not wanting to come." He started the engine.

"Think your recorder picked anything up?"

"Let's go find out," Cameron responded as he slipped the Jeep's transmission into 'D' and pulled away from the burial ground.

"UNFORTUNATELY, THE SPEAKER ON THIS thing's pretty tiny," Cameron said, placing the cassette recorder on his coffee table. "I like using the big reel-to-reel in my bedroom, but obviously couldn't haul it out to the graveyard."

The detective plopped onto the couch. "Well, fire it up. Let's see if we captured anything."

Cameron carried a chair across the room and sat. He leaned forward and pushed the 'play' button; the tiny spindles began to slowly rotate. The men unconsciously leaned forward, toward the cassette recorder, straining to hear anything as the thin recording tape flowed through the machine.

Seconds after Cameron's usual greeting to anyone present, the disconsolate sound of faraway sobbing floated from the cassette player. Startled, Cameron started to speak, but Moe shook his head, exhorting silence. The mournful sobbing faded to nothingness. Stillness ensued.

Cameron looked at his watch; only twenty seconds had elapsed. He glanced over at the detective, who stared intently at the cassette recorder as the tape continued to play, though no additional sounds emerged. After a few more seconds they heard a rustling sound then an abrupt click.

"That's where I turned it off and moved across the room," Cameron said. Moe nodded. A moment later, Cameron's voice again invited anyone in attendance to speak. They thereafter heard a soft thud when he placed the cassette recorder on the earthen floor of the crypt. Although they concentrated on the two-minute recording that followed, they were unable to discern any anomalous noises on the tape. The sound of Cameron's clicking the recorder off terminated the recording. Moments later, the third session, recorded in the second charnel house, began. Moe closed his eyes while they listened to Cameron's customary introduction, as if to focus all his senses on his hearing.

The penultimate segment produced nothing. Cameron reached forward and clicked the recorder off. "It doesn't surprise me that we're not hearing much," Cameron remarked. "I usually need head phones to hear anything at all."

"Well, we've still got one to go," Moe said, referring to the fourth two-minute recording. "After we listen to it, we'll go back and replay the first one with the crying on it."

Cameron pushed the 'play' button and the listening exercise dutifully resumed. The silence on the tape was punctuated two minutes later, when they heard the sharp sound of Cameron clicking the cassette recorder off. For a moment, the men looked at one another without speaking.

"Rewind it and play the first one over," the detective finally broke the silence. Cameron nodded, pushed the 'rewind' button, then the 'play' button. The delicate tape began to slide across the recording heads of the machine. Cameron focused his attention on the second hand of his watch in order to ascertain the precise inception of the sobbing they previously heard, and to time its duration.

"Who is that with you?" The voice on the tape was so abrupt, so startling, that both men literally jumped. "Who is that?" the voice again imperiously demanded.

"What?" Cameron spontaneously blurted. The detective looked stunned.

"It's so dark I can barely see you," said the voice after a sustained pause. "I don't know who that is with you." It sounded distant, feeble, and was difficult to discern over the ambient rushing noise.

"Who is this?" Moe crossly interjected. He rapidly scanned the interior of the room, though he was unsure what he expected to see. Cameron looked at his watch, hoping to pinpoint the exact spot on the tape where the voice began speaking.

The spindles of the cassette recorder continued to slowly rotate, though no additional sounds emanated from it. After two minutes Cameron reached forward and clicked it off.

"What the hell was *that*?" Moe burst out. "Did you recognize the voice? It apparently recognized *you*."

"How do you know it was talking to me?" Cameron responded. "How do we know *who* it recognized, or if it recognized anyone at all? Maybe it was just more trickster phenomena."

The detective nodded. "You're right," he conceded. "But, whatever it was, how did it manage to record on a tape that was in the 'play' mode?"

"I don't know how it all works," Cameron confessed, "but people have recorded voice phenomena even when their tape recorders were switched completely off. It must have something to do with electromagnetic waves or something, because the voices are somehow able to record irrespective of the status of the recording device." He paused and glanced around uneasily. "Whoever it was may be here, now."

"Play it over," Moe urged.

Cameron rewound the tape and pushed the 'play' button before carefully placing the cassette recorder back on the coffee table. Cameron wondered whether Moe's heart was beating as fast as his.

A turbulent sibilation issued from the small tape recorder. Cameron glanced at the impassive detective, who stared at it fixedly.

"Please come get me, Cam," the voice suddenly emerged from the background interference. It was nearly inaudible. "It's so dark here."

"Chet?" Cameron cried. A troubled frown darkened Moe's face.

"It's so dark and I'm cold," the voice murmured. "Are you there?"

"Yes, yes! We're here! Is this Chet?" Cameron looked anxiously about the room.

"I can't see you anymore but you have to come for me. I have to go." The rushing noise on the tape increased in intensity.

"Where are you?" demanded Moe.

"Yes, I'm here. Please come for me."

"Where are you?" the detective repeated.

"Yes, yes, I have to go now. Why aren't you coming? I'm cold." The voice began to fade into the background.

"We're not coming *anywhere* until you tell us who you are," Moe barked.

"The house. Come to the house." The voice was so faint as to be nearly imperceptible. "Don't wait. Come now." Then it was gone, replaced by the sounds of rushing wind. After listening another minute, Cameron reached forward and flicked the recorder off.

The detective slumped back onto the couch. "Do you think that was Chet?" he asked.

Cameron sighed. "I couldn't tell, but you heard whoever it was call me by name." He looked intently at Moe. "What 'house' do you think he was talking about?"

Moe reflected before answering. "Maybe he was talking about that big house that Nancy and I saw in Esperanza, the one we told you about."

"But you said it was deserted. Why would he want us to go there?"

"The charnel house?" Moe suggested.

"We were just there...do you think he was telling us to go back there?"

The detective slowly shook his head. "I have no idea, Cam. I have no idea about any of this."

ANNO DOMINI NOSTRI IESU CHRISTO
1822

"THE VILLIAN RESPONSIBLE FOR THE depredations among the *campesinos* has been espied, Excellency," the *Capitán* confidently announced.

The *alcalde* looked up from his ink pot as though bored. He stroked his beard thoughtfully. "Oh? And who is this blackguard, Diego? Has he given an account of himself?"

The Capitán lowered his voice. "Two *campesinos* saw him while they were out gathering fire wood, Excellency. He was stalking them!"

His interest piqued, the *alcalde* carefully placed his quill on its blotter and laced his slender fingers together. He looked intently at his cumbrous subordinate. "What is his name and why is he abducting my *peones*?"

"Unfortunately, Excellency, the *campesinos* were unable to capture the rascal because he fled before they could apprehend him."

"Fled?" the *alcalde* sharply responded. "Then go to his *casa* with some of your men and arrest him, *Capitán.* Surely the *campesinos* recognized him; there are not that many *habitantes* in the *pueblo.*"

Diego could feel sweat beginning to trickle down his face. "He was not of this *pueblo*, Excellency."

The *alcalde* leaned back in his chair and looked skeptically at his inferior. "This man was an Apache?"

"He was neither man nor Indio, Excellency," the Capitán replied with hesitancy. "He is not of this world."

The *alcalde* burst out laughing at Diego's grim mien. "You sound like that idiot *monje*, Diego! Pray, tell me, what did this apparition look like? Did the *peones* get a good look at him before they bolted in terror?"

"With respect, Excellency, this is not an occasion for mirth," soberly intoned the Capitán.

"Really, *Capitán*? I find it all quite amusing. Now, describe for me the creature encountered by the *campesinos.* When did this occur?"

Diego cleared his throat. "It happened two days ago. Beto Gomez and his wife were out in the *desierto*, south of here, scrounging for wood for their cooking fire. Although they feared attack from the ferocious Apaches, they had to travel to a remote area because all the wood in the immediate vicinity of the *pueblo* had been collected long ago. Beto's wife told me that they stumbled upon the remains of an ancient *hacienda*, possibly dating from the times of the *conquistadores.* The creature was living there."

"What did this creature look like?" the *alcalde* skeptically inquired.

"Beto told me that it was small, like an *enano,* scarcely a *vara* in height, but that its face was that of an old man. Its legs were furry and it wore a *poncho.* But most remarkable was its head! It had horns on its head like those of a *vaca,* Excellency! And Beto's wife said that it smelled very bad, like it was dead."

"Perhaps it was nothing more than a poor *ermintaño,* Diego," suggested the *alcalde.*

"No, no, Excellency," the Capitán deferred. "It was not human."

"How do you know this?" The *alcalde* impatiently retorted. "You trust the report of two illiterate *peones* whose credulous minds are filled with fancies and terrors? I suspect they were both drunk on *pulque* and their tale was nothing more than the product of their fevered minds. Are you as big a fool as them?"

"No, no, *Don Alcalde,*" the Capitán strenuously objected. "Gomez and his wife are God-fearing souls who would not risk eternal damnation by inventing such a story. It is true." Diego solemnly crossed himself.

The *alcalde* was silent a moment. "Though not human, does this being possess a name?" he probed.

"He has many names, Excellency: Sargatanas, Marbas, Asmodeus, Moloch. The name by which he is known changes, depending on where he is found, but he is the Father of Lies."

The soldier's credulity vexed the *alcalde,* whose face glistened with perspiration. "Whatever his name, this *fantasma* is apparently well-traveled."

"He is no *fantasma,* Excellency. He is as real as your own hand and he is the sworn enemy of our Blessed Savior. He goes about the world sowing discord and strife, and capturing people to use as his personal slaves."

The magistrate sighed. "So what did Gomez and his longsuffering wife do after confronting this peripatetic creature?"

"Gomez abjured it in the name of our Savior."

"And that was sufficient to dissuade the fiend from kidnapping him?" the *alcalde* coldly smiled.

"*Si,* Excellency. When Beto's wife displayed her holy rosary the monster fled."

The *alcalde* stroked his beard in thoughtful silence for a few moments while his subordinate continued to stand stiffly before him. "Bring me this Beto," he finally instructed. "I wish to speak to him...make certain to sober him up first," he added.

"As you wish," Diego crisply assented. "But, Excellency, Beto and his wife do not partake in *la bebida alcoholica.* More honorable *campesinos* do not reside in the entire *pueblo.*"

FOURTEEN

A CLOUD OF WHITE SMOKE BELCHED from the muzzle of Ham's '73 Winchester as the 200 grain .44-40 slug plowed into Moloch. A ghastly wound immediately burst on the creature's throat, from which fragments of tissue erupted. No blood emanated from the massive hole; the half-smile on Moloch's lips never faltered.

"Shoot him again!" Bill bellowed. He abandoned his stricken horse and raced back toward Ham.

In a single motion, Ham levered another cartridge into the chamber and yanked the trigger a second time. Again the rifle barked as the lead bullet flew from the muzzle and acrid smoke filled the air. The heavy projectile thumped audibly into the creature's chest. "It ain't doin' nuthin'!" he snarled.

"Bop him with it!" Bill screeched. Ham stepped forward and attempted to club Moloch with the butt of the Winchester, though the creature merely brushed it aside. He wrenched the rifle from the cowboy's hands and flung it away. Slapping Ham across the face with a leprous hand, the creature stepped over to Bill and drove him to the ground.

Ham instantly recovered from the assault and, as Bill clambered to his feet, leapt on Moloch's back. "Help me with this son of a bitch!" he yelled at Bill as the creature whirled about, trying to dislodge the determined cowboy.

Bill rapidly retrieved the Winchester from where it lay in the dirt and attempted to aim it at the spinning duo. "For Christ sake, slow down! I can't draw a bead on him!"

"Then grab the bastard!" Ham shouted as they careened across the collapsed porch. He wrapped an arm around the creature's sinewy neck in an attempted strangle hold.

Bill dropped the rifle and launched himself against Moloch's legs, the three of them crashing to the ground. Grunting and straining, they brawled in the dirt.

Moloch's strength was prodigious. "I got holt of him tighter than a tick!" Ham grunted through gritted teeth, redoubling his grip. With his free hand, he began to pound the creature's face to the extent his awkward position would permit. The stench that emanated from the thing nearly made the cowboys gag, though neither man relented. Bill continued to hug the creature's legs, committing all his strength to grip them as they thrashed about.

"I ain't lettin' go," Ham growled. "I broke hosses with more spunk that you got." He punctuated his remark by punching the creature's scaly head. The creature strained and twisted in an effort to unburden himself, but the men wouldn't yield.

"Damn, this rascal's tough as a one-bit steak," Bill panted.

Although Moloch's strength appeared undiminished, it was more than matched by the cowboys' tenacity. Ultimately sensing this, the creature finally yielded and lay unmoving, on his stomach, in the dirt near Bill's rifle, the panting men still anchoring him.

"Reach acrost with one hand, grab that Winchester, and hand it to me," Ham directed his companion from astride the creature's back. Bill complied. Ham laid the rifle flat across Moloch's neck and, spreading his hands, leaned forward and forcefully pushed downward on it, grinding the creature's deformed head into the earth. "Sit on that end and don't be gentle, Bill," he said, tipping his head. As his companion arranged himself at the butt-end of the rifle, Ham assumed a position close to the muzzle.

"Ain't you afraid we'll break the poor bastard's neck?" Bill speculated aloud.

"Whacha think, ugly?" Ham asked, addressing the creature lying in the dirt beneath them. "You comfy?"

"How come he ain't dead?" Bill marveled. "You shot the rascal twice from no more'n three feet away, and that Winchester'll kill a bar. He should be deader than Pompey if'n you actually hit him."

"It'd be a helluva trick *not* to hit him from that distance," Ham retorted. He looked down at the scaly creature beneath them. "You some kinda ghost, ugly?" And where's ever'body else in this damned town?" He shifted his position slightly because the Winchester's slender barrel dug into his rump.

The basilisk remained silent but stared balefully.

"Well, what ya think we outta do?" Bill asked, looking around. "Mouse is lookin' pretty feeble on account o' this feller, but I sure as hell don't feel much like *walkin'* outta here."

"Brig's still where we left him, out yonder at that corral," Ham responded. "I reckon we can ride Mouse that far, then vamoose on him."

Bill shook his head ruefully. "Like a coupla damned squaws again. Ain't they any hosses in this town?"

"Hey, ugly," Ham punched Moloch in the side of his head. "You got any hosses?"

"Both of you will soon be dead," the creature rasped.

"I guess that means he ain't got no mounts," Ham concluded, matter-of-factly.

"He's pretty game for somebody layin' in the dirt, bein' sat on," observed Bill. "What ya reckon we outta do with him?"

Ham shifted his position again. "Well, he's rough as a cob. If we let him up, he's liable to start swingin' again. But we sure as hell can't sit here all day 'cause I'm already hotter than an outlaw's six-gun." He glanced at the rifle on which he and Bill were uncomfortably perched. "But the Winchester don't seem to put much of a dent in him," he concluded in disgust.

"Well, he can't whup the both of us," Bill reasoned. "Otherwise, we wouldn't be sittin' on him. I say we let him up and get outta here afore it gets any hotter."

Ham slowly nodded.   He looked down at creature pinned beneath the rifle. "Hey, ugly. We're gonna let you go.   But if you try anything funny, me and Bill are gonna be on you like a duck on a June bug. You savvy?"

Moloch said nothing.

The two men warily eased themselves to standing positions. Bill leaned down and lifted his rifle from the creature's neck, who slowly sat up. "Remember what I told you," Ham warned as the cowboys backed away from the creature, toward Bill's tethered mount. "It would suit me just fine to knock the piss outta you again."

"Both of you will soon be dead," he seethed, though he made no effort to pursue the cowboys.

"C'mon, Mousie," Bill said when they reached his horse, "we's gonna blow outta here." He gently stroked the animal's neck as he slid his rifle back into the scabbard attached to the saddle. Ham untied the reins that secured Mouse to the railing. The animal nickered softly and its labored breathing continued; Bill realized that Mouse was trembling as he patted the horse's damp pelage. He glanced behind but Moloch had disappeared. "Where'd that varmint go?" he asked, uneasily.

"Don't matter to us," Ham responded. "I don't reckon he's in much of a hurry to et another mouthful o' dirt. Ya think Mouse is up to carryin' the both of us? I'd like to give 'im some water, but there don't appear to be any about. Brig could use some, too."

"The Good Lord made hosses to ride, so I reckon we'll ride," Bill philosophically replied. "Ole Mouse been through worse than this, ain't ya Mousie?" He affectionately rubbed behind the horse's ears. "Maybe we can scare up some water back at the corral." He placed his foot in the stirrup and swung into the saddle. Ham handed Bill the reins, then pulled himself onto Mouse's rump, behind the saddle's cantle. Bill smoothly tugged the reins and clucked his tongue. "Let's go, Mouse." The horse turned from the railing and began plodding down the dusty street toward the corral where Brigham awaited them.

"What you reckon was wrong with that poison slinger?" Ham puzzled from behind Bill, referring to the Winchester. "It outta knocked that sonofabitch on his ass."

"I coulda hit that feller with a rock," Bill retorted. Where the hell'd you learn to shoot?"

Ham made a disgruntled face. "If you're thinkin' that I missed that ugly bastard, you're dumber than you look. You seen them bullets hit him, but they didn't do shit!"

"I ain't gotta be very smart to be smarter'n you," Bill countered. "And at least I can shoot."

Ham shrugged. "I'm thinkin' the powder mebbe got old or wet, or they don't put enough powder in when they make 'em in the first place. The bastards figure they can save a few pennies by short-weighin' the cartridges when they make 'em and, if we get et by a bar or kilt by Injuns, we ain't gonna be around to bitch about it."

"If you cain't hit what you're aimin' at it don't matter how old the powder is," Bill replied.

Ham was quiet a moment. "Bill, I'm kinda worried about Brig. Neither of these hosses been right since we got to this damned place." The other cowboy didn't respond as Mouse trudged through the purlieus of the deserted town.

THEY SAW THEM AS they approached the corral.

Three helmeted figures clad in peculiar, blousy clothing caked with filth were huddled inside the enclosure, the battered steel morions on their heads glinting in the sun. Distorted by the heat waves that flared through the scorching air, the silent, numinous figures seemed oblivious to Mouse's sluggish approach. Brigham lay on his side at their booted feet, insentient. The air reeked with the stench of rotting meat.

Mouse abruptly stopped 200 feet from the corral. "What in hell?" Bill blurted. "It'd stink a dog off a gut wagon around here! Did that feller follow us?"

"Brig!" Ham cried over Bill's shoulder as he slid off the horse. "Brig!" Ham scrambled across the parched earth toward the corral. Simultaneously, Bill slid his rifle from its scabbard and spurred Mouse, but the exhausted animal refused to budge. Again Bill applied his spurs, but the animal squealed and reared, refusing to advance.

"Goddammit, Mouse!" Bill cursed. He flung the reins aside and leapt from the saddle, levering a cartridge into the Winchester as he raced after his companion.

"Git away from my hoss!" Ham panted as he ran.

Bill drew up and raised the rifle to his shoulder. Taking aim at one of the figures, who still appeared oblivious to the cowboys, he snapped off a shot. Both men heard the distinct thump when the lumbering bullet struck flesh but the figure seemed completely unaffected.

When Ham reached the corral gate, the figures finally turned to stare dumbly in the direction of the commotion, their feral beards tangled and matted with blood. Shaggy black eyebrows overhung pink sockets devoid of eyes.

"Good God o' Mighty!" Ham gasped as Bill joined him. From where they stood, they could see that the figures had been feasting on Brigham. The horse had been torn open and its glistening entrails hung from its body cavity. "Gimme that rifle!" he barked, yanking the Winchester from Bill's hands. He levered another cartridge into the chamber and fired into the nearest figure, now less than 15 feet away. The figure registered no reaction as the projectile bored into it. None of them appeared to comprehend what was happening, but stood unmoving, wordless.

"Git the hell outta here!" Ham shouted, levering another cartridge into the Winchester's chamber. He snapped off a second shot, then a third, with the same fruitless result.

The figures stood facing the bewildered cowboys for a few moments, weaving almost imperceptivity in the shimmering heat, before silently turning away. Mutely, they began to shamble across the dusty corral, their disintegrating leather boots making no sound as they shuffled like mindless automata. Bill and Ham watched from outside the corral, dumbfounded.

"Hey, you sonsabitches!" Ham shouted at the retreating figures as they drifted away. He snapped off a final shot when they neared the far side of the corral. Without pausing, the three figures passed through the wooden boards that enclosed the corral. Like sleepwalkers, they ambled away from the cowboys into the surrounding desert where they finally disappeared, their methodical pace unaltered.

"Fuck me," Bill mumbled in awe. "Them bastards walked right through."

Ham swung open the corral gate and strode to Brigham's ravaged body. "Goddamn them," he moaned as he knelt in the dirt by the animal. "Look at poor ole' Brig. He never hurt nobody and look what them fuckers done to him." He gently stroked the animal's dead cheek, its lifeless eye milky and dull. Ham looked up at Bill. "Why would anybody kilt a innocent cayuse?"

"Because they's fuckers, Ham. You said so yerself."

"That feller back in town put 'em up to it," Ham said. "He's the one that done it." He stood.

"Well, I'll go back if ya want and we'll get to the bottom o' it, but Mouse ain't entirely hisself. I think that feller back there hexed him. Otherwise, we either gotta stay put or head outta here, and stayin' put prob'ly ain't in the cards 'cause we've neither food nor water. I vote that we ride Mouse as far as he'll take us. Ain't nuthin' been right since we got here and we need to git whiles we still can."

Ham gazed sadly at the unoffending horse lying at his feet. "I sure am sorry, Brig," he whispered. "You was a good hoss and I'm sorry you ended up like this. I sure as hell didn't want ya to git et. Forgive me, friend. Maybe we'll cross paths on the next go-round." He turned away from the animal's body and walked to the side of the corral. There, he removed the wooden canteen attached to Brigham's saddle with a length of rawhide and walked out the gate without looking back.

"You think we should follow them's that et Brig?" Bill asked as he trailed Ham back to Mouse, who stood, head down, where they'd left him.

"I don't know what them things are, but they ain't men," Ham responded. "The Winchester don't have no effect on 'em and they's too many of 'em to wrassle, like we did that one back in town. I don't know about you, Bill, but I'm thinkin' we outta just git the hell outta here, *pronto*."

Bill slipped his rifle back into its saddle scabbard. "Yep. I'm just hopin' that Mouse's got enough pepper left in him." He patted his listless mount's neck.

"Well, we're sure as hell gonna find out. Hop up so's I can get behind you," Ham urged, hooking his canteen over Mouse's saddle.

The two cowboys climbed onto the horse's back, Bill clucked his tongue, and Mouse wearily turned back up the trail, away from Esperanza.

"I GUESS I'M GAME IF YOU ARE," Moe said. "What about Nancy?"

"I already ran the idea past her and I think she'll agree as long as you do. We'll need a couple more people, too, and I've already talked to them."

The detective looked dubious. "You ever done anything like this before?"

Cam shook his head. "Not exactly, but I've read a lot about it. There's no shortage of information on séances. Porphyry made the first reference to a séance in the third century; even before that, Pliny the Younger wrote about a house in Athens that was supposedly haunted by a ghost, complete with rattling chains. But the first formal account of an actual séance was published in England in 1659. They've been around for centuries."

"What exactly happens at one?"

"A séance is basically an interface where the dead are supposedly able to communicate with the living. The participants don't have to have any psychic abilities but it usually works better if they do. There shouldn't be more than six or eight people involved. Everybody forms a chain by holding hands or placing them on a table with their fingertips touching."

Moe sipped his Diet Coke. "Don't you need a medium for a séance? Every scary movie I ever saw about a séance had a medium in it, usually some crazy nut-job. Where are you going to get a medium? Craiglist?"

Cameron chuckled. "Yeah, people generally associate a medium or 'guide' with séances. But I'm thinking that, because Chet's already contacted us, we can probably dispense with a medium and establish contact ourselves. Chet's obviously receptive to hearing from us. Besides, my suspicion is that there's probably a lot of fake mediums...Houdini made a career out of exposing 'em. I figure, what could a medium do that we can't? I've read enough to know how to conduct a séance."

"If it *was* Chet," Moe cautiously reminded him.

"Well, even if it wasn't Chet, it was *somebody*," Cameron stubbornly contended. "And I don't think we need a professional medium to contact them."

The detective nodded thoughtfully. "Fair enough. You know a lot more about it than I do." He finished his soft drink. "So now what?"

"I've gotta talk to Nancy again, to tell her that you're in, then start putting everything together. I'm not too worried about it but, out of an abundance of caution, I don't want to be in Esperanza after dark so, although it'll be hot, I want to conduct the séance within the next couple of weeks because it'll still be light until pretty late in the day."

"You don't want to do it at night? In the movies, they're always at night and it's always storming outside."

"You can conduct a séance at any time of the day. And, from what I've read, storms actually detract from the success of a séance. Dry conditions are supposedly better than wet ones."

"What kind of equipment will we need? Tambourines?" Moe couldn't resist the playful jab.

Cameron refused to be baited, even in jest. "Some people think that music or singing creates vibrations that contribute to the likelihood that a séance will actually produce psychic phenomena. But a famous medium named Stainton Moses said that music wasn't necessary and was actually a distraction. So, no, we won't need tambourines or anything else...just us."

"I thought you said we needed a table, too."

"We really don't need a table or chairs. We'll just sit on the floor."

"So we're all just gonna show up and have a séance. It's as simple as that?"

"Well, I've gotta do a little more research, but yeah, that's pretty much it."

The detective assumed a somber expression. "After what happened to your Jeep last time, I don't think anyone should park their vehicles out there."

"I already thought of that," Cameron said. "I'm going to have somebody drop us off and wait for us."

Moe looked skeptical. "After what happened to Chet, you think it's smart to have people waiting out there?"

"Chet was alone," Cameron reminded him. "I plan on having a group who'll be ready for anything."

"I guess that's about all you can do," Moe conceded. "But there's no cell phone service out there, so we can't call anyone to come pick us up. So what's the next step? What do you want me to do?"

"I don't think there's anything you *can* do, Woody. I'll talk to Nancy and tell her that you're on board. Once she hears that, I'm sure she'll agree, too, though she's not too keen on the whole idea. Then I'll talk to everyone to see which Saturday they'll be available this month. You got a preference?"

The detective shook his head. "You tell me when and where and I'll be there. And I think I'll do a little homework myself. I'm tired of being jerked around by whoever, or whatever, we've been dealing with.... they're obviously not benign."

"Well, if it's Chet, he's not a threat," Cameron protested.

"Yeah, but I don't think it's Chet," replied Moe. "Do you really think Chet would hurt Daisy?" He paused, but continued before Cameron could respond. "When we go back this time, Cam, I'm gonna be loaded for bear."

"How's that?"

"Whatever we're dealing with, I intend to bring every weapon that I can carry."

Cameron was puzzled. "What kind of weapon are you talking about, Woody? A gun? Don 't you always carry a gun, anyway?"

The detective shook his head. "That's where my homework comes in. I'm gonna do some research on protection against poltergeists, or tricksters, or ghosts, or whatever you want to call 'em. If people have been conducting séances for hundreds of years, like you said, then there's bound to be lots of information about what to do if things go south."

"Magical grimoires have been around for centuries," Cameron said. "They're basically folklore spells and incantations for protection against demons and whatnot. But I'm not sure those are what you're talking about."

"No, I'm not talking about magic circles and wolf's bane," Moe demurred. "I'm talking about something that, if something comes after us like it came after Daisy, we can blow it into next week!"

Cameron reflected a moment. "In the 1920's and '30's a nutty priest named Montague Summers wrote a bunch of books on witches, ghosts, werewolves, vampires, the devil, and related stuff. He was gullible as hell and most of what he wrote is crap, but his books might contain something useful, I suppose. I have some of Summers' stuff if you want to look at it."

"That's as good a place to start as any," the detective assented. He glanced at his watch. "I have to get back to work. You gonna be around later?"

"Whenever you say," Cameron said.

Moe slid from the booth and stood. "I'd like to come by and snag those books after work."

"Call my cell when you're on your way."

"Done," said Moe.

Cameron grabbed their check, exited the booth, and headed for the cashier near the front of the pizza joint. "I got this one, Woody. Next time, when it's your turn, we're goin' to the 'Chez Louie.'"

"I believe it," Moe laughed. "I'll call you later, when I get off." He donned his sun glasses and braced himself for the wave of scorching air that would assault him the moment he stepped from the restaurant. He hesitated only a moment before swinging open the heavy glass door and stepping into the blinding heat. Cameron paid the tab and followed a few moments later.

MOE HAD NO IDEA WHERE TO BEGIN, so he started with the Internet. His resulting research, consistent with every B horror movie ever made, advised that the sign of the cross was the most potent weapon against demons. In addition, water, bells, saints' relics, and minerals such as chalcedony, chrysolite, and agate, as well as plants like mandrake, rue, anise, clove, and peppermint, were supposedly effective. Garlic, of course, as well as roosters and salt were also recommended on several websites. In French folklore an herb called *permanable* was said to be especially powerful, though the detective was unable to determine exactly what "permanable" was. Aglaophotis, an herb that supposedly grew in the Arabian Desert, was also supposed to be efficacious against demons. One could, Moe concluded after more than two hours of surfing the Net, be forced into bankruptcy simply acquiring all the substances recommended for protection against purportedly hostile metaphysical agencies.

More intriguing was information he discovered about pacts with Satan.

"Satan," the detective learned, was nothing more sinister than a Hebrew word meaning "adversary." It originally referred to a divine entity whose purpose was simply to test men's loyalty to God. Not inherently evil, the concept of Satan became transmogrified over time into the antithesis of God, an arch-fiend, tempter and tormentor, the supreme adversary of everything good and wholesome in the universe.

Notwithstanding his fearful nature, throughout history people, either through naiveté or in the deluded expectation of earthly wealth and pleasure, have purportedly agreed to assist Satan in his cosmic mission to mock and ultimately subvert God. As a reward for their everlasting loyalty, Satan supposedly promises his votaries wealth, protection against all mischief, the power to inflict harm on their enemies, the secret of invisibility, the ability to fly, and a host of other worldly inducements. In exchange, Satan's adherents freely deliver into the demon's grasp as many additional souls as they are able to entice. Satan's puissance is said to increase in proportion to the number of souls he thus ensnares.

Cast into a funereal netherworld, Satan and his minions subject these unfortunates to exquisite, agonizing tortures in a mocking demonstration of God's utter impotency, or simply for the pleasure derived from inflicting pain. When their victims are finally released from their excruciating misery through the expedient of death, or simply because their infernal master grows weary of them, their bodies are consumed and their animating substance extracted. They are thus reduced to nothing more than simulacra of the living, shadows emptied of substance.

Finally overwhelmed by the profusion of information on the Internet, the detective wearily logged-off, rose from his desk, and walked across his living room, where he stretched out on a couch. The room was rapidly growing dark, so he propped his head on a pillow and reached up to switch on a reading light at the head of the couch. The handful of books by the self-styled "Reverend" Montague Summers that he borrowed from Cameron were piled on the floor beside him, as well as treatises written by other supposed experts.

He'd previously thumbed through some of the volumes and, as far as Moe was concerned, the eccentric Summers had indiscriminately embraced every absurd fantasy throughout history regarding the supernatural, no matter how illogical or preposterous. The detective found Summers' discussion of such subjects as 'flying ointment', the evil eye, and the black mass to extraordinarily naïve, and his solemn reproofs of them laughable. Resignedly, he reached down, pulled the topmost volume from the stack, and resumed reading.

After a tedious hour perusing the Reverend's jejune observations about Satan, werewolves, witches, and vampires, Moe grew listless and laid aside Summers' *Popular History of Witchcraft*. He wearily picked a moldering discourse on witches' "familiars" from the pile of books on the floor next to the couch and carefully opened it.

The volume reeked of mildew and its yellowed pages were brittle with age. The detective gently flipped through it. He was getting sleepy and hoped that something would catch his eye before he completely lost interest and dozed off. He sighed and began reading.

According to the treatise, there exists a hierarchy of demons, with Lucifer occupying the preeminent position. As a reward for serving him, Lucifer awards his earthly devotees a subordinate demon, a "familiar," which typically assumes the form of an animal. The familiar is thereafter the constant companion of its owner, its function to provide advice and perform sundry malignant tasks, including property destruction, uncontrolled bleeding, arson, causing women to be barren and food to spoil, inducing illness in children, and murder. Familiars are especially insidious because, by mimicking the form of mundane animals, they are easily able to dupe the unwary, thereby rendering it a simple matter to effectuate their demonic intrigues.

A farmer in Gifford's *Dialogue,* written in 1593, for example, expressed a very real fear of familiars when he confessed that, "When I go into my gardens, I am afraid, for I see now and then a hare, which my conscience giveth me is a witch, or some witch's spirit, she stareth so upon me. And sometimes I see an ugly weasel run through my yard, and there is a foul great cat sometimes in my barn, which I have no liking unto."

While generally appearing in the form of domesticated creatures, familiars can take a myriad of forms: rabbits, crows, rats, oxen, lambs, owls, even newts and toads.

Moe shut the book and placed it on his chest.   He was perplexed and, frankly, annoyed, by the childish naiveté of Montague Summers and his ilk.   He yawned and stretched luxuriantly, weary of reading.   Aside from the illumination provided by the reading light at the head of the couch, the living room was enveloped in darkness. Growing drowsy in the quietude, he closed his eyes.

The sound of soft rapping intruded upon his torpor.

Initially, Moe wasn't even certain he actually heard the faint sounds, but a regular tapping definitely seemed to emanate from an unlit corner of the living room.   Thinking it attributable to some innocuous activity in the neighboring apartment, the detective did his best to ignore the percussive sound.   Although muted, he mildly resented the disturbance, but it persisted and, indeed, became more imperious. In that pleasant twilight between wakefulness and sleep, Moe became absorbed in listening to the rhythmic tapping.

Something roughly grabbed his shoulder.

Moe's eyes instantly flew open and he sprang to his feet, his heart thumping.   He frantically scanned the dim interior of the room, seeing nothing.   The area at the head of the couch was empty, devoid of anything that could account for jostling him. Irrespective of the distinct sensation that someone had just seized him, the detective had no alternative but to conclude that he'd simply drifted off to sleep and dreamt the unnerving episode. His frantic heart beat began to slow.

He reached forward and swiveled his reading lamp toward the corner where the soft rapping continued its rhythmic tattoo. The volume of tapping increased. Moe peered intently in the direction of the sound.

The soft illumination of the reading lamp revealed a large white cat sitting quietly in the corner, its golden eyes fixed on him. It raised a paw, licked it, and unconcernedly used its paw to wash its face. A chill thrilled through the detective's body.

"Hey, buddy," he blurted. "How'd *you* get in here?"

He instinctively stepped toward the animal, which calmly glided behind a nearby upholstered chair. As he moved to pursue it, two tiny birds, resembling iridescent finches, landed on the back of his couch and briefly hopped about before flitting away.

"What the hell ..." the detective mumbled under his breath, half-suspecting that he must be dreaming.

The rapping abruptly changed. Originally resembling the rhythmic cadence of finger tips drumming softly on a table top, it abruptly changed to a scratching noise, as of someone dragging their finger nails across wood or burlap. The reading light at the head of the couch spontaneously extinguished and, with it, the scratching noise. In its place, the unlit room rang with a jarring clang, followed by a sound akin to heavy furniture sliding across a bare floor.

The unnerved detective raced across his living room and flicked a wall switch adjacent to his front door; the overhead light blazed to life. A pandemonium of crashing detonations instantly rocked the apartment, the cacophony thundering off walls and ceiling. The floor beneath his feet bucked and heaved and the walls shook.

Moe snatched a flashlight and an automatic pistol from atop a bookshelf. The first panicked thought that raced through his brain was that his apartment had just suffered a massive explosion. A quick visual inventory of the room confirmed, however, that the room remained intact. Though the deafening tumult did not subside, but seemed to actually increase in violence and intensity, lamps did not tumble to the carpeted floor, windows did not implode, and furniture was not reduced to splinters.

Moe raced to his front door, flung it open, and bolted from his apartment into the sweltering, if tranquil, evening air. Standing on his porch, the detective was utterly unable to hear the booming crashes that reverberated within his apartment, notwithstanding that, scarcely two feet behind him, the door gaped open. Baffled, the detective stepped back inside, where he was instantly assailed by the noise of shattering glass. As before, however, the interior appeared completely unscathed in spite of the uproar.

Moe quickly retreated to his porch. Although well past sunset, sufficient ambient light remained for him to see easily. He looked up and down the street in an effort to determine the origin of the violent commotion rending the interior of his apartment, but discerned nothing unusual.

He was uncertain what he should do. The overwhelming din inside his apartment rendered it impossible for him to reenter, though the detective could hardly stand on his porch all night waiting for the commotion to subside if, indeed, it ever would. Moe cautiously poked his head back though the open door.

Stillness prevailed. The maelstrom appeared to have terminated, as though it had never occurred.

Moe slowly reentered the quiescent apartment, not realizing until that moment that he still clutched his flashlight and pistol. The harsh light from the overhead fixture still illuminated the living room and he peered anxiously about, fearful the bedlam would resume.

Everything remained orderly and still. Moe quietly shut the front door behind him and proceeded to explore the remaining rooms of the apartment in order to satisfy himself that everything was intact. Nothing appeared out of place. He switched off the lights in each room that he successively examined and padded back to the living room, where he returned his flashlight and pistol to their customary places atop the bookshelf. Shaken by the bizarre incident, the detective knew he had to inform Cameron. His cell phone lay on the floor near the pile of books at the head of his couch; shaken, he cautiously walked across the room to retrieve it. En route, Moe passed a decorative mirror mounted at eye-level on his living room wall. A sudden chill enveloped him as, from the corner of his eye, he saw reflected in it a human face. He abruptly stopped and turned to directly face the mirror.

Although only about four inches tall, every feature of the male image was perfectly distinct.

The countenance was pockmarked and deeply furrowed, as through prolonged exposure to the sun. Despite this, the face did not appear to be that of an elderly man because the stubble on its unshaved chin was copious and black. Appearing to be some sort of soldier, the figure wore an antiquated steel helmet, spattered with rust. As Moe gazed in astonishment, the face's eyes moved and it smiled, exposing missing front teeth. The detective instinctively reached out and placed his fingertips on the cold glass, blocking the image. When he removed his hand the face moved its lips, as if undertaking to speak, though no sound emanated from it.

Moe turned away from the mirror, seeking the source of the reflection. Behind him, the room was empty. Flummoxed, he looked back at the image, whose lips continued to move as though engaged in silent conversation. The skin on the back of Moe's neck began to tingle and the tiny hairs stood erect. He reached forward and unhooked the mirror from the wall. Notwithstanding the movement, the image remained centered in the mirror.

Moe carried the mirror to his kitchen, the reflection continuing to smile and talk unabated, where he placed it face-down on the counter. Instead of using his cell phone, as he originally intended, the detective removed from its cradle the handset of the adjacent wall-mounted telephone and rapidly punched-in Cameron's cell number. Cameron answered on the second ring.

"Cam?"

"Woody, I was literally in the process of calling you." The fear in Cameron's voice was palpable. "You're not gonna believe what just happened."

FIFTEEN

CAMERON WAS RECLINING ON THE couch, watching TV, when he thought he heard the soft knock. Because his overhead neighbor could simply have dropped something by accident, he ignored it. A moment later, though, he heard it again: this time, a series of sharp, distinct raps at the front door of his apartment. Cameron muted the TV and listened more intently. Nothing. He looked at his watch: 8:12 p.m. He wasn't expecting anyone this time of night and was perplexed, and annoyed, by the intrusion. And why didn't whoever it was just ring the doorbell, rather than knock?

Cameron placed the television's remote control on the arm of the couch, stood, and stepped to his front door. Switching on the porch light, he peered out through the peephole. His mouth literally fell open.

Chet stood on the vestibule outside. He was clad in the same hiking clothes he wore when Cameron last saw him, though they were soiled and disheveled. Notwithstanding the intervening weeks since his disappearance, Chet was clean-shaven though his face was puffy, like a grave worm. What appeared to be a bulky canvas bag was slung across his chest.

"Oh, my God!" Cameron gasped. He reached down and frantically fumbled to unlock the door. "Chet, hang on!" he shouted as his sweaty hands slipped off the latch. Finally succeeding in unbolting the door, Cameron flung it open.

The porch was vacant.

Cameron bolted outside, to the walkway leading from the street to his apartment. He initially ignored the overpowering smell of rotten meat that permeated the baking air. "Chet! Chet!" he shouted into the stifling night as he anxiously looked about.

No one was there.

Cameron checked up and down the street before slowly retracing his steps back to the porch, absolutely dumbfounded. His front door still gaped open, so he pulled it shut before stepping around the corner of his apartment building. By the uncertain glow of a streetlight, he surveyed the wide lawn that separated his building from adjacent apartments. The landscaped expanse, dotted with neatly-trimmed palm trees and shrubs, was destitute of any human presence.

"Chet, are you here?" he anxiously called into the void, though his supplication went unrequited. After waiting in vain a few more minutes, Cameron trudged bitterly back to his apartment. It was an absolute certainty that someone had been standing on his stoop only moments ago, and Cameron was convinced it was Chet. How was that possible? Where had he gone?

As he approached his front door Cameron was again assailed by the putrid stench of decomposing flesh. He wrinkled his nose, suspecting that a neighborhood cat had either died, or had ambushed a bird, behind the hedge. Cameron peered into the shrubbery but the languid illumination provided by his porch light revealed nothing. Moving closer, he used his hand to gingerly ease the spiky hedge away from the exterior wall, seeing only shadows and dirt.

Cameron released the shrubbery and it flopped back against the wall. Though he couldn't be certain, the nauseating smell seemed to have dissipated slightly. He turned from the hedge and again looked into the darkness. Whoever had previously been at his door had simply vanished into the night. A feeling of unease gripped him.

Cameron reentered his apartment, carefully bolting the door behind him. He was immediately assaulted by the stench of decomposing flesh. He strode into his living room.

Daisy's putrescent body was spread on his couch, her stuffed penguin and water bowl placed neatly beside her. Her fur was matted with dirt, the rictus of death twisting her mouth into a lifeless snarl.

"Oh, fuck!" Cameron wretched. "Oh, my God!"

His immediate thought was that Daisy was still alive, that she'd frantically managed to dig herself free from her desert grave and make her way home. But even though his heart wanted to believe that, his brain knew it couldn't be true. Daisy was dead. Something out at the cemetery had killed her, and he personally buried her, weeks ago. The person at his door had obviously disinterred Daisy's fetid corpse and deposited it in Cameron's living room, having entered the apartment through the open front door while Cameron was outside. Although resembling Chet, it could not have been him. Why would anyone go to such trouble or indulge in such a despicable prank?

The smell was nauseating. Cameron knew he had to get Daisy's body outside, into the open air, without delay. But where was the man on the doorstep? Cameron kept his Walther .22 on his bedside table, but had no assurance that the intruder wasn't lurking in his bedroom.

Cameron stepped quickly to a hall closet where linens were stored. He swiftly removed an old, faded counterpane. Unfolding it as he walked, he approached the couch and flung it over Daisy's prostrate body. Close to vomiting, he leaned over and began tucking the bed spread beneath her, the foulness causing his throat to burn. As he feverishly worked, Cameron glanced up from his dolorous task to confirm that he remained alone.

After more-or-less wrapping Daisy in the counterpane, Cameron grasped either end of the roll and lifted it off the couch, onto his living room floor. It was lighter than he expected, owing to the desiccated condition of Daisy's body. Averting his head in an effort to minimize the fetor, he bent, grasped two corners of the bundle, and dragged it toward his front door. Once there, he unbolted and opened the door, then muscled the cerement over the elevated threshold, into the sultry night air. Cameron rested the bundle containing Daisy's body on his porch and straightened to pull the door shut. The odor of her decaying body penetrated the fabric of the bed spread and Cameron hoped to keep it from filling his apartment. He looked anxiously around, uncertain what to do next. He couldn't just leave Daisy on his porch, but was loathe to unceremoniously place her body in the apartment complex's dumpster.

At a loss, Cameron decided to call Woody. Through the closed door, he heard his cell phone begin to ring. He bounded into his apartment and snatched it from the arm of the couch. It was the detective.

Breathlessly, Cameron apprised Woody of what had just occurred. When he finished, the detective related his own experience.

"Is the mirror still like that?" Cameron asked.

Moe cradled the phone with his neck and slowly lifted the mirror, which remained face-down. In it was reflected only the pattern of the laminated counter top. "No, it's okay now. I honestly thought I was going crazy, Cam." He replaced it on the counter, face-down.

Cameron glanced toward his front door, beyond which Daisy's body lay on his porch. "No, you're not going crazy, Woody," he murmured. "But I'm freaked out."

The detective glanced at his watch. "I'm coming to your apartment, Cam. I'm not sure what to do at this moment but, if nothing else, we've got to do something with Daisy's body."

"I don't know what to do with her," Cameron dejectedly confessed.

Moe reflected a moment before responding. "We need to rebury her as quickly as possible. We'll put her in your Jeep and roll all the flaps up. With two of us digging, we can get it done pretty fast." Sensing Cameron's grief, he quickly added, "I'm so sorry, Cam."

"No, you're right. We need to take care of Daisy. I'll see you when you get here, Woody," he sighed. "I'm sorry for getting you mixed up in all this."

"You didn't get me mixed up in anything, Cam. Don't worry about it. I'm on my way." Moe hung up the phone and, without looking at the mirror again, grabbed his keys, pistol, and cell phone and headed out the door.

"C'MON, MOUSE." Bill pulled impatiently on his horse's reins, urging him forward.

"I ain't walked this damned far since I wore short pants at my momma's knee," Ham complained, tripping over a rock. He removed his battered, sweat-stained hat and squinted into the scorching late afternoon air. "You reckon there's another town hereabouts?"

Having fled Esperanza more than two hours earlier, the two cowboys slid from the exhausted horse and began trudging along the desert floor, Mouse plodding wearily behind them. Although neither man was desirous of walking, they decided it prudent to preserve the animal's strength. Once they located water, all three of them would be able to rest.

"It don't make sense they'd just be one town," Bill opined as they stumbled along. He stopped momentarily to mop his face with a threadbare bandana. "But if they ain't a town, they's gotta be at least a ranch around hereabouts...not ever'body lives in a town."

"That's fer damned sure," affirmed Ham. "You think the only one who lived in that town back yonder was that little smelly feller?"

"Maybe him and them three what we saw at that corral, what kilt Brigham," Bill responded. "Dunno. All I know fer sure is that he was uglier than scabs on puke!"

"The Salt River s'posed to drain through here someplace," Ham continued, changing the subject. "A *hombre* I was breakin' horses with in Texas told me about it 'bout a year ago. Not perzactly sure where it is, but it's s'posed to be pretty big and where they's a river, they's people. And where they's people, they's whisky!" he cackled.

Bill scanned the barren landscape. "Well, if they's a river around here, it must be hidin' and I ain't worried 'bout whisky. But if we don't find some water *pronto*, I ain't sure how much longer Mouse can go." He solicitously patted the animal's neck.

Ham nodded sympathetically. "Sleepin' on the ground tonight don't sound too appealin', neither." He kicked at the dry, rocky soil. "It's harder than a preacher's dick." Although neither man wanted to admit it, both were still shaken by their experience in Esperanza and eager to distance themselves from it. Ham pointed to a distant ridge, shimmering in the heated air. "Les take a peek from that high ground, Bill. Mebbe we can spot a town. The sun's startin' to drop and we outta keep movin'." He didn't relish spending the night in the open desert with the possibility of the three personages from the corral remaining anywhere in the vicinity. "Ya think we outta try ridin' Mouse again?"

His companion looked at his horse affectionately. "Whacha think, Mousie? You feel like haulin' Ham and me fer a little bit? We's jest about there." He reached up and stroked Mouse's nose, which was as dry and rough as the surrounding desert. "I reckon he can carry us for a while," he concluded. "Otherwise, we prob'ly won't make it to that ridge afore dark." Like Ham, Bill was uneasy about spending a vulnerable night in the desert.

Because of the animal's dehydrated condition, Bill slung the stirrup fender over the saddle horn and reached beneath Mouse's belly to check that the two cinch straps remained secure. Satisfied, he unhooked the fender, placed his foot in the stirrup, and swung into saddle, its scarred leather polished smooth through years of use. Mouse snorted, squirmed, and hopped a bit before settling down, and Bill extended his calloused hand to Ham. The other cowboy grasped Bill's hand and pulled himself onto Mouse's back, just forward of the animal's rump. Once Ham was settled in, Bill clucked his tongue and Mouse resumed plodding forward.

The ridge was farther away than it initially appeared and, by the time they finally crested it, the sun was already sliding beneath the horizon, an angry, burnished disc casting its final, baleful rays across the exhausted, scorched landscape. Far to the south, the dying light glittered off what appeared to be water.

"I reckon that be the Salt River," Ham remarked, peering over Bill's shoulder.

"How far?" Bill softly asked, gazing at the alluring reflection.

Ham squinted into the hazy distance. "Six, seven, miles...mebbe a mite more."

"Reckon we can make it afore it gits too dark?"

Ham glanced around uneasily. "I don't imagine so. Once the sun starts droppin', it gits dark mighty fast and I sure as hell don't want Mouse trippin' and fallin' into a damned hole, 'specially with us perched on him."

"What ya reckon we outta do?"

"I guess we'd best try and find a place to hole-up for the night," Ham reluctantly suggested. "I'm thinkin' we probably outta take turns stayin' awake in the event any of them sonsabitches gits a mind to pay us a visit."

Bill nodded. "I don't figure on gittin' much sleep, anyway. Like you said, this ground ain't exactly goose hair," he noted, meaning a feather bed. A breeze kicked up and Bill could sense Mouse shiver beneath them in the rapidly fading light. "What about right here?" he suggested, glancing around.

"I reckon one place is as good as the next," Ham replied. He tilted his head backward to look at the darkening sky overhead. A faint dusting of stars was already visible in the twilight. "I think it's gonna be pretty close to a full moon tonight. If somebody tries to creep up on us, we should be able to see 'em." He slid off the horse's back onto the stony soil. Bill quickly followed by swinging his leg over the saddle plopping onto the ground.

As Mouse patiently waited, Bill hooked a stirrup over the saddle horn and reached beneath the horse's belly to uncinched the saddle. Ham stood on the other side of the animal and, once the straps were released, dragged the saddle and blanket off Mouse's back and deposited them onto the ground. "Now, I ain't gonna hobble ya, Mousie, so don't wander off," Bill warned the animal, scratching its ears. "Mebbe you can find somethin' to eat around here 'till we git to town tomorrow." Mouse snorted and pawed the flinty earth.

Ham squatted and unbuckled one of Bill's saddlebags. Flipping it open, he removed an oilcloth bundle which he carefully unfolded, revealing a handful of stale biscuits and a chunk of dried beef. "How much water we got?" Bill called to him. He was gathering dry weeds and brush with which to start a fire.

Ham shook the two canteens attached to Bill's saddle. "'Bout a third between 'em, maybe a mite less," he replied. "We got some grub, too."

"If we eat we'll prob'ly just choke on it," Bill opined. "Best each take a sip o' water and give the rest to Mouse. We'll need him to get to that river tomorrow." Ham nodded and replaced the victuals in the saddlebag. He rose to his feet and began to collect the ancient chunks of dead wood scattered about the site. The horse wandered nearby, snuffling the ground, vainly seeking something to eat.

The cowboys heaped the fuel into a bristling pile on the bare earth and piled the remainder nearby. "They's some Lucifers in my other saddle bag," Bill told Ham, who quickly retrieved them. Notwithstanding the blistering daytime heat, the temperature in the desert plummeted once the sun went down, often dropping forty or more degrees. But the shiver that passed over Ham wasn't entirely due to the declining temperature.

Squatting next to the brush pile, Bill flicked one of the wooden matches to life with his thumbnail and applied its flame to some of the dried sticks at the bottom of the pile. After a moment's hesitation they began to burn, the crackling blaze licking upward to envelope the larger pieces of wood at the top of the jumble. The cowboys gazed into the fire in silence.

"It's liable to get cool tonight," Ham finally said, idly. Bill nodded wordlessly. "How long you reckon the fire will last?"

"That wood's dry as my grandma's cunt and there ain't much of it," Bill laconically replied. "I don't figure it'll last more'n a hour." He adjusted an errant branch with the toe of his boot.

"I don't reckon we'll be gittin' much sleep, anyway," Ham philosophically remarked.

"Reckon not."

Ham walked over, bent, and grasped the horn of Mouse's saddle; in his other hand he picked up the saddle blanket. Straightening, he lugged both into the fire light and tossed the blanket to Bill before depositing the saddle on the ground. Ham flopped down next to the saddle, leaned back against it, and stared contemplatively into the fire.

Bill placed the saddle blanket over his shoulder. "I'd best give Mouse a drink o' that water." He walked over to where Ham sat and retrieved one of the canteens. "Come over here, Mousie," he called to the horse as he pulled the stopper from the canteen. The animal ignored him and continued to search the parched earth for food.

Bill removed his battered hat and poured some water from the canteen into it. He clucked his tongue. "Here, Mouse, here. Drink this afore it soaks into my hat." He awkwardly walked to the horse and placed his hat on the ground, near the animal's head. Mouse tentatively nuzzled it before attempting to drink the little pool of water in the bottom. "There ya go. That's a good hoss." Bill stroked the animal's lowered neck. It was now completely dark and noticeably cooler. Although the illumination provided by their modest campfire was marginal, a three-quarter moon had climbed into the night sky and cast its cold light across the barren landscape.

"You got that Winchester with you?" Bill called to Ham while Mouse drank.   He felt strangely restive.

"Yessir, right here aside me," Ham assured him from his place by the fire.

Bill retrieved his hat from the ground and patted Mouse a last time before returning to the campfire.   He sat opposite Ham, wrapped the saddle blanket around him, and stared into the flames.

Moloch came that night.

ANNO DOMINI NOSTRI IESU CHRISTO
1822

"YOU ARE BETO GOMEZ?" the *alcalde* gruffly demanded.

"*Si, alcalde.*" The terrified peasant was literally shaking as he stood before the magistrate. It was impossible to ascertain the original color of his coarse shirt and shapeless trousers because of the filth caked on them. In his callused hands he clutched a torn straw hat. The peón's face, blistered and corrugated through protracted exposure to the relentless sun, resembled a leather mask.

The *alcalde* leaned back in his chair and stroked his beard as he disdainfully surveyed the shabby man. "*Capitán* Diego informs me that you have seen the person responsible for the abduction of my *peones*. Is this true?"

"*Mi esposa* and I saw something out in the *desierto, alcalde,* though, if it was a person, I cannot say."

The *alcalde* could not conceal his disgust. "If not a person, what, then?" he barked. "Perhaps you were both too drunk to know what you saw, or whether you saw anything at all!"

The peasant's face assumed a look of horror. "No, Excellency!" he protested. "I swear by the blood of Christ that we were *sobrios*. What we saw was *real!*"

"Tell me exactly what you saw," the *alcalde* evenly replied. "You need have no fear, Gomez." He leaned forward, placed his elbows on his ornate desk, laced his slender fingers together, and gazed expectantly at the peasant.

The grizzled peón swallowed nervously. He wished his wife were there; she was much better at talking than he was. However, the *alcalde* had no interest in indulging the hysterical ravings of an excitable female. It was bad enough that he had to explicate the husband's credulous fantasies. "*Mi esposa, Lupe,* and me," Gomez finally began, "were gathering firewood, Excellency."

"When?"

Gomez paused and furrowed his brow as he pondered the question. "Four days ago, I think. *Lupe* wandered some distance away but I paid no attention until I heard her shriek. Because I feared that she'd been bitten by a snake, I dropped the wood I was carrying and ran to her."

"Where did this occur?"

"We were more than dos *kilómetros* south of the *pueblo,* Excellency. There is no firewood closer than that and we cannot cook our food without firewood," the peasant explained.

"Yes, yes," the *alcalde* sighed, swiftly losing patience with the credulous peasant. "Your cooking practices are of no interest to me."

"I thought his Excellency might wonder what we were doing so far from the *pueblo*," Gomez stammered.

"It is not your place to think," his superior snapped. "I care only what you saw."

Gomez nodded as though he understood. "We saw the devil," he gravely responded.

The *alcalde* leaned back in his chair and folded his arms. "Describe to me exactly what you saw. If you lie or attempt to deceive me, I will have you flogged."

"*Si, entiendo,*" the peasant acknowledged. He shifted his battered hat from one hand to the other. "*Lupe* was about fifty *varas* from me. She had discovered the foundation of an old building and was poking about, looking for anything of value. When I heard her shriek, Excellency, I flung the wood I was carrying to the ground and ran to her." The nervous peón hesitated.

"What did you see? Speak!" the *alcalde* impatiently demanded.

"I saw the devil no more than ten *pasos* from *Lupe*, Excellency. He was standing there, watching her."

"The devil?"

"*Si, señor,* it was the Evil One himself."

The *alcalde* could scarcely conceal his disgust with the artless peasant's naiveté. "How did you know it was the devil?"

"When I was a child, my nana taught me about such things, so I recognized him at once. He is small like a child, Excellency, not even one and a half meters tall, but his face is that of an old man."

"You had never seen him before that day?"

The peasant shook his head vigorously. "No, Excellency. At first I thought he was an *enano.*"

"How do you know he wasn't?" the *alcalde* probed.

"Its legs! Its legs were hairy, like an animal's! Instead of feet it had hooves and its face was that of a *demonio!*"

"How could you possibly see his legs beneath his *pantalones*?" the *alcalde* scornfully challenged.

"No, no," Excellency," the peasant protested. "Although the devil wore a long shirt, it did not cover his legs. He wore no *pantalones* and his legs were like those of a goat! And the smell, Excellency! The smell of death clung to the devil...it almost made us *vomitar!*"

The *alcalde* resumed slowly stroking his beard. He knew the surrounding desert contained the remains of long-abandoned *haciendas*, some supposedly dating from the time of the *conquistadores,* but was unaware of anyone actually living in them. Why would they choose to live in the hostile desert, given that Esperanza was nearby? If, however, the *peón* was telling the truth, *somebody* was apparently occupying one of the old *ranchos*. "Did he speak?" he inquired of the timorous peasant.

"*Mi esposa* was struck dumb with fright, *alcalde,* but, after making the sign of the cross in front of the devil, I demanded, in the name of our Blessed Savior, to know why he was there and what he wanted."

"What was his response?"

"He hissed like the cursed serpent that he is!"

"Indeed? Your devil did not possess a voice?" The *alcalde* enjoyed baiting the gullible peasant.

"*Si, si,* but when he began to speak, his voice sounded like a buzzing insect. It was very scratchy."

"He spoke our mother tongue?" The *alcalde* was aware that the Apaches routinely raided isolated villages, where they captured Mexican peasants to use as slaves. Some unscrupulous *Mexicanos* even kidnapped their own countrymen and sold them to the Indians. Perhaps the curious intruder was one such slave trader.

"The devil can mimic any tongue in the world. He speaks all languages, Excellency."

The *alcalde* nodded, which the peasant mistook as concurrence. "What was your devil's response to your probing questions, Gomez?"

"He laughed and said that he lived there and that, although he has lived among us for centuries, no one believes he really exists! As he spoke I could see that his teeth were pointed like those of an animal, and that his mouth was bright red, like your jacket, Excellency." The peón pointed a grimy finger at the *alcalde's* elegant tunic.

"For *centuries*? Indeed! Your devil sounds more demented than devilish," the magistrate wryly remarked. "Is he not remarkably small in stature for one of such a prodigious age? And where was his forked tail and pitchfork?"

Gomez hastily crossed himself. "With respect, it is not wise to mock such things, Excellency."

The *alcalde's* features grew hard. "You presume to lecture me of wisdom? What do you know of wisdom, a man who can neither read nor write? Perhaps you should be sitting here and I should be the one begging for scraps of food, rather than the other way around."

Realizing his blunder, the abashed peasant immediately backtracked. "I meant only, Excellency, that the devil knows much. Nothing more. I beg your forgiveness." He poignantly clasped his hands before him, crushing his hat, and lowered his eyes, fully aware the *alcalde* wielded over him the power of high justice.

The magistrate coolly surveyed the trembling peasant before responding. "'Wisdom' would dictate that you moderate your tongue," he finally advised.

"*Si, señor. Lo siento mucho.*"

"What ultimately became of your devil? Did he vaporize in a puff of smoke, a ball of flame, or did he simply run away?" The *alcalde* resumed his interrogation as though nothing had happened.

"*No, señor.* He slithered down a hole in the earth, like a *gusano.*"

"Indeed? If your devil is as evil as you say, why did he flee? Why did he not harm you?"

"Because he had no reason, *Alcalde.* The devil waits until he has need and can locate anyone he wishes at his leisure."

"What 'need' would anyone have of someone as contemptible as you?"

"The devil uses both the living and the dead to serve him, Excellency."

The *alcalde* frowned unconsciously. "You are no doubt aware that someone has been abducting my *peones.* Do you think the man you encountered may be responsible for this villainy?"

"As I said, *señor,* I saw no 'man.'"

The peasant's superstitious ignorance was beginning to grate on the *alcalde*. He painstakingly restated the question. "Do you believe this man, whom you believe to be the devil, may be responsible for preying on my *peones?*"

"*Si.*"

The *alcalde* reflected momentarily before speaking again. "Can you find this place again?"

"*Si*, though I do not think you should go there, Excellency. It is *muy mal lugar.*"

"Your thoughts, such as they are, do not interest me. You will lead *Capitán* Diego to this place as soon as a patrol can be assembled. You know *Capitán* Diego?"

"I do not know him, Excellency, but I know who he is," the peasant conceded.

"Locate him and return here with him at once. Have you a horse?"

"I cannot afford a horse, Excellency."

"In that case you will walk. Instruct your wife to prepare food for your journey and return here at once with *Capitán* Diego."

The *peón* could not conceal his dismay. "How long am I likely to be gone, *alcalde*? *Mi esposa* and *niños,* they rely on me."

The *alcalde* looked at him stonily. "I have no doubt that you are a dutiful husband, but your family is not my concern. Let us hope that your devil has no need of you, as you apparently fear. For, unless your faith protects you, your children are likely to find themselves fatherless. Now, go fetch *Capitán* Diego immediately!" He snapped his chin upward, dismissing the peasant.

Gomez bowed awkwardly and began shuffling backwards, toward the door, still clutching his crumpled hat.

THE TWO MEN PRESENTED THEMSELVES thirty-five minutes later. The seated *alcalde* wordlessly surveyed them from behind his carved desk as they stood rigidly before him. "*Capitán* Diego," the *alcalde* finally began, "I have instructed this *peón*," he casually flicked his fingers to indicate Gomez, "to guide you to the place where he recently encountered the miscreant who is responsible for the disappearance of several *peones*. You will find the trespasser and bring me his head, and you will not return until you have done so. Do you understand, *Capitán*?"

"*Si,* Excellency," Diego smartly acknowledged, his eyes focused straight ahead.

"The *peón*," continued the *alcalde*, "has displayed reluctance to assist you in this endeavor. Should you find his cooperation wanting, you will bind him and drag him behind your horse until his flesh hangs from his body in ribbons. You will thereupon sever the rope and leave his miserable carcass in the *desierto* as carrion for the vultures to feast on."

"*Si, entiendo.*"

"You will depart within the hour," the *alcalde* concluded, summarily returning his attention to a sheaf of documents on his desk.

CAPITAN DIEGO ALLOWED THE LUCKLESS peasant to climb aboard his horse and ride double once they were beyond Esperanza and the astringent gaze of the *alcalde*. His motivation was less compassionate than practical: with the peón leading the way on foot, it would take the patrol several hours to reach their destination and Diego was eager to complete their mission before nightfall. Behind him plodded a half-dozen liveried soldiers, resplendent in gaudy shakos and armed with gleaming swords and halberds.

"How far is this place?" he asked over his shoulder.

"Not far, *Capitán*. *Mi esposa* and myself walked there in one-half day and Maria, she is very fat and cannot walk fast. It is not far," Gomez reiterated.

The gold buttons and trim on the men's Imperial Blue woolen tunics glittered in the malevolent sunlight as it burned through the dusty atmosphere. Although originally white, their linen trousers were impossible to keep clean in the uncongenial environment. The absurdly stiff collars of their uniforms chafed their sweaty necks as the soldiers gently swayed in their creaking saddles.

Given the nature of its mission, the *alcalde* originally intended that the priest accompany the patrol into the desert. However, the cleric was nowhere to be found and the magistrate was determined to dispatch *Capitán* Diego with a minimum of delay. He would deal with the absentee priest later.

"I told his Excellency it was unwise to disturb the devil," the peasant confided from where he sat just forward of the horse's rump. "I fear we will both go home today by a road that we do not know," he mourned.

"Shut up!" *Capitán* Diego barked. "If you fail to return to the arms of your fat wife and jabbering children it will only be because I flung you from my horse after growing weary of listening to you whine like a contemptible woman! Let the wolves eat you, for all I care! His Excellency the *alcalde* will congratulate me for getting rid of you." The peasant lapsed into chastened silence and the column pressed resolutely onward.

They drew near the place two hours later.

"It is just over the next ridge, *Capitán*," the peón advised. "But I must make water; I am not used to bouncing on the back of an animal."

Diego motioned the patrol to a weary halt. "Do not make us wait," he cautioned.

The peasant slid from the back of the horse. The moment his sandaled feet touched the baked earth, he spun and dashed into the desert, his listless escorts taken completely by surprise. The startled soldiers initially gawked at one another, then at *Capitán* Diego, with indecision.

"Shall I pursue him?" one of them finally asked as, from atop their mounts, they idly observed the peasant's frantic exodus.

"No, spare your animals." Diego grunted. "The *peón* is of no further use. The *alcalde* will have him executed if he dares return to the *pueblo,* and he will die soon enough if he remains in the *desierto* without water. Either way, it is as one to us." The soldier nodded his acquiescence. "Our destination lies beyond that ridge," the Capitán continued, pointing. Tugging his horse's reins, he clucked his tongue and the patrol resumed its vapid expedition.

THE SITE WAS UNREMARKABLE: the cracked foundations of a few long-vanished buildings, some piles of rocks, a scattering of squared stones, the melting vestiges of adobe walls, an array of large holes bored into the rocky soil.

Diego surveyed the area from the saddle, seeing nothing.

"What are we looking for, *Capitán*?" one of the men ventured.

"The *peón* says he encountered someone living here who has been carrying off *peones* from the *pueblo*. The *alcalde* has ordered us to see that it stops."

The perplexed soldier looked around. "'Here' where, *Capitán*? There is nothing here."

"Barbosa! Maldonado! Lopez! Rodriguez!" Diego barked, swiveling his head around. "Ride around the perimeter and see if you can find anything alive around here. Medina and Ruiz will remain with me."

"What are we looking for, *Capitán*?" Lopez inquired.

"Anyone or anything that is not us," the Capitán responded. "Slay and bring to me whatever you encounter."

"What if there is nothing?"

Diego shrugged. "Then it will not matter."

The men spurred their horses toward the periphery of the decrepit settlement as Diego and the other two soldiers dismounted. They secured their mounts to a bedraggled mesquite tree growing through a crack in a low stone wall and proceeded to wander the site.

"Who built this place, *Capitán*?" one of them asked as he poked about.

Diego dragged a bandana from his trouser pocket and began mopping his face with it. "*Quién sabe*? *Colonos, ganaderos, refugiados.* I care only that we find who we're looking for and return to the *pueblo* before nightfall." He squinted into the cloudless sky, toward the blistering sun.

"It has not been inhabited for a long time," Ruiz observed.

"Not according to the *peón*," Diego snorted. "He said a *monstruo* lives here!" He jammed the bandana back into his pocket.

"A *monstruo*? Why would even a *monstruo* want to live out here? There is no water, no shade, no *nada*."

Medina's shout interrupted the Capitán's response.

"*Capitán!*" Medina yelled. "Come look at this!"

Diego and Ruiz hastened across the broken ground.

Medina pointed. "*Allá está.*"

Yawning in the earth before them was a large vertical shaft. The fetor of rotting meat wafted from its mephitic interior.

"It smells like whoever lived here fell down there and died," Medina opined, wrinkling his nose.

Diego nodded. "Perhaps." He bent close to the ground and examined the earth surrounding the mouth of the shaft. Plucking something from the soil, he straightened and held it aloft in the brilliant sunlight. "The *peón* claimed that whatever lived here had legs like a goat's," he said as he scrutinized the substance. He handed it to Ruiz, who unconsciously frowned as he peered at it. Diego squatted and carefully examined the entire circumference of the hole. "There is an abundance of the same material here," he announced.

"It looks like wool or hair," Ruiz concluded after a moment. I suppose it *could* have come from a goat, *Capitán*. Do you think the animal tumbled down this hole and perished?" He transferred the object to Medina, who wordlessly inspected it.

"The *peón* said that it only *looked* like a goat, but that it was a small human," Diego responded. He backed away from the noxious hole, followed by Ruiz and Medina. "Even if this stench *does* come from an animal, there is too much of it to have come from only a single goat tumbling into the shaft. Either an entire herd of goats fell in, or single animals fell in over a period of time."

Ruiz was perplexed. "*All* of them fell in, *Capitán?* And if, as the *peón* said, the inhabitant was a human and not a goat, what sort of human has furry legs like that?" He glanced at Medina, who merely shrugged. Diego didn't respond either. Additional speculation was necessarily postponed by the return of the remaining four soldiers, who trotted over in a haze of dust.

"We saw nothing and no one, *Capitán,*" Lopez announced from the saddle. "The place is deserted. It does not look like anyone has been here for a long time and the soil is too hard to preserve any tracks." All of the mounted men struggled to maintain control over their agitated horses, which inexplicably reared and plunged.

Diego nodded. "That may be. But if we do not present the *alcalde* with tangible proof of success, he will be angry," he warned. "The *alcalde* is convinced that someone here has been abducting the *peones.* If he is not provided confirmation, we will all suffer for it."

"Confirmation? What 'confirmation' does the *alcalde* expect us to provide?" Medina challenged, the angst in his voice palpable.

Diego looked gravely at each of the men in turn. "The *alcalde* demands that we return with the miscreant's head, a task obviously impossible if this place is uninhabited."

"His head? There is no head to provide the *alcalde*! We cannot produce a head out of nothing! The *alcalde* must understand that we are blameless."

The Capitán turned to face Medina, who had last spoken. "The *alcalde* understands only that his orders are to be obeyed."

"I know where a head may be found," Barbosa quietly interjected. The men turned their attention to him. "There is a small village of *Indios* not far from the *pueblo*," he continued. "They live in secrecy because they fear violence if their existence became known. Each of them has a head, *Capitán*."

Diego smiled coldly. *"Muy bien.* One head is very much like another, no? Once we provide his Excellency the *Alcalde* with a head, we will have fully discharged our duty." He looked at Barbosa. "Where is this place with the *Indios?"*

"Not far. We can ride there, and return to the *pueblo,* before nightfall."

"Excelente. I do not like this place, anyway. It is *sobrenatural* and smells of death. Vá*monos, hombres!"*

Diego and the other two soldiers strode to their horses and, with the other men, spurred their mounts away from the ruin.

"YOU HAVE RETURNED ALREADY?" the *alcalde* barked with asperity. Although it was after 7:00 p.m. the temperature remained sweltering and the ambient sunlight stubbornly refused to dwindle. Diego presented himself at his superior's private apartments immediately after the patrol's return to Esperanza, where the *alcalde* had previously retired, shed his uncomfortable tunic, and placed damp cloths over his face in a fruitless effort to cool off. He was displeased by the *Capitán's* intrusion.

"*Si,* Excellency. The *peón* led us directly to the place and we located it without difficulty."

"And what did you find there, *Capitán?"*

"It was exactly as the *peón* described it."

"How so?

"*Ruinas* of an age impossible to determine, but very old."

"They were inhabited?"

"*Si*, Excellency, but are no longer."

The *alcalde* smiled coldly. "Show me."

Diego turned smartly aside to allow his superior to brush past. The *alcalde* stepped from the comparative dimness of his room into the fiery air of the late evening, where the *Capitán's* men huddled near their horses on the opposite side of the plaza. They snapped to attention when they saw the *alcalde* emerge, trailed by Diego.

"*Ruiz!*" the Capitán yelled. "Show his Excellency what gifts we bear!"

One of the soldiers hastened to his horse, where he untied a large bundle swathed in canvas; it tumbled to the ground with an audible thud and he stepped away to rejoin his companions, who remained chiseled in place, their eyes fixed straight ahead.

The *alcalde* and Diego approached the wrapped bundle. "Open it, *Capitán*," he ordered.

Diego bent and flipped back the dusty canvas to reveal two human heads, their cropped black hair matted with blood. Fragments of spine protruded from the stump of necks that had been crudely chopped with a *machete*. Although it was impossible to ascertain either the age or genders of the grisly remains, one was appreciably smaller than the other.

The *alcalde* looked dubiously at Diego. "The *peón* spoke of only one inhabitant, *Capitán*."

"*Si*, Excellency. This one was an unexpected boon." He nudged one of the lifeless heads with the side of his boot. "We were confident you would be gratified to recover these two villains." Diego and his men had previously decided to return to Esperanza with two heads, rather than one, as a demonstration of their diligence and in hopes of currying favor with the magistrate.

The *alcalde* scrutinized the gruesome display with more than casual interest. "They look like nothing more than *Indios,*" he remarked. "The *peón* confirmed these are the creatures he encountered?"

"*Si, señor.*"

"Where is the *peón*? I wish to talk with him."

"The *peón* fled into the desert when the creatures attacked us, Excellency," Diego smoothly responded. "He was frightened out of his wits. Had my men not stood firm against the creatures, I fear they, too, would have perished." He gravely crossed himself.

"Indeed? You did well, *Capitán,*" the *alcalde* finally concluded, turning away. "Inform me should the *peón* return to the *pueblo*. And dispose of those."

"*Si,* Excellency." Diego could scarcely believe that his subterfuge had succeeded so effortlessly.

The *alcalde* hastened back to his apartments without looking back, eager to get out of the ferocious heat.

The predations continued.

SIXTEEN

AFTER CRESTING THE HILL, Cameron's friends, Harry, Leonard, Sam, and Phil parked their vehicles in an open circle before clambering out to stretch large blue plastic tarps between them in an attempt to provide a shady respite from the blazing March sun. Sam lowered the tailgate of his pickup truck and dragged a cooler full of sodas, beer, and bottled water from the bed as Phil began setting up a propane stove and some collapsible lawn chairs. Notwithstanding that sunrise had occurred scarcely an hour before, it was already rapidly approaching 85 degrees.

"We'll be here when you get back," Harry assured Cameron as the rest of the group piled out. "Don't worry about us. Phil's gonna cook up some breakfast, and a mess of ribs for lunch. If anything tries to screw with us, we'll put a few lumps on their head."

"Damn straight," Sam agreed, twisting the cap off a bottle of orange juice.

"Hey, where was your Jeep parked when they trashed it?" Leonard called from the rim of the plateau.

Cameron ambled over. "There," he indicated, pointing. While the others availed themselves of the marginal shade provided by the tarps, Moe walked over and joined the two men.

"And where'd they disappear to?" asked Leonard.

"When they saw me, they stepped away from my Jeep and just started walking through the desert. Aside from the general weirdness, they acted like they were sleepwalking."

"So what finally happened to 'em?"

"I think they went down an old mine shaft," Cameron replied, realizing how improbable that must have sounded.

"You didn't take a picture of 'em with your cell phone?" Leonard probed, skeptically.

"It wouldn't have mattered because phones don't work out here, not even cameras. Besides, I was so freaked out that I never even thought about it 'till it was over," Cameron explained.

"Yep, I'd probably have freaked, too," Leonard admitted. "I think I would have probably peed my pants if I'd seen those guys!" Cameron and Moe grinned, perhaps more out of nervousness than amusement.

"Hey!" Nancy called from the vicinity of the parked vehicles. "We're gonna bag the whole thing and hang around for bacon and eggs unless you two are ready to head out."

Although Phil intended to prepare breakfast at the base camp, Moe, Cameron, Nancy, and the others participating in the séance had breakfasted more than two hours earlier. They met at a coffee shop at 5:00 that morning before returning to Cameron's apartment, where they rendezvoused with Harry and his friends. Aside from Moe and Nancy, Cameron managed to cajole three others into participating in the Esperanza séance, though it hadn't been an easy sell. In addition, he'd prevailed upon Harry, Leonard, Sam, and Phil to ferry them out to the desert and act as guards. After discussing it with the detective, Cameron decided not to mention to anyone the recent event involving Daisy's body. Although he felt guilty about his lack of candor, Cameron feared that, if he spoke of the incident, it would have proven impossible to recruit anyone for the séance. Moe also kept silent about the face he observed in the mirror which, thankfully, hadn't returned.

"On our way," Cameron called. He stepped away from the edge and began walking back toward the group.

In addition to food, water, and a bottle of salt tablets, the backpacks assigned to each séance participant held a whistle, Band Aids, a signaling mirror, a point-and-shoot camera, a small wooden crucifix, a pocket-sized New Testament, a flashlight with extra batteries, a small roll of paper towels, a knife, a bandana, and a walkie-talkie. Those that felt comfortable with them were also invited to carry firearms, if only for protection against snakes. Cameron was gratified that all of them had complied, including Nancy, whose beat-up .38 Special revolver was in her pack. Harry and his friends were armed with even greater potency: distributed among them were two 12-gauge shotguns, several .45 caliber automatic pistols, at least three aluminum baseball bats, and a flare gun. "If you're gonna be a bear, be a grizzly," shrugged Sam. Everyone wore stout hiking boots, a hat, and had slathered themselves with sunscreen.

"Okay, here's the deal," Cameron called out to the throng upon reaching the vehicles. "Everybody that's heading down into the valley for the séance, grab your packs from the back of Leonard's Jeep. Double check your packs to make sure that everything's that supposed to be in 'em is there before you put 'em on and clip your walkie-talkies to the outside of your pack, or put 'em in a front pocket, so you can get to 'em in a hurry." He turned to Harry. "We'll be using channel two so you'll be able to monitor us the whole time we're gone. If you pick up anything that doesn't sound right, call the county sheriff."

Harry nodded. "Yeah, we'll call the sheriff, then me and the boys," he nodded toward his companions, "will jump in Leonard's Jeep and bust a gut getting' down there to you. You just hang on 'till we get there, 'cause the cavalry's comin'...you can bet your life on it."

Both Cameron and Moe grinned, which relieved some of the tension they both felt.

"There's a big pile of dirt and rocks blocking the trail from a cave-in," Moe informed Harry. "I don't think even a Jeep could climb it."

Phil wandered over to listen to their conversation, handing bottles of cold water to Cameron, Moe, and Harry.

"Leonard's Jeep can climb a glass wall," Harry said, taking a swig of water. "Don't worry about it. You just worry about doing what you have to do and getting your butts outta there before nightfall. We'll be here waiting." He took another sip of water. "And like I said earlier, if anything tries to mess with you *or* us, we'll put the hurt on their ass." He and Phil touched water bottles in an impromptu toast.

Moe took a drink of water. It was icy cold and it tasted like heaven.

"I figure it'll take us a couple of hours to get down there, an hour or so for the séance, then a couple of hours to get back here...five, six hours at the outside," Cameron said.

Phil looked at his watch. It's just after 7:00 now, so you figure on being back by around 2:00?

Cameron sipped his water and nodded. "Yeah, thereabouts."

"What if we're not?" Moe asked. "What do you want to do if, for whatever reason, we're not back when we're supposed to be?"

Cameron reflected a moment before responding. "Our radios will be on the whole time, so you'll be able to hear what's going on," he repeated to Harry. "If something happens, or somebody gets hurt, you'll know right away. But use your discretion about calling the cops," he cautioned. "They charge out the wazoo for rescues and I don't want to call them unless it's pretty much life or death. Otherwise, like you said, you guys can come get us in the Jeep." Leonard and Phil nodded. "But I don't think anything's gonna happen," he hastily added.

"So how long should we wait before we send in the cavalry?" Phil asked.

Cameron looked searchingly at the detective, who volunteered the answer. "If we're not back by 5:00 and you don't hear from us before then, come get us."

"Done," Harry acknowledged. "If things start popping down there, all ya gotta do is give us a yell on the radio. We'll be off faster than a prom dress."

Nancy, wearing her backpack, approached the conversing men. "Everybody's ready to go, guys. We need to get started before it gets any hotter." Cameron and Moe nodded. The men shook hands then rejoined the rest of the group. Aside from the nucleus comprised of Cameron, Nancy, and Moe, the other members of the team were Tina, Andres, and Darlene.

"Everybody buddy-up and stay within sight of everybody else," Moe instructed them. "If you have a problem, or even *think* you may have a problem, yell for help or get on the radio. We'll stop to rest periodically on the way down but, if you need to stop before then, just holler out." Everyone nodded. "Well, I guess that's about it," he concluded, looking at Cameron.

"I'll buddy with you, Woody, if you don't mind getting stuck with me," Nancy volunteered.

The detective grinned. "I was hoping you'd say that."

Cameron partnered with Darlene, Andres with Tina and, after checking their counterpart's backpack to insure that everything was in order, the group began plodding down the trail toward Esperanza. The scent of frying bacon wafted into the morning air as, behind them, Harry and his companions unconcernedly laughed and joked while Pete cooked breakfast.

THE INITIAL STAGE OF THE hike proceeded without incident, until the party encountered the enormous pile of earth and debris that intersected the path. Moe, Nancy, Cameron, and Darlene carefully picked their way up the impediment where, drenched in perspiration, they awaited Andres and Tina atop its broken crest. Nancy reached into Moe's backpack, removed a bottle of water, and took a deep swallow before handing it to the detective.

"I can't believe how hot it already is," she grumbled. She wiped her sweaty forehead using the sleeve of her shirt.

From the top, Cameron called down to Andres and Tina. "Who's next?"

"I guess I'll go," Tina said, without enthusiasm. "Grab me if I come flying down on my ass," she instructed Andres.

"That's cool, but who'll grab me when it's *my* turn," he grinned.

Jagged boulders of various sizes comprised the bulk of the earthen barricade. Tina cautiously placed a booted foot on its rocky surface to undertake its tentative ascent.

The abundance of loose rock covering its surface, coupled with the steepness of the incline, rendered direct ascent of the pile impossible. Where snapped tree limbs and dead brush protruded from the heap, Tina leaned forward and grasped them in an effort to steady herself as she climbed. "So far, so good," Andres assured her from his position at the foot of the heap as she slowly began zigzagging her way upward.

Slightly less than half-way up the mound, Tina stumbled when the toe of her boot snagged the sharp edge of a boulder half-buried in the soil. A shower of dirt and rocks cascaded downward as she floundered, seeking to regain her balance. Instinctively, Tina grabbed a piece of desiccated wood that jutted from the rocky surface of the mound.

"Whoa! Are you okay?" Cameron cried in alarm from the summit.

The branch that Tina grasped wasn't anchored to the soil and simply pulled free as she attempted to right herself. Tina became overbalanced and tumbled onto the rocks, her struggle producing an avalanche of debris that surged down the face of the mound.

"Ow! Dammit!" she groaned.

"You okay?" Andres anxiously called from below.

"Not really," Tina grumbled, unsuccessfully struggling to regain her feet. "I cut my hand trying to break my fall, and twisted my knee." She smiled ruefully. "Worse, I tore the crap out of my new pants."

"Wait there. Don't move," Andres said. "I'll come up there. Just stay put." He began clambering up the mound. From its summit, Moe and Cameron began descending toward Tina.

Fearing their approach might dislodge an entire section of the pile that would surge downward, burying her, Tina craned her neck upward. "I think it would be better if just one of you came!" she yelled. She gestured in a sweeping motion with her hand. "It's not stable and the whole damned thing is liable to start sliding. You guys stay up there; Andres can help me."

Cameron and the detective retreated to the top of the mound where, with the other two, they apprehensively watched Andres slowly crab his way toward Tina.

"Everything's gonna be all right," Nancy called to Tina. "You doin' okay?"

"Yeah, I'm okay," Tina sighed. "Except for my hand, knee, and pants. Oh, yeah, and my dignity," she added as an afterthought. Wincing, she attempted to shift her awkward sitting position, thereby dislodging more soil that slithered down the face of the mound toward Andres.

"Dammit, sit still!" he ordered. Chastened, Tina eased back onto the unstable ground. After a few minutes of delicate climbing, Andres reached her and planted his feet on the sloping surface to steady himself.

"Okay, hang onto me," he instructed Tina, extending his hand.

Tina reached up and grasped Andres' wrist. He wrapped his fingers around her wrist and braced himself as she awkwardly struggled to her feet, initially using her free hand to push against the face of the stony heap.   Rocks slid from beneath their shaky foothold and bounced to the foot of the mound.

"Ouch!" Tina yelped when she attempted to put weight on her leg. She'd torn the knee of her jeans when she fell and a small spot of blood seeped onto the fabric. Andres continued to firmly grip her arm.

"You guys okay?" Nancy called down to them.

Tina swiveled her head upward. "Not really. I think I did something to my knee. But look at my pants!" she said with disgust.

"Are you able to walk, Tina?" Cameron asked.

She shook her head. "I don't think so, Cam. I can't put any weight on my knee."   She cautiously attempted to take a step, wincing in pain.

"Crap," Cameron muttered beneath his breath.

"Can you make it back to the vehicle?" Nancy asked.

"Crap," Cameron repeated.

"So what are we gonna do?" Nancy softly asked him, hoping Tina wouldn't hear. "If she can't walk, she can't make it back to the vehicles. And she obviously won't be able to hike the rest of the way down into the valley with us."

"Do you think those guys could drive one of the Jeeps down here and retrieve her?" Cameron suggested.

Nancy looked dubious. "I don't know, Cam. The trail is pretty narrow. I'm not even sure a Jeep could get down here. Besides, we've barely even started and we're *already* gonna ask 'em to come rescue us?"

"I don't think we have a choice, Nance," Cameron responded. He glanced at the detective, who nodded.

Cameron peered over the lip of the mound, at Tina and Andres, who looked up at him expectantly. "Hang on; I'm gonna see if Harry can come get you." He unhooked his walkie-talkie from the strap of his backpack and pushed the 'send' button. Although a warbling call should have emanated from the unit, connecting him with the men at the trailhead, the radio was silent. Cameron checked to ensure the unit was switched on. It was.

"Dammit!" he grumbled. "Something's wrong with my radio...try yours." Nancy pulled her walkie-talkie from her shirt pocket and depressed the 'send' button. Dead. Perplexed, she clicked the on-off switch a couple of times and turned the volume to 'max.' She squinted at the unit's digital screen, shielding it from the sun's blinding rays with her hand. The screen was completely black.

"Mine's dead, too," she said, puzzled. "How is that possible? I checked it this morning before we started down and it worked fine. The batteries are brand new."

Moe and Darlene also tried their walkie-talkies, with the same futile result.

"What do you guys wanna do?" Andres yelled, somewhat impatiently, from below.

"Hang on, we're tryin' to figure it out," Cameron responded. "Do either of your walkie-talkies work? Ours just took a dump." While the others watched, Andres unsteadily pulled his radio from his pocket. He moved with deliberation in order to maintain his balance on the steep, uneven grade.

After fiddling with his walkie-talkie for over a minute, Andres frowned. "I guess mine must've taken a crap, too." He repeatedly slapped the recalcitrant device against the palm of his hand, as if to jar it into action, then scrutinized it. He looked at Tina. "Is yours working?"

Tina shifted her weight onto her uninjured knee and bent to remove her radio from the pocket of her cargo pants. She nearly fell when she straightened and frantically grabbed for Andres, sparking another landslide.

"You're okay," Andres reassured her, gripping Tina's arm. "Hand me your radio; it'll be easier for me because you can hardly stand up."

Still hanging onto Andres, Tina cautiously transferred her walkie-talkie to Andres with her other hand. "My knee hurts like hell," she confided.

Andres depressed the 'call' button on Tina's radio and held it close to his mouth. "Cam, can you hear me? Hello? Phil? Anybody?"

Nothing.

Andres craned his head upward and saw their four companions watching him intently over the edge of the mound. "Can you hear me on your radios?" he yelled to them, forgetting their radios were inoperative.

Cameron shook his head. "All our radios are dead. Can you get through to those guys?" He meant Phil or Harry back at camp.

Andres pushed the 'send' button again and repeated his greeting, with the same result: silence. He switched the radio off, then back on, and glanced at the small red light that glowed when the walkie-talkie powered up. It remained unlit. Frustrated, Andres rotated the switch again, with the same result.

"Did you check the batteries in this thing before we left?" he asked Tina.

"They're brand new," she told him.

Andres repeatedly turned Tina's walkie-talkie on and off, to no avail. "You're telling me that *everybody's* radio abruptly just stopped working? Really?" He vigorously shook the radio, not knowing what else to do. "Cheap Chinese junk," he muttered, handing it back to Tina.

"So now what are we gonna to do?" she asked. "My knee's swelling and I don't think I can walk on it. Do you just want to leave me here, while you guys go on ahead? Maybe it'll be better by the time you get back here."

"Are you kidding?" Andres scoffed. "We're not gonna leave you here! Are you nuts?" He looked upward, toward the crest of the mound. "Hey, Tina's radio's dead, too!" he hollered. "What the hell's going on?"

Though not entirely surprised at the revelation regarding Tina's walkie-talkie, Cameron was no less dismayed. He turned to the other three atop the mound. "Well, what do you think we should do? We can't get through to Harry so he can't drive down to retrieve Tina, even if the Jeep could make it this far. And Tina can't walk...now what?"

"I don't like this place," Nancy responded. "I don't know about you guys, but if we bag it today, I don't intend to come back."

"We can't just leave Tina behind," Darlene, short, plump, with bobbed blonde hair, added. Her pale skin was already becoming flushed from the heat and the exertion of hiking.

Moe listened thoughtfully before speaking. "It seems to me that we can either pull the plug right now and head back to the truck, or go forward as planned," he eventually said. "If we pull the plug, though, it may be impossible to get everybody back together in the future." He nodded toward Nancy. "And, of course, we're already here. But if we go ahead, we'll have to do so without Tina and somebody's gonna have to stay behind with her until we come back later today. Between all of us, we'll be able to help her back to camp, even if we have to carry her." He paused. "I don't know any other way of looking at it and I'm prepared to defer to whatever everybody else wants to do."

No one spoke for a moment. Although the changed circumstances now rendered them ambivalent about continuing the hike to Esperanza, Nancy and Darlene feared ridicule if either volunteered to stay behind with Tina, notwithstanding their suspicion that none of the men was likely to do so. They glanced at one another uneasily, loathe to break the awkward silence.

"I think we should ask Tina what she wants to do," Nancy advised.

"What the hell's happening up there? Did you guys doze off?" Andres testily shouted from below.

"If Tina can't walk, I guess I'll stay with her until you guys get back," Darlene finally offered. She stepped to the edge of the mound, followed by Moe, Cameron, and Nancy. "Tina, can you walk well enough to climb back down from there?" she called.

Tina grasped Andres' shoulder and tested her knee by putting weight on it. "It hurts like hell," she responded, wincing, "but I obviously can't just stand here the rest of the day. What do you guys want to do?"

"If you can make it to the bottom, into some shade, Darlene said she'd stay with you while we go on," Moe yelled. "Are you okay with that?"

"I don't need a babysitter," Tina retorted. "I'll hobble back down by myself. By the time you guys get back, my knee will probably be okay."

"No, we don't want you to be alone, Tina," Nancy responded. "If you don't want somebody to wait with you, then we'll just bag the whole thing and get you back to camp right now." She glanced at Cameron and the detective, who both nodded in affirmation.

Tina looked at Andres. "What do you think I should do? What do *you* want to do?"

"It's up to you," he said. "Nobody will resent it if you can't go on. But Nancy's right: it's not safe to be out here by yourself with no radio."

"Well, we've come this far and it doesn't make sense to deep-six the whole thing now," Tina said. She looked up the slope at the four faces peering down at them. "If Darlene wants to stay behind, okay. But it's not necessary and I'll feel guilty about it."

"Don't," Darlene interjected. "I wouldn't volunteer if I didn't want to." In truth, she was far from crestfallen to have escaped the strenuous hike farther into the valley, but concealed her relief. "Have Andres help you back down. I'll climb down once you reach the bottom, so that any rocks I dislodge won't bounce into you." Darlene stepped away from the edge.

"Both of you have guns, right?" Moe confirmed.

"I have a .22 pistol in my pack and I think Tina brought one, too," Darlene assured him. "But I'm more worried about heatstroke than snakes."

Moe didn't tell her that neither snakes nor heatstroke were his primary concerns.

"And plenty of water?"

Darlene smiled indulgently. "Yes, plenty of water. Stop worrying, will ya?"

Below them, Tina held onto Andres as they gingerly began to retrace their way down to ground level.

"I feel so stupid," Tina rued as they scrabbled across the face of the mound. "I've ruined it for everybody."

"Don't be a dope," Andres dismissively responded. "You didn't ruin anything. As long as you're cool just hanging with Darlene until we get back, everything's going as planned. I just feel bad about your knee."

"*You* feel bad," Tina laughed humorlessly. She slid on some loose rocks and had to catch herself. "Dammit! That hurt!"

Andres paused to allow Tina to regain solid footing. "We'll put some ice on your knee once we get back to camp. Just sit in the shade and stay off it until then." Tina bit her lip, waiting for the pain to subside, before continuing their downward trek.

From the summit of the mound, Nancy, Cameron, Moe, and Darlene monitored their descent.

"You guys doin' okay?" Nancy anxiously called down to them.

"Yeah, everything's good," Tina responded with forced buoyancy, though her voice quivered with pain. "Just tweaked my knee...gimme a minute." Andres continued to firmly support Tina until she was able to continue. She took a deep breath. "Okay, I'm good."

"You sure?" Andres probed. "Don't hurry, Tina. We've got as much time as you need."

She shook her head. "No, I'm okay. I've held everybody up long enough already. I'll be better once I get on level ground and can prop my knee on my pack. I just need to get weight off it."

"Well, we're almost there," Andres affirmed. He twisted his neck upward and saw the others watching them attentively from atop the mound. "Darlene!" he yelled. "Start down; we're almost to the bottom!"

"If Tina's able to walk, head back to camp if you think you can make it," Moe instructed Darlene before she departed. "Just don't push it. If she can't walk, fine. Just find some shade and wait for us. And keep trying your radios because they may start working." Although the detective believed that an impossibility, he felt compelled to tender the advice.

"Okay, dad," Darlene chuckled. "We'll be fine. Don't worry." She adjusted the weight of her backpack on her shoulders, trying to minimize chafing from its straps, before cautiously stepping over the edge of the mound to retrace her steps groundward.

"We should be back here in no more than about four hours," Nancy said as Darlene's boots immediately began sliding on the loose scree.

"We'll be here," Darlene assured her, trying to concentrate on not duplicating Tina's mishap. Hoping to maintain her balance, she instinctively tilted her body from side to side as she delicately picked her way down the unstable surface. Andres and Tina watched her descent from the mound's base, the latter trying to keep weight off her knee by leaning on Andres. She could already feel her knee growing stiff and she dreaded attempting to walk on it.

Darlene sprightly hopped the last couple of feet from the mound onto level ground after a five-minute descent. "I'll take over from here," she smiled, taking Tina's arm. "Can you walk at all?" she asked as Tina steadied herself.

Tina gingerly tested her knee. "I don't think so...it hurts too much to put weight on it. I feel like such an idiot."

"Sush!" Darlene scolded her. "They're gonna go on and do their thing," she continued, referring to Moe, Nancy, and the rest of their party, "while you and I wait here, in the shade, until they come to get us."

"Everything okay?" Cameron called to them from atop of the mound, eager to resume the trek to Esperanza.

"Yeah, we're fine," Darlene waved to him with perhaps too much enthusiasm. She glanced around. "C'mon, Tina, lean on me and we'll head toward that mesquite tree and some shade." Andres stepped clumsily aside as Darlene wrapped her arm around Tina's waist and began to half-drag her toward the comparative oasis.

"You'll be okay here..." Andres' voice trailed off as the two women limped away from him. It was unclear whether he was asking a question or making a statement.

"We're fine," Darlene assured him over her shoulder. "But you'd better get movin' before Cam has a cow." Andres nodded, ambled to the base of the rocky hill, and began clambering upward.

Cameron turned to the others on the summit of the mound. "I have no idea why the radios quit working but, hopefully, we won't need 'em."

"They quit working because this place is messed up," Nancy grimly responded.

"I don't like it, either," Moe concurred. "Especially since it's now down to only four of us."

"So what do you want to do?" Cameron sighed. "Pull the plug on it? We can still have the séance with only four people but, if you guys don't want to go ahead with it, I guess that's it." He looked at them expectantly and shrugged. Nancy glanced at the pensive detective.

"I'm still willing to go forward if Nancy is," Moe finally responded. "Frankly, the most worrisome thing for me is having to leave Tina and Darlene behind. I don't like that one bit," he emphatically concluded. In the background, they could hear Andres grunting and swearing as he noisily fought his way up the mound.

"I agree," Nancy concurred. "But if we just pack up and leave now, what was the point in coming in the first place? I mean, we're already here; let's just get it done and get out of here." The detective nodded in agreement just as Andres scrabbled over the rim of the mound.

"Damn! Who piled all this up?" Andres gasped, out of breath, as he stumbled toward them across its summit. He paused to look around, unhooked a leather *bota* from his belt, and gulped water from it. "It can't be mine tailings because there aren't any mines around here big enough to produce this much debris. Somebody actually had to *pile* all this crap here." Andres' khaki baseball cap was soaked with perspiration.

"That's what we wondered the first time we were here, too," Cameron replied.

"In case you haven't already noticed, this whole place is weirded out," Nancy added. "But you ain't seen nuthin' yet."

Moe walked quietly to the edge of the mound to check the status of Tina and Darlene. The two women had removed their backpacks and were sitting on the ground about fifty yards from the base of the mound in the sparse shade afforded by a ragged mesquite tree. Tina elevated her bruised knee by placing it on her pack.

"You two okay?" the detective hollered down to them.

Darlene grinned up at him. "Yep, we're fine. You guys gonna go ahead?"

"Yeah, it looks that way," Moe responded. "You got plenty of water?"

"We're good," Darlene assured him. "Don't worry about us. But Tina's knee is really swollen and I don't think we should try to hike back to the vehicles by ourselves. We'll just wait here for you guys. Between all of us, we'll be able to get her back."

"As long as you're okay with that, we'll see you this afternoon," Moe said. "You guys be safe until we get back."

"We're cool here. You guys just be safe and don't do what I did," Tina groused, looking at her contused knee.

SEVENTEEN

HE DIDN'T EVEN REALIZE that he'd been dozing until Mouse's screaming woke him with a start. Momentarily disoriented, Bill jumped to his feet, flinging to earth the saddle blanket he'd previously wrapped around himself. His eyes darted about in the darkness as he attempted to orient himself.

Bill must have been sleeping for an appreciable period of time because, although it was still night, the campfire that lay between he and Ham had been reduced to glowing ash. Icy light from the myriad stars overhead pierced the blackness notwithstanding that the moon had disappeared from the firmament.

Mouse was nowhere to be seen though, receding into the distance, Bill could hear the fading sound of the animal's pounding hooves.

"Mouse!" Bill hollered into the darkness. His plaintive cry was greeted with crushing silence, unbroken even by Ham's snoring.

Bill shivered. Only now did he become aware of the faint scent of decaying meat that floated in the air. He regretted leaving the Winchester with Ham on the opposite side of the dying campfire. The hair on the back of his neck began to prickle as he took a tentative step forward.

"Ham," he hissed. "Wake up!"

Ham didn't respond.

"Ham, goddamn it, wake up! You smell that?" Bill stood rigid, straining his eyes into the darkness. He was relieved when rustling sounds began to emanate from the gloom, hinting that Ham was finally stirring.

"Mouse runned off," Bill continued, uneasily. "I don't know what spooked him, but we better stoke up the damned fire. It's darker than the inside of a black cat."

He squatted, snapped a piece of dry wood, and used it to stir the smoldering embers. A plume of crackling sparks soared into the night sky. Bill reached over, gathered a handful sticks, and tossed them onto the struggling fire. He watched as, after a moment, thin tendrils of flame began to lick the wood. He glanced across the growing blaze, toward Ham.

The trunk of his companion's body was propped against Mouse's saddle, legs extended outward in the dirt. Ham's lifeless hands were cupped around his head, which had been placed in his lap, facing outward. Gouts of sticky blood had soaked both Ham's clothing and the saddle against which he slumped, forming a muddy patch in the earth surrounding his body. The Winchester lay across his knees.

"Fuck me!" Bill cried, leaping to his feet. He looked frantically about for the perpetrator of the gory display. Shocked and panicked, he rapidly began to add additional wood to the burgeoning campfire in order to provide greater illumination.

"Who done that to you, pard?" he groaned as he broke the brittle, desiccated branches over his knee and fed them into the flames.

Tendrils of orange flame devoured the fuel as the fire blazed to life, the resulting heat forcing Bill to quickly retreat into the shadows. He scanned the expanded area revealed by the flames but saw nothing that could account for the ghastly injury done to his friend. Though his eyes didn't linger on Ham's disfigured corpse, he knew he had to retrieve the Winchester from Ham's body. Bill feared that whoever invaded their camp and decapitated Ham was probably still nearby, watching.

Taking care to keep to the shadows beyond the perimeter of the firelight, Bill edged toward Ham's slumped body. He hunkered down as he crept, attempting to suppress his ragged breathing so as not to betray his position. When he drew near Ham, he paused and surveyed the area before stepping into the firelight to secure the rifle.

"Your friend's braggadocio seems to have abandoned him," rasped a familiar wheedling voice from nearby in the darkness. Bill's head whipped around in the direction of the sound. He craved to have Ham's Winchester in his hands at that moment.

"You done that to Ham?" Bill demanded, though his bravado was tinged with perceptible fear. He strained his eyes into the desert night, hoping to fix the creature's location, his heart hammering in his chest.   Seeing nothing, Bill reluctantly glanced toward Ham's body.

Curdled streams of blood that previously flowed down the stump of Ham's denuded neck, still sticky in the night air, glistened in the firelight. Notwithstanding that his head rested in his lap, Ham could otherwise have simply been sleeping. As Bill watched in amazement, however, Ham's eyelids gently fluttered. His eyes, gleaming in the half-light, slowly opened and his lips began to quiver.

"Ah, your garrulous friend wishes to speak," the minatory voice taunted from the gloom. "But you must listen closely if you wish to profit from his advice. Do not be afraid to approach him. I assure you that you have nothing to fear. Had it been my desire to harm you, you would already have shared the fate of your unfortunate friend."

His heart pounding, Bill slowly emerged from the shadows. He looked furtively about before approaching Ham, but Moloch remained invisible.

"Don't you try and sneak up on me, you bastard," he warned.

The creature responded with cackling laughter. "And what will you do to prevent me?"

Bill ignored the challenge. He stepped warily toward Ham, whose dead eyes appeared to follow him. He squatted on the ground two feet from the corpse and, to steady himself, hesitantly grasped the rifle that lay across Ham's knees. Leaning forward slightly, he placed his ear near Ham's trembling lips.

"Run," the head whispered.

THE REMAINER OF THE HIKE into the heart of the valley was uneventful and, just over an hour after separating from Tina and Darlene, the group approached the disintegrating corral.

"I gotta sit down a minute," Andres panted as he unshouldered his pack and unceremoniously flopped down onto the scorching earth in the marginal shade cast by a spindly creosote bush. He uncorked his *bota* and took a long draught of warm water. "I can pee colder than this. I thought *botas* were supposed to keep stuff cool," he scowled.

Moe slouched against a wooden fence post that was in danger of falling completely over. He knew better than to sit on the bare ground, where the surface temperature was often twenty degrees hotter than the ambient air. "Did you soak it before you filled it?" he asked. "You're supposed to soak a *bota* before you use it; they cool by evaporation."

"I didn't know that," Andres admitted. "It didn't come with directions. I just thought it looked cool," he shrugged.

Nancy and Cameron walked toward the corral. She rotated the switch on her walkie-talkie to the 'on' position, hoping to contact either Darlene or the base camp, but the radio remained inoperable. Nancy's sunglasses repeatedly slipped down the bridge of her sweaty nose as she squinted at her radio in the brilliant sunlight. "Try yours," she finally urged Cameron in frustration, pushing her sunglasses back into place. He had no better luck. The detective also switched his radio on and off repeatedly, but to no avail.

"This makes me really mad," Nancy muttered. "How is it possible that the atmosphere, or whatever, just sucks the juice out of brand new batteries? Andres," she called to their seated companion, "try your radio. None of ours are working."

Andres shifted his position and pulled his walkie-talkie from his pants pocket. He switched it on. Nothing. "Nope," he announced. He returned the radio to his pocket and withdrew a granola bar. "I'm thinkin' the whole lot of batteries must've been bad." He finished the snack in three bites, jammed the wadded-up wrapper into his backpack, and climbed to his feet. "Let's get moving; it's hotter than hell out here." He hoisted his pack onto his back and trudged over to the other three.

"If the batteries all came from the same lot and were all bad, how come they worked okay earlier this morning, when we tested them at camp?" Nancy asked him pointedly.

Andres shrugged. "Beats the hell outta me," he said. "I'm a salesman, not an engineer. I suppose that, if they came from the same lot, it's possible they could all take a crap at the same time...what else could it be? There's no other explanation." He glanced over Nancy's shoulder. "Hey, is that a horse?" he asked, pointing to the brittle corpse lying inside the corral.

"It used to be," Nancy told him.

"Man, that's really sad," Andres said, shaking his head. "What the heck happened to it?"

"We don't know. It's been here a long time. Woody thinks it may have died of thirst." Nancy glanced at Moe, who remained impassive.

"God, that would be awful," Andres said. "Poor thing."

"We better get going," the detective finally spoke. "We don't want to leave Tina and Darlene any longer than we have to."

The foursome sipped water from their canteens and adjusted their backpacks before stepping single file onto the faint trail that led past the corral to Esperanza.

"WOW! CAMERON EXCLAIMED. Like Andres, he was seeing Esperanza for the first time, notwithstanding that, several months ago, he and Nancy were able to discern some of its buildings from several miles away.

The hamlet appeared unchanged from Nancy's previous visit. If anything, it looked even more derelict and forlorn. Nancy felt a chill pass over her when the narrow path widened into what passed as Esperanza's shabby main street.

"Does anybody live here?" Andres asked, gawking around.

"We're not sure," the detective responded. "Cam saw a light coming from here but, when Nancy and I were here before, we didn't see anybody."

"A light? From where?" Andres quizzically inquired.

"I couldn't tell," Cameron answered. "But I was thinking maybe it was Chet. That's why Woody and Nancy hiked down here in the first place."

Andres nodded. "Well, it looks pretty cool. It wouldn't surprise me if somebody lived here, a bunch of bikers or some kinda loony cult."

"If bikers lived here, I don't know how they'd get in and out," Moe replied. "They'd have to lift their bikes over that pile of crap back there."

"Yeah, I guess that's true," Andres acknowledged. "I didn't think of that. Still, it's hard to believe that nobody knows about this place."

"Where was the big house that you guys saw?" Cameron interjected.

"Clear at the other end of town," Nancy said, pointing.

Moe looked at his watch. "We've made pretty good time, but we'd better hit it. I don't know how long the séance will take but I don't want to hang around here any longer than necessary."

"It's after eleven," Cameron noted. "I think we should eat something now because we won't be able to interrupt the séance once we start." The other three nodded their assent. "Let's find some shade," he added.

The foursome tentatively entered the decaying settlement. They surveyed the crumbling structures that lined the dusty thoroughfare, seeking an area that provided a modicum of shelter from the blistering sun where they could rest and eat lunch.

"When was this place built?" Andres asked as they walked.

"Probably sometime in the mid-1800's," Cameron replied. "At least that's probably when people started settling here on a more-or-less permanent basis.

"You mean these buildings are nearly 150 years old?"

"Some of them probably are."

"So how come nobody comes here?" Andres asked. "It's like a museum."

Cameron smiled. "How long have you lived in Phoenix, Andres?"

"I was born here; you know that."

"Exactly. You were born here, yet had no idea this place was even here. Nobody comes here because they don't know it exits."

"So how did *you* find it?"

Cameron smiled. "It's a long story."

"There," Moe interrupted. "A place we can sit." He nodded toward a relatively intact, though roofless, adobe structure that resembled a bunker. The disintegrating remnants of a neighboring wooden building leaned haphazardly against its exterior wall, creating beneath it an attenuated patch of shade. "We'll have to sit on the ground, but at least it's out of the direct sun." They made their way toward the comparative oasis.

"Check for snakes," Nancy cautioned as they approached.

Cameron warily poked his head under the sagging boards and glanced about. "I don't see any," he announced over his shoulder.

"In that case, let's eat," Andres chirped. He ducked inside the makeshift lean-to and, using his foot, cleared a space to sit among the dry weeds. He unshouldered his pack and placed it on the ground, then sat next to it and leaned against the exterior wall of the adjacent adobe building. He looked at the others expectantly. "You guys gonna eat, or what? We're burnin' daylight," he grinned.

The detective and Cameron followed Andres beneath the shelter, with the unenthusiastic Nancy bringing up the rear. After arranging themselves in the sparse shade, they removed sandwiches from their backpacks and began eating.

"How long do you think the séance will take?" Andres asked between bites.

"Well, I've never actually done one," Cameron admitted. "But, based on what I've read, they usually take about an hour, maybe ninety minutes. Shouldn't take too long..." his voice trailed off.

Nancy flashed her eyes at Moe, who wordlessly returned her glance.

"You think you'll actually be able to contact Chet?" Andres probed. He fished a packet of trail mix from his pack and tore it open with his teeth.

"Well, that's the plan," Cameron said. "It's the only way I know to figure out what happened to him."

"So what are you actually gonna say, assuming that we're even able to contact him? 'Hey, Chet, what the hell happened to you?'"? Andres poured the trail mix into his mouth.

Cameron smiled thinly. "I honestly don't know. I guess I'll figure it out at the time."

Andres slowly nodded. "So, if you don't actually *see* Chet, how will you know that it's actually him you're talking to? Doesn't all kinds of weird shit happen at séances?"

"I think sometimes it does," Cameron guardedly conceded. "You have to ask 'control' questions in order to confirm the identity of whoever you're talking to." He took a last bite of sandwich and pulled a banana from his pack. "I brought a video camera and tripod to record everything."

Until that moment, Moe was unaware that Cameron intended to record the séance. He recalled the cassette recorder that nearly brained him during his previous excursion to Esperanza with Nancy and didn't relish getting clobbered with an even heavier video camera. "How are you going to make sure that no one gets clocked upside the head if that thing goes flying?" he asked.

Andres looked blankly at the detective, then at Cameron. "'Goes flying'? Is this something I should know about?"

"The last time Nancy and I were here, in fact the *only* other time we were here, my cassette recorder went flying across the room and nearly KO'ed us," Moe informed him. "I don't want it to happen again."

"Damn! *That's* nice," Andres frowned. "You guys piss off one of the spooks around here?"

"I don't know about that, but it surprised the hell out of us," Moe asserted. "I just don't want it to happen again. If anybody gets their skull cracked, we're a long way from help."

"I guess that falls under the category of the 'weird shit' I referred to a second ago," Andres noted.

The detective turned toward Cameron. "I'm serious, Cam. A video recorder would be the equivalent of a brick sailing through the air. We're already down to four and I don't want anyone else to get hurt."

"I'm with Woody on this one," Nancy added. "You weren't there, Cam. Whatever's here isn't exactly friendly."

Cameron look puzzled. "You mean Chet?" he asked.

"I'm not sure *who* I mean," Nancy affirmed. "All I know is that there are some bad vibes in this place."

Cameron nodded thoughtfully as he chewed. "I'd not considered that recording the séance might be a hazard, but you may be right. So are you suggesting that we shouldn't record it?"

Nancy glanced at the detective. "I'm not suggesting anything," Moe responded. "I'm just saying that we need to keep our heads up."

"I'm startin' to think that I may have gotten myself into something," Andres muttered as he listened to the exchange. "Do you think I'll need this?" He patted the 9mm pistol strapped to his hip, then began rummaging through his pack looking for additional ammunition.

"Unless you can shoot a flying tape recorder out of the air, I'm not sure how much good a gun will do you," Nancy laconically replied.

Andres sighed as he laid his pack aside. "It just gets better and better, huh?"

"So what should we do?" Cameron asked no one in particular. "I think we should record everything, but I'll defer to you guys." The remaining members of the group looked at one another wordlessly. Nancy finally broke the silence.

"I agree with Cam that we should record what happens, but I also agree with Woody that a video camera is basically a weapon...if for whatever reason it goes flying, it could do some serious damage. If we're all concentrating on the séance and not paying attention, it could very easily smack into somebody's head. On top of that, if it smashes into something it's probable that the resulting damage to the recorder might make whatever it had recorded up to that point unrecoverable." She looked directly at Cameron. "Cam, what's the absolute minimum number of people you need for the séance?"

"Based on what I've read, three," he responded. "No more than twelve and no less than three."

"Well, there's four of us. If you only need three, I'll use your camera to record everything while you three do the actual séance. With me holding onto the camera, there will be less chance of it flying around the room and hurting someone." She looked at the three men, seeking concurrence.

"I've got a better idea," Andres suggested. "Since you guys have done this kind of stuff before and I'm just basically along for the ride, why don't *I* man the camera while you guys do your thing? I'll hang on to it like there's no tomorrow ... the fucking Vulcan death grip!"

Nancy and the detective glanced at each other. Though she was tempted to respond that she'd *never* been engaged in anything like this and had agreed to participate only because of her longstanding friendship with Cam, Nancy didn't disabuse Andres of his belief.

Cameron sipped water from his canteen before responding. "I think that actually might be a good idea," he agreed. The three of us," he nodded toward the detective and Nancy, "already have a *simpatico* because we've been involved with this thing for months, which is important. I also think it's important to have a mixture of sexes at the séance, rather than all men or all women. And Andres is right: he's physically stronger than Nancy so, if something *does* go south, he can immediately deal with it. Nancy?" Cameron looked at her probingly.

"Fine by me," she said. "Like I said, I think it *should* be recorded and the recorder should be anchored to something. It doesn't matter to me who it's anchored to."

"Well, since we've settled that, we'd better get going," Moe suggested. He stuffed his lunch debris into his pack and stood as his companions slowly got to their feet. The detective hoisted his pack onto his back. "The house is just down the street."

The foursome ducked from beneath the shelter and comparative shade of the collapsed building onto the arid thoroughfare that bisected the abandoned settlement. Moe noted that Andres kept one hand on his holstered pistol. The detective glanced at his wristwatch. "We've got less than two hours," he informed his companions as they trudged forward in the heat. Nancy's sunglasses kept sliding down the bridge of her sweaty nose and she repeatedly pushed them back into place.

"A séance shouldn't ordinarily last more than an hour or so," Cameron assured them as they walked. "We should have plenty of time."

Andres stopped to take a picture of the decrepit town with his cell phone. "Hey, my camera took a dump!" He attempted to shield the phone's screen from the brilliant sunlight by cupping his hand over it. "It says the battery's dead but I charged it last night. How can it be dead?"

"The same way our radios went dead," Nancy replied. "This place has that effect on things."

"So how come your cassette recorder worked when you were here before? How come it didn't crap out, too?"

"It worked because they wanted it to work," Moe said, without breaking stride.

"'They' who?" Andes pressed, trailing after him.

"That's what we intend to find out," the detective asserted as they turned left at a dogleg, around a small, rock-strewn hill.

THE EDIFICE THAT REARED BEFORE THEM in the desolate bleakness shimmered in the superheated desert air. The structure appeared unchanged from the day Moe and Nancy stumbled upon it several weeks previously.

"Holy shit!" Andres exclaimed. "What's *that* doing here? It looks like it was built yesterday!"

He looked around, as though expecting the house's occupants to return at any moment. Notwithstanding that Moe had previously apprised him of its existence, Cameron had never actually seen the impressive structure and, like Andres, was viewing it for the first time. "I thought nobody lived here," Andres asserted.

"As far as I know, nobody does," the detective replied. "The house is empty."

"Who built it?" Andres marveled as they made their way toward the building. No one answered.

"Although it'll be hot inside, this is really the only suitable place to conduct the séance," Cameron informed the group after they'd assembled on its wraparound porch. "I don't trust any of the other buildings not to fall down on top of us and I don't want to just sit out in the open. We'll leave the door open and open the windows while we're here. Hopefully, we won't be inside very long."

Andres peered through a dirty window pane, past gauzy, yellowed curtains, into an empty room. "Where are we gonna sit?"

"On the floor," Cameron replied.

As the others watched, Moe stepped forward and tested the oblong brass doorknob on one of the double doors that communicated from the interior of the house onto the porch; it yielded to his touch and the portal shuddered open with a groan. He stepped aside and looked at Cameron expectantly.

"Well, I guess we should get started," Cameron remarked as he stepped past the detective into the building's stifling interior. The others filed in after him. As they did so, a movement inside the room immediately captured their attention. A huge black toad squatted along an interior wall, balefully surveying the intruders.

Andres involuntarily jumped as the anomalous creature began to hop clumsily toward them. "Christ! Where'd *he* come from?" he yelped as the toad lumbered over the threshold, onto the porch. It continued its ungainly transit across the weathered boards before tumbling over the edge onto the desiccated ground below.

Nancy looked at the others, her mouth agape. "What the heck was *that*?"

A cold shiver rippled up Moe's spine. He strode across the porch and looked over the railing, but the animal had apparently squirmed beneath the house and was no longer visible. "A toad, but toads have no business being here," he said quietly, returning to his companions.

"Well, it was obviously here," Andres observed. "But how did it get in? I thought toads usually hang around water. Where's the water in here?" He looked quizzically about the interior of the suffocating room.

"It probably just got in from outside," Cameron dismissively responded. "We need to get started. C'mon." He walked to the center of the room, unshouldered his backpack, and deposited it on the floor. "Try to open some windows," he suggested as he squatted and began rummaging through his pack.

Nancy glanced worriedly at the detective before walking to a row of windows along one wall. Moe and Andres followed. When she attempted to push aside the diaphanous curtains they disintegrated between her fingers; years of dust embedded in the stiff fabric boiled into the stifling air. The detective stepped forward and unceremoniously yanked the curtains from the window and tossed them to the floor. Nancy moved to one side as Moe placed his palms against the wooden frame and strained to shove it upward. It didn't move. He gritted his teeth and redoubled his efforts. Nothing. "Try one of the other windows," he urged Andres over his shoulder.

Already soaked with perspiration, the detective brushed away some of the accumulated filth that appeared to impede the window's movement. To no avail: it obstinately refused to budge. He wiped away the sweat that streamed down his face and bent to examine the immovable window.

"Somebody painted the window shut," he announced, straightening up.

"Huh?" Nancy asked, perplexed.

"Whoever painted this place in the past slopped paint onto the window frame. When it dried, it basically glued the window shut. Now I can't open it."

"Same with this one," Andres said from an adjacent window. "Stuck tighter than a duck's asshole. You think we should just smash 'em? I don't know how much longer I can stand this heat!"

Moe rapidly stepped to the remaining windows to confirm that all were similarly inoperative, his shirt plastered to his body with sweat. "No," he sighed, after completing his circuit. "We don't have the right to damage somebody else's property."

"'Somebody else's property'!" Andres protested. "There's *nobody* here! You said nobody even *lives* here!"

"Woody's right," Nancy said. She wiped her sweaty forehead on the sleeve of her shirt. "Even if nobody lives here this house belongs to somebody. We're just gonna have to make due by leaving the door open and getting out of here as fast as possible." They looked over at Cameron, who sat cross-legged on the dusty floor. A Ouija board was on the floor in front of him and he cupped a small video camera in one hand.

"I'm ready when you guys are," he said.

EIGHTEEN

BILL SNATCHED THE WINCHESTER from Ham's lifeless hands and spun about. With one motion, he levered a cartridge into the rifle's chamber and snapped off a wild shot into the darkness. The concussion reverberated through the night, filling the air with a plume of white smoke.

"Come out, you son of a bitch!" he shouted. "Show yourself!" He levered another cartridge into the chamber and fired the Winchester a second time. "If you wasn't such a piss ant coward you'd face me like a man!" Wild-eyed, Bill frantically searched the blackness beyond the uncertain light of the campfire, swinging the rifle first one way, then another.

Moloch hooted and laughed from the darkness. "Now what do you intend to do, my friend? Your horse has abandoned you and your friend is dead. It appears your options are rapidly diminishing."

Bill fired randomly twice more into the night. "I'll show you what I'm gonna do!" he shouted defiantly. When he attempted to lever a fifth shot into the chamber, the rifle's hammer fell with an audible click. Empty. "Son of a bitch!" he snarled. Additional ammunition for the rifle was in the saddle bags near Ham's body, though he was disinclined to dig for it.

Bill flung the useless rifle aside and, after deliberating only a moment, dashed away from the camp, into the enveloping darkness. He crouched in an effort to minimize his profile and, as quickly as his eyes adjusted to the gloom, rapidly scanned the area immediately around him. Seeing nothing, he a tentative step forward.

"Do you think you can so easily elude me?" Moloch cackled from somewhere nearby.

Bill involuntarily jumped, startled by the apparent proximity of the being, then began running headlong into the desert. Heedless of the uneven terrain, crashing into unseen obstacles, and sliding across loose rocks, the terror-stricken cowboy ran pell-mell through the darkness. More than once he fell, sprawling, onto the hardpan but immediately jumped to his feet to resume his chaotic flight. Even over his panicked breathing Bill could hear Moloch's howling laughter behind him.

The slick leather soles of the cowboy's boots, ideal for sliding into a stirrup, were less suited for running. It was for that reason that, despite spotting at the last moment the fissure that yawned before him in the desert floor, he was unable to arrest his mad escape. Though he frantically back-peddled in a desperate effort to avoid the chasm, Bill's boots slid wildly on the scattering of pebbles that surrounded its sunken mouth.

His shriek rent the darkness as he plunged into the sepulchral abyss.

"HERE," CAMERON SAID, offering the video camera to Andres. "Sit there." He nodded toward a spot near the wall about eight feet away. "You'll be able to lean back while you're recording." He switched his attention to the detective and Nancy. "Woody, why don't you sit on that side and, Nancy, you can sit on this side."

Andres unshouldered his pack and took the camera from Cam's outstretched hand. He then sat, Indian style, on the floor where indicated. Moe and Nancy piled their packs on the floor before dutifully assuming their assigned places on either side of the Ouija board. The heat inside the room was wilting.

"How long's this gonna take?" Andres asked as sweat streamed down his face.

"We'll be in an out," Cameron assured him as he leaned forward to adjust the Ouija board's planchette.

"So how do we start?" Moe asked, glancing uneasily at Nancy.

Cameron straightened. "I'll start like I do voice recording, by inviting anyone here to communicate with us. Then we'll go from there."

"When do you want me to start recording?" Andres asked, fiddling with the video camera.

"When I say 'go,'" Cameron said. He looked at Moe and Nancy. "I don't know what, if anything's, gonna happen, but just hang with me," he instructed them. Both nodded. "Okay, put your fingertips on the planchette." The three bent forward and gently placed their fingertips on the wooden pointer. "Go," Cameron instructed Andres.

Nancy was basically familiar with the Ouija board, having toyed with it when she was a teenager. Whenever the planchette moved across the smooth surface of the board, as it invariably did, she and her friends would accuse one another of surreptitiously moving it, an accusation all would, of course, hotly deny. Although she didn't know what previous exposure, if any, the detective had to the Ouija board, she felt a little foolish sitting there, as an adult, attempting to summon spirits through the use of a child's parlor game. She glanced at Moe; the detective's intense concentration on the planchette betrayed no emotion.

"Good afternoon. You are among friends. If anyone is present, you are in a safe place," Cameron began in a low voice. My name is Cameron Wylie and with me are Nancy, Woody, and Andres. If there is anyone here who knows me and who wishes to communicate, either by speech or through the Ouija board, please do so now. Chet, if you are present, please give us a sign. We welcome all who may be with us today and invite you to manifest yourselves if it pleases you to do so. We invite anyone who can see us or hear my voice." Cameron paused, though his fingertips remained glued to the planchette.

Nancy wasn't sure what was supposed to happen next. She stole a glance at Andres, who appeared to be concentrating on the video camera's small display screen. Her back was already beginning to ache from the strain of hunching over the Ouija board and cold rivulets of sweat flowed down her sides beneath her shirt.

She feared that she might actually pass out because of the suffocating heat. Moe remained imperturbable.

"Spirits, please acknowledge that you are present and can hear me," Cameron resumed. His face glistened with perspiration and his baseball cap was soaked with sweat. "We ardently wish to communicate with you and humbly request that you reciprocate. Chet, if you're here, please give us a sign."

The planchette started to move.

Slowly, almost imperceptibly at first, the pointer on which their fingertips gently rested began to inch a trembling path across the Ouija board. Startled, Nancy kept her fingertips planted on the planchette and looked first at Cameron, then at the detective, fully expecting to discover one of them intentionally impelling the pointer across the surface of the board. The eyes of both men were locked on the leisurely, yet seemingly deliberate, movements of the planchette.

"I hope you guys are doing that." Andres whispered.

"Friends, are you with us?" Cameron breathed, focusing on the Ouija board and ignoring Andres.

The planchette glided insensibly across the board's smooth surface until its pointer drew abreast of the letter "N," where it momentarily lingered. After a pause, it resumed its meandering transit until reaching the letter "O," where it rested

"No?" Cameron read aloud, doubtfully.

'No' what?" Moe asked. "'No' there's no one here, or 'no' something else? But if there's no one here, who moved the planchette?"

Cameron slowly shook his head and started to respond. Before he was able to utter a word, however, the double doors through which they'd previously entered the house abruptly swung shut with a violent crash, causing the room's sealed windows to rattle in their frames.

The concussion caused both Nancy and the detective to whip around from their places on the floor, the séance immediately forgotten.

"Jesus Christ!" Andres exclaimed.

Moe sprang up and strode to the doors, where he roughly twisted their ornate brass knobs. "They're locked," he tersely announced. He turned back toward the others. "We're gonna have to break one of the windows."

Are you kidding?" Cameron protested. "You want to end it already? We just barely started!"

"Cam, the only air flow we had are the doors. If I can't open 'em, there's no ventilation and in about two minutes the temperature in here's gonna go through the roof. If we don't smash a window, we're all gonna collapse from heat stroke."

The detective scanned the barren room for something he could use to break the sealed windows. Seeing nothing, he unholstered his Python, approached the nearest window, and tore its rotted curtains from the rod. He then gently tapped the pane with the butt of the weapon. When it failed to yield, he cocked his wrist and struck it more forcefully, punching a hole in the glass. Nancy rose and joined Moe at the window while Andres continued to record the event.

"Do you think we should break another one?" she asked as the detective gingerly knocked shards of glass from the broken pane with his revolver. A shower of fragments clattered onto the wooden porch outside.

He nodded without looking up, his hair plastered to his head with sweat. "Yeah. Use your gun. Just be careful not to cut yourself."

She retrieved her backpack from where she'd deposited on the floor and extracted from it her .38 revolver. Moving to an adjacent window, she rapped smartly on the pane until it shattered. After the largest pieces of glass tumbled out, Nancy used the barrel of her revolver to brush the residual shards from the frame. Although the scorching air outside was scarcely cooler than the steaming interior of the house, at least there was a possibility that a slight breeze might arise to stir the stale air inside the room. Besides, they'd need an exit if they were unable to force open the double doors leading outside once the séance ended.

"Good job," Moe smiled.

"You think we'll need more?" Nancy asked.

The detective reflected a moment. "We'd best stop at two, at least for now. I don't want to wreck more than we have to."

"Well, I guess if anyone was home they'd have come charging in by now," Andres observed. "'What the hell are you doin' to my house!'" he impersonated a hypothetical, outraged homeowner.

Cameron remained seated on the floor with the Ouija board in front of him, while Andres continued to record.

"Well, I think we know the answer to your first question, Woody," Cameron said. The detective holstered the Python and waited while Nancy returned her revolver to her backpack.

"First question?" he asked, puzzled, as he and Nancy returned to their places on the floor near Cameron. "What are you talking about?"

"You asked if there was anyone here," Cameron responded. "I guess now we know."

"Why would they slam the door?" Nancy wondered.

I asked them to manifest themselves," Cameron shrugged. "They were just complying."

"Yeah, maybe," Moe skeptically responded. "If somebody actually slammed the door, 'no' obviously can't mean that nobody's here."

"How do you know the door didn't close by itself?" Andres asked from behind the video camera.

"I don't," Cameron conceded. "Maybe it did. But the only way to figure it out is to continue."

Nancy listened thoughtfully. "Your question had two parts, Cam," she finally said.

"Huh?" Cameron looked at her without comprehending.

"Think about what you asked. Your exact question was, 'Friends, are you with us?' Right after you asked that, the Ouija board spelled out the word 'no.'"

"So?"

"So your question basically had two parts, one implied and one explicit: 'Are you friends?' and 'Are you here?'"

"Okay," Cameron acknowledged. "So what?"

"Well," Nancy continued, "the answer to the second question is obviously 'yes,' since you believe that some spirit, or whatever, is here and physically slammed the door. So the 'no' response couldn't have applied to the second part of your question, the 'are you here' part. Whoever it is, is obviously here."

"I don't understand where you're going, Nance," Cameron said.

Moe grasped the point Nancy was trying to make. "She's saying that whoever is here isn't our friend."

"That's exactly what I'm saying," Nancy affirmed. "They couldn't have made it more clear."

"Maybe you misunderstood the answer," Andres uneasily suggested. "Or maybe one of you unconsciously moved the planchette."

Yeah, maybe," Nancy responded, unconvinced. "Or maybe the answer meant exactly what it said." She looked directly at Cameron. "I think we should leave, Cam."

"Leave? Nance, you can't be serious," Cameron protested. We barely got here and you already want to leave?" He looked pleadingly at Moe.

"I'll do whatever everybody wants to do," the detective said. "But we're already here, we can't be trapped inside, even with the doors locked, because we broke the windows and, if we just take our ball and bat and go home now, everybody's gonna wonder why we bothered to come in the first place. But, like I said, I'll go with the flow."

Cameron appealed to the other member of their party. "Andres?"

Andres switched the video recorder off and placed it in his lap. "I'm pretty much with Woody. I can either stay or go but, since we're already here, I think we should probably see it through to the end. Like Woody said, otherwise, why'd we even bother? Besides," he grinned, "we're all armed, so if a ghostie tries to hassle us, we'll give him a hot lead injection." He wiped his sweaty forehead on the sleeve of his shirt.

Cameron looked at Nancy. "Nance?"

"Yeah, okay, I guess," she sighed. "I don't want to be the bad guy here...I suppose we can go ahead with it. In about ten minutes it's gonna be so hot in here that we'll *have* to leave."

"Thanks, Nance," Cameron smiled, visibly relieved. "I really appreciate it." He placed his fingertips on the planchette again and looked expectantly at Nancy and Moe, who followed his lead. "Fire the camera up again," he directed Andres.

"Friends," Cameron resumed when Andres was ready, "I fear that we may have misunderstood your last message. I promise you that you have nothing to fear. We especially wish to communicate with Chet if he is present." He paused to watch the immobile planchette. Nancy unconsciously held her breath as she concentrated on holding her hands completely still. Her tee shirt was plastered to her body with sweat. Beside her, the detective remained stoical.

"Chet, please let us know that you're here," Cameron importuned, his appeal tinged with more than a modicum of desperation.

Moe glanced at Nancy, whose attention appeared riveted on the Ouija board. Although he couldn't be certain, the detective thought he discerned a mild vibration coursing beneath them through the floor.

The smell of rotting meat wafted into the room.

"God damn!" Andres blurted. "What just died?" He slowly panned the room with the video camera, hoping to detect the origin of the nauseating stench. Although Cameron seemed oblivious to the aberrant fetor, Nancy and Moe looked up from the Ouija board and wrinkled their noses. The detective removed his hands from the planchette and began to stand in order to investigate its origin when a peal of thunder shook the house. As the rumbling died away it was immediately followed by the sound of objects striking the exterior of the structure.

"Hail?" Nancy asked, mystified. She looked toward the windows, where brilliant sunlight continued to pour into the room from a cloudless sky.

The curious drumming noise, initially modest and sporadic, rapidly increased in intensity until it reached a deafening crescendo. The spontaneous tempest buffeted the house like a roaring wind, though the thin curtains covering the remaining windows hung motionless in the listless air.

MOE STRODE TO ONE OF the smashed windows. Pressing his body along the wall, he peered outside. As he did so, he felt Nancy steal up behind him. She slipped her hand into his and nervously squeezed it.

"Can you see anything?" she shouted over the din.

Not hail, but an avalanche of stones pelted the house. Rocks, some more than two inches long, rained down, striking the siding with a violent crash and ricocheting off the wooden porch.

Nancy peeped cautiously over the detective's shoulder as Cameron and Andres crept to the window.

"What the hell's going on?" Andres nervously demanded. "How can it be hailing on a cloudless day when it's so fucking hot?"

"It's not hail," the detective yelled. "Somebody's pelting the house with rocks."

"Rocks? What the hell for? Who's doing it?"

"I don't see anything," the detective tersely responded as, through the shattered window, he studied the immediate vicinity. "There's nobody out there."

The noisy torrent raged unabated. Curiously, notwithstanding their obvious momentum, the cascade of stones that rained down bounced off the intact windows without breaking the glass.

"Christ, there's got to be a horde of people out there," Andres yelled. "How can there not be anybody?"

Moe slid away from the window as the tumult continued. "Take a look," he gestured. I'll be damned if I can see anyone."

Andres switched places with the detective and cautiously looked out the broken pane.

Although a blizzard of rocks hurtled toward them, the area in the immediate vicinity of the house appeared bereft of life.

One of the stones struck the window frame near Andres' head, denting it, and he hastily ducked inside.

"What do you think we should we do?" he shouted over the racket.

Moe was about to respond when a handful of rocks that were in mid-flight thudded into the house. Abruptly, the cascade of stones ceased. The group nervously looked at one another, breathlessly awaiting the resumption of the lithic assault.

"Is it over?" Nancy whispered, almost as though she feared being overheard. She continued to grasp the detective's hand.

The detective peered out the window again, but all was quiet. "I don't know," he murmured. "Let's give it a second."

Overhead, a loud crash emanated from one of the house's upper stories. Startled, their heads swiveled upward as one.

"Jesus! Now what?" Andres hissed.

The group remained perfectly still, staring at the ceiling.

Something struck the floor above them, bounced, and began to roll about. Then another. And another.

Moe looked questioningly at Cameron, who shook his head.

The number of objects hitting the floor began to increase.

"It sounds like marbles," Andres whispered, frowning.

The overhead drumming abruptly intensified as wave after wave of objects began hurling down onto the wooden floor above them. Like the deafening shower of stones the group had just experienced, the sound resembled that of a violent rainstorm. The entire house seemed to shudder under the onslaught.

"We need to get out of here!" Moe shouted to the others.

"No way," Andres retorted. "We'll step outside and get lambasted by one of those flying rocks."

"Wait, did you guys find a way upstairs when you were here before?" Cameron hollered.

Nancy shook her head. "No, but we didn't really look, either. Even if we did, I'm not going up there." She looked at Moe for confirmation.

The detective glanced out the window. Although the porch was previously littered with hundreds of stones, it was now barren of them. It was as though an invisible broom had swept them all away.

"It sounds like the whole roof may cave in!" Moe shouted. "If I can get the doors open we need to blow this place. If the doors won't open, we'll have to climb out through one of the windows."

He abandoned his position by the window and made his way to the double doors that disembogued onto the porch. With the others arrayed around him, he grasped a knob in each hand and simultaneously twisted them; to his surprise, they turned easily.

"They're open!" Moe shouted excitedly.

The detective swung the portals open but did not immediately step out onto the porch. Instead, he shielded himself along the jamb while he studied the area outside. The maelstrom of noise that reverberated throughout the room was becoming unbearable and the pervasive stench of decaying meat was nauseating.

Discerning no activity within his immediate purview, Moe stepped tentatively from the sweltering interior of the house onto the porch. As his companions watched anxiously from the open doorway, he stole to the edge of the porch and looked along its length in both directions.

"Do you see anything?" Andres called to him in a hushed voice.

Moe didn't verbally respond, but shook his head in the negative.

Looking about, Nancy marveled at the bare porch. "What happened to all the rocks? And the broken glass?"

Somewhat emboldened, the detective walked to the head of the stairs and trod them to the ground. Nancy, Cameron and Andres warily emerged from the house and followed him, where they gathered in front of the house. Only then did it occur to them that the cacophony inside the house had ceased.

"Well, so far, so good," Andres remarked, looking around. "Nobody's been hit with any fucking rocks yet."

Moe glanced at his watch. "We've been here just over an hour. What's everybody want to do? I vote that we get out of here before anything else happens."

"I'm with you," Nancy concurred. "There's no way I'm going back in there," she nodded toward the house. "I'll take my chances out here."

"Our stuff is still inside," Moe reminded her. The detective looked at Cameron. "Cam and I'll go round up everything. You guys wait here."

"I'll go, too," Nancy volunteered.

Moe placed a hand on her shoulder. "No, we got it. Please just stay here, okay?"

"You sure? I don't mind," she persisted.

"*I* mind," the detective said. "Just wait here. We'll only be a minute, I promise. We need to get out of here before another shoe drops."

"Amen to that, brother," Andres gravely added.

Moe turned and ascended the stairs with Cameron trailing him. Stepping back into the house, they immediately saw that their backpacks had disappeared from where they'd previously deposited them on the floor. Gone, too, were the video camera and Ouija board. The room was utterly barren.

"This is really beginning to piss me off," the detective seethed as he surveyed the empty room.

"Should we try and look for any of it?" Cameron queried.

"Aside from our water, I couldn't care less about our packs," Moe said. "And I don't know about you, but *I'm* not looking for anything. Andres still has his *bota* and we'll share whatever water remains in it until we get back up the hill.

We're just gonna have to tough it out." Cameron nodded but said nothing.

"You guys all right in there?" Andres yelled from outside.

"Yeah, we're fine," the detective responded. He turned to Cameron. "Let's get out of here," he urged. "I'm about ready to melt and God only knows what could happen next."

Cameron nodded wordlessly as they turned to rejoin their companions.

ANNO DOMINI NOSTRI IESU CHRISTO
1824

MOST OF THE REMAINING INHABITANTS huddled together in three collapsing structures, hoping that such propinquity would guarantee their safety, notwithstanding the evidence of their own eyes to the contrary. The *alcalde,* of course, refused to indulge such naiveté and remained ensconced in his private apartments.

Nearly six months had passed since Diego's return to the *pueblo,* brandishing the heads of those purportedly responsible for carrying off the *peones,* with assurances to the *alcalde* that the predations would end. The disappearances resumed scarcely two weeks later. Though the *alcalde* angrily demanded an explanation from the *Capitán,* Diego protested his rectitude and reiterated his utter fidelity. Clearly, complained the frustrated *Capitán*, there existed a pernicious nest of creatures, only two of which he and his men had managed to bag. The rest had obviously managed to flee before resuming their rapine.

The *alcalde* stroked his beard thoughtfully. "That *idiota* Don Luis cares nothing for his *peones,* but that is beside the point. Their disappearance reflects poorly on me at Court. If, in Don Luis' eyes, I am unable to adequately safeguard worthless *peones,* how can I possibly be entrusted with even greater responsibilities? No, Diego, my entire appointment to this thankless post has yielded nothing but grief," he morosely reflected. "It is certain that my enemies in *Sevilla,* who wish to discredit me, have Don Luis' ear and prevailed upon him to abandon me to this wasteland." He cast a penetrating gaze on his subordinate. "Did the *peón* ever return from your previous sojourn into the desert ... what was his name? Gomez? Perhaps he will prove of some value in ferreting out the lair of the rascals."

"*Si,* Beto Gomez, Excellency." Capitán Diego shifted uncomfortably. "Unfortunately, I am informed that the *peón* failed to return to the *pueblo.* His wife has despaired of seeing him again and begged *Padre* Guerrero to say a prayer for his eternal soul at mass, and to light a candle for him."

"*Padre* Guerrero's prayers are a fool's errand, as effective as using a rake to push water uphill," the *alcalde* dryly remarked. He leaned forward, tented his elegant fingers, and fixed a cold smile on Diego. "However, because you are obviously incapable of ridding the *pueblo* of this scourge, perhaps I should ask Guerrero to pray for divine succor...his efforts can certainly not be of less efficacy than yours."

Diego shifted again but said nothing. His eyes were focused straight ahead.

"Are we simply to sit idly as the population of the *pueblo* continues to dwindle, *Capitán*? Who will labor in the fields to cultivate such meager crops as we are able to grow in this pestilential *desierto* after all the *peones* have disappeared? You?" he scoffed.

Diego remained staid.

The *alcalde* leaned back in his chair and folded his arms. "Here's what you will do, *Capitán*. You will immediately gather a patrol and return to the place where you previously encountered the creatures. You and your men will remain there until such time as you are satisfied that all of them have been extirpated. It is matter of indifference to me how long it may take...a week, a month, six months. Neither you nor your men will return to the *pueblo* until the task is finished. I am tired of trying to catch the mice *after* they are already in the house."

Diego cleared his throat but did not shift his gaze from the wall behind the *alcalde's* baroque desk. "Do you consider it prudent, *Excellency,* to leave the *pueblo* virtually unguarded during our absence?"

"Leave a sufficient number of men here to protect the *pueblo, Capitán.* However," the *alcalde* looked icily at his subordinate, "you will personally lead the patrol of which I speak, which will depart no later than vespers today."

"*Si, señor,*" Diego acknowledged, softly clicking his heels.

"You may go, *Capitán*. Waste no time in assembling your men." With that, the *alcalde* turned his attention to the confusion of papers scattered atop his ordinarily immaculate desk.

Diego took a step backward, turned smartly, and withdrew.

As ordered, Capitán Diego duly commandeered a dozen men and provisions sufficient for two weeks ... beyond that he was not disposed to speculate. The detachment rode from Esperanza just as the raging sun began its hesitant descent behind the surrounding hills.

"Do you think it safe to travel at night?" Barbosa asked with evident trepidation as they cantered.

"I fear it is not safe to travel at all, irrespective of the hour," Diego responded with disheartening candor. "But the *alcalde* gives us no choice." They subsequently rode in silence, each man contemplating his own terrors.

Capitán Diego and his men failed to appear after a fortnight. A third week passed, then a fourth; still there was no sign of the patrol. After two months it became obvious, even to the *alcalde*, that the detachment was unlikely to return. Murmurings from Esperanza's inhabitants inevitably reached his ears, resulting in the issuance of an edict: anyone overheard discussing or speculating about the fate of *Capitán* Diego's detail would be summarily exiled from the *pueblo*. Although the whisperings did not thereafter cease, the *alcalde* managed to convince himself otherwise.

Certainly, it was possible the patrol chanced upon those responsible for preying on the *pueblo*, with disastrous consequences. But the *alcalde* suspected it was far more likely that the faithless Diego had simply abandoned his mission. Sonoita was scarcely 50 *leguas* to the south, a distance the *Capitán* and his horsemen could easily traverse in only three days. Although it was a poor excuse for a town, the *Capitán* was completely unknown there; he and his men could easily meld into the local population. As for their wives and children abandoned in the *pueblo,* they were mere hostages to fortune. Sonoita was filled with an abundance of potential wives, and nothing is easier, or more pleasurable to generate, than children.

Yes, that is what undoubtedly happened to that worthless Diego. The *alcalde* sighed as he dipped his quill in the ink pot and began to compose his report to Durango.

NINETEEN

THEIR EXODUS FROM THE TOWN was without incident. Having exhausted the remaining contents of Andres' bota early in their flight, they hastened without pause past the bleak corral that marked Esperanza's purlieus and finally approached the imposing earthen mound. Though none were eager to voice it, all were fraught with anxiety over Tina and Darlene's welfare. They were unnerved, hot, tired, and thirsty.

Andres was the first to reach the barrier and, without looking back, began to ascend its formidable surface. His three companions watched from the base as dirt and rocks cascaded downward. As he climbed, Nancy glanced at Moe, who nodded for her to follow once Andres neared the crest. "Why don't you go after Nancy, and I'll bring up the rear," suggested the detective, looking at Cameron, who nodded his concurrence.

"Hey, you guys!" Andres waved excitedly after gaining the summit. He was staring down the opposite side of the mound, in the presumed direction of their two stranded companions. He turned back toward the other three as Nancy cautiously picked her way upward. "They're still here," he announced. Returning his attention to Darlene and Tina, Andres shouted, "Everything okay?"

Nancy eventually gained the top of the hill, where she bent, hands on her knees, gulping air and trembling, next to Andres. Sweat poured down her face and dripped onto the parched ground. "I can't believe how hot it is," she panted. She glanced over the edge to see Cameron angling his way up the face of the mound. The detective monitored the progress of all three from its base. Finally able to catch her breath, Nancy straightened and stepped to the far edge; Tina leaned on Darlene as both stood gazing upward from the foot of the hillock.

"You guys weren't gone very long," Tina called to Nancy. "You get everything you needed?"

"And then some," Andres retorted. "You two doin' okay?"

"Yeah, we're fine," Tina shrugged. "My knee hurts like a bitch and we're hot and sweaty, but we'll live," she grinned.

"We thought you'd be gone longer," Darlene added.

"We were attacked," Andres informed them as Cameron pulled himself to the top of the mound. He dusted himself off and stepped to the far edge of the mound, where Andres and Nancy stood.

"Attacked?"

"Somebody was heaving rocks at us. You wouldn't have believed it!" Andres reiterated.

"Was anybody hurt?" Darlene asked in alarm.

"Where's Woody?" Tina frowned.

"Woody's fine; we're all fine," Nancy assured them. He's still coming up the other side; he'll be here in a sec." She paused. "You guys, did anything weird happen while we were away?"

"Weird? Weird like what? Tina responded, perplexed.

"Never mind. We'll talk about it when we get down there."

"Nobody threw rocks at us, if that's what you mean," Darlene laughed. "I want to hear about *that*."

"You guys have any water left?" Andres interjected.

"Yeah, we have some...where's *your* stuff?" For the first time Darlene noticed that their companions were bereft of their backpacks.

"We had to leave everything behind."

"'Leave it behind? Why?"

"We'll explain," Nancy promised. "Are you gonna be able to make it back to camp?" she asked Tina.

"I'm sure as hell not gonna stay out here!" she snorted, "even if you guys have to carry me back!"

As Tina spoke, Nancy heard Moe scramble onto the top the mound behind her. She walked back to him and gently touched the detective's hand. "Everything okay?" he asked, squeezing her hand as he caught his breath.

"Tina and Darlene are fine. You okay?"

"I'll be a lot better once we get out of here," the detective affirmed, nodding in the direction from whence they'd just come. "We'd better keep moving, though. Is Tina able to walk?"

"I think so. She doesn't really have any alternative."

Moe nodded and, with Nancy, crossed to the far edge, where they rejoined Cameron and Andres. "You want to go first, Nancy?" he asked.

"Absolutely," she replied. "The sooner I get out of here, the better." She stepped over the lip of the mound and began to carefully pick her way to its base.

While she descended, the detective called to the women waiting below. "Can you walk, Tina?"

"Well, my knee is swollen and still hurts like a bastard but, if I take it slow, I'll be able to make it back up the hill. What choice do I have?" As if to demonstrate her resolve, Tina hobbled a few steps, then looked up at Moe with a grin. He tipped his baseball cap to her just as Nancy hopped the last few feet to the ground. "Cam?"

Cameron nodded and began clambering down the precarious slope.

"What was Andres talking about being attacked?" Tina quizzed Nancy as the latter guzzled water from Darlene's canteen.

Nancy wiped her mouth and waited for Cameron to finish climbing down the face of the mound. Once he reached its base, Andres began his descent; Nancy met Cameron at the bottom and handed the canteen to him as Moe vigilantly scanned the surrounding desert from his vantage point atop the pile.

"We were sitting in an old house, just starting the séance', when somebody started throwing rocks at the outside of the house," Nancy finally responded as Cameron gulped the tepid water.

Darlene looked dubious. "Why would anyone throw rocks at you?"

Cameron finished drinking and returned to Darlene her canteen.

"You'd have to have been there. It wasn't like somebody was just tossing a handful of pebbles...it sounded like a hailstorm!" Andres chimed as he scuttled down the mound.

"Who?" Tina probed, looking directly at Cameron. "And why?" He didn't respond. "So maybe it *was* a hailstorm," she wryly suggested.

"A hailstorm? Are you fucking kidding me?" Andres grunted. He stopped his descent and pointed upward. "Do you see any clouds?"

"It was no hailstorm," Nancy said. "They were rocks, a boat-load of 'em. We thought they were gonna knock the whole house down!"

Andres slid the remaining few feet to the ground and hastened away from the pile. "Welcome back," Tina smiled as she handed him her canteen. "Sounds like you had quite an ordeal."

"'Ordeal' is right," Andres replied before taking a swig. "It was the damnest thing I ever saw!"

Nancy looked over Cameron's shoulder toward the mound, where Moe was carefully picking his way downward. She hurried over to await him at the foot of the mound and, together, they returned to the others. The detective gratefully accepted the canteen that Darlene proffered him.

"What the heck happened to you guys back there?" Tina asked Moe while he drank.

The detective drained what little water remained in the canteen before returning the container to Darlene. "Ask Cam," he responded.

Tina looked at Cameron expectantly. He hesitated before speaking. "Poltergeist activity," he finally said. "It was classic poltergeist activity." He looked at Moe, though the latter remained stoical.

"So poltergeists were throwing rocks at you?" Tina asked, dubiously. "Why?"

"Who knows why? All I know is that rock-throwing is classic poltergeist activity," Cameron replied. "I have a book that talks about a rock-throwing poltergeist as far back as 858 A.D., when the Romans thought an evil spirit was throwing rocks at them during a battle with the Gauls."

"So what did you guys do?" Darlene probed.

"We got the hell outta Dodge!" Andres cried.

"That's what I was asking you before," Nancy interjected. "Did you guys experience anything weird while we were gone?"

Tina reflected a moment before responding. "Well, I don't know if it qualifies as 'weird,' but while Darlene and I were sitting, waiting for you, a big jack rabbit casually walked, not hopped, walked, out of the brush and sat down right in front of us, literally about six feet away. I could have reached out and touched him. He just sat there, staring at Darlene and me for about, what," she looked at Darlene, "two or three minutes, probably, before just walking away. It was kinda strange but I figured that they must not be hunted much around here and was just curious."

"Fortunately, he didn't throw any rocks at us," Darlene added.

Cameron appeared reflective. "Do you remember exactly when that happened?"

"The rabbit? I didn't look at my watch, but it was probably about an hour ago," Tina guessed.

Cameron looked at Moe. "We were in the middle of the rock shower an hour ago. I checked my watch."

"So?"

"So rabbits don't just walk up to people. I don't care *how* little they're hunted; they just don't do it."

"Maybe it *was* just a rabbit, Cam," the detective postulated. "Nothing more. 'Sometimes a cigar is just a cigar'."

Cameron shook his head. "I don't think so. Nothing in this place is what it seems."

Tina was dubious. "It sure *looked* like a rabbit. If it wasn't a rabbit, what *was* it?"

"A familiar," Cameron affirmed.

"Huh?"

"A demon," said Cameron. "Sometimes they appear in human form, but more often 'familiars' assume the form of animals...goats, lizards, birds, dogs."

"So the jackrabbit we saw was actually a demon?" Darlene chuckled. "Cam, we're in Phoenix, not Salem, Massachusetts."

"I think it was more likely a familiar than a rabbit," Cameron matter-of-factly insisted. "You can laugh if you want."

"Wait, are you guys serious?" Tina made a wry face. "A demon? Really?"

The detective turned to her. "Believe it or not, there were familiars in my own apartment earlier this month, a cat and some birds. If you seriously want to know, I'll tell you about it when we get back." His gaze was strange, unsettling.

Andres frowned unconsciously as he listened to the exchange. "That big toad back there, was it..." he began. Cameron nodded silently. "I don't know squat about poltergeists, demons, whatever," Andres continued in an effort to defuse the growing unease, "but I *do* know that something very weird happened to us in that town. Maybe it was demons, maybe it wasn't, but I suggest we get out of here before anything else happens."

Nancy finally spoke. "Andres is right. We need to go. Now."

"Did you try your radios again while we were gone?" Cameron asked Tina as, with Darlene's help, she turned and hobbled toward her backpack, which lay on the ground.

"Yeah, we tried a couple of times. They're still dead."

"You gonna make it?" Andres asked Tina as she scooped her pack up.

"Yeah, I'll be fine," she said, shouldering her pack. "I'll just have to take it easy."

The group began trudging out of the valley. The remorseless sun seared through their clothing as they struggled up the rocky trail, Cameron in the lead. Darlene and Andres assisted Tina as she limped along, while Nancy and the detective brought up the rear. As they climbed, the latter paused regularly to intently scan the desert behind them, though he wasn't sure what he expected to see. Nancy waited while Moe reconnoitered, after which they hastened to rejoin the others.

"Wait, I've gotta rest," Andres gasped after twenty minutes of struggling. He removed his boonie hat, already soaked with sweat, and fruitlessly attempted to mop perspiration from his face with it. "Do you suppose those guys have any beer left?"

Cameron laughed. "I wouldn't count on it. I'll be happy with just a big glass of ice water."

Darlene passed a canteen around and each of them took a sip of stale water. "I'd settle for that and some shade." She looked at Tina. "You doin' okay?"

Tina smiled thinly. "Yeah, I'm okay. I'll just be glad to finally sit down and take the weight off my knee."

"We'll put some ice on it as soon as we get back to camp," Moe promised. "Don't be afraid to stop and rest whenever you need to...we'll be at the top pretty quick." He surveyed the floor of the lifeless desert before resuming their ascent.

THEY CRESTED THE PLATEAU NINETY minutes later. It was devoid of their companions and the vehicles.

Tina could scarcely stand upright and promptly collapsed onto the rocky ground, exhausted. "Where is everybody?" she nearly wept. "This is the right spot, yes?"

"Yeah, this is the right spot," Cameron affirmed, looking around in dismay.

"What happened to them?" Andres wondered aloud. "Why'd they leave?"

"Can we call 'em?" asked Tina, anxiously.

Nancy shook her head. "Cell phones don't work out here."

"Jesus! What *does* work?" Nancy didn't respond. She, Cameron, and Moe looked at one another, dispirited, as the others huddled together near the perimeter of the ridge.

"Well, now what?" Nancy asked, the disgust in her voice apparent. "I don't think Tina can walk another step and we're almost out of water."

"I'll hike to the road," the detective volunteered. "Whoever wants to come with me is welcome, but I think either you or Cam, or both of you, should stay here. I don't think it's a good idea to leave these guys up here by themselves." He gestured with his head toward Tina, Darlene, and Andres. "I'll go just far enough to get a cell signal, so I shouldn't be gone too long."

"What do you think could have happened to Phil and them?" Cameron asked. "Why would they just drive off and leave us?"

"I *hope* that's all it was, that they just drove off," Nancy said. "Though I don't know why they would."

Moe walked over to their three companions. "I don't know what happened to the others, but I'm gonna hike out far enough to get a cell signal. Something must've come up; I don't know why else they would have left."

"Yeah, well, it's pretty damned lame if you ask me," Andres grunted. Tina and Darlene nodded their agreement.

"I should be back inside a couple of hours," the detective continued, though he wasn't entirely sure that was strictly true.

"You're gonna leave us out here?" Darlene cried in alarm.

"No, I'll wait here with you guys," Nancy replied as she walked up behind the detective. "I'm worn out, anyway." Though tired, Nancy was no more fatigued than any of the others and she'd really have preferred to accompany Moe. "Besides, you're in no condition to do any more hiking, Tina ... you're hardly able to put any weight on your knee as it is. We'll just wait here until Woody gets hold of those guys and returns with some help. No biggie." Nancy hoped the others would find her forced insouciance convincing.

"I'll go with Woody, if that's okay with you, Nancy," Cameron said. "It's probably not a good idea for him to hike out alone."

"I was just about to make that very suggestion," she acknowledged.

"How much water do we have left?" Moe addressed his question to the group. Tina and Darlene produced their canteens.

"I've got about a fourth," Darlene said, sloshing her canteen.

Tina shook her water container. "I've got less than that."

The detective reflected a moment before responding. "Cam and I will each take a sip and leave the rest for you guys. We'll bring more water when we come back."

Darlene handed her canteen to the detective. He immediately passed the receptacle to Cameron to allow him the opportunity to drink. After a couple of sips, Cameron returned the canteen to Moe, who took a shallow drink.

"You ready?" the detective asked Cameron, as he returned the container to Darlene.

"I guess it's probably not gonna get any cooler," Cameron said. "We might as well head out."

"Be careful, Woody," Nancy quietly urged.

The detective gently squeezed her arm. "We'll be fine. We'll be back as quick as we can, I promise. Just make sure those guys don't lose their cool in the meantime. And keep trying your radios and cell phones...maybe you'll be able to get through to Harry. There's no shade up here, so try to keep your movements to an absolute minimum." He leaned over and gave Nancy a peck on the cheek. "I'm ready now," he winked at Cameron.

The two men stepped away from their companions, onto the faint trail leading down to the cemetery.

THEY WALKED IN SILENCE FOR three-quarters of an hour. Far in the distance, sunlight flashed off the windshields of vehicles driving along McDonald Drive.

"What do you think happened to everyone?" Cameron finally asked. He started to slide on some loose shale but quickly regained his balance.

"I don't know," the detective responded. "I'm not sure whether we should be worried or pissed. Right now I'm more pissed."

"Do you think something happened to them?"

Moe drew to a weary halt and leaned down to unbutton a pocket on his cargo pants. Removing his cell phone, he straightened. Using his hand to shield its screen from the blinding sun, Moe speed-dialed Harry's number, which he'd previously programmed into his phone. "Still no signal," he sighed after a moment.

"We're gonna have to get a lot closer to the road."

The detective nodded resignedly.

They approached the cemetery after another forty minutes, trudging past it without stopping. "I'm sorry I ever saw this place," Cameron softly commented, nodding in the direction of its rusted fence. Moe didn't respond.

Dry weeds whipped against the men's legs as they pressed resolutely onward. Fifteen minutes beyond the cemetery, Moe again stopped to try his cell phone again. McDonald Drive was close enough for them to actually hear the traffic on it.

This time his call went through.

"Hey, man, where are you?" Harry cheerfully greeted him.

"Me?" Moe barked. "Where the hell did you guys go?"

"I don't know exactly where we are," Harry breezily replied, seemingly oblivious to the anger in the detective's voice. "Hang on a sec. Hey, Phil!" Moe heard him yell through the phone, "Where are we?" The detective could hear a miscellany of indistinct voices in the background. "We're at 'Rosa's Cantina'," Harry finally informed him. "Where are you guys? Did you find what you were looking for?"

"Why the hell did you leave us out here?" Moe heatedly demanded. He put the cell phone on 'speaker' so Cameron, who crowded near him, could hear their conversation.

Harry was clearly taken aback by the detective's combative attitude. "Huh? What are you talking about? You *told* us to leave! Why are you yelling, Woody?"

"*Told* you to leave? We told you to *wait* for us. Nobody told you to leave...what are you talking about, Harry?"

"Wait, wait," Harry responded. "Hang on 'till I can get someplace quieter." There was a pause while Harry found a more sedate location in the restaurant. "Okay, I'm back. Now, where are you, Woody?"

The detective struggled to maintain his temper. "Cameron and I are on McDonald, near the cemetery. We hiked here. The others are still up where we left you earlier today. Tina hurt her knee and can't walk. So why'd you leave us?"

"Jesus! Is Tina okay?"

"Everybody's okay, but we don't have any water. You've gotta come get us."

"Not a problem, Woody. Look, the only reason we left is because, about forty-five minutes after you headed out this morning, you called me on the radio and said that you guys found another way out that was quicker, and that we should go because you didn't need us anymore."

"None of us called you on the radio, Harry. Our radios don't even work!"

"Well, I don't know about that, Woody," Harry defensively responded, "but *somebody* called us on the radio. I don't know if it was you, personally, but it was somebody...why else would we have left?"

Hearing Harry's explanation, Woody felt his anger begin to abate.

"Well, did it *sound* like me?" the detective probed.

Harry reflected before responding.   "Not really, I guess. It was sorta raspy, scratchy, but I just figured they were cheap, shitty walkie-talkies. You identified yourself and told us that we could go. I told the other guys and we packed up and came here." He paused. "Woody, if it wasn't you I don't know who else it could have been. There's no way we would have just gone off and left you guys."

"Harry, it's Cam," Cameron interjected. Moe handed him the phone. "Like Woody said, none of us called you. Do you have any idea who it was? Did you recognize the voice?"

"I don't know, Cam," Harry responded. "He called me by name and said he was Woody. What was I supposed to do?"

"Well, right now you've gotta come get us," Moe urgently interjected.   "We don't have any water and everybody's still up the hill, waiting for us to get back!"

"We're on our way, Woody. Are you close enough to the cemetery to meet us there? We'll pick you up on the way."

"Yeah, we'll walk back there," Moe concurred. "But you have to leave *now* and make sure you bring water."

"We'll be there in twenty minutes," Harry promised. "Just hang tight and meet us at the cemetery. We're on our way."

The detective ended the call and slid the phone back into his pocket.

"Thank God you were able to get him," Cameron said with relief.

"If I hadn't been able to get hold of Harry, I'd have called somebody in the Department," Moe responded. "Believe me, I'd have gotten us out of here."

They turned to retrace their steps back to the cemetery. "So who do you think called Harry on the radio?" Cameron asked.

The detective paused. "I don't know, Cam, but it was malicious, whoever it was. They obviously want to hurt us, or worse. Harry had better get here in a hurry."

"Tricksters?"

"I don't know, Cam." Moe murmured. "I honestly don't know."

TWENTY

HE WAS ENVELOPED IN COMPLETE darkness. Although vaguely aware that he was lying supine on a cold, hard surface, Bill had no inkling of exactly where he was nor of how he had arrived there. The nebulous image of having stumbled while running at night flitted about the periphery of his muddled brain, though he could recall no sensation of actually falling. The only definitive movement he could discern was the chattering of his teeth from the penetrating cold.

Bill remained motionless while he tried to collect his thoughts, a stratagem he'd learned over many years of getting bucked off innumerable unruly horses. Before attempting to stand, he would lay on the ground, immobile, in order to settle his mind and determine whether he'd broken anything. Only when satisfied that he wasn't seriously injured would Bill ultimately clamber to his feet.

Because of the intense cold, Bill couldn't feel his limbs. He cautiously attempted to extend his right arm but, perhaps benumbed by the chill, it did not respond. When he tried to move his other arm it, too, was unresponsive. The ambient temperature continued to plummet.

Even though his teeth chattered uncontrollably, Bill tried to speak. No sound emerged from his throat. Stiff with cold, his efforts to lift his head were no more successful. He strained to roll onto his side but was unable to move.

From somewhere in the vast emptiness the faint sound of weeping reached Bill's ears. For the first time in his life, Bill was genuinely afraid.

After an eternity of ineffectual struggle, a tingling, burning sensation began to stir within Bill's prostrate body. His blood grudgingly resumed its sanguinary flow, ineluctably imbuing his torso with a semblance of feeling. Simultaneously, Bill's head began to throb; he guessed that he must have struck it at some point, rendering him unconscious.

"Why do you struggle so, my helpless friend?" inquired a wheedling voice from the surrounding darkness. "It will avail you nothing."

Bill whipped his head in the direction of the sound, but his eyes were unable to distinguish anything in the impenetrable murk. Although he still remained unable to move his limbs, a dull throb of pain began to radiate through the trunk of his inert body.

Bill attempted to swallow but his mouth was bereft of saliva. "Where are you, you bastard?" he managed to rasp. "Where am I?"

"What is it your companion recently asked me? Surely you remember: are you 'comfy'?" taunted the unseen inquisitor.

"You ain't gonna be too comfy once I'm on my feet, I promise you that," Bill threatened, renewing his feckless attempts to reanimate his deadened limbs. Blinding pain immediately seared through his trunk, forcing him to terminate his exertions. Copiously perspiring despite the cold, Bill feared he was once again on the verge of blacking out.

Moloch's mocking laughter rang in his ears. "I wish only to repay the solicitude you recently accorded me by doing you the honor of inviting you and your friend, Ham, to be my guests. Because you will have no further use of them for the duration of your stay, I also took the liberty of relieving your body of certain superfluities.

"Speak the Queen's English, you ugly bastard," Bill croaked in the frigid darkness.

"As you wish," Moloch accommodatingly replied. "Although you are probably only now becoming aware, you are no longer burdened with eyes or limbs because I removed them while you slept. I feared you might consider your presence an imposition and took steps to disabuse you of such foolish reservations. Now you may freely avail yourself of my hospitality in perfect ease, given that you are no longer capable of either standing or seeing." He paused as a distant wail pierced the freezing air, followed by a chorus of desolate sobbing. "Those agreeable sounds will be your unending companion," Moloch resumed. "I regret that your friend will be unable to savor its extraordinary beauty for, as you know, I found it needful to remove his head."

Bill's heart pounded as he struggled to breathe, his shivering now almost convulsive. If what the creature said was true, the source of the agonizing pain that was beginning to wrack his inert body was obvious.

"You're a lyin' sonofabitch," Bill whispered.

"If you are convinced of that," replied Moloch, "I invite you to rise. Should you succeed, you will be free to depart. Indeed, I will reward you with as much gold as you can carry."

Bill arched his back and thrashed frantically about in hopes of articulating his unresponsive limbs. His futile attempts were rewarded only with exquisite bursts of pain and he was rapidly forced to abandon his fruitless efforts and collapse back onto the cold floor.

"You are needlessly tiring yourself," Moloch smirked from somewhere nearby. "I would suggest that you wipe your undoubtedly sweaty brow, but that would prove quite impossible given your armless condition. Nor, my generosity notwithstanding, could you have carried any amount of gold whatsoever. No matter; you have an eternity to ponder your condition. Your companion, Ham, is here, too. Perhaps he will one day encounter you. Until then, I shall leave you to your thoughts." A harrowing shriek from somewhere nearby pierced the void, then all fell silent.

Mutilated and sightless, Bill was abandoned in the frozen darkness.

ANNO DOMINI NOSTRI IESU CHRISTO
1825

ONLY A HANDFUL OF PEOPLE WERE LEFT.

The *alcalde'* received correspondence two months previously, ordering his immediate return to Victoria de Durango. Rumors abounded that unrelenting attacks by warring Navajos, Utes, and Apaches had finally driven *Don* Luis from the largest and most congenial of his Floats, 150 leagues to the east. He and his family had retreated southward, where he marshalled his surviving men-at-arms and summoned his senior officials from the remaining Floats. To the extent the *alcalde'* was able to divine the rationale behind the summons, either *Don* Luis was displeased with his agent and wished to personally berate him for the unremitting dissipation of his *peones,* or he wished to personally reward the *alcalde'* for his exemplary service. Given *Don* Luis' present, embarrassing circumstances, the *alcalde'* chose to believe the latter. In any case, he promptly decamped from the *pueblo,* taking with him the remaining handful of men that *Capitán* Diego had left behind as guards when he, over a year ago, left on his abortive mission to locate the culprits responsible for abducting the *peones.* The *alcalde'* would require the troops' protection during the arduous overland journey to Durango, far to the south, because the intervening desert swarmed with marauding *Indios* and *bandidos.*

In truth, the *peones* were glad to be rid of the *alcalde',* as well as the troops he commandeered, who spent most of their time drinking *pulque* and fighting among themselves. Their absence represented no loss to the *pueblo.* Certainly, the soldiers did nothing to slow the continuing diminution of the population, and the *alcalde'* no longer even bothered to emerge from his quarters. At least when *Capitán* Diego was around he pretended to be concerned about the welfare of the *peones*; the *alcalde* engaged in no such pretense. Their seedy priest, who eagerly volunteered to accompany the *alcalde* on the trek to Durango, "in order to attend to his spiritual needs," was equally ineffectual in providing either material or spiritual comfort to the townsfolk. The *pueblo* had apparently been forsworn by both men and God.

In their wretchedness the *peones*, through fear of death, prayed to die.

"When will His Excellency return?" mourned one. Her husband and son had previously disappeared while searching for food, and she and her infant daughter were crowded together with the others, mostly old men, women and children, in a stifling room previously used to store dried beans.

"Does it matter?" responded another. "The *alcalde'* did nothing to protect us from the Evil One's grip, nor did that worthless priest. I'm glad they're gone. We can be no worse without them."

"But who will administer the Holy Communion?"

Her companion scowled. "God has abandoned us; the Eucharist is worth less than nothing. We have nothing to eat and our menfolk are gone. Are you so blind that you do not see that, if we wish to survive, we must repay God in the same coin?"

Initially detached from the conversation, the women around them began to listen attentively.

"You don't know what you are saying. The Evil One has seized your tongue." The woman edged away.

"Who is the 'Evil One,' Juana? Is not the God who has forsaken us and left us to perish in the wilderness truly the 'Evil One'?"

"You speak blasphemy!"

"If it is blasphemy to speak the truth, then I freely confess my guilt."

Another woman leaned closer. "What are you saying, Xochitl? Surely you cannot be saying that we should renounce our Blessed Savior!"

Xochitl turned to her. "There is no need to renounce him. He renounced us long ago...is that not apparent?"

The room fell silent except for the fussing of infants.

"So what are you saying?" the woman finally repeated.

"If God will not help us, we must turn to wherever help may be found."

"There is no help except through the blood of *Jesucristo*," Juana gravely intoned.

"But where is help to be found?" the other woman persisted, ignoring Juana's gloomy admonition. "My *niños*, they are starving."

Xochitl, clearly savoring the sudden attention, looked at her questioner with palpable confidence. "I have, myself, already found one who has promised our salvation. If," she knowingly added, "we are prepared to give in return."

"Give? What have we to give? We have nothing."

"He seeks only our loyalty. Surely a small thing in exchange for great rewards, to say nothing of the very survival of our children."

"Who is this Good Samaritan whom you praise so lavishly?" Juana sharply demanded.

Xochitl looked at her evenly. "He calls himself 'Moloch'."

"'*Moloch*?' I know no one by that name. Why, if he is *Mexicano* and resides in the *pueblo,* have we never heard of him?" Juana glanced at the stoical faces of the other women listening nearby, seeking confirmation.

"He does not live in the *pueblo*," Xochitl answered. "He lives in the *desierto* and, if we devote ourselves to him, we will be reunited with our vanished *maridos* and *niños.*"

"Your 'Moloch' is the serpent in the Garden of Eden," Juana spat.

"*Si*," Xochitl mockingly responded. "I'd forgotten what an Eden this is." She spread her hands expansively. "That is why our lives are filled with such ease and we are surrounded by our loving husbands and children."

"I miss my Pedro and my *niños*," another woman in the room admitted. She turned to Xochitl and, in a plaintive voice asked, "Why have they abandoned us for this man that you speak of? Why have they not returned home?"

Xochitl didn't immediately respond. "I don't know," she ultimately admitted. "Moloch promised me only that we can be reunited with them."

"He is a demon and a liar! A murderer!" Juana cried. She clumsily crossed herself.

The other woman ignored Juana's histrionics. "But where has everyone gone?" she pleaded. "Why does Moloch not deliver them to us?" Xochitl remained silent.

"I will do whatever Moloch requires that does not menace the lives of my children," a woman vowed. Other women in the immediate area nodded silently. "Where is he to be found?"

"I summon him by going into the *desierto* at night after everyone is sleeping," Xochitl confided. "I arrange certain objects on a flat rock...luck stones; a lizard's skull; the dried heart of a *paloma*; black goat's hair; candy made from brown sugar, mud and alum; and burn dried grasses. Moloch quickly reveals himself to me. When he does so, I give him a magic cake."

"But how did you learn these things, Xochitl?"

"My *madre* taught me many things when I was a girl," she said. "I remembered them all these years and, when God deserted the *pueblo*, I returned to them."

"Moloch is the devil," Juana grimly warned. "You risk your eternal soul."

"I will happily risk my soul if doing so reunites me with my family," another woman softly affirmed.

Juana turned to her. "Do you know what is in a 'magic cake,' *tonta*? It is made with *maize* mixed with the flesh of unbaptized children. What sort of evil creature would demand such an offering? Only a *demonio!*"

The women looked at Xochitl in alarm, who blandly shrugged.

"In the absence of *mi esposo,* Moloch gives food to me and my *niños* and, in return, he asks for almost nothing. I do not know what is in the magic cake, for he gives me the ingredients and I merely prepare it. I do not inquire further because its contents are neither here nor there to me." Xochitl paused and lowered her voice. "Moloch also told me there is much treasure in the *pueblo* and promises to reveal it to me," she concluded.

"Treasure!" scoffed Juana. "If the *alcalde* possessed treasure, why would he live here, rather than at his ease in Durango? And why would he not have taken such treasure with him when he departed? Do you suppose the *alcalde* would simply leave his 'treasure' lying around for anyone to find?"

"The *alcalde's* treasure is hidden," Xochitl insisted, undaunted. "Moloch told me that it is nearby, that it is guarded by a *diablillo,* and that, like a seed, it continues to grow beneath the earth. The *alcalde* will return for it after he concludes his business in Durango."

Juana looked at her incredulously. "You are a fool, Xochitl."

"In what manner do you help him?" another woman warily inquired, changing the subject.

"Moloch has a small red book that he directed me to make my mark in. I also swore to assist him, in exchange for which he promised to help my *niños* and me. Beyond that, he asks nothing of me. It is a trifle..." Xochitl's voice trailed off.

"He has no need to ask anything further of you," screeched Juana, "because you have already marked his book of death and bargained your soul for a crust of bread! Your contract was purchased at the expense of your soul!"

"*Cállate!*" A woman glared fiercely at Juana. "You are a foolish old woman who no longer has children to feed. Many of us still have little ones for whom we must care and, in the absence of our husbands, will do what we must. Making one's mark in a book seems a meager price to pay." She turned to Xochitl. "In what other manner did you agree to assist your friend?"

Xochitl hesitated.

"You see!" Juana howled. "She fears speaking because she is mindful of her wickedness and rightly trembles at the prospect of eternal damnation!" The remaining women ignored the harangue as they waited for Xochitl to respond.

"In return for food for my children," she woodenly resumed, "I am to renounce God and the Most Holy Trinity, as well as my baptismal vows. I promised to submit myself to Moloch in both body and soul, forever into eternity." She looked imploringly at the women seated around her. "If my *niños* had enough food to eat, I would despise such sins."

"You are doomed, Xochitl," Juana intoned.

"I do not wish a life here, or in the hereafter, without my *familia*," a woman said. "Will you show me how to contact this Moloch? I will mark his book and do what he wishes if he will provide for my *niños*." The women around her nodded their collective assent in silence.

"You are consigning your souls to hell," Juana rebuked them.

"We will go into the *desierto* this very night, after it begins to cool," Xochitl said, uncaring of Juana's censure.

TWENTY ONE

OUTSIDE, A STRAY CAT YOWLED and hissed. Using his fingers, Cameron parted the venetian blinds covering the window and peered into the alley. In the yellowish glow of a street light, he was able to clearly view the area immediately beyond his window. Although the volume of the caterwauling increased as he peered outside, the alley appeared empty of life. Cameron pulled his hand from between the cheap plastic slats and stepped away from the window.

The only illumination in the room was provided by the series of tiny indicator lights on the front of the TEAC. Cameron resumed his seat in front of the tape recorder and flicked on the small reading light adjacent to it. Sliding open the top drawer of the desk, he removed a yellow legal pad and an ink pen. He flipped through several pages on the pad, glanced at his wrist watch, and began jotting notes. When he'd finished, Cameron placed the legal pad and ink pen atop the desk then clamped the set of earphones on his head. He paused momentarily to gather his thoughts, then pressed the TEAC's 'record' button. As its large plastic reels slowly began to rotate, Cameron spoke.

"Chet, if you're here give me a sign."

Cameron was distressed by the continued screaming of the cat in the alley outside, which he could hear despite his headphones. It sounded as though someone was slitting the animal's throat.

"Chet," he repeated, louder this time. He closed his eyes and concentrated, trying to blot out the din just outside his bedroom window.

The howling abruptly ceased. Surprised, Cameron opened his eyes, grateful for the interlude, yet half-expecting the cacophony to resume.

Something thumped into the window.

Cameron jumped. His gaze flew in the direction of the disturbance. Startled by it, he was apprehensive about opening the venetian blinds to investigate its source. Mindful that an intruder, if that's what it was, might be able to peer into his bedroom through the narrow spaces between the closed slats of the venetian blinds, he quickly reached forward and extinguished the reading light. Cameron's heart raced in his chest.

Sitting in gloom, Cameron continued to stare toward the window, scarcely daring to breathe. The ghostly blinds appeared vaguely luminous in the glow of the streetlight outside. Realizing that the TEAC was still recording, Cameron quietly switched the machine off.

A low growl emanated from beyond the window. Something began rapping on the pane.

Silhouetted in the window was an anthropomorphic form which appeared to be standing in the alley, directly outside his window.

Cameron gasped softly. He feared moving, lest the figure outside see him through gaps in the blinds. The smell of decaying meat filled the air.

A vaporous cloud began to materialize around the interior of the window, visible in the half-light passing through the closed venetian blinds. The mist seeped lazily from between the closed slats and began drifting, wraithlike, in a phosphorescent stream toward Cameron. The ambient temperature inside the room plunged.

"Jesus Christ!" Cameron spontaneously blurted. He spun in his chair and snapped the reading light back on. The ethereal stream instantly vanished.

Cameron looked toward the window. The trespasser's outline could no longer be seen because of the interior light. He again clicked the reading lamp off. The silhouetted figure appeared to have vanished, though the diaphanous emanation around the window had formed itself into a gossamer bridge stretching to Cameron's desk. He stood and warily stepped around the swirling mass; the contiguous temperature was glacial.

Shivering in the frosty air, Cameron was transfixed by the eddying stream of vapor. Leisurely whirling and spinning, the translucent accretion began, like a spider's web, to completely envelop the small desk on which the TEAC recorder sat. He gingerly extended his hand to touch the fragile material; its coldness eddied and curled around his fingers. Cameron withdrew his hand and instinctively stepped backwards, his eyes still focused on the shimmering cloud that was beginning to obscure his desk. He glanced across the room, where the closed venetian blinds remained dimly illuminated by light passing through the window from the alley beyond.

Cameron's desk was by now completely cloaked in the ethereal substance. It flowed outward from the base and began to carpet the entire floor. The temperature in the room was now nearly freezing and he was shaking uncontrollably and nearly gagging from the fetor.

"To hell with this," he growled to himself, with more bravado than he actually felt. He turned and walked to the overhead light switch on the bedroom wall. Hesitating only a moment, Cameron flipped it on.

Instantaneously, the vaporous effusion evaporated in the harsh overhead light. In its place, a score of what appeared to be white mice tumbled to the floor and frantically darted beneath Cameron's bed, squeaking madly. He didn't even have time to react.

"What the fuck?" he exclaimed, stunned. No vestige of the mist was in evidence. The temperature in the room immediately returned to normal and the nauseating stench dissolved.

Cameron remained with his hand on the wall switch, uncertain what to do next. His eyes flitted about the bedroom. Beneath his bed he could still hear the creatures rustling and chittering. The bed skirt that hung nearly to the floor prevented him from specifically identifying them and he was leery of the prospect of peering under the bed in order to do so. Cameron looked toward the table where his legal pad still rested next to the tape recorder.

On an otherwise blank page of the yellow tablet someone had scrawled several sentences.

Even from where he stood across the room, Cameron could see that the handwriting was unfamiliar.

Cameron's eyes widened and his pulse quickened. Although it seemed utterly impossible, someone had evidently managed to steal into his bedroom in the darkness of the last few minutes. Perhaps the intruder was there still, the noise emanating from beneath his bed betraying his presence.

Cameron rapidly weighed his options. His .22 pistol rested in the drawer of his bedside table, necessitating that he walk past his bed to retrieve it, a venture he was reluctant to undertake. He could call the police...his cell phone lay on the living room coffee table. And tell them what? That he thought someone might be hiding under his bed? Aside from the embarrassment factor, the police would undoubtedly ask probing questions that Cameron would prefer not to answer. He could call Woody or Nancy, but it would take either of them at least a half-hour to drive to Cameron's apartment. And, once they arrived, what then? Moreover, if Cameron left to get his cell phone from the coffee table, what might happen in the few moments he was absent from the bedroom?

The stirring beneath his bed subsided. Cameron listened intently for a few seconds, but all was still. Leaving the overhead light on, he cautiously left his place near the wall switch and, deliberately skirting the bed, returned to the small table holding the tape recorder and legal pad. He bent to read what had been written on the latter.

Written in ponderous lower-case cursive, the composition seemed to have been written by a child, its letters comprised of large, uneven, canted loops of varying heights. There were numerous run overs and the spaces between the letters were irregular. Although Cameron's ink pen lay atop the yellow pad, the note appeared to have been written in pencil, of which there were none in the room.

The first line of the apparent message, two-thirds down the page, looked to Cameron's eyes as nothing more than a shapeless doodle. Beneath it, a second line stated, "it is not there." Slightly below, and to the right of this, was written, "you are." The latter two words seemed the product of an entirely different hand, for the letters were diminutive, feminine, evenly spaced, and well-formed. The terminal line on the page contained only the words "wrong" and "yes," written in the same juvenile manner as the first sentence of the note. Beneath the final two words was drawn a rough image of a human face, though Cameron was unsure whether it was intended to be male or female. The composition was unsigned.

He involuntarily shivered as he read the enigmatic communication. Cameron straightened and looked over his shoulder, toward the bed. Nothing seemed amiss. Although not eager to do so, Cameron knew that he had to determine what was beneath it, notwithstanding that the previous rustling noises had subsided.

Cameron walked from the small table to his bedroom closet, where he removed a wooden yardstick. He tossed the yardstick onto the floor a few feet from the bed before going to his bedside table, where he opened the drawer and removed his Walther pistol and a flashlight. Holding one in each hand, he dropped to his hands and knees next to the yardstick on the carpeted floor.

Cameron could discern nothing under the bed because the space between the bottom of the bed skirt and the floor was too narrow. He laid his pistol on the floor, muzzle pointing toward the bed. Warily lifting the bed skirt with the yardstick, Cameron directed the beam of the flashlight beneath the bed and rapidly scanned the carpeted floor.

The space was empty.

Relieved though puzzled, Cameron used the illumination afforded by his flashlight to scrutinize the floor from one end of the bed to the other. There was absolutely nothing there. He held the bed skirt up with his free hand and used the yardstick to sweep the carpeted floor. Thankfully, nothing scampered out.

Perplexed, Cameron released the bed skirt, rolled onto his back, and stared at the ceiling while he contemplated what to do next. His reverie was broken when his cell phone began buzzing from the next room.

Cameron climbed to his feet and tossed the flashlight onto the bed before bending to retrieve his pistol. He exited the bedroom, leaving the communicating door open.

The living room was largely illuminated by light streaming in through the open bedroom door and Cameron laid the Walther on the couch before scooping up his phone. The screen indicated "unknown caller." He mechanically flipped the phone open and held it to his ear.

"This is Cam," he said.

Faint rushing sounds filled the tiny speaker, as though a windstorm was raging in the distance.

"Hello? This is Cam," he repeated.

"Under the bed," a sepulchral voice finally responded. "Under the bed."

Cold rivulets of sweat began to course down Cameron's sides beneath his shirt. "Who is this?" he barked into the phone.

"The bed," repeated the lifeless voice before being enveloped in the background noise.

"Fuck you!" Cameron spat. He abruptly terminated the call by pushing the "end" button on the cell phone's faceplate. He was shaking.

Cameron placed the phone back on the coffee table and sank onto the adjacent couch. He sat on the edge and stared at his cell phone, fully expecting it to ring again. His heart was pounding and cold beads of perspiration glistened on his forehead. He grasped his pistol with his right hand.

The cell phone remained silent.

After sitting what seemed an hour, Cameron stood and returned to the bedroom, carrying with him the pistol and cell phone. Everything in the room appeared as he had left it a few minutes previously. He retrieved the flashlight from atop his bed then knelt on the floor. Clicking the flashlight on, Cameron lifted the bed skirt and once again surveyed the space beneath his bed.

It was inconceivable that Cameron had, during his initial survey, completely overlooked what appeared to be a sheet of thin cardboard lying directly beneath the bed in the center of the carpeted floor. Using the yardstick, he guardedly dragged the object toward him.

Cameron laid the yardstick aside then climbed to his feet. He bent to pick up the stiff material and sat on the edge of his bed to examine it in the overhead light.

The object was prosaic dull white paperboard, about eight inches square. Three of its edges were cut smoothly, while its fourth edge was rough, as though it had been torn rather than cut. The side facing Cameron was blank, so he flipped it over.

Printed in bold letters was the word "cemetery."

ANNO DOMINI NOSTRI IESU CHRISTO
1825

IN THE SWELTERING TWILIGHT, a dozen women trouped into the baking desert. Most were accompanied by stumbling children; a few carried infants in their arms or swaddled them in wide strips of faded cloth slung from their bodies. Although the angry sun had reluctantly dipped behind the surrounding hills almost an hour previously, the temperature remained torrid. Each of the women carried an offering for Moloch: a few tortillas, a small earthenware bowl of *frijoles* or *pozole,* an old pair of *huaraches.* The pious Juana refused to participate in the women's foray into the desert, declining even to guard their children during their absence. She remained in the village, clutching her rosary and muttering devout prayers. The children began to quietly whimper as the small band picked its way through a rugged landscape indifferently illuminated by an apathetic moon.

"How far do we have to walk, Xochitl?" one of the women grumbled.

"There is a peculiar rock where we meet," Xochitl replied from her place in the lead. "As soon as he sees me, Moloch emerges from the *desierto*."

"If he knows the whereabouts of treasure, as you say, surely he will not be satisfied with our meagre offerings," remarked another.

"He does not care a fig for treasure," Xochitl assured her. "He expects only loyalty."

Beyond the looming hills, a myriad of stars started to reveal themselves in the celestial vault overhead, their glacial light spearing the firmament. A pack of coyotes undertook a mournful howling in the distance. The women, with the exception of Xochitl, shivered collectively.

"Are we close, Xochitl?" one of them asked. As she spoke, she tripped over the uneven earth and nearly fell, dropping her gift to Moloch onto the ground.

"*Mama!*" yelped the child floundering behind her in the darkness. The youngster abruptly stopped in his tracks and began to cry.

"No, no, *hijo.*" The woman turned, abandoning the splash of *frijoles* at her feet. She stooped and took the sobbing child in her arms. "You see? *Mama está bien. Todo está bien,*" she cooed as she stroked his head. The remaining women clustered protectively around her while the children watched gloomily.

Ignoring the sobbing child, Xochitl pointed to a large flat stone several yards away, resembling an altar. "That is the place," she announced.

"Where is Moloch?" one of the women asked, straining her eyes in the direction of the cynosure.

"He is near and sees us already," Xochitl assured them. She turned and looked detachedly at the crying child. "He is attracted to weeping."

"How long must we wait here?" The yowling coyotes seemed to be encroaching on them and a few of the women fancied they could see the forms of animals skulking in the fringes of the moonlight.

"He will be here soon," Xochitl promised. "We must not stop now." Without waiting for the others she resumed shambling in the direction of the lithic platform.

"Ugh! What is that smell?" a woman exclaimed as the unexpected odor of decomposing flesh drifted over the group.

"He is here," Xochitl confided as she quickened her step, ignoring the outburst.

"Greetings," rasped a strange, piping voice from somewhere in the darkness.

Xochitl abruptly stopped. "*Saludos*," she returned the salutation into the void. Xochitl bent and piled a handful of curiously shaped stones and some quail feathers atop the flat stone. The sickening sweetness of rotting meat began to permeate the oppressive air, prompting the women to hastily press the hems of their tattered skirts to their noses. They instinctively drew closer together. "*Hijole!*" one of them exclaimed. "What *is* that?"

"It is nothing," Xochitl quickly assured her. "Do not be alarmed."

"You have done well, my child," said the spectral voice. "How many have you?"

"Over a dozen," replied Xochitl.

"Splendid!"

"They have come to be with their husbands and children," Xochitl guardedly added. She uneasily scanned the encompassing gloom.

"And so they shall. They are with me here at this moment." Hearing this, the women began to murmur.

"Where is my Roberto?" cried one.

"Put yourselves at your ease. He is here, as are all of your loved ones, eager to see you once again," Moloch smoothly replied from somewhere in the murk. "You will see them all in due course when I take you to them."

"I want to see him *now*," the woman stammered. "Xochitl, where is Roberto? Where are the others?" she whispered. "It smells very bad here."

"Place your things on the stone," Xochitl instructed, indicating the flat rock adjacent to her. "Moloch must see that we come in good faith and with pure hearts."

One by one the women hesitantly shuffled forward in the dimness to deposit their modest gifts, afterward huddling together uneasily.

"Look." Their attention was arrested when one of them raised an emaciated arm to point into the distance. A number of ill-defined, shaggy creatures crouched in the dimness, silhouetted against the pale earth of the desert floor.

"*Coyotes*," a woman muttered. "They are drawn to the smell of rotting meat."

"I do not like this place," said another, the fear in her quivering voice evident. "Why does your friend not show himself?" She turned toward the flat stone but Xochitl had vanished. *"Orale! Where did she go?"* she exclaimed in dismay.

The women began to frantically mill about, desperately crying aloud, as they anxiously searched the darkness for the woman who'd led them into the desert. In their despair, they initially failed to detect Moloch's unobtrusive emergence from the shadows.

"Cállate!" he barked above the tumult. *"Cállate!"*

Stunned, the women abruptly stopped their keening and focused their collective attention on the intruder.

In the pallid moonlight a dwarfish goat-like figure, smaller in stature than even the women themselves, stood next to the alter-shaped stone.

A putrid fetor clung to the bare-headed form whose physiognomy was masked by the enveloping darkness. He seemingly wore furry trousers and a coarse mantle that fell to his waist.

"Quién eres?" one of them guardedly asked, instinctively shrinking to one side. "Where is Xochitl?"

"She has joined the family that has patiently awaited her here, as I promised she would," Moloch replied. "Just as you, yourselves, will."

"I have no family here. I want to return to the *pueblo.*"

"Indeed? I thought it was your desire to be reunited with your loved ones," Moloch scoffed in mock surprise. He edged closer to the huddled group of frightened women.

"Where are they?" a woman skeptically responded. "There is no one here."

"They are here, and others besides. They have been awaiting you," he unctuously replied.

Some of the women stole glances into the contiguous desert. The coyotes that had earlier prowled the fringes had stealthily reformed themselves into a loose ring that surrounded the group, creating an effective barricade. Their tongues lolled from mouths from which long strings of saliva dripped. A child began to wail but her mother quickly pressed a calloused hand over her mouth to silence her.

Observing this, Moloch resumed. "Why do you fear? I wish only to reward your constancy by granting you riches, as well as the power to exact vengeance on your enemies and all those who have abused you. We will become partners, you and I, in a just crusade against the inequities of this world."

"Being reunited with Roberto is enough. I seek nothing more."

"In that case, you will be amply rewarded," Moloch said. "Look!" He extended one of his misshapen, hairy arms and, with an open palm, gestured behind the group of women.

From the gloom a figure slouched toward them through the desert. Impossible to recognize in the exhausted moonlight, it dragged its feet and stumbled as though inebriated. Looming beyond it in the distance the women were able to discern the dim outlines of additional, motionless forms which appeared to be mutely observing them.

"Roberto?" one of the women spontaneously blurted in a whispered query. She glanced with unease at the woman beside her, who remained silent, her attention consumed by the shambling figure.

"You see, *mujeres*, I did not deceive you!" Moloch cackled. "Your loving husbands await your embrace and beg you to join them!"

A woman took a halting step in the direction of the lurching figure.

"Rosa!   No!   Whoever that is, it is not Roberto!" Her friend extended a restraining hand.

Roughly brushing off the impediment, Rosa pushed toward the figure, which had wobbled to a halt and stared dumbly in the direction of the assembled women, neither acknowledging their presence nor speaking.

The individual was clad in filthy, tattered hemp trousers and shirt, and was barefoot. His disheveled hair hung in his face and drool bubbled from his slack, stubble-covered jaw.

"Roberto, Roberto!" cried the woman as she bolted toward the figure. *"Mi querido!"* The others watched, stupefied, as she flung herself to the earth and passionately wrapped her arms around the calves of the figure's legs. *"Mi amor,"* she wailed, pressing her face into his fetid clothing.

"Your husbands, sons, brothers, sisters, and daughters are all here!" cried Moloch, dancing gleefully as clouds of effluvium billowed into the dead air. "My daughter, Xochitl, has told you of treasure concealed about the *pueblo*. Will it surprise you to learn, my children, that the treasure of which she speaks is not hidden, nor is it mere worthless baubles buried in the earth? Nay, *you* are the treasure!" With a skeletal appendage more animal than human, he animatedly gestured toward the encompassing desert.   "Behold your loved ones, gathered in expectation of your arrival tonight. They beg you to repudiate your former lives and join them in their new abode, where you will be revered and venerated.   You have come this far and your families long to be reunited with you. Put aside your anxieties and misgivings; your place lies here now."

"We are not your 'children,'" one of the women defiantly asserted, her outward fortitude betrayed by the quiver in her voice. "We are the children of God in heaven who is our father, as the Apostle Pablo reminds us in Romans."

"Juana spoke truly at the *pueblo*," added another. "You and this place are evil. We must leave."

Moloch screeched with bitter laughter. "Leave? You wish to slink back to your hovels, where you and your children are free to prostrate yourselves before your false god, who entertains little regard for you? Why, despite your devotions, did your divine father callously take your menfolk from you, thereby allowing you and your children to starve? Why has he abandoned you to this wilderness, where only the ravenous wolves will profit by your imminent deaths? Are those the acts of a just and loving father? Small wonder that your loved ones despise your impotent god, who heaps upon you nothing but suffering and anguish.

Anxiously pressed together in the gloom, none of the women ventured a response.

"What he says is true." Rosa's frail voice finally emerged from the silence. Startled, the women looked in her direction. She'd released her grip on Roberto, who remained standing before them, glassy-eyed and swaying slightly from side to side, seemingly oblivious to the conclave taking place around him.

"What are you saying?" one of the women importuned.

"God has abandoned us," Rosa declared. "We are as nothing to Him."

"God and his blessed son and lord, Jesus Christ, love us as their own children," a woman hollowly insisted.

"If that is so, where are they? I do not see them, nor have I seen any evidence of them in a long while. If this place is evil, as you say, why are they not here to protect us? We pray constantly with open hearts, as we have been taught since childhood, but are rewarded with only endless sorrows. Even the *alcalde* and his *monje* have abandoned us to our wretched lot, to say nothing of God and Christ Jesus. They do not care a straw for us."

"You are wise," Moloch gravely observed. "It would be well for your sisters to heed you." He turned to address the women collectively. "Is it not obvious that you have been duped by an uncaring god who demands cringing devotion, yet repays you with unending misery? You have only to join us and your sorrows will be at an end. You will be at liberty to enjoy perfect ease, exactly as your loved ones have already discovered. Who could possibly blame them for choosing such repose over a life of unmitigated suffering? It is not you who have sinned against god; it is god who has sinned against you!"

"Do not allow yourselves to be tricked," cautioned a woman. "Although he speaks honeyed words, he cares nothing for us and desires only that we deny God, the Blessed Virgin, and the holy saints." She turned to Rosa. "*Tu esposo* is not here, Rosa. I do not know who, or what, that is," she pointed to the silent form standing over the seated woman, "but it is not Roberto."

Rosa tenderly grasped the mute figure's tattered cuff. "Even if he is only one-half of *mi esposo*," she whimpered, "that is one-half more than I have now."

"You are mistaken," Moloch smoothly responded, ameliorating her anxieties. "Roberto is much superior to what he previously was. Before, he was little more than a sleepwalker, burdened with care. Now, he is fully awake and eager for you to join him...a *novum hominem*."

"He looks very far from awake," asserted a woman. "What happened to him?"

"Can you not see that he is merely overwhelmed with joy?" Moloch answered. "All will be well once your loved ones have you near them once again."

"Where is *José Ruiz*?" another woman demanded. "I do not see him. Is he here?"

"And *Ignacio Ramirez*?" added a third.

"*José*, and all your loved ones, patiently await your embrace." Moloch gestured toward the vague figures standing mutely in the distance. "They wish for you to join them in your new home."

"*Donde?*" A dubious woman glanced nervously about; the coyotes that had previously surrounded them had soundlessly melted into the night.

"We have prepared places for all of you," Moloch promised. "You will soon be rejoicing in the company of your dear ones. Do not be afraid." He began to impatiently goad the women and children toward the open desert.

A woman pointed to the alter stone. "And our offerings, shall we leave them here?"

"Bring them with you," Moloch soothingly responded, knowing the viands represented the last meal his captives would ever eat. "You may do with them what you will once you arrive at your new home."

The anxious women allowed themselves to be herded in a tremulous march into *terra incognita*, where sunless fissures yawned into the depths of the earth.

TWENTY TWO

CAMERON, NANCY AND MOE occupied a table on the Mexican restaurant's misted patio. Moe and Nancy moved their chairs close to one another in order to hold hands.

"So what are you proposing?" Nancy asked. She idly swatted at a large, persistent fly that had annoyed them since they sat down.

"Going back to the cemetery," Cameron responded. "That's clearly what I'm supposed to do."

"And do what?" Nancy scoffed. "We've already been there, twice, and other than losing Daisy, nothing came of it. Besides, you don't even know who, or what, wrote that, or even what it means." Before them on the table was the card that Cameron found under his bed.

"Not true," Cameron corrected her. "When Woody and I did voice recording at the cemetery, the voice asked us to come to 'the house.' I assumed it meant the house in Esperanza, but what if it meant the charnel house?"

"Why would it ask you to go someplace if you were already there?" Nancy said. "That doesn't make any sense."

The fly continued to torment them, buzzing loudly around their heads. It finally alit near Nancy and began a herky-jerky perambulation about the table.

"Damn!" the detective exclaimed. "What the hell kind of fly is that? A horse fly?" The creature was iridescent blue with red eyes, the length of a man's thumbnail. Stiff hairs grew from its body.

"I think so," Nancy opined. "It's too big for a regular house fly. Are there stables or something around here?"

"Not that I know of," Moe said. "I guess he just likes the food here," he smiled.

The fly sprang into the air with a loud tremolo and flew directly at Nancy. Although she attempted to dodge it by leaning toward the detective, the insect landed on her neck with an audible thump, where it locked itself onto her skin.

"Owe! Dammit!" she cried. "It hurts!" She rapidly reached up to dislodge the creature. "It burns!" she yelped. "It feels like it's biting me!"

Both Moe and Cameron sprang from their chairs.

"Don't smash it!" Cameron warned.

The detective gently lifted Nancy's pony tail away from her neck. Her skin, which was beginning to redden, was clasped in the insect's bristly legs. Without taking his eyes off Nancy, Moe reached down with his free hand and retrieved a napkin from atop the table and gathered it into his hand. Cameron reached forward to help hold Nancy's hair aside.

"I'm gonna grab it in this napkin he whispered. 'Don't move."

"Hurry up!" Nancy hissed from between clenched teeth. "It hurts like hell!"

Moe cautiously raised the napkin toward Nancy's neck. The fly remained immobile.

"Almost there," he whispered. With a rapid sweep of his hand the detective enveloped the insect in the napkin and plucked it from Nancy's neck.

"Ouch!" she winced. "Did you get it?"

Pinched inside the napkin between his fingers, Moe could feel the fly buzzing angrily.

"Yeah. You okay?" The detective and Cameron resumed their seats, the former clutching the captive insect.

"I swear to God it felt like somebody was poking a red-hot ice pick into my neck," Nancy groused. "What the hell *was* that? Am I bleeding?" Nancy gingerly touched her neck with her fingertips.

Cameron leaned forward to scrutinize her neck. "You're not bleeding, but it looks like there's kind of a little welt there."

"Can you see anything, Woody?" Nancy tilted her head to one side.

The detective scooted his chair closer and scrutinized the area. "I suppose it *could* have bit you," he concluded after a moment. "Does it still hurt?"

Nancy stroked her neck again. "Not like it did, but it's still tender. You sure it's not bleeding?" She withdrew her fingers and looked at them for evidence of blood.

"No, not bleeding," Moe reiterated. He planted a quick kiss on her neck. "That should help," he smiled.

"It feels better already, Dr. Woody," Nancy grinned. "How much do I owe you?"

"We'll talk about that later," he winked.

Nancy nodded toward the napkin the detective still held. "What are you gonna do with that?"

The detective glanced somewhat sheepishly at the napkin in his left hand. "I know it probably won't make much sense to you guys, but I don't feel right about killing something just for doing what nature created it to do."

"You mean bite me?" Nancy sarcastically responded.

"Well, that's sometimes what flies do..." Moe noted. "Flies behave like flies because nature didn't give them a choice."

"So what are you gonna do with it?" Nancy again asked.

Moe stood. "Hang on a sec...I'll be right back." He began walking toward the restaurant's parking lot.

"If you're gonna let it go, do it where it won't come flying back here," Nancy called after him.

"I'd have just smashed it," Cameron confided as the detective disappeared around the corner.

"Yeah, I know," Nancy sighed. "But Woody comes from a different culture. He looks at nature differently than we do. You know how the Sikhs in India carefully sweep their porches so as not to harm any insects that might be there? Woody's kinda like that." She smiled almost wistfully.

"I'd have smashed it," Cameron repeated.

The detective returned five minutes later.

"No problems?" Nancy teased.

Moe slid into his chair. "No, but it was pretty pissed off. It flew right at me when I unwrapped it! Thought it was gonna take my head off!"

"Did it bite you?" Nancy asked in alarm.

"No, but I had to keep ducking. I've never seen anything that aggressive...not even a pissed-off wasp! It finally flew away, thank God."

"What kind of fly attacks people?" Cameron mused.

Moe shrugged. "No idea, but I hope it doesn't come back." He looked at Nancy. "Your neck okay?" She nodded. "Well, where were we before the arrival of our dive-bombing guest?"

"Cam was discussing going back to the cemetery," Nancy drily replied, "specifically, those two tombs."

"Charnel houses," Cameron corrected her.

Moe was unable to disguise his skepticism. "Every 'house' we've been to, either the charnel houses or the Esperanza house, has been a disaster. We're no closer to finding Chet and we've just about got ourselves killed. In fact, even our *own* houses aren't safe anymore."

Cameron tapped the card with his fingertip. "Then why would they have written this?" he challenged.

"Who *cares*?" Nancy cried in exasperation, throwing her hands up. "We don't even know who 'they' are! Whoever 'they' are, they're just screwing with us and we continue to play along with them. Instead of *acting* we're always *reacting*." Nearby diners looked up from their plates with curiosity.

"So what would you suggest?" Cameron retorted. "Should we just forget the whole thing and call it a day?"

Moe gazed soberly into the distance. "Well, for whatever reason, somebody wants Cameron to return to the cemetery," he finally said. "But I agree with Nancy that we always seem to be one step behind whoever it is." He paused. "The problem is, I don't see what other options we have at this point. It seems to me that we either return to the cemetery, or we do nothing." The detective grasped Nancy's hand and looked at her almost apologetically. "No one expects you to keep putting yourself at risk," he said.

"Too late now," she snorted. "I'll go wherever you guys go. Looking back on it, I should have gone back to the cemetery with you when Cam did voice recordings there. Maybe I could've talked some sense into you." She smiled thinly, a futile effort to project an air of confidence.

No one at the table was persuaded.

"Okay, so now what do we do?" Nancy continued after a moment. She arched her eyebrows and looked expectantly first at Moe, then at Cameron. With an equivocal expression, the latter turned silently toward the detective.

Moe looked slightly disgruntled. "Well, I guess we'll go back to the cemetery," he said.

"Day? Night? When?" Cameron queried.

Nancy shook her head. "I'm willing to go back out there with you guys, but I'm not goin' at night. No way."

The detective took a sip of Coke Zero. "I agree. It's bad enough in broad daylight."

"So when should we go?" Cameron pressed.

Moe looked at Nancy, who said nothing. "I suppose there's no sense in waiting," he finally said. "Whatever's gonna happen is gonna happen, no matter when we go."

"Should we ask any of those guys if they want to come, too?" Cameron asked, referring to Tina, Darlene, and Andres.

"Yeah, good luck with that!" Nancy laughed. "After what happened out at that house you'd have to *pay* them to come. Andres, anyway."

"She's right," Moe concurred. "None of 'em will probably want to come." He looked ruefully at Nancy. "Who could blame 'em?"

The arrival of a waiter with multiple plates balanced on one arm interrupted their conversation.

"Very hot plates," the waiter cautioned as he slid dishes onto the table.

"Looks good," Nancy declared. She grinned at the detective. "I'm glad you thought of this place."

"Can I get you anything else for now?" the waiter inquired.

Moe looked at Cameron and Nancy, who shook their heads. "No, I think we're good. Just keep the Coke Zeros comin'."

"I'll check on you in a few minutes," the waiter assured them before departing.

"Well, eat, drink, and be merry, for tomorrow we die," Moe grimly proposed as he began to slice the *quesadilla.*

"Very funny," Cameron groused.

"Yeah, I don't like the sound of *that,*" Nancy added.

"I just figured that, under the circumstances, a little graveyard humor might be appropriate," the detective suggested.

"You forget that 'graveyard humor' is just an expression," Nancy drily remarked as the detective slipped a slice of quesadilla onto her plate. He then beckoned Cameron to pass his plate.

"Yeah, but it probably originated in a cemetery," Moe responded. "Otherwise, they'd call it 'laundry humor' or 'Mexican restaurant humor.'" He grinned at Nancy.

"Well, if it's okay with you guys, I'm gonna call 'em, anyway," Cameron resumed. "Maybe Harry and Phil and those guys will want to come for the hell of it."

"Yeah, I'd forgotten how reliable they turned out to be last time," Nancy said with feigned seriousness.

Cameron looked at her acerbically but didn't argue. He retrieved his plate from Moe and took a bite of quesadilla instead.

The detective placed some Mexican food on his plate. "I suppose there's no harm is asking them," he conceded. "When do you guys want to go?"

Nancy shrugged as she nibbled at her *quesadilla*. Moe turned expectantly to Cameron.

"This weekend?" Cameron suggested, looking at Nancy, who shrugged again.

"Done," said Moe. "Call your friends and see if they wanna come."

Cameron nodded wordlessly as he finished off his remaining quesadilla before digging into a cheese enchilada.

IN THE GLOOM, A DISCORDANT buzzing heralded his emissary's return.

"Ah, *Liebchen*, what tidings do you bear?" Moloch crooned, cocking his deformed head in the direction of the inharmonious sound.

The iridescent blue insect, the length of a man's thumbnail, alit on his cheek, the stiff hairs on its body abrading his crusted skin. Moloch reached up with a scaly hand and lovingly stroked it.

"What did you see on your sojourn, I wonder? You undoubtedly observed that, notwithstanding the helpless intercession of their laughable god, the world spirals unceasingly into Pandemonium. Will we have additional tenants soon; do you think?"

The insect began a soft trilling, its body throbbing in unison.

Moloch smiled, running his split tongue over yellowed, pointed teeth. "Splendid. For too long we have been forced to content ourselves with desiccated corpses or the occasional straggler. Let us make certain our anticipated new arrivals are made welcome. You have done well, *bien-amie'*."

The insect continued trilling for a moment, then waddled across Moloch's feculent cheek and climbed into one of his nostrils.

"Rest well, *deliciae meae.* We will soon enjoy the company of new disciples."

TWENTY THREE

"I WAS THINKING WE MIGHT COULD build a sorta main ranch house here. You know, kinda like Cinderella's Castle. Could sell cowboy hats and such...maybe put in a family-style restaurant. There's probably a lot of old stuff buried around here that we can use to decorate it. Maybe sell some of it, too."

"Yeah, I suppose that would be doable," his companion amiably agreed. "Be a pain in the ass to haul in lumber and equipment, though. We sure as hell don't want it to get out that we're building a wild west Disneyland. Don't want some other bastard gettin' the jump on us."

The first man looked around. "We could probably tear down some of these old buildings and salvage the lumber. A lot of them are close to falling down and wouldn't pass code, anyway. Besides, using the original lumber will make 'em more authentic."

His friend nodded noncommittally. "What are we gonna do about electricity and plumbing?" he asked. "There sure as hell ain't no power or water all the way out here."

"We'll use outhouses and a generator," Dave responded, undeterred. "It'll give the place a more authentic atmosphere."

Arizona had been a state for less than fifty years and the scattered accoutrements of the Old West, including wagons, buckboards, saddles, firearms, and mining equipment remained widespread. Collectors were beginning to recognize the potential value of such objects and prices were steadily increasing, fueled in large part by prime-time television westerns like 'Gunsmoke,' 'Rawhide,' 'Bonanza,' and 'Have Gun, Will Travel.'

Hoping to cash in on the Old West mania, the two men made repeated forays into the raw desert in order to investigate rumors of a ghost town they'd heard about from various hikers. Aside from purportedly being located "in the hills around Scottsdale," they knew nothing of its exact whereabouts and had devoted months searching for it. Although they managed to locate a circle of cement foundations and a scattering of abandoned, roofless stone cottages in the desert near the base of Thompson Peak, far to the north of Scottsdale, their location rendered it improbable those few structures represented the "town" they were seeking. They kept looking.

It was Ed who spotted the old cemetery as they drove slowly along McDonald Drive.

"Hey, stop the car," he ordered. Dave applied the brakes and they lurched to a halt in the middle of the one-lane dirt thoroughfare, choking dust boiling up and enveloping their car. "You see that?" He flicked his cigarette butt out the open window then extended his arm and pointed north.

Dave squinted into the glare. "Stinking Desert Estates, you mean?"

"No, a cemetery. See it?"

"Yeah, I guess," Dave dubiously responded.

Ed swiveled his head to see where Dave was looking. "No, *there*." He vigorously flexed his wrist up and down to emphasize where he was pointing.

"Well, I see a big patch of weeds with some crap sticking out of 'em," Dave finally conceded. "That?"

"It's a cemetery, or what's left of one," Ed declared. "And where there's a cemetery, there's a town." He flung the car door open and bailed out of the vehicle.

Dave pulled to the edge of the roadway and turned the engine off. "It's already hotter than the devil's dick," he grumbled. "How long's this gonna take?"

But Ed was already out of earshot as he bounded through the desert.

"Hey! What'd I tell you!" Ed shouted excitedly over his shoulder.

"What is it?" Dave called as he tromped through the sage brush. His shirt stuck to his body with perspiration.

"Just what I said: a cemetery!"

Ed stood at the edge of the grave yard, panting from exertion. With a shirtsleeve, he wiped the sweat that streamed down his face and leaned against a tilted fence post while he waited for Dave to catch up.

It was obvious that the derelict cemetery hadn't been used in a long time. The fence that had apparently once enclosed it had collapsed and the graves were all but obliterated by overgrowth.

"Well, it *was* a cemetery," Dave conceded as he approached. He scanned the contiguous desert. "So where's the town?"

"Gotta be here somewhere," Ed speculated. "They sure as hell didn't haul all these stiffs out here and bury 'em just for the hell of it."

"How old you think this place is?"

Ed shook his head. "No tellin'. Fifty, a hundred years?"

The men fought their way through the bushes growing around the perimeter of the graveyard, not knowing what they were looking for. Both were drenched in sweat.

"Looks like a trail here," Dave announced from the far side of the cemetery.

"Where's it go?"

"Hard to say, but it looks like it heads that way." Dave pointed northward.

Ed looked in the direction indicated. "Well, from what we know, the ghost town is supposedly 'in the hills around Scottsdale.' We're 'around Scottsdale' and those look like hills to me."

"More like mountains than hills, but..." Dave's voice trailed off.

"I wouldn't be surprised if there's a town up there," Ed continued. "They were probably mining for silver or copper."

"Maybe. So what do you wanna do?"

"Let's check it out," Ed enthusiastically urged.

"We can't do it now because we don't have water or supplies," Dave cautioned. "We may be able to drive part of the way up, depending on the terrain, but it might be a pretty long hike from there. Especially since we don't know where the hell we're goin'."

"Think your heap'll make it?" Ed asked, referring to Dave's car.

Dave shrugged. "Depends on how rough it is. But I sure as hell don't want to break a tie rod 'cause it don't look like anybody's been out here in a while."

"That's good for us 'cause, if there's a town up there, nobody's probably been up there to pick through it yet."

"Yeah, I guess," Dave responded without conviction. "But I wanna get outta the damned heat."

The two men turned from the cemetery and began trudging back toward McDonald Drive.

They returned a week later.

Dave managed to maneuver his car a hundred yards beyond the cemetery but was unwilling to proceed any farther. "I don't want to risk bending a rim or bustin' something," he explained as he switched the ignition off.

"It's a long way to those hills," Ed grunted, unhappily.

"Then we'd better get movin' while I'm in the mood."

They exited the vehicle and stepped to the rear, where Dave inserted a key into the lock and popped the truck lid.

"How far you think it is?" Ed asked as they grabbed canteens and day packs.

Dave squinted through the heat at the hills shimmering in the distance. "Hard to say. Three, four miles, maybe less. Probably take us a coupla hours."

Ed nodded. "If there's anything up there we should be able to see it pretty quick."

Dave jammed a cowboy hat on his head and slammed the trunk shut. "The quicker the better. It's already too fuckin' hot." He returned to the front of the car and locked the doors before stuffing the key in the front pocket of his jeans. Ed unhooked a canvas water bag from the chromed mirror on the passenger's side, uncorked it, and took a deep draught. He handed the bag to Dave, who followed suit. "Well, let's get at it," Dave said, wiping his chin on the sleeve of his tee shirt. He looped the water bag's sisal handle back over the outside mirror and strode into the desert.

They managed to locate the town with surprising ease.

Slightly more than two hours of hiking brought the men to the top of the hill closest to the cemetery. While they rested from their exertions, Ed used an old pair of war-surplus binoculars to survey the valley on the far side of the hill and was quickly able to identify what appeared to be distant buildings.

"I think I see it!" he excitedly informed Dave.

His companion took the binoculars and was able to confirm the existence of structures in the distance. "It sure *looks* like something," he agreed. "You think that's it?"

"What else *could* it be?" Ed rhetorically responded. "Look," he pointed toward the valley behind them. "There's an old cemetery down there so, at one point, there obviously had to have been a town nearby. Since there doesn't appear to be a town adjacent to the cemetery, and we *know* there's supposed to be a ghost town out here someplace, it stands to reason that that's it."

"Why's it so far away?" Dave wondered. "Wouldn't they have put it closer?"

"Who knows?" Ed dismissively responded. "If they were mining silver or something, they built the town wherever they found veins. Besides, they probably didn't want to get robbed by banditos. But if A equals B and B equals C, A equals C." Dave looked at him quizzically. "What I mean," Ed explained, "is that if there's a cemetery there's gotta be a town to go with it. And, since there's obviously buildings down there, that's gotta be it!" He folded his arms and looked triumphantly at Dave.

"No, I meant why is the *cemetery* so far away?" Dave corrected him.

Ed ignored the question. "How long do you think it'll take to hike down there?" He enthusiastically asked.

"An hour, maybe a little better."

"Let's check it out!" Ed began scrambling down the hill.

The meandering trail leading downward into the valley, though overgrown with sagebrush in areas, was easy to follow and, as Dave predicted, they came upon an old corral just over an hour later.

"I'll bet there's a lot of old stuff in there." Ed pointed to a collapsing tack room.

"Yeah, maybe," Dave responded. "We can check it out later. I think we outta see first if there's actually a town nearby. *That's* where most of the collectible stuff'll be."

Ed hastened across the baked earth to the tack room. After cautiously testing his weight on the rotted boards of the slightly elevated porch, he stepped confidently forward and looked through the open doorway leading to the storage room's narrow interior. Sunlight streamed through gaps in its rough boards, causing the dust motes that filled the air to sparkle.

"What's in there?" Dave yelled from near the corral.

"Nuthin'," Ed responded over his shoulder. "It's empty."

"Not surprised," Dave said. "Can't imagine there'd be anything in there after all these years."

Ed turned from the tack room and stepped from the porch onto the rocky soil. "No harm in looking."

"No, guess not," Dave acknowledged. He nodded toward the interior of the corral. "Dead horse."

Ed followed his gaze to the luckless animal's desiccated body, lying on its side and largely obscured with blown dirt. "How long you think it's been here?" he wondered aloud.

"A while," Dave shrugged.

His companion shook his head sadly. "Why would anybody just leave a horse out here to die?"

"I don't know," Dave responded, "but it ain't our problem. We better start lookin' for a town. We can check this place out some more on our way back to the car."

"Yeah, I guess," Ed sighed. In the near distance, the trail on which they'd hiked into the valley widened into what at one time had evidently been a fairly substantial roadway.

"You think that leads to a town?" Dave postulated.

"It's gotta lead *somewhere*," Ed affirmed. "Hopefully, wherever that is ain't too far away." The men walked away from the corral, onto the dusty roadway.

Twenty minutes later they found themselves on what clearly was once a main thoroughfare, surrounded by a collection of moldering structures. The two men walked slowly down its length, overawed by their discovery. The facades of the buildings around them simmered in the heat.

"Wow! What'd I tell you!" Ed chortled. "This place looks like a movie set!"

"Why do you suppose nobody's ever come across this place?" Dave wondered aloud as they walked.

"They have," Ed responded. "*We* heard about it, didn't we?"

"No. I mean, why isn't this place overrun with people? Everybody's heard of Jerome," a 19th century copper-mining town in northern Arizona, "supposedly the most famous ghost town in the west. Except that Jerome isn't, and never was, a ghost town...somebody's always lived there. But this place looks like a genuine by-God ghost town."

"Well, their loss is our gain. When do you think this place was built? Do you think it has a name?"

Dave stopped and looked around. He rubbed his chin in thought. "It's sort of a mishmash of styles. It looks pretty damned old, though. Hard to say..." his voice trailed off.

"What do you suppose happened to everybody?"

"I'm sure everybody just moved away once the mines played out. Just like all the other ghost towns in Arizona...Charleston, Gleeson, Cleator. A bunch of 'em don't even have names."

"Well, it doesn't matter to us!" Ed exclaimed. "We just hit the jackpot, Buddy! "We'll call it 'Ed-and-Daveville!'" He scuttled off to explore a nearby adobe building.

Dave continued wandering down the main street, marveling at the number and variety of structures. Most were still standing, albeit precariously, and were constructed of various materials: adobe, wood, scraps of tin siding. It was inconceivable to him that the place seemingly remained intact and he was excited at the prospect of exploring, and exploiting, the place. He paused here and there to poke about in the rubble.

"Hey, Dave, how come there's so many mine shafts?" Ed shouted from somewhere out of sight.

Dave stopped and looked around, trying to locate Ed. "Where are you?" he yelled into space.

After a moment, Ed emerged from behind a large pile of dirt in a lot overgrown with creosote bushes. "Did you see all the mine shafts?"

"What are you talking about?" Dave blandly responded.

"This place is honeycombed with mine shafts." He pointed vaguely toward the area behind the buildings lining the road. "Would they build a town directly on top of the mine? Seems kinda dangerous."

"Show me," Dave instructed him. With Ed leading the way, the two men left the main street and made their way across the overgrown lot.

"There." Ed pointed to a yawing hole in the earth. "There's lots of 'em around here. Just don't fall in."

Perplexed, Dave crept near the edge of the gaping orifice, about ten feet in diameter, and carefully leaned forward to peer into its murky interior. He was unable to see beyond the first few feet.

"What do you see?" Ed asked from a safe distance.

Dave retreated from the hole. "Nothing. It just goes straight down. I can't see anything."

"It's a mine shaft?"

"It doesn't look like one," Dave replied. "Mine shafts aren't usually vertical and, even when they are, they're a lot bigger than this...this looks way too small to be a mine shaft. They've also gotta have derricks or some kind of rigging above them to lower men and equipment. It doesn't look like anything like that was ever here. This just looks like a big hole in the ground."

"What's it for?"

"I don't know," Dave confessed. "Maybe it used to be a well or something."

"If that's the case, they must've been pretty damned thirsty to dig so many of 'em because they're all over."

"Who knows why people did stuff years ago? Hell, who knows why people do stuff *now*?"

"You're right about that," Ed laughed. "Just don't fall into a hole while you're farting around!"

The men separated, Dave picking his way through the brushy lot back to the main street while Ed hustled over to investigate another sagging habitation.

Dave meandered down the dirt thoroughfare slightly more than a block, where it doglegged around a small, rocky hillock. He bore left and continued walking until the road abruptly terminated. On his right the desert had apparently been scraped clear of chaparral and cactus and levelled at some time in the past, evidently in anticipation of erecting something. Only Mexican poppies and some stunted green tumbleweeds grew on its parched surface. He left the roadway and stepped onto the levelled area. An eddy of hot wind stung his face.

Dave contemplated the anomalous, enigmatic place in silence. He turned when he heard the crunch of Ed's footsteps on the road behind him.

"You seen any rabbits or anything?" Ed inquired as he drew near.

"No, I don't think so," Dave responded. "But I haven't actually been looking for 'em, either."

"It don't matter, 'cause there ain't any," Ed affirmed. "At least none that I've seen. And it isn't just rabbits...there's no birds, either." He stepped from the roadway and walked across the flat ground to join Dave. "I even turned over some old boards to look for lizards...nary a lizard *or* a scorpion or any bugs at all! Other than the two of us, there don't appear to be a living thing in this place. How do you figure that?"

"Well, I guess that's why they call 'em 'ghost towns'," Dave noted as he continued to study the area. His companion nodded noncommittally.

"How we gonna get people down here?" Ed asked. They sure as hell ain't gonna hike in like we did."

Dave clucked his tongue. "It wasn't *that* bad." He pointed to the hills behind them. "We'll scrape out a parking lot up there, bulldoze a road down here, and shuttle everybody around in big school buses. By bussing them down here, they'll pretty much be marooned while they're sittin' around waiting for the next bus and we'll be able to gouge 'em for food and souvenirs."

"Where are all these people gonna come from?" Ed asked, doubtfully. "Phoenix sure as hell ain't got enough people to keep us in business. Besides, they're all drivin' to Disneyland just to get outta the heat."

"We're not gonna have to rely on just the locals. Don't you read the papers? You never heard of Sputnik? The damned Russians just launched some kinda satellite into outer space with a rocket. TWA's even got airplanes that can haul people from coast to coast in less than a day! And now they're talking about cuttin' the work week down to twenty hours. People are gonna want someplace to spend all their free time, especially when they can just jump on a plane to get there. We'll fly 'em in by the planeload!"

Ed looked dubious. "I guess that'll make it easier for Ike to fly around the country so he can play more golf. But what's to keep everybody from just flying to Disneyland instead of here?"

"Apples and oranges, buddy," Dave grinned. Who the hell's gonna wanna fly half-way 'round the country to see a big rat? Besides, with all the money and spare time that ever'body's gonna have, there'll be plenty to go around. We ain't greedy."

Ed nodded thoughtfully. "I like the way you think." He looked curiously at the ground on which they stood. "It looks like somebody already graded this."

"Yeah, I was thinking that, too. I'm guessing that they leveled it expecting to eventually building something on it, but shit-canned the idea once the mines gave out."

Ed wrinkled his brow. "How ya figure they manage to get it so flat?"

"Probably the same way the ancient Egyptians used to build the pyramids...dig a trench completely around the perimeter, fill it with water, then use the water level as the baseline for leveling the foundation. It doesn't take a theodolite or anything."

"Well, whoever did it, and *however* they did it, they did us a favor."

"That's why I was thinkin' about putting the main house right here. The land's already been leveled and, if we use lumber from some of the old buildings that are about to fall down, anyway, we could get a pretty good start on it. It'd be sorta like a Welcome Center."

"Does anybody already *own* this place, do ya think?" Ed speculated. "I mean, we can't just come in here start tearin' shit down, can we? What if somebody already owns it?"

Dave shook his head. "We're on county, not private, land. Nobody owns it. It's just an old town that used to be here, and now isn't. Other than a handful of hikers that accidentally stumbled on it, I doubt whether anybody even knows this place exists. We'll just 'homestead' it, like they did in the old days, and claim it as ours."

"We can still do that?" Ed asked, incredulous.

Dave grinned. "Hell yes! Don't forget Wyatt Earp's only been dead about thirty years and Arizona's only been a state for about fifty years. The Old West ain't that old!"

"Well, let's get started, man!" Ed excitedly urged. "Who knows how long it'll be before somebody else comes along and steals our idea."

THEY RETURNED THREE WEEKS later with a crew of eight Mexican laborers. They promised the Mexicans fifty dollars, to be split as the Mexicans saw fit, plus two-dozen bottles of A-1 Beer at the end of each workday. The Mexicans were responsible for supplying their own tools, pry bars, hammers, and a couple of hand saws, and had to provide their own lunch, which consisted of tortillas wrapped around some cold, mashed beans.

One of the Mexicans spoke marginal English and, through a combination of pantomime and rudimentary Spanish, Dave managed to explain that he wanted them to tear down as many of the old wooden buildings as possible, and place the resulting lumber in stacks. Ed had meanwhile secured five cases of dynamite, fuse, and blasting caps from a local mining supply company and set about filling in many of the pits, holes, and mineshafts that dotted the area. Ed had learned the rudiments of demolition during World War II and set about his task with alacrity.

In order to maintain secrecy, Ed informed the inquisitive proprietor of the mining supply that he intended to blast the many tree stumps that littered his property; the proprietor appeared satisfied with this innocuous elucidation and gladly provided the means to do so. The Mexicans carried the dynamite and associated hazardous materials down the trail on their backs, along with their tools.

While the Mexicans noisily hammered, pried, and sawed, Dave wandered the site, thinking and sketching. Periodically, a tremendous boom would rock the earth, and a plume of dust and rocks would rise skyward, as Ed displayed his explosive proficiency.

Though its ruined condition rendered it difficult to precisely ascertain its exact proportions, it was apparent the town had once been fairly substantial. Not immense by any means but, insofar as Dave could judge, it had probably supported at least three hundred or so households at some point. Although it was impossible to determine when it had last been inhabited, its overall state of disrepair suggested that the town had been abandoned long ago. With any luck, his Mexican demolition crew would uncover something that would shed some light on the city's history. Although he was convinced that, like virtually all similar places in Arizona, the town was created when somebody discovered gold, silver, or copper, in the surrounding hills, Dave was puzzled by the absence of any mining equipment. Western mining towns were uniformly characterized by the existence of ore cars, crushing mills, sluices, and slag heaps of greater or lesser extent. Because such accoutrements were simply too large and cumbersome to move when the towns were eventually abandoned after the nearby mines grudgingly yielded up the last of their ore, they were simply left behind. The sole evidence of mining activity in *this* town was the numerous pits that riddled the area. Aside from those, however, there was nothing to suggest that any mining had ever occurred in the vicinity.

The rhythmic tattoo of the Mexican crew's hammering could be heard in the distance when another jarring explosion flung a cloud of dirt and rocks into the blistering afternoon air. Unruffled, Dave completed his transit of the ruins and turned back toward the center of town. As he ambled along the main street, Ed emerged from behind a dilapidated building, covered in grime and grinning broadly. A limp Lucky Strike cigarette dangled from his lip.

"Just like ridin' a bike," Ed announced. "You never forgot how to blow shit up." He removed the cigarette from his mouth, scrutinized it, then stuck it back and resumed puffing.

"You think it's a good idea to smoke around dynamite and stuff?" Dave cautiously inquired.

"What are you, my mother?" Ed sourly responded. "Don't worry about it."

Dave decided to change the subject. "You makin' any progress?"

Ed wiped his perspiring brow on a dirty shirt sleeve. "Yeah, but there's a lot of holes to fill and they're all connected. I detonate one and, fifty yards away, smoke comes out of a different one. The ground around here must be like Swiss cheese. I'm surprised the whole damned town hasn't caved in."

"You seen any actual mining equipment around here? Ore carts, mills, crushers, narrow gauge track...anything like that?"

Ed shook his head. "Nope. I guess they took everything with 'em when they left."

"Yeah, I guess," Dave responded without conviction.

"What ya got the Mexes doin'?"

"I was just now heading in their direction."

"In that case, I better get back to work fillin' in holes," Ed informed him. "If you need me, I'll be around here somewhere."

"You got enough dynamite?"

Ed nodded. "Dynamite's pretty potent stuff. It don't take much to fill in a hole."

"Well, don't blow yourself up 'cause it's too damned hot to haul your corpse outta here."

"The beauty of dynamite is that you gotta pretty much *try* to blow yourself up," Ed assured him. "It ain't as unstable as they make it out to be in the movies."

Dave turned away and resumed his sojourn back to the group of workmen. Though he'd been away less than an hour, the crew had already managed to dismantle one modest structure and had started on another.

"*Las casas están en malas condiciones, señor,*" shouted the spokesman for the Mexican crew when he saw Dave approach. "We no work much hard," he explained, switching to English after seeing the empty look on Dave's face.

"How long to tear down the rest of 'em?" Dave asked with a vague sweep of his arm. The Mexican spokesman looked at him quizzically. "*Mucho tiempo más?*" Dave haltingly ventured.

Clearly puzzled, the spokesman turned to his companions, who began conversing simultaneously in Spanish in hushed tones. Dave now regretted that he'd bothered to ask, given that it was unlikely he'd be able to understand anything the Mexican said in response.   After a few moments of muffled discourse, the spokesman turned back toward Dave.   *"Poco tiempo,"* he grinned, exposing two front teeth rimmed in gold. *"No mucho,"* he reiterated.   His companions beamed and vigorously bobbed their heads in collective affirmation, though none of them had the slightest idea whether the response proved agreeable to Dave.

"Bien," Dave said, uncertainly, no wiser than before. The Mexican crew resumed pounding and prying as Dave wandered off to find some shade where he could eat his sack lunch. In the distance, a thunderous explosion reverberated through the scorching air as Ed enthusiastically continued to dynamite mine shafts.

THE MEXICANS SUCCEEDED IN razing many of the old wooden structures by the end of the week.   While half the crew continued to demolish the remaining buildings, the other half began construction of the envisioned "Welcome Center."

Because of the impracticability of hauling into the valley both the components and the cumbersome equipment used to prepare them, Dave elected to dispense altogether with an underlying cement foundation.   Drawing on previous construction experience, he drew up plans utilizing a foundation comprised entirely of wood, a material he now possessed in abundance. Communicating his decision to the Mexicans as best he could, Dave watched with satisfaction as the workmen began fabricating the Center's post-and-beam skeleton. Within three days they had completed framing most of the ground floor and were progressing to a second story.

"The heat don't seem to bother Mexicans at all," Ed remarked as he watched the men work.

"They're probably about as hot on the inside as they are on the outside because of all the chilies they eat," Dave responded. It was unclear whether he was serious or making a joke.

Ed acted as though he didn't hear. "How long you think it'll take 'em?" he asked, referring to the Welcome Center. "There gonna be enough lumber?"

"There outta be," Dave said. "I still got the other guys tearin' down what's left of the town. We'll probably have to put about a hundred coats of whitewash on it, though, because the lumber's so weathered and porous." Ed nodded absently, seemingly lost in thought. "Did you get all the shafts filled in?"

Ed emerged from his reverie. "It's hard to say. I think I've just about got 'em all then, like I said, smoke starts billowin' out of a hole a hundred yards away that I didn't even know was there. I blow it up, and more smoke starts comin' out of more invisible holes. God only knows how many damned holes there are around here, and He'd only be guessin'. Even the holes I blew up left some pretty deep pits that we're eventually gonna have to backfill."

Dave nodded. "We'll get a 'dozer down here to clean everything up."

"How we gonna do that? Get a dozer all the way down here, I mean."

"It'll blade its own road," Dave responded. "There's not many places a 'dozer can't go."

The two men continued to watch in silence as their industrious crew labored to complete the Welcome Center beneath a blistering sun.

TWENTY FOUR

CAMERON, NANCY, AND MOE pushed through the overgrown cemetery toward the forlorn charnel houses. It was just past dawn; Nancy informed them that, if they expected her to accompany them, they had to get there as soon as it was light enough to see. Although Cameron had telephoned them earlier that week, none of their friends--Harry, Leonard, Sam, Phil, Andres, Darlene or Tina-- had agreed to participate in this latest mission. While none had explicitly said so, Nancy suspected the men's egos remained bruised after the scolding they suffered following the previous fiasco into the desert.

Cameron's cassette recorder was tucked in the pocket of his shorts; holstered on his belt was his Walther .22 pistol. Behind him, the detective was packing his customary Colt Python .357 revolver. As they walked, Nancy slashed at the tangled weeds around them with a machete. Because Cameron was able to park his Jeep nearby, none of them carried backpacks or water; a cooler filled with ice and bottles of water rested on the floorboard of the vehicle.

"Tell me again what we're supposed to accomplish here today," Nancy said.

"I'm not sure, exactly," Cameron responded over his shoulder. "Hopefully, we'll find out today."

"Well, I, for one, am getting pretty tired of this place," Nancy asserted.

Cameron stopped and turned to look directly at her. His face already glistened with perspiration. "Are you telling me that you're not the slightest bit intrigued by anything that's happened?"

"Honestly, Cam, I'm just tired of it all," she answered. "Ever since you saw whatever you saw standing out here in the rain that night, nothing good has come of it. I'm willing to admit that some intelligence, or some *something*, is involved, and that's exactly the problem. Who, or whatever it is, has always been one step ahead of us. Like Woody said at the restaurant, the whole point, originally anyway, was to find Chet. Despite everything we've been through since then, Chet's still missing, Daisy's dead, and we've been close to getting ourselves killed. Call me a baby, or unimaginative, or whatever, but I just think there are some things we shouldn't be messing with, and this is probably one of 'em." She paused and glanced at Woody, who stood a few feet away, listening.

Cameron, taken somewhat aback by the passion of Nancy's declamation, slowly nodded without speaking. He sighed and turned to Woody. "Well, what say you, detective? Yea or nay? Are we just wasting our time?" Nancy turned her attention to Moe with an air of expectancy.

"Well," he began after a moment of reflection, "I signed on to find Chet. Nance's right that we haven't been able to determine what happened to him so, if that's the criterion we're using, it's pretty much been a bust." He paused a moment before continuing. "But, based on everything that's happened, it's pretty obvious that we struck a nerve with, as Nance said, someone or *something*. Whether it has anything to do with Chet's disappearance, I don't know. *Why* it's happening, I don't know, either, but I can't help believing that everything's connected."

"So what should we do?" Nancy pressed.

"We're already here, it's daytime, and the Jeep is close by. We might as well go ahead as planned. After today I think we should rethink things, though."

"Fair enough," Cameron said. "I'll record for a few minutes in each building then we'll bug out of here and have breakfast."

"You buy," Nancy said.

"I second that," Moe concurred, smiling.

"Done," Cameron agreed. He turned and resumed pushing toward the forlorn structures.

Despite the early hour the morning air was already growing hot, though Nancy shivered as they approached the decaying tombs. She halted momentarily to allow the detective to catch up to her. Cameron continued plowing forward through the weeds, oblivious.

"You okay?" Moe softly asked her, gently squeezing her arm.

"Yeah, I guess. I just hate this place," she said, placing her head momentarily on his shoulder. "I'm glad you're here, though."

He kissed the crown of her head. "My mom taught me never to miss a free breakfast."

Nancy made a wry face. "That's all I'm worth to you? Breakfast?"

"Worse-a *free* breakfast," he shrugged with pretended nonchalance.

She playfully pushed him away. "If a ghost gets you *I'll* be the beneficiary of your free breakfast."

Moe was about to respond when Cameron stopped and looked back at them. "Hey, you guys need to get a room!" he yelled. "C'mon!" The detective sighed and released Nancy.

Cameron skirted one charnel house and approached the neighboring tomb. He rapidly scanned the interior through its collapsed doorway.

"Nobody home!" he shouted to the others after withdrawing his head.

"Yet," Nancy added under her breath as she and Moe continued to plod forward.

"So what's the plan?" the detective asked as they drew near.

"Just like we did before, when you and me were here the first time," Cameron said. "We'll go inside each building and I'll do some recording. We'll just have to see what happens next. Remember, we were invited back here, so it seems to me that *something* will probably happen."

"Yeah, that's what I'm afraid of," Nancy said.

Moe turned to her. "Nance, do you want to wait here? It's pretty cramped inside, anyway. With you outside, you'll be able to see anyone approach. And, if something bad happens, which I don't expect," he quickly added, "we won't all be stuck inside."

Nancy looked at Cameron. "Cam?"

"I think that's a good idea," he concurred. "Like Woody said, there's hardly any room inside and, with you outside, you can keep an eye on the Jeep and stuff."

"But stand right in front of the opening," Moe cautioned. "We've seen too much weird stuff happen and I don't want to lose sight of you."

Nancy stepped aside to allow the two men to duck into the tomb. They stepped over the threshold and entered the moldering crypt. Acrid dust boiled up from the earthen floor as they carefully stepped over mounds of detritus.

"You were over there last time," the detective pointed.

The small, relatively flat area on the floor that Cameron had previously created by kicking into the grime was still there and he returned to it. He pulled the cassette recorder from his pocket as Moe glanced toward the tomb's gaping door, through which Nancy wordlessly watched them. Although he smiled at her reassuringly, Nancy's expression remained tense. The detective moved to the opposite side of the cramped room. He nodded at Cameron.

Cameron pushed the two 'record' buttons on the cassette recorder and held it close to his mouth. "Good morning," he began. "This is Cameron Wylie and I'm here with Detective Woody Moe. If anyone here wishes to communicate with us, I invite you to do so now." He bent and carefully placed the tape recorder on the dirt floor then straightened and backed away as its tiny reels silently rotated. Moe again looked in Nancy's direction, but she was no longer standing at the aperture. Alarmed, he instinctively began to exit the tomb, but Cameron gently touched his arm and pointed at the tape recorder. The detective begrudgingly relented and remained stationary, though his eyes remained fixed on the crumbling structure's vacant doorway.

After twenty seconds, Cameron stooped to retrieve the cassette recorder and clicked it off. Moe bolted to escape the tomb, leaping from its cheerless interior just as Nancy reached him from outside the sepulcher.

"Jesus Christ! You scared the hell out of me, Nance!" Moe passionately hugged Nancy and she reciprocated his embrace. After a few wordless moments, she raised her head to look directly into his eyes.

"I couldn't stand to watch it anymore, Woody," she explained. "It's just too much...the whole thing is just too much." She leaned forward and kissed him on the lips.

"Wow! I need to go ghost hunting more often!" he smiled.

Cameron poked his head through the open doorway. "Good grief! Are you guys already back at it? Can't you even wait 'till we're done?" he laughed.

"Well, you'd better get crackin', mister," Nancy retorted, releasing Moe.

Cameron exited the tomb and stepped to the adjacent structure, where he paused before entering its dolorous interior. "Who's comin' with me?"

Nancy arched her eyebrows as she looked at the detective.

"We're already half done," Cameron coaxed. "We'll be sitting down to breakfast in no time."

"I'm right behind you," Moe said. "You okay out here for another few minutes, Nance?"

She spread her hands in a helpless gesture. "I hate it in there, but I hate being stuck out here, too. I'm creeped out, either way."

"Look," said Cameron, "if you'd feel better being near Woody rather than waiting out here, why don't you just come inside with us? It won't be *that* cramped and you can stand close to the opening. Besides, we're only gonna be inside for a minute or two."

Nancy looked questioningly at Moe.

"It's up to you, Nance," he said.

She sighed. "I'm sorry for being such a baby, guys. I didn't think coming out here would bother me so much. But I don't really like standing out here by myself, so I guess I'll go with you inside. Like you said, it'll only be a couple of minutes...short and painful, I suppose." Nancy stooped to place her machete on the ground and smiled awkwardly.

"Let's do it, then," Cameron urged. He placed the palms of his hands on either side of the gaping crack in its wall and, leaning forward, poked his head into its squalid interior. "Looks okay," he said over his shoulder.

Cameron squeezed through the fissure and entered the moldering crypt, followed by Nancy and the detective. Cameron moved to the far corner of the interior while his companions positioned themselves opposite him.

Although the interior of the structure was imperfectly illuminated by the morning sunlight that pierced the fissure in the wall, it was by no means well lit. Dust motes shone in the shaft of light that ameliorated the general dimness. Nancy shivered and slipped her hand into Moe's.

Exactly has he'd previously done in the neighboring tomb, Cameron removed the cassette recorder from his shirt pocket and, after switching it on, carefully and slowly enunciated his customary salutation. Having done so, he bent and placed the recorder on the dirt floor, then took a step backward as its tiny spindles whorled silently. Nancy glanced nervously at the detective and squeezed his hand; Moe's eyes were riveted on the cassette recorder.

Something outside the sepulcher blocked the opening in the wall, plunging the interior into darkness.

"Hey!" Cameron yelped, whipping his head toward the entry.

Moe dropped Nancy's hand and lunged toward the wall in the gloom. Extending his hands, he felt the uneven interior surface, but the aperture through which they'd previously entered the structure had seemingly vanished. He ran his hands up and down the wall as far as he could reach, but its surface was unbroken.

"What's happening, Woody?" Nancy whispered, reaching for him in the murk.

"I don't know," the puzzled detective murmured as he continued his tactile exploration. His hands failing to encounter the gap through which they entered the tomb, Moe took a tentative step forward, testing the wall's irregular surface as he groped his way in the darkness. "Cam, you okay?"

"Yeah, I'm okay," Cameron's voice quivered from the blackness. "What the hell is going on?" For the first time, the fear was palpable.

"I don't know, but intend to find out," Moe assured him as he continued his cursory circumnavigation of the interior.

"Do you think somebody's out there?" Nancy hissed.

"Looks that way," Cam responded. "They obviously blocked the entry from outside."

"What do they want? Why would they try to trap us in here? A prank?"

"It's not a prank," the detective said, but did not elaborate. His toe caught on the debris-strewn floor and he stumbled.

"Woody! Are you all right?" Nancy cried in the gloom.

"Yeah, I'm fine. Just can't see a damned thing."

"Can we get out?" Nancy asked. Remembering her cell phone, she slipped it from the pocket of her jeans. Holding it at chest level, she used its flashlight app to illuminate the area immediately around her. The detective stood in the shadows ten feet away. Nancy swung the cell phone to the opposite wall, where Cameron was revealed in its indifferent glow.

"Yeah, we'll get out," Moe grimly responded. "Nance, can you get a signal on your phone?"

She flipped the cell phone's face toward her. "No bars," she stated after a moment. "What's with that? We've made calls from the cemetery before. It's up in the hills where's there's no signal."

"All the calls you made before were from *outside*, not from inside these tombs. For whatever reason, the signal's evidently blocked in here."

"Can you guys get a signal?"

"If you can't, we can't," Moe said. He looked toward Cameron. "Cam, can you get to the wall nearest you?"

"Um, I guess so," Cameron dubiously responded.

"If you can, try to see if you can feel the outline of a doorway or something. Nance, you may want to kill the light from your phone for now...we may need it later. I brought a flashlight and Cam has his phone that we can use for light if we need to. But I don't think we're gonna be in here long enough to need them."

"You realize that it's gonna be like an oven in here before long," she reminded him, reluctantly tuning her phone off.

"Yeah, I know," the detective said. "But we'll be out of here before that happens." He heard Cameron flounder in the suffocating blackness. "You okay, Cam?"

"I'd be a lot better if we were out of here," Cameron groused. "I just kicked the tape recorder."

"We'll worry about that once we're on the outside. Did you feel anything that feels like it may be an irregularity in the wall?"

"I didn't feel shit yet. I'm lucky I managed to find the wall without breaking my damned neck. What, exactly, am I supposed to be feeling around for?"

"A doorway. They used adobe bricks to seal these old tombs. Although they generally plastered over the entrance once the tomb was sealed, we should be able to feel the doorway from inside. The mud mortar they used between the bricks often cracked and fell out...that's probably what happened to the other tomb that caused its doorway to collapse. When we find the door to this tomb, one good shove should probably be enough to push the whole thing over, plaster or no." Moe dragged his fingertips over the unbroken surface as he carefully felt his way along the interior wall of the unlit tomb.

"But what happened to the big crack in the side that we used to get in here in the first place?" Nancy nervously interjected. She strained her eyes in the opacity but was unable to discern any hint of the aperture.

The detective was about to respond when the fetor of rotting meat began seeping into the dismal room.

"Good God! What the hell is *that*?" Cameron exclaimed in dismay. "I thought there weren't any bodies in here!" He spun around and stared anxiously into the blackness. Perspiration streamed down his face, though not because of the airless interior.

"There aren't any," Moe confirmed. "Nance, use your phone and try to see where that smell is coming from," he ordered.

Nancy clumsily retrieved her phone from her pocket and tremblingly shone it about the interior.

A human figure slumped in the far corner. What had once been clothing hung from the intruder's shriveled frame in tatters, caked with dirt. Though shoeless, filthy socks covered its feet. The tremulous illumination provided by Nancy's cell phone disclosed a gaunt face whose hollow eyes were shadowed beneath shaggy brows. The tang of decaying flesh rolled from the figure.

"Chet?" Cameron blurted, opening his eyes wide as he stared at the mute figure. "Chet?" Cameron took a half-step forward.

"Cam, stop!" the detective barked. He unsnapped the holster on his hip and drew his revolver. "Cam, Nancy, don't move, either of you!"

Moe's eyes never left the figure.   "Identify yourself!" he demanded.

"Woody, it's Chet!" Cameron plaintively beseeched.

Nancy lunged toward Cameron and grabbed his arm.   "No, Cam."   She positioned herself between Cameron and the figure, as if to shield the former, and aimed her phone toward the corner of the tomb again.

"How did you get in here?" Moe snarled. He pointed his Colt Python directly at the figure, which remained stoical, outwardly apathetic to their presence.

"To hell with how he got in," Nancy interpolated. "How do we get *out*? I'm about ready to puke from the smell."

The figure pointed dumbly downward, toward a lightless pit near the foot of the adjacent wall.

"He got in here through *that*?" Nancy gulped.   "It leads outside?" She released Cameron's arm and took two steps in the direction of the opaque depression, craning her neck to look into its ebon maw.

"No, stay there, Nance," the detective cautioned. She directed the light from her phone toward him. "Cam, you sure that's Chet?" he asked.

Cameron slowly shook his head. "I don't know, Woody. I thought it was, but how *could* it be? If it's Chet, why doesn't he speak?" The interior of the tomb was enveloped in the deep shadows created by the sickly light from Nancy's cell phone.

"That's not Chet," Nancy said. "I don't know who he is, or what he's doing here, but we need to get out of here."

A curious rustling sound emanated from within the room, instinctively causing Nancy to swing her phone in that direction.

With movements measured and deliberate, a hirsute creature climbed from the pit at the foot of the wall. Though its features were difficult to precisely ascertain in the crepuscular light, its waxy, misshapen head appeared to be covered by a thin layer of hair. A stunted pair of wooly legs became visible as the being pulled itself from the earth, its upper body covered with what appeared to be a rough smock. Once free of the noisome hole, the dwarfish figure stood upright. A mephitic fetor oozed from the creature, intensified by the closeness of the interior.

"What the hell is going on?" Cameron croaked.

"The answer to your question is contained in the question itself," the figure spoke in a singular, rasping voice. "Is it not obvious? I'm pleased that you finally deigned to join me, though I confess that it took much longer than I anticipated,"

Nancy's cell phone winked out, immersing the chamber in blackness. She frantically slapped it in her palm of her opposite hand, but the light did not reappear. "Woody, Cam, flip your lights on," she said, tersely. To her left, she heard the detective fumbling in the dark as he attempted to access the flashlight clipped to his belt while still gripping his revolver. Still clasping her dead phone, Nancy blindly extended her arms in an effort to locate Cameron in the aphotic vault. Her hands encountered nothing. "Cam!" she cried.

Nancy began to flail about in the blackness. "Woody, I can't find Cam! He's not here!"

"Stand still, Nancy!" Moe barked from nearby.

The sepulcher reverberated with the intruder's screeching laughter. "There is no returning!" he convulsed. "My hierodules have seen to it that you will remain here!"

The detective's flashlight blazed on. Nancy whipped her head around in the spear of light, frantically seeking Cameron.

"Cam's not here, Woody! He's gone!" she wailed. The detective's flashlight revealed that only he, Nancy, and the stunted creature still occupied the charnel house; both Cameron and the initial ragged intruder had vanished.

"Nancy, move over here," Moe quietly urged. He directed the beam of his flashlight downward, to the tomb's rutted floor, to enable her to join him without tripping in the darkness.

"I have for too long been reduced to revivifying the desiccated corpses from Esperanza's cemetery," Moloch thoughtfully stated, almost as a soliloquy. "They serve me well enough, though it is hardly worth the effort to reclaim them from the earth."

Nancy rejoined the detective, pressing herself close to him. Still holding his revolver, the detective aimed his flashlight toward the creature. He could feel Nancy trembling beside him.

"I was so engaged the night your friend apparently observed me."

"Where is he? Where's Cameron?" Moe growled.

The chimera gestured toward the pit whence he'd previously emerged. "Your friend finally found what he sought. *Cave quicquam incipias quod paeniteat postea.*"

"What does that mean?" Nancy whispered to the detective.

"'Be careful about starting something you may regret,'" the creature responded, unbidden.

"The prudent counsel of Publilius Syrus, whom you will presently have the signal pleasure of meeting."

Moe thumbed the hammer of his revolver rearward, the mechanical click echoing ominously inside the narrow tomb. "You'll have the pleasure of meeting a mortician unless you cut the bullshit and let us out of here."

Moloch clucked his tongue reprovingly. "You are here through your own volition. Why do you threaten others for the consequences of your own decisions? *Stultum est queri de adversis, ubi culpa est tua.*"

"What are you? What do you want?" Nancy demanded, hoping to project as much authority as she could muster.

"You are here at this moment only because of your unslakable curiosity," the being said in a wheedling voice. "You are the authors of your own fortunes. Your friend, Chet, attempted to provide you with presentiments; these you deigned to treat as invitations rather than as warnings. So be it." He was about to continue but the detective interrupted.

"Cover your ears, Nance," he ordered.

Nancy scarcely had time to jam her fingers into her ears before Moe squeezed the Python's trigger.

The revolver bucked in the detective's hand, flames bursting from its muzzle. The interior of the crypt blazed with light as the gun's report reverberated off the walls. Over all, Moloch's screeching laughter could be heard.

"You are too late!" he gleefully cackled as he danced and gibbeted about. "The great god Pan is dead!"

TWENTY FIVE

"*SEÑOR ROBERTO, HE NO* here."

Dave looked up from the schematics he was examining, annoyed at the intrusion. "What?"

"Roberto, he no here."

Because Dave knew none of their names, he had no idea which of the workmen was 'Roberto.' "Where is he?" he condescendingly addressed the agitated laborer.

"He no here," the man dumbly repeated.

"I understand ... *entiendo*," Dave patiently acknowledged. "Do you know where he is?"

"He no here," said the laborer for a fourth time.

Dave sighed and rapidly rolled his documents into a loose cylinder then bent to insert them into the canvas rucksack resting on the ground beside him.

The Mexican crew had already finished construction of the Welcome Center and, under Dave's supervision, were staking out the "Gunman's Sidewalk," the main thoroughfare bisecting the proposed Western town.

"That thing sticks out like a turd in a punch bowl," Ed dryly remarked as, earlier that week, he watched the crew put the finishing touches on the Welcome Center.

"It may now, but it'll be the centerpiece for the whole park. Cinderella's Castle was the first thing they put in when they built Disneyland because they knew they could put all the other shit in later...they just needed some place for all the customers to flock to in the meantime. We'll haul in an air conditioning unit and put in a restaurant and big gift shop. We'll have gun fights out front, too, so everybody can spend their money while they're waitin' for all the rides to be built; we'll need the cash flow to bankroll all the other attractions, anyway. Maybe if we really want to be authentic, we'll even add a bordello!" he laughed.

"How we gonna get an air conditioner and restaurant equipment all the way down here?" Ed asked, dubiously.

"I got the Spics out marking the main drag. Once we get that squared away, we can haul whatever we need down here, includin' a big gas generator." Ed nodded in agreement. "I wanna print some advertising brochures, anyway," Dave continued, "and the Welcome Center will look pretty damned impressive in the pictures."

Ed had to admit that Dave clearly had things under control. But now one of the damned Mexicans had apparently gone missing; hopefully he hadn't tumbled into one of the remaining holes that dotted the area, or been crushed by falling debris while scavenging one of the collapsing structures. In all likelihood, Roberto had merely stolen away from his companions, to a secluded pocket of relative shade, where he was taking a protracted *siesta*.

Dave lifted his rucksack and slung it over one shoulder. *"Como se llama?"*

"Primo," replied the Mexican laborer.

"Okay, *donde,* Primo?" The man pointed vaguely past the Welcome Center, in the general direction of the wretched hamlet's center. *"Ir!"* Dave ordered with a thrust of his chin.

The two men trudged beneath a blistering sun toward the presumed site of Roberto's disappearance. The remaining members of the crew watched them sullenly as they made their way down Gunman's Sidewalk. Dave glanced about as they walked, looking for Ed, but the latter was not in sight.

Primo ducked behind a crumbling adobe building, where he stopped and turned to look expectantly at his trailing boss.

"Aqui?" Dave asked when he rejoined his escort.

"Si," Primo nodded, pointing downward.

Gashing the earth was a large hole, identical to the multitude of others that punctuated the area.

"Aqui?" Dave asked a second time. Primo nodded.

Dave placed his rucksack on the ground and circumspectly approached the cavity. He leaned forward to peer inside. The sickening odor of rotting meat radiated from the crepuscular void. He squatted to examine its rim, hoping to identify disturbed soil or other confirmation that the missing Roberto may accidently have tumbled in. Nothing.

Dave rose to his feet, nauseated by the cloying odor of decay that rose from the pit. He felt light headed. Primo stood silently behind him.

"*Donde?*" he turned to ask the worker. As he spoke, Dave pointed to the area of the pit immediately in front of him. "*Este? Este?*" He used his finger to indicate various locations around rim of the chasm.

Primo shook his head, as though he failed to comprehend. "*No lo se,*" he shrugged.

"*Cuando?*"

"*No mucho tiempo.*"

"*Una hora? Dos? Tres?*"

"*No mucho tiempo.*"

Dave stepped away from the noisome pit. He couldn't be sure that a laborer named 'Roberto' even existed or, if he did, that he'd accidentally fallen into a hole or some other mishap had befallen him. For all Dave knew, 'Roberto' had simply grown weary of the hard work and low pay and had unilaterally decided to decamp.

He heard footsteps and turned as Ed emerged from behind an adjacent pile of rubble.

"What's goin' on?" Ed asked as he approached.

Dave gestured toward the abyss. "He says one of the Mexicans fell in here."

Ed peered over Primo's shoulder, toward the hole yawning in the earth. "Which one?"

"Roberto."

Ed scoffed. "Which one's he? I thought they were all named 'Roberto.'"

"Don't ask me...I'm just telling you what he said."

Ed frowned and walked closer to the chasm. He contemplatively scrutinized the black void.

"Well," he remarked after a moment, "I don't hear anything. If he fell in there, he ain't comin' out."

Dave turned again to Primo. Using his right arm and hand to mimic a diving motion, he pointed again to the hole. *"Roberto está? Si?"* Primo nodded gravely.

"So what do ya wanna do?" Ed asked, stepping away from the edge.

"Not a helluva lot we *can* do," Dave responded. "If he's down there, I don't see how we can possibly get him out."

"What's that one's name?" Ed asked, pointing to Primo.

"Primo."

"I thought 'primo' meant 'cousin.'"

"I don't know, that's just what he said. Maybe he's Roberto's cousin."

"Do you know how to say 'shout' or 'yell' in Spanish?"

Dave shook his head. "Nope."

Ed turned to Primo and pointed toward the pit. *"Hablar con Roberto."*

"Que?" Primo responded, clearly puzzled by the directive.

"Hablar con Roberto," Ed repeated, more emphatically this time.

Primo didn't budge. *"Muy malo,"* he intoned.

Ed edged nearer the pit. *"Mira. Muy fácil, no problema,"* he demonstrated. *"Hablar con Roberto."* He pointed downward, into the shaft.

Primo glanced nervously at Dave, who remained impassive.

"I think he thinks I'm gonna push him in!" Ed hooted. He imperiously motioned for the worker to come closer.

Primo dutifully crossed himself and reluctantly complied. While the workman watched, Ed cupped his hands around his mouth, creating an impromptu megaphone. *"Hola, Roberto!"* he shouted into the cavity. He flamboyantly placed a hand behind his ear and rocked slightly forward on the balls of his feet, tilting his head as though listening. Straightening, he looked directly at Primo. *"Tu,"* he said, pointing to the chasm.

Primo inched forward and leaned toward the hole. *"Soy yo!"* he halfheartedly shouted. He straightened and looked expectantly at Ed, who officiously waved his hand for him to continue.

The unhappy workman leaned forward again. *"Estás muerto? Qué quieres que haga?"*

"Can you tell what he's sayin'?" Dave asked.

"I think he asked if he was dead," Ed indifferently replied. "Otherwise, I have no idea."

Primo backed away from the shaft and looked again at Ed. *"Quién sabe?,"* he grunted.

"What'd he say?"

"*'Who knows?'*"

The three men gazed in silence at the lifeless orifice. "Well, what now?" Dave finally asked. "I got work to do."

"Yeah, me too," Ed concurred. He looked at Primo, shrugged, and lifted his hands to shoulder level, palms upward, in a token of defeat.

"Sí," the Mexican acknowledged.

"Well, I guess the rest of 'em'll have more money and beer to split between 'em," Dave concluded. He lifted his rucksack from the scorched ground and turned to walk away.

"Yep, Roberto's loss is their gain," Ed guffawed. "This one sure don't seem too broken up over the whole thing." He pointed to Primo, who trailed after the men.

"Fill that hole in as soon as you can," Dave continued. "Don't want any more of the workers fallin' in."

"I'm workin' my way this direction," Ed assured him. "I'll have it filled in in the next day or two...shouldn't take more than half a stick. What are you gonna tell the other Mexicans?"

"About Roberto?" Dave asked over his shoulder. "Nuthin'. I'll leave it up to Primo. He can tell 'em whatever he wants."

"You're not afraid that the rest of 'em will take a powder?"

"For what? Because one of 'em fell in a hole? Where else are they gonna get work? Even if they *do* leave, we'll just go round up some more." He paused to wipe the sweat from his face. "Besides, Primo will probably just tell 'em that one of their *amigos* ran off. Why should they give a shit? Like you said, his loss is their gain."

ANOTHER WORKER VANISHED two days later.

In the interim since Roberto's disappearance, Primo had more-or-less arrogated to himself the role of *de facto* Spanish translator and foreman of the crew, notwithstanding that his ability to speak and understand English remained problematical. Undeterred by his dubious linguistic expertise, Primo appeared to listen attentively as Dave, accompanied by an abundance of hand-gestures, pointed to two members of the crew and explained that he wanted them to raze the remains of an old adobe wall, the waist-high vestige of a former habitation. Primo then repeated, in Spanish, Dave's laborious instructions, at least to the extent that he actually comprehended them. The taciturn workmen nodded; one gathered up a crow bar, the other a sledge hammer.   Both men also shouldered battered shovels before trudging in the direction indicated.   Though it was not yet noon, the ambient temperature was already soaring.

Ed was still engaged in the explosive backfilling of the remaining shafts that perforated the town, including the hole that Roberto had purportedly fallen into two days previously.

"Did that Mexican who fell in the hole ever show?" he asked Dave.

Dave shook his head.

In his left hand Ed held a length of thick fuse leading to a black-powder blasting cap.   In his right hand the quivering flame of his Zippo lighter fluttered over the ragged end of the cord. After a moment, it began to sputter.   Ed casually tossed the sizzling fuse to the ground, snapped the Zippo shut, and sauntered away.

"How do you know how much time you have?" Dave asked as he hastened after Ed.

"The stuff I'm using burns at about 30 seconds per foot.   We've got plenty of time," Ed assured him.

The dynamite erupted just as the two men ducked behind a large dirt pile. They hunkered down as a plume of dirt and rocks soared into the air.   After the concussion subsided and the resulting cloud of dust dissipated, they emerged from their shelter.

"Well, if Roberto was in there, he won't be coming out now," Ed laconically observed as they made their way back to the site of the pyrotechnics.

The quondam abyss had disappeared beneath tons of earth displaced by the explosion, its former existence marked by a shallow crater.

"I'll smooth everything out when we bring the grader down here," Ed said. "There's a bunch more that I'll have to do the same for."

"How many more shafts are left?"

"To fill?" Ed wrinkled his brow in thought. "Hard to say 'cause they're so scattered. I don't know...coupla dozen, maybe a little better."

Dave nodded. "We should have Main Street completely staked by the time you're finished and can use the blade to level it, and to knock down and bury the biggest piles of scrap." He paused. "You got enough dynamite to finish the job?"

"More than enough," Ed replied. "Like I said, it don't take much to backfill a hole."

Dave turned to depart when he saw Primo hastening through the desert in their direction.

Ed squinted into the brilliant sunlight, toward the approaching figure. "I never saw a Mexican move that fast before," he absently remarked.

"*Qué pasó?*" Dave called.

"*Señor, Nacho se ha ido!*" Primo excitedly blurted when he finally reached the men. Streams of perspiration rolled down his face and his chest heaved from his exertions.

"What's he sayin'?" asked Ed.

"Beats me," Dave responded, "but he's pretty damned excited." He looked sternly at the panting workman. "*Qué?*"

Primo managed to catch his breath long enough to respond. "*Nacho no está aquí.* Gone."

"'Gone' where?"

"*No lo sé,*" the worker panted.

"Another one of the Mexicans fly the coop?" Ed deduced.

Dave sighed. "Looks that way. *Donde?*" Primo pointed in the direction he had just come. "*Vamos,*" Dave ordered, with a nod of his head.

"I wanna see why the Mexicans keep fallin' into holes, but I ain't gonna hike through the damned desert," Ed declared. "I'm thinkin' we may wanna cut back on their beer ration."

The agitated worker leading, the three men made their way back toward Main Street. Primo hastened ahead and regularly glanced rearward, where Dave and Ed struggled to keep pace.

"Jaysus!" Ed wheezed, "I think that wetback's been eatin' too many chili peppers."

In short order the men found themselves in an isolated section of the settlement, surrounded by a handful of tumbledown buildings. A scattering of creosote bushes sprouted from the baked earth. Primo nervously approached one of the scraggly plants and held aside its oily branches, revealing a gaping hole at its base. He looked expectantly at Dave and Ed.

"There?" the latter asked, pointing downward toward the cavity. Primo nodded. "How'd he fall in?" Ed continued. Primo didn't comprehend the question and looked puzzled. He removed his calloused hands from the spindly branches of the creosote bush and they flopped back to their former position.

Ed turned to Dave. "How the hell could anybody fit into that little hole?"

"Well, it ain't *that* little," Dave observed. "But *my* question is, what was he doin' over here in the first place? I didn't send any of the Mexicans over to this area...all but two of 'em are workin' on the main drag and the other two are supposed to be knockin' a house down. He turned toward Primo. "Nacho *aqui?*"

"*Si,*" the workman nodded vigorously. He pointed to the hole beneath the creosote bush. "*Ahi abajo.*"

Clenching his fists and extending them outward from his chest, Primo then drew his parallel arms sharply back toward his body.

"I think he's sayin' that Nacho may have been dragged here," Dave said.

"*Dragged?*" Ed exclaimed. "By who? One of the other Mexicans? Why would they drag him over all the way over here and stuff him in a hole?"

Dave stepped forward and squatted on the balls of his feet to examine the cavity at the foot of the bush. "Damn! It stinks like the one where the first guy fell in," he announced. "But if they dragged somebody in here, I don't see any sign of it." He stood.

"You believe him?" Ed asked, skeptically.

"Why would he lie?"

Ed shrugged. "I didn't say he lied. Maybe he's just confused."

"Yeah, maybe," Dave muttered, unconvinced. He turned back toward Primo, who watched the men in stony silence. "Primo, Nacho is *en el hoyo?*" He pointed to the aperture as he spoke.

"*Si, si,*" Primo emphatically responded.

"*Quién?*" Ed interjected.

"Nacho," the worker answered, puzzled that the two Gringos continued to ask the same question repeatedly.

"No," Ed continued. "*Quién* put him there? Who?"

Primo and Ed both looked at Dave in mutual frustration, hoping for assistance in translating. He shrugged helplessly.

"Well, I don't think anybody's down there," Ed affirmed. "The lazy-ass Mexicans are just looking for an excuse not to work."

"If they don't want to work why don't they just leave? Why make up stories about getting dragged down a hole?"

Ed clucked his tongue. "Mexes are like that. They'd rather climb a tree and lie, than stand on the ground and tell the truth."

"Yeah, maybe," Dave responded. "But we're gonna have to start lookin' for more workers if this shit keeps up."

"Mexicants are a dime-a-dozen," Ed grunted, turning away. "I'll add this hole to the ones already on my list. I didn't even know it was here because it's under a bush." Dave nodded wordlessly.

"You no help Nacho?" Primo lugubriously asked as the men walked away. Neither of them responded.

ED RACED DOWN MAIN Street, frantically waving his right arm over his head to get Dave's attention. Since discovering the abandoned settlement, the crew had managed to more-or-less clear a road to it, thereby rendering it possible to drive to the site every morning rather than undertake the laborious hike on a daily basis. Dave was at the truck, retrieving his transit, when he saw Ed.

"What the hell's the matter with you?" Dave nonchalantly inquired once Ed finally reached him, gulping mouthfuls of torrid air.

"You ain't gonna believe what I just saw," Ed panted.

"Don't make me guess. Make it easy on me," Dave retorted.

Ed's chest heaved as he strove to catch his breath. He took a final wheezing inhalation before responding. "I swear to God that you're gonna say I'm crazy, but I just saw a guy without a head walkin' around."

Dave pursed his lips, uncertain how to respond to Ed's singular disclosure. "A guy without a head? What are you talkin' about?"

"I'm not fuckin' with you, man. I was fillin' some holes out behind Main Street, mindin' my own business. I thought I heard somethin' and, when I looked up, I swear to fuckin' Christ there was a guy standing there, not thirty feet away, and he didn't have a fuckin' head! I just about shit a brick!" Ed was becoming increasingly agitated as he spoke.

"Ed, for Christ's sake calm down," Dave sternly ordered. "What do you mean he didn't have a head? Have you been smokin' more of your whacky tabacky?"

"I haven't had a reefer in days," Ed scowled. He took a deep breath. "I know what you're thinking, man. You're thinking that I'm either full of shit or that I'm makin' shit up. But I'm telling you what I saw, Dave. There was a guy just standing there, in front of God and everybody, and he didn't have a fucking head! As sure as I'm standing here, I saw him!"

Dave was at a loss. He and Ed had been tight for years and he knew his friend to be level-headed and conscientious. "What'd the guy look like?" he ventured.

"You mean aside from bein' minus his fucking head?" Ed blurted. He continued without waiting for Dave's response. "I sure as hell didn't hang around long enough to inspect him, but he kinda looked like a cowboy, I guess: grungy clothes, chaps, spurs."

"You sure it just wasn't one of the crew?"

"It wasn't one of the damned Beans! They were still rounding their tools up when I saw him. It couldn't have been one of them. Besides, every Mexican I ever saw had a head."

"So where'd he go after you saw him?"

"The hell if I know! I got the hell out of there!"

Dave reflected a moment before responding. "Buddy, I have no idea what you saw, but think about it a second: how could it possibly have been somebody with no head? Maybe it was an old store mannequin or something. Now that I think about it, it's possible it was a hobo who lives in one of the old buildings...it wouldn't surprise me. There's a few buildings around here that are probably still livable. Did he see you?"

Ed looked tiredly at Dave. "Dave, he didn't have a fucking head...how could he see me?"

"Show me where you saw him," Dave sighed. "If there's somebody living here, we need to know about it." The two men stepped away from the vehicle and began retracing Ed's panicked route down Main Street.

"I wouldn't say anything to the crew about what you saw," Dave cautioned as they walked. "They're already spooked about the other Mexicans disappearin'."

"I couldn't say anything even if I wanted to because I don't know how to say 'headless guy' in Spanish," Ed replied in disgust.

"THERE," ED POINTED WITH HIS extended hand.

They'd skirted several crumbling structures before arriving at the place where Ed claimed to have seen the figure.

Dave surveyed the dusty, nondescript area. "Where, exactly, was he when you saw him?"

"Standin' right there, facing me," Ed indicated. "He scared the bejesus out of me."

"Where were you?" Ed pointed. "And you have no idea what happened to him after you saw him?"

"No clue. I just dropped my tools and split and didn't look back."

"Did he move around or anything?" Ed shook his head. "Not that I saw. Just stood there."

Dave walked to the nearest building and looked inside. There was no sign of human habitation. He bent to scrutinize the surrounding soil; it appeared undisturbed, devoid of footprints.

"Well, if somebody was here, they must've levitated," he remarked as he stood. "Did you look inside the rest of these buildings?"

"Yeah," Ed nodded. "They're all dumps, fallin' down. Nobody's livin' in 'em that I could tell."

Dave reflected a moment. "Well, assuming you actually saw somebody, and there's no reason to think you didn't," he quickly added, "it's gotta be a bum who either lives here or just wandered in. But if he lives here, I don't want any hassles so, if you see him again, let me know. Meanwhile, I'll try to tell the Mexicans to be on the lookout for anybody."

"It wasn't a bum," Ed grunted. "Bums have heads."

Dave folded his arms and glared at him. "So what would you recommend we do, Ed? Just pack up and go home? If that's what you want, all ya gotta do is say the word. We'll just let somebody else step in and run with our idea, which is exactly what's gonna happen. Hey," he needled, "maybe they'll give us a discount since it was our idea to turn a worthless hunk of desert into a genuine money machine. Seems like the least they could do, especially since we've already put a ton of work into the place. But if that's what you wanna do ... "

Ed looked at him peevishly. "Did you hear me say that I wanted to split? I just figured we outta to know what the hell's creepin' around out here."

"Okay, Ed, *you* saw him. What *is* creepin' around out here? A cowboy with no head? Does that really make any sense to you? And even if that's what you actually saw, what would you recommend we do about it? It seems to me we either keep on keepin' on, or we deep-six the whole shootin' match. You tell me."

Ed was silent as he reflected on Dave's words. "I guess it don't make sense to quit now," he finally said.

Dave slowly nodded. "Yeah, I guess it don't."

"But I'm gonna start carryin' a damned gun," Ed avowed.

"Fine with me," Dave said. "But if the guy's able to walk around without a head, I'm not sure how much good a gun'll do you." He couldn't resist smiling.

Ed scowled. "I'll shoot the bastard in the legs. He might be able to walk around without a head, but he damned sure won't be able to walk without legs."

"Lemme know the next time you see him and I'll join you for some target practice," Dave laughed.

ED SCRAMBLED OVER THE ROUGH ground as he concentrated on slowly uncoiling fuse from a heavy spool. Three more crew members had vaporized during the week and he was jumpy. It had been two weeks since his encounter with the headless apparition and Ed was beginning to believe that Dave's skepticism was probably warranted.   Still, workmen continued to vanish.   It was one thing for an individual, perhaps even a couple of laborers, to desert a jobsite...the wholesale disappearance of five workers was altogether different.

Notwithstanding that Ed possessed no incontestable proof, he couldn't shake the conviction that the seemingly abandoned settlement was inhabited.   While he never actually *saw* anyone except Dave and the Mexican workers, Ed's tools would disappear from where he had previously laid them, or were moved from one place to another.   One time, while he was on hands-and-knees carefully attaching the end of a fuse to a blasting cap, Ed thought he heard people nearby conversing in Spanish, followed by a cascade of brittle laughter.   Thinking the source was merely the Mexican crew, Ed glanced up from his work to warn them away from the area.   No one was there.

A gust of wind stung Ed's sunburned face, carrying with it the smell of decaying meat. Using the palms of his hands, he slapped the dirt from his pants and squinted into the burning sunlight to survey the immediate area.

Nothing stirred in the simmering heat. Aside from two eroded mounds of earth nearby, there were no other objects in the vicinity. Discerning a metallic clinking sound, Ed swiftly turned in that direction but saw nothing.   Again he thought he heard the indistinct murmur of voices.

"Fuck me," he muttered under his breath. The heat notwithstanding, Ed shivered.

Abandoning the demolition, he quickly gathered his tools and headed in the direction of the Welcome Center, where he expected to find

Dave. As he rounded one of the adjacent piles of dirt, he encountered a largish black bird hopping about. It abruptly stopped, cocked its head, and looked at Ed, seemingly unafraid. It was the first creature Ed had encountered in an area otherwise barren of wildlife.

Startled, Ed blurted, "Hey, what are you doing here?" He took a hesitant step toward the incongruous creature, which fluttered its wings and hopped beyond his reach. The bird coolly assessed him with an anthracite eye. Because of its boldness, and because crows are uncommon in Arizona, Ed suspected that it might be someone's escaped pet. He squatted, extended his hand, and clucked his tongue. "Come here, buddy."

The creature ruffled its feathers but otherwise remained stationary. Ed leaned forward on the balls of his feet and placed one hand on the ground to steady himself. He extended his free hand and gently snapped his fingers in an effort to lure the bird toward him. "C'mon, buddy, c'mon. I'm not gonna hurt you"

The creature opened its beak and emitted a harsh squawk then turned and fluttered a short distance into the desert. Ed slowly stood and watched it hop to the base of a spindly creosote bush, where it stopped and looked back at him. His curiosity piqued, Ed followed.

Partially concealed by the chaparral, a narrow hole disappeared at a slight oblique into the stony earth. The bird poised momentarily at mouth of the defile before plunging downward into its ebon depths. Ed strode to the orifice and, shading his eyes from the sun with his hand, bent to peer inside.

The bird had vanished. Characteristic of the other holes Ed had demolished over the past few weeks, the fissure exuded a rank odor. He and Dave previously concluded that the source of the fetor was probably the decaying bodies of small animals which, over the years, had fallen into the cavities and perished. Ed wrinkled his nose and straightened. Though he had never seen a bird that appeared to be tame dart into a hole in the ground, many things about this place were eye-opening. He turned away from the creosote bush and resumed trekking toward Main Street.

TWENTY SIX

DAVE HASTENED OUT TO MEET Ed as the latter approached the Welcome Center.

"We lost two more," Dave panted when he drew near.

"'Two more' what?   Mexicans?"   Dave nodded. "What do you mean 'lost' 'em? Like in an accident?"

Dave shook his head. "No, like the others. Just gone.   Maybe an accident ... who the hell knows."

"When did anybody last see 'em?"

"I sent 'em out to clear some brush earlier today. Primo just went to check on 'em and they were gone. Their tools were there, but *they* weren't."

"Where's Primo now?"

"Back at the Welcome Center. He's about ready to pee his pants."

"Yeah, I'll bet," Ed responded. "Let's head back there; I'm about to roast and gotta get outta the damned sun."

The two men made their way back to the Welcome Center, where they found Primo sitting on the steps leading to the front deck, wearing a mournful expression. The self-appointed foreman didn't acknowledge their return and they clumped past him up the steps without speaking, and plopped down in the comparative shade of the porch.

Ed removed his sweat-soaked baseball cap and used it to mop his face. He nodded toward Primo. "He say anything else?"

Dave shook his head. "Just what I told you."

Ed stared pensively through the carved wooden railing, into the surrounding desert. "Well," he finally began, "I had something funny happen to me just now, but I doubt whether it has anything to do with the Mexes." Dave looked inquisitive while Ed described his encounter with the curious bird; he omitted any mention of the disappearance of his tools or of hearing voices converse in Spanish.

"Arizona doesn't have crows," Dave pedantically remarked after Ed had finished speaking. "We have ravens but no crows, and even the ravens are only found in the northern part of the state...like around Flagstaff. What you saw was probably grackle."

"No," Ed protested, "it wasn't a grackle. I know what a grackle looks like. And it was too small for a raven. It was a crow."

"How do you know what a crow looks like if there are no crows in Arizona?" Dave pointedly asked.

"I know what a crow looks like," Ed insisted.

"Well, the only bird I know that lives in the ground is a burrowing owl," Dave affirmed.

"It wasn't an owl. It was a crow...maybe somebody's escaped pet," suggested Ed.

Dave said nothing further and the men grew quiet.

"So now what?" Ed broke the silence.

"'What', what?"

"The Mexicans...now what? We've gotta have a crew."

Dave removed his cowboy hat and ran a calloused hand through his damp hair. "Yeah, I know," he sighed.

"Ask him if he has any idea what happened to his *amigos*," Ed urged, indicating Primo.

"Primo!" Dave barked. The ersatz foreman turned to look at him. "*Donde otros?*" Dave asked in pidgin Spanish.

Primo slowly wagged his head. "*El monstruo, el diablo,*" he mumbled.

"Monster? Devil?" What the hell is he talking about?" Dave scoffed. "Methinks Mexicans are just too damned lazy to work. We should've hired whites from the get-go!"

"'Lazy' hell! Goddammit, Dave! He's tryin' to tell you that he saw that fuckin' headless bastard I told you about!"

"Primo!" The worker swiveled his head again and looked at Dave apathetically. "Did you see un *hombre sin cabeza?*" Dave asked in hybrid English-Spanish.

"*El monstruo, el diablo,*" Primo listlessly responded.

"*Donde el monstruo?*" Dave asked.

"*Aqui,*" the Mexican responded with a sweep of his arm. "*En todos lados.*"

"I think it's the tequila talkin'," Dave grunted. "The monster, or whatever it is, is everywhere and nowhere. But, without a crew, we're up shit creek without a paddle." He looked at Ed. "How close are you to havin' the rest of the holes filled in?"

"Just about got 'em wrapped up...only a few left that I can see, anyway. Should be done in the next coupla days."

"Once a Mexican gets a few dollars in his pocket, and a few beers in his belly, he pretty much loses interest in working," Dave complained. "At least until he's broke and thirsty again."

"I guess the good news is they got the Welcome Center pretty much finished before they went AWOL," Ed remarked.

"Yeah, the Welcome Center's not perfect, but it's good enough for the women I date!" Dave laughed.

"We'll just have to find some more broke, thirsty Mexicans." Ed continued. He gestured toward the remaining workman. "Ya think this one can convince some of his buddies to come on board?"

"That depends on how broke and thirsty they are."

Ed looked as though he was about to respond, but paused. He grew somber. "Dave, I don't like to say it, but I don't like the feel of this place. I haven't said much about it to you, but I been thinkin' about it for a while, ever since I saw whatever I saw the other day. I *know* somebody's watchin' us. It's even more than that...sometimes when I put stuff down and come back to it later, it ain't there. Somebody moved it. I'm not kidding, man. And the fact that the Mexicans keep disappearin' ain't right. One or two, maybe, but now seven? What are the odds that *all* of 'em suddenly got tired of working and decided, out of the blue, to hot-foot it out of here? Don't you think it's possible that *something* may actually be cartin' 'em off? Not a 'monster,' but maybe a mountain lion or bear? Why else would they make up stories about it?" He stared contemplatively into the distance. "I hate to say it, but this whole thing is getting' a little too strange for my taste."

"Maybe your crow carried them down into his hole," Dave dryly proposed. Ed looked at him acidly. "Look, either the crew just walked off the job or a monster kidnapped 'em. Which do you really think is the most likely?"

"Obviously, that they walked off the job. But, like you said: why make up stories about getting dragged away if that's not what happened? Primo could have just said that he didn't know what happened to the Mexicans...why invent a story about a monster takin' 'em?"

"You, yourself, said it," Dave explained. "Mexicans would rather climb a tree and lie, than stand on the ground and tell the truth."

Ed slowly shook his head. "I'm not so sure anymore."

NOTWITHSTANDING THEIR BEST EFFORTS, including the promise of unlimited beer, Dave and Ed were unable to recruit replacement workmen. It was as though word had gotten around that working at the site was dangerous, unhealthy, or both. At a subsequent dawn, Primo was not at his customary pick-up spot on the sidewalk in front of a run-down Phoenix grocery store in a predominately Mexican neighborhood.

"Godammit!" Dave spat.   He impatiently pressed the Bakelite button in the center of the truck's steering wheel with the heel of his hand; its raucous horn pealed down the deserted, littered street. "Don't tell me *he* bailed, too!" The two men fidgeted in the idling truck while Dave repeatedly honked its ear-piercing horn. "I can't believe that Spic stiffed us, too," he grumbled.

"Now what?" Ed asked after three minutes of listening to Dave honk the horn.

Dave leaned back into the bench seat in disgust. "Well, there's still plenty of work out there that me and you can still do. It'd be nice to have Mexicans, but I'll be damned if I let their lazy asses torpedo our plans. We'll do our best to replace 'em but, until then, I wanna keep working. We may have to break down and hire some white guys but, like you said, we'll have to pay 'em more."

"If we can't replace the Beans we ain't got a choice," Ed noted.

Dave slid the transmission lever into 'D' and the truck rattled away from the curb.

WHEN THEY BUMPED THEIR WAY into Esperanza over two hours later, it was obvious that someone had been there in their absence.

Dave's delicate theodolite, which he had carefully placed on the Welcome Center's porch before departing the previous evening, lay in pieces in the center of Main Street. Lengths of dynamite fuse had been uncoiled and strung between creosote bushes. The sturdy hickory handles of shovels, rakes, and scythes had been snapped like so many pipe stems and the tools thrown about. Even from the cab of the pickup truck it was apparent that numerous new holes had been dug during the night.

"Mother fuck!" Dave spat in disgust. He threw the transmission lever into 'P' and switched the ignition off. "It's one thing for the Mexicans to walk off the job, but why'd the bastards wreck our stuff?"

"I don't think it was the Mexicans," Ed cautioned. "Nobody, not even a Mexican, would dig holes just for the hell of it."

"Yeah? So who did this? And why? There's nobody here but us!" Dave swung the driver's-side door open and stepped out of the truck, onto the arid soil.

"The thing I saw?" Ed ventured as he exited the opposite side of the vehicle.

"I don't know *what* you saw," Dave responded with disgust. "But why would anybody do this?" He bent to retrieve a piece of the theodolite, which he lovingly placed in the bed of the truck. "Seems to me the *last* thing he'd want would be to call attention to himself."

"I gotta go see if they messed with the dynamite. That shit's expensive," Ed said. "I keep it in one of the old buildings, so they may have overlooked it." He strode away from the truck. "I'll catch up with you at the Welcome Center." Dave continued to recover fragments of the theodolite without responding.

ARRIVING AT THE DILAPIDATED HOVEL where he'd previously cached it, Ed was relieved to find the dynamite unmolested. Using his extended index finger, he counted beneath his breath the remaining boxes. Aside from the lengths they'd seen draped along the bushes, most of the coiled fuse appeared to be there, too, as were the blasting caps. He carefully replaced the warped boards that were formerly propped across the doorless entry and walked over to examine a hole that had not been there the previous day.

Ed estimated the new cavity, which disappeared into the ground at a diagonal, was about eighteen inches in diameter. Curiously, there was no mound of fresh earth piled near its mouth, as he expected would be the case with such a recent excavation. He bent to look into its interior but saw nothing exceptional. Although the familiar nauseating smell radiated from the orifice, it looked like nothing more than the burrow of a fairly large animal.

Ed straightened. If animals kept digging holes as fast as he could dynamite them, he'd *never* get them filled in. His reverie was interrupted when he heard Dave honking the truck horn in the distance.

"Yeah, yeah, keep your shirt on," he grumbled. Casting a final look around the area, Ed headed toward the Welcome Center.

SOMEONE HAD WRAPPED LENGTHS of fuse diagonally, like a barber pole, around the columns that supported the Welcome Center's veranda. Parked before it in the hard-packed dirt, Dave's pickup was unoccupied. Ed glanced into the truck's bed, where fragments of the theodolite remained scattered. He turned away from the vehicle.

"Hey, Dave!" Ed hollered into the already-torrid air. Silence. "Dammit," he muttered to himself. He was inexplicably jittery. "Dave!" he again called.

The odor of decaying meat assailed Ed's nostrils. "Godammit, Dave!" he shouted uneasily, strangely reluctant to leave the vicinity of the pickup. A curious, gurgling sound emanated from an area of the veranda that was obstructed by a corner of the Welcome Center.

"Godammit, Dave!" Ed hollered. "This isn't funny, godammit!" He reached through the open driver's side window and depressed the truck's horn button.

Eliciting no response, Ed moved to the other side of the truck, hoping to identify the source of the singular noise without having to approach the building any closer. The edge of the Welcome Center still blocked his view. He glanced into the bed of the pickup and, among the debris, spotted a splintered shovel handle, about two feet long. As furtively as possible, Ed reached over and began moving aside the pieces of theodolite that lay atop it. Having freed the shovel handle from the surrounding rubbish, he grasped it then quietly stepped away from the vehicle.

Forcing himself to take slow, modulated breaths through his open mouth in order to calm himself, Ed crept toward the Welcome Center, though he feared his palpitating heart would betray him to whoever was on the veranda. His hands trembled and he felt as though he was suffocating. The alien sounds coming from the opposite side of the building continued unabated.

Ed eased one foot onto the first step of the short flight of wooden stairs leading to the porch, where he stopped to listen. Concluding that his presence remained undetected, he slowly began ascending. Upon reaching the porch, Ed paused again to gather his thoughts. He carefully switched hands with the broken shovel handle and wiped his sweaty palm on his trousers.

The incongruous noise abruptly ceased. Ed froze and held his breath. Were he able, he'd have willed his pounding heart to stop hammering in his chest.

The enveloping reek of rotting meat nearly caused him to gag, but Ed remained motionless, gripping the shovel handle until his knuckles grew white.   After what seemed ten minutes, the gurgling resumed.

Ed was about twenty-five feet from the corner of the Welcome Center, beyond which the incongruous noise seemed to originate.   He hazarded a step forward, wincing unconsciously, hoping the boards of the veranda wouldn't squeak beneath his work boots. The porch didn't yield; somewhat emboldened, Ed risked another step, then another, and another, until he was within a few feet of the corner.   Rapidly closing the distance, Ed pressed himself against the Welcome Center's exterior wall, seemingly within a few feet of his goal.

Drawing a series of rapid, shallow breaths through his open mouth, Ed bent and carefully placed his shovel handle on the porch, parallel to the wall. Quietly, almost in slow motion, he then lowered himself onto his hands and knees.

Ed crept forward and, with breathless concentration, slowly peeped around the corner.

About a dozen feet away, Dave's inert body lay on its back in a pool of blood, limbs akimbo and entrails trailing onto the veranda. Hunched over it with its back toward Ed was an animal of uncertain provenance.   Transfixed in stunned horror, Ed watched the creature dip a cloven hoof into Dave's body cavity and withdraw it, dripping with gore. Movement in the adjacent desert lured Ed's eyes away from the appalling spectacle.

Two bearded figures clad in peculiar, blousy uniforms caked with filth stood near the veranda's carved railing. Battered shakos rested on their heads and rusted swords dangled from their cracked leather belts. The men appeared oblivious to Ed. Mouths agape, their attention was dumbly focused on the goat-like creature squatting next to Dave's body on the other side of the balustrade. Despite their seemingly fixated stare, Ed could discern only vacant pink eye sockets beneath the figures' tangled eyebrows. Beyond them in the desert stood the headless being Ed had previously encountered. Like the other two figures, he appeared transfixed. The pervasive nauseating odor of decaying flesh was beginning to sicken Ed, who had to steel himself from simply lunging to his feet and racing away from the Welcome Center.

It was obvious that the four beings, whatever they were and for whatever reason, had killed Dave. Alone, Ed could do nothing to retaliate. He suspended his ragged breathing and began backing away from the corner of the Welcome Center, terrified that his presence was about to be detected. After crawling backwards a yard, Ed slowly got to his feet, convinced that his pounding heart would betray him. He stood, unmoving, and strained to hear any evidence that he'd been discovered. Ed wasn't sure whether he ought to be relieved or horrified when the previous gurgling, lapping sounds resumed.

Ed silently hastened across the veranda and down the short flight of steps to the ground. Glancing back toward the Welcome Center, he was relieved to see no one in pursuit. He ducked behind Dave's pickup to think, panting from terror.

Obviously, no one would believe Ed should he return to town with the wild tale that his partner had been killed and eaten. Odds are, he'd probably be suspected of the crime, or locked up in the crazy house. Under the circumstances, discretion must be the order of the day until Ed figured out what to do. The immediate thing was to ensure that those creatures, whatever they were, were unable to attack anyone else...although Ed was powerless against them alone, he could sure as hell keep them bottled up until he figured out what to do.

Ed carefully stood to confirm that the keys were still in the pickup's ignition. Notwithstanding that starting it would be hazardous, he needed the vehicle to effectuate his plan. Keeping low, he skulked away from the truck, looking back regularly to confirm that he wasn't being followed.

IT TOOK ED TWO TRIPS, and an appreciable portion of the morning, to ferry the necessary supplies back to the truck. It ordinarily would have taken far less time, but he had to be circumspect in order to remain undetected, creeping from building to building and lying in wait until he was satisfied that he remained unobserved. He carefully laid all of his materials in the bed of the truck, confronting none of the monstrous figures he'd encountered earlier in the day.

Following his last trip to the pickup, Ed gently eased open the door and slid into the driver's seat. With the door still open, he reached down to twist the ignition key and was elated when the engine immediately roared to life. Ed slammed the door shut, shoved the transmission lever into 'R,' and stomped on the accelerator. The truck shot backwards as he cranked the steering wheel hard to the left. Ed hit the brake, whipped the transmission lever into 'D,' and goosed the accelerator again. The pickup slewed out of the dirt parking lot in a shower of dirt and rocks.

Ed nervously monitored the truck's rear-view mirror as the vehicle rocketed down Main Street, throwing up clouds of dust. Either because his precipitous flight from the Welcome Center had gone unnoticed, or had been a complete surprise from which they had not yet recovered, no one pursued Ed as he careened out of town. He'd reduce speed only when he passed the old corral on the outskirts of town, where the hills that rose beyond it would force him to slow. Until then, he intended to keep the accelerator mashed to the floorboard.

Rocks spewed from beneath the pickup as Ed barreled away from the Welcome Center. He whipped the steering wheel hard to the right and the truck slid across the rocky soil until its tires regained purchase on the dirt, whereupon it shot forward again. Ed had to grip the steering wheel tightly to avoid being thrown about the cab as the truck plunged ahead, though his head banged repeatedly against the roof of the vehicle as the pickup twisted and bounced over the uneven surface. He was oblivious to it, focused entirely on his headlong exodus.

Reaching the disintegrating corral, Ed gunned the engine and the truck skittered onto the path leading away from town. The constriction he sought was only about a mile and a half up the trail; provided he didn't wreck first, he should get there in only minutes.

ED SLAMMED THE BRAKES on and the pickup slid to a stop in a swirl of dust, which billowed into the cab of the vehicle through its open windows. With his foot on the brake pedal, he turned as best he could on the bench-seat to survey the landscape behind the idling truck. From this point forward, the trail grew increasingly steep and rugged as it began its ascent from the floor of the valley. Though still passable in a vehicle, the route had to be negotiated with care to avoid tumbling into the steep ravine that ran parallel to it. On the opposite side, a beetling precipice loomed over the path. On the trail ahead a switchback loomed between two prominent bluffs.

Finally satisfied that he wasn't being pursued, Ed eased his foot off the brake and the truck began to crawl forward, up the steepening grade. He'd be able to effectuate his plan once he was beyond the switchback.

The pickup lumbered forward, rocks crunching beneath its tires. Ed constantly checked the rear-view mirror to satisfy himself that no one was there. Since encountering the headless specter he'd carried a revolver with him everywhere, though Ed doubted whether it would afford much protection now. Several times while the Welcome Center was being constructed the entire crew had been forced to camp overnight in the town. Though without incident, they'd periodically heard curious sounds in the darkness and smelled the odor of rotting meat. They rationalized it by convincing themselves that the town was simply old and musty. Such things were to be expected. Periodically, tools would also disappear, but Ed endeavored to ascribe it to nothing more than misplacing them, or pilferage by the Mexicans.

The pickup swayed like a ship at sea as Ed wrestled the steering wheel back and forth, negotiating the truck around the largest rocks protruding from the hardpan. He slowed to nearly to a stop when he approached the switchback and torqued the steering wheel hard to the left. The truck inched upward. Stones dislodged beneath the pickup's tire bounced and tumbled into the ravine on Ed's right and the vehicle's fender nearly brushed the cliff on his left. Desiccated sagebrush that grew adjacent to the trail scraped along the sides of the pickup as it crept forward, the noise of its surging engine reverberating off the rock face.

Once beyond the most treacherous section of the incline, Ed drew to a stop. He threw the transmission lever into 'P' and studied his surroundings from the cab of the truck.

He'd already climbed an appreciable distance above the floor of the valley. Looking downward, in the direction of Esperanza, the desert appeared devoid of life: no dust trails announced the presence of pursuers.

Ed finally switched the ignition off and swung the door open. Sliding out, he stepped to the bed of the truck and swiftly began to gather his equipment. Slipping a long coil of fuse over one shoulder, he removed fourteen heavy sticks of dynamite from their wooden crate and carefully placed them in a canvas bag. He shoved a box of blasting caps into the hip pocket of his jeans. Patting his other pocket to insure that he still had his lighter, Ed began trudging back down the path, toward the switchback.

UNLIKE HARD ROCK MINING, WHICH TYPICALLY required drilling equipment in order to bore holes in which to place the dynamite charges, the demolition that Ed had undertaken in Esperanza was much simpler: he had merely to dig a small pit next to the larger hole he wished to backfill and place a quarter stick of dynamite in it. Once detonated, the larger hole would simply collapse on itself from the resulting explosion and displacement of earth. Though the absence of drilling equipment was an impediment to Ed's plan, he wasn't sure he'd have adequate time to utilize it even if he possessed any.

In order to maximize the destructive effect of the dynamite, after attaching a blasting cap to each one Ed crammed the sticks into crevices in the rocky face of the cliff nearest the trail. Linking them together with lengths of fuse, he spliced the resulting tangle onto a single fuse, which he unrolled as he retreated back to the pickup. Laying the remaining spiral of fuse on the ground, Ed climbed into the truck and drove slowly up the trail another 500 feet. He stopped, placed the transmission in 'P', and jumped from the cab. While the pickup idled, Ed raced back down the trail. He bent to retrieve the coil of fuse and quickly fed it out, hand-over-hand, as he walked backwards toward the idling pickup. Its modest burn rate should give him plenty of time to distance himself from the imminent explosion.

Back at the truck, Ed paused. By his estimate, there was easily enough dynamite to cause the entire cliff face to plummet downward onto the trail, completely obliterating it beneath tonnes of rock and soil.

Until he could figure out what to do about Dave's death, he'd at least keep the evil bottled up.

Ed cut the fuse then removed his lighter from the pocket of his jeans. Flicking it open, he spun the tiny corrugated wheel with his thumb and a flame sparked to life. With a trembling hand, he held it against the frayed end of the fuse. After only a moment, it hissed to life.

Ed threw the sizzling fuse to the ground, clambered into the idling vehicle, and shoved the transmission into 'D.' The pickup lurched forward.

After travelling about 100 yards farther up the steep ascent, a searing explosion rent the atmosphere; Ed's eyes flitted to the rearview mirror.

A plume of white smoke boiled skyward, carrying with it a column of dirt, rocks, and scorched brush. The earth beneath the truck shook perceptibly as the ejecta floated languidly in the torrid air. Ed refocused his attention on the trail ahead, anxious to rapidly distance himself from the valley below.

ANNO DOMINI NOSTRI IESU CHRISTO
1826

ESPERANZA WAS VIRTUALLY DESERTED. Aside from a handful of aged peasants too feeble to brave the murderous desert, the remaining inhabitants had already fled or had simply disappeared. Finally weary of caring for them, the townspeople traded the few surviving children left in their care to peripatetic Apaches in exchange for modest quantifies of food: rancid bacon, wormy flour, gritty tortillas. The Indians used these unfortunates as slaves, sexual and otherwise; those that survived ultimately disappeared with their marauding captors into Mexico's *Sierra Madre.*

Juana heard long ago that the *pueblo*, and all of its citizens, actually belonged to a nobleman in *España*, and that the *alcalde* was merely appointed to do the nobleman's bidding. If that were so, where was this supposed nobleman and why had he allowed the *pueblo* to perish? Why had he not marshalled forces sufficient to resist the relentless predations that plagued them? And what of that venal priest, who spent all his time licking the *alcalde's* boots and extorting money from the peasants.

Nothing further had been heard from either the *alcalde* or his sacerdotal toady following their abrupt departure over five months ago. Wherever they ended up, Juana prayed that both of them suffered unending misfortune or, better still, that the Evil One, himself, had seized them during their flight from the *pueblo* and was now subjecting them to ceaseless torments.

More than one resident feverishly claimed to have encountered *Capitán Diego* and his men, dumbly roving the desolate alleys of the *pueblo*, their empty eye sockets focused on nothing. When accosted by name, the soldiers did not respond, but continued their noiseless plodding. No one dared approach the phantoms, for Juana had emphatically pronounced them demons. Anxiously crossing themselves, the pious citizens averted their eyes and retreated to their homes where, accompanied by ardent prayers, they lit their few remaining candles and appealed to the Holy Mother to protect them from evil. Despite such fidelity, stragglers from the community continued to vanish notwithstanding the intercession of the Blessed Virgin.

At Juana's urging, the *pueblo's* few remaining denizens huddled at dusk in the *alcalde's* former quarters. It was far too hot to gather there during the daylight hours, though they lacked sufficient candles to light the interior after darkness fell. It was critical that they make their way back to their individual hovels before the Evil One emerged from the earth to roam Esperanza's barren thoroughfares.

"Our food is gone," Juana announced to the frightened remnants. "If we are to survive we must immediately depart the *pueblo* and cast our lot with our dear Savior and the blessed saints, who will never forsake us. Gather only those foodstuffs as you are able to carry on your backs. We will leave at dawn and walk until we are unable to continue because of the heat. By resting during the day and traveling only by night, we will make our way to another *pueblo*." She paused to survey the hushed assemblage clustered around her.

"Our Savior and his saints abandoned us long ago," a withered old man softly declared. "We do not know the location, or even the direction, of any other *pueblos*. Besides, look around, Juana. We are all old and enfeebled. Attempting to walk from here will prove an impossible task. The *desierto* will consume us as fire consumes dry twigs. It is all the same whether we stay or go...we are all doomed." The remaining citizens were simply too wretched to care anymore, though some of them nodded detachedly.

Juana directed a fiery gaze at the audacious interloper. "God has given you freewill, *Ramón*. You are free to remain in the *pueblo* and, as Xochitl and the others did, barter with the Archfiend for a crust of bread." Her voice became shrill and she extended a quivering finger. "You commit your soul to hell by such infernal bargains! For myself, I choose our blessed Savior over a bowl of soup." She turned to the old man's mute companions.   "I leave here tomorrow. Anyone who wishes to join me must be in front of my *casa* at daybreak. The rest of you should pray for your eternal souls." Juana turned to leave.

"Our souls are already lost," murmured a crone wearing a soiled *mantilla.*

Juana stopped. "Our Dear Savior forgives all who request it."

"Even those who trade their own children to the *Indios* for food?" The old woman shook her head, sadly. "I fear there must a special place in hell for such people, along with cowards, whoremongers, the faithless, the immoral, murderers, idolaters, and liars."

"Do not concern yourself with such trifles," Juana sniffed. "Our Lord provides food, that we may have adequate strength to praise Him, as commanded by Scripture. Who are you to second-guess our Savior about the manner in which he provides for His children? You should remain mindful that God has also reserved a place in hell for the faithless."

"I no longer care," the old woman replied, painfully rubbing her rheumatic joints. "The hell that awaits me can be no worse than the one I currently occupy."

Juana shrugged. "In that case, as Roberto stated, it would appear to matter little whether you join me or remain behind. I must go now, before the creatures of the night emerge from their lairs." Juana stepped to the door; the remaining citizens remained seated on the floor without responding.

"I am glad the shrew is leaving the *pueblo,*" the old woman affirmed after Juana's departure. "She does nothing but scold us for a lack of faith. It is easy to be self-righteous when one's stomach is full."

"Juana felt the pinch of hunger no less than the rest of us," someone corrected her.

"Even so, I am glad she is gone," the old woman reiterated, unrepentant. She was about to continue her denigration of Juana when another woman interrupted her.

"*Cállate!*" she hissed. The others looked on in surprise as the woman stared intently about the room. "Do you not feel that?"

"I feel nothing," a man affirmed, looking to his companions for confirmation.

"You do not feel the walls tremble?" the woman asked in alarm.

"It is merely the rumbling of your empty stomach that you feel," someone suggested.

The woman began to awkwardly clamber to her feet a moment before the room's floor collapsed beneath them.

FORMS GRADUALLY BEGAN TO STIR in the featureless gloom.

"Where am I?" someone called feebly from the blackness. "Is this *purgatorio?*"

"*Nacho?*" stammered a quivering female voice.

"*Marco?*" another pleaded. "Who is here? Where are we? I cannot move; my legs are crushed, I think." Her sobs were intensified by the freezing air.

"*Maria?*" floated an elderly male voice from the emptiness.

A handful of people managed to drag themselves to their feet and sightlessly began to feel their way through the enshrouding murk. In the distance, an anguished scream abruptly tore through the lightless vacuity, followed by incoherent babbling. Then silence.

"Is anyone near me? Please come toward my voice," a man importuned as he vainly groped about.

"I am here, my friend," a peculiar, unctuous voice responded, "as are many of your dear companions. All of us have been eagerly awaiting you."

"Where are you?" the man cried as he frantically swiveled his head in the frosty darkness.

"Your *alcalde* deceived you. The hoard of *conquistadors'* gold that he and his masters in Victoria de Durango made bold to recover was but a laughable delusion. Beguiled by puerile fantasies of endless riches, they gladly discarded their wits," stated the ethereal voice. "Those venal fools have now abandoned you to your fate."

"I am cold and want to return to my *casa*," a woman begged from somewhere in the dark.

"Put yourself at your ease!" the disembodied voice gleefully replied. *Your alcalde* considered all of you nothing more than disposable chattels, strong backs useful only for feeding and clothing him, your daily hardships a source of indifference to him. But your *alcalde's* faithlessness has spun fortune's wheel in your favor, for you now possess genuine value. Having substituted one lord for another, you shall have the honor of nourishing and serving me. Were he here, the *alcalde'* would gladly accept your thanks for imbuing your meaningless lives with such a laudable purpose," the voice mocked.

"Who *are* you?" a man wept in terror.

"Is it not clear who he is?" a woman wailed in the blackness. "He is the one Juana spoke of: the devil, Moloch." The distinct sound of twigs snapping reached the ears of the terrified *peones*.

"He has broken my arms!" the woman shrieked from somewhere nearby. "Please, Blessed Mother, protect me!" A shrill tremolo of her piteous screams rent the air.

"Carmen!" a man screamed as he stumbled blindly in the darkness. "Carmen! Carmen!"

"Yes! Yes! By all means invoke your saints and your relics, your bones and your trinkets!" Moloch crowed. "Though they did not previously deign to succor you, perhaps they will find your present circumstances more deserving of their ministrations!" A loud thud betokened a head forcefully striking the cold floor, whereupon Carmen's screams instantly terminated.

"Your women are old and physically repellant," Moloch apathetically resumed. "Even so, we acquire comparatively few females. Their talents, to the extent they still possess any, will be well utilized."

The doomed peasants broke into poignant weeping, above which Moloch's screeching laughter reverberated.

JUANA ARRANGED MOLDY TORTILLAS, chunks of dried goat meat, and a handful of dried corn in a shawl and wrapped it around her waist. She slung two skins of water over her shoulder and stepped outside, into the half-light that precedes the dawn.

The air temperature was already stifling. In the dimness, Juana impatiently surveyed the desert surrounding her crumbling one-room a*dobe* home. She would not wait, not even a *minuto*, for any of the others to join her. She was, in fact, hoping they were still sleeping, for she had no intention of sharing her provisions with anyone on the trek from Esperanza. She had scarcely enough for herself and, even then, had been forced to loot the communal pantry in order to secure even the modest viands she carried with her. Juana felt not the slightest twinge of guilt for appropriating an appreciable portion of the *pueblo's* food supply, comforting herself with the assurance that the Lord would provide for those who remained behind. Had not the *Baptista* admirably survived on mere locusts and honey during his sojourn in the wilderness? Even so, Juana was pleased not to have been placed in the awkward position of having to explain her actions to the others; they were too simple minded to understand their necessity. No one would even discover the missing foodstuffs until finally dragging themselves from their hovels. By then, Juana would be far away from the doomed *pueblo,* even afoot.

Not having ventured more than a few miles from Esperanza during the past decade, Juana was unsure how many other *pueblos* were in the vicinity, or even in which direction they lay. She could not recall tradesmen ever coming to the *pueblo,* bearing news of other settlements. The occasional hunter, or those who gathered firewood, who traveled greater or lesser distances from Esperanza and managed to survive the inhospitable desert, spoke of nothing but desolation and brutal heat. They made no mention of neighboring communities.

Juana had been told the stony track leading from Esperanza led ultimately to its cemetery, located somewhere in the wasteland, but she had never been there. Why would she bother? Because most of its citizens simply vanished, Esperanza's priest, even prior to his departure from the *pueblo,* was conveniently spared the boorish necessity of conducting funeral masses. The disappearances eliminated the necessity for the remaining inhabitants to undertake the hazardous sojourn to the distant burial ground. With respect to the few natural deaths that actually occurred in the *pueblo*, typically children suffering from fevers, malnutrition, or dysentery, the priest tut-tutted that it would be highly pleasing to God if the earthly remains of such innocents were entrusted to his solicitous care. He would thereupon summarily toss the lifeless bodies into one of the curious holes that punctuated the earth throughout *pueblo*.

Juana had heard rumors that the graves in the distant cemetery were very old and dated from Esperanza's founding. Most, it was said, had been emptied of their quondam tenants long before, though by whom, and for what purpose, none vouchsafed to speculate. No matter: Juana had little doubt that demons feasted on the corpses that once reposed there, the same demons to whom Xochitl and the other fools had mortgaged their eternal salvation. Demons certain to converge inevitably on the remaining inhabitants of the *pueblo*.

Juana tightened the shawl encircling her waist. Glancing furtively about in the quickening dawn, she stepped onto the path leading out of Esperanza. Keeping to the shadows as best she could, she crept noiselessly from the settlement, the cracked soles of her *huaraches* creating tiny puffs of dust as she walked. Though it had confined no horses for several months, Juana would be able to walk as far as the outlying corral before the sleeping *pueblo* even took note of her absence.

She was heedless that the very things she sought to avoid roamed unhindered in the desert beyond the corral.

TWENTY SEVEN

"THAT JEEP'S BEEN PARKED THERE for over a week. It hasn't budged." He pointed through the windshield, into the desert that flashed past the vehicle.

"How do you know?"

'Cause I've been looking, stupid."

The other man scowled. "Maybe it's stolen."

"Yeah, maybe. We should go look at it," he said, hopefully.

"Knock yourself out. I'll pull over for you," his companion grunted. "It's only about 175 degrees out there." He pretended to slow down as he pulled onto the dirt shoulder of McDonald Drive, spewing gravel.

The other man looked at him dubiously. "I'm gonna check it out over the weekend."

His friend swerved back onto the tarmac. "You're nuts. It probably belongs to some rock hound who's out in the fucking desert, looking for whatever rock hounds look for."

"For over a week?"

"What are you, his keeper?"

"Naw, it's just weird. That's all." He turned to look at the receding desert through the vehicle's rear window. "It looks like there's a building, and some other shit, out there, too. That's where it's parked."

"So maybe it's the guy's house. Maybe it's even one of those 'bait cars' that the cops put in mall parking lots, tryin' to get people to steal 'em. Why are you getting your panties in a wad over it?"

"Yeah, they put 'bait cars' out in the middle of the desert because so many car thieves hang out there. Good thinking."

The driver glowered at him and responded by turning the radio up.

THE JEEP HAD OVIOUSLY BEEN PARKED there for days. Its clear plastic windows were unzipped and both the interior and exterior were covered with a blanket of wind-blown dirt. The keys were missing from the ignition.

Jimmy squinted against the harsh sunlight to survey the contiguous desert. Although he wore sunglasses, he shaded his eyes with his hand.

"You think it's stolen?"

Jimmy dropped his hand from his eyes and turned toward his companion. "Well, it's a pretty nice Jeep. I can't imagine why'd somebody'd just leave it out here."

"The battery dead?"

Jimmy reached into the Jeep and depressed the button on the steering wheel. The horn responded with a harsh squawk. "Yep, but it don't take much juice to honk a horn."

"Look in the glove box. See if the registration's there. Maybe the owner got lost in the desert or something."

Jimmy walked around the Jeep and opened the passenger door. He unlatched the diminutive glove box, which fell open with a thud. He rummaged through its contents: an old pair of sunglasses with one ear piece missing, a torn topographical map, various receipts, restaurant coupons, a non-working flash light, a tire pressure gauge. At the bottom, the vehicle's registration and certificate of automobile insurance. His companion watched intently through the open driver's window.

"Here it is," Jimmy announced.

"Who's it belong to?"

Jimmy unfolded the registration and scrutinized it. "Somebody named 'Cameron Wylie.'"

"That the same as on the insurance card?"

Jimmy placed the registration on the dusty passenger seat and retrieved the certificate of insurance from the glove box. "Yeah: Cameron Wylie."

"You think it's stolen?"

Jimmy stuffed everything back into the Jeep's glove box and slammed it shut, thereby disturbing the accumulated dirt and creating whorls of spinning dust inside the vehicle. "I don't know," he said. "But even if it is, it's pretty easy to spot from the road...if the owner reported it stolen, how come it's still here?"

The other man shrugged. "Maybe he got lost in the desert and nobody's missed him yet." He looked around. "This place looks pretty cool. Did you know there was a cemetery back here?"

Jimmy shook his head. "No, but I told you I could see some buildings and stuff from the road."

"Apparently, so could Cameron Wylie." The other man stepped over a strand of rusted barbed wire, into the burial ground. "Maybe he drove back here to check it out?"

"Could be," Jimmy responded. "But what happened to him?"

"I'm gonna check out those tombs. Maybe there's something in 'em." He began striding through the overgrown bushes.

"Yeah, dead people," Jimmy replied, trailing his friend.

"Or Cameron Wylie," the other man laughed over his shoulder.

Jimmy stopped. "Hey," he said, "maybe he went up into those hills." He pointed northward.

His companion turned to look. "Yeah, maybe. But he can't be too smart to have left his Jeep unlocked while he's out farting around in the desert."

"I guess he didn't plan on bein' gone very long," Jimmy remarked.

"GOT A REPORT OF AN ABANDONED vehicle off McDonald." The dispatcher sounded like she was bored to tears as she transmitted the information to any patrol car in the general vicinity.

"Unit 754," crackled a response after a moment. "Where on McDonald?"

"West of Scottsdale Road," she responded. "Unclear how far. The guy who reported it was pretty vague. He said he and a buddy found it abandoned in the desert, next to an old cemetery."

"What 'old cemetery'?" Without waiting for a response, 754 continued. "If it's west of Scottsdale Road it's not in our jurisdiction...probably Paradise Valley or Phoenix, maybe even the rez. But I'll head over in that direction. What's the make?"

The dispatcher consulted the computer screen in front of her. "Yellow Jeep Wrangler, evidently in good shape. I ran the plates the guy gave me and it's clean. Registered owner is somebody named 'Cameron Wylie' who lives in Phoenix. No wants or warrants."

"The guy who found it still there?"

"Negative. He said that because he couldn't get any cell reception, he had to drive 'till he could and didn't want to go back. He said you can see the Jeep in the desert on the north side of McDonald."

"He must have a cheap-ass cell phone. He got a name?"

"Negative. Said the vehicle looked like it had been there a while and thought we should know, but didn't want to get involved otherwise."

"10-4," sighed the cop. "On my way."

"754," INTONED THE COP.

"Go ahead, 754," the dispatcher instructed him.

"Abandoned Jeep off McDonald. Not in Scottsdale's jurisdiction but checked it out, anyway. False alarm. Nobody around and no sign of foul play. Owner probably just out hiking in the desert. Recommend forward info to Phoenix or Paradise Valley PD, or whoever, and they can do what they want with it."

"Which one?"

"Pick one. All I know is that it isn't in our jurisdiction."

"10-4. Was there a cemetery out there?"

"Yeah, an old one out in the middle of nowhere. I didn't even know it was there. Looks like it hadn't been used in forever."

"10-4. Out."

The cop replaced the handset on the radio and glanced at his watch. Lunch time.

TWENTY EIGHT

IN THE STILLNESS, NANCY THOUGHT SHE could discern elusive, faraway sobbing. She was engulfed in illimitable darkness, so intense as to be almost unbearable. The air temperature was near freezing and she shivered uncontrollably.

"Woody? Cam?" she cried into the emptiness. Her voice was absorbed by the blackness.

Cautiously, Nancy extended her hands into the glacial void. Encountering nothing, she took a tentative step forward and immediately stumbled. Though knowing it a futile gesture, she opened her eyes as wide as possible in a fruitless effort to capture any ambient light, and reached down to touch the offending obstacle. Her exploring fingertips encountered an undulating expanse of irregular, dome-shaped objects. Wresting one loose, she straightened and held it near her face. It smelled musty, deathlike.

Nancy turned away in revulsion and, with quivering finger tips, began the sightless exploration of the object's curved surface. Even in her blindness, she immediately realized that it was a human skull, patches of hair still clinging to its cranial vault.

Nancy flung the grisly relic aside. "Where am I?" she shrieked into the icy desolation. "Woody! Cam! Where are you?"

"They are here, with innumerable others." The disembodied response floated from the blackness. It was the same rasping voice as that of the creature she, Moe, and Cameron had previously encountered in the charnel house.

"Where the fuck are you, you bastard?" Nancy challenged as she vainly strained her eyes into the darkness.

"We have far too long been denied the society of a desirable female," the creature laughed derisively. "And you are a very beautiful young woman, a true *rara avis*. You should be flattered to learn that, even from the beginning, it proved necessary to cast lots in order to determine who among us would be the first to enjoy you." From the gloom, he extended a cadaverous hand to cup one of Nancy's breasts through her blouse. She slapped it away in disgust and stumbled backward in the blackness. The gelid air was thick with the nauseating fetor of decaying flesh.

"Get away from me, damn you!" she spat.

Moloch howled with mirth. "You should be very glad that it was I whom fate decreed should be the first to enjoy your favors. I fear that, once the rest avail themselves of your charms, but little of them will remain."

"Where are my friends?" Nancy demanded, angry and terrified in equal measure.

"I already told you. Both are nearby and well," the creature responded. "You need not concern yourself with them."

"I want them here, with me."

Moloch smiled in the blackness. "'I am with you always, even unto the end of time.' Is that not what your feckless Matthew promised?" A pause. "Welcome home."

THE END

TERMS OF USE

This is a copyrighted work and WF Waldrip and his licensors reserve all rights in and to the work. Use of this work is subject to these terms. Except as permitted under the Copyright Act of 1976 and the right to store and retrieve one copy of the work, you may not decompile, disassemble, reverse engineer, reproduce, modify, create derivative works based upon, transmit, distribute, disseminate, sell, publish or sublicense the work or any part of it without WF Waldrip's prior consent. You may use the work for your own noncommercial and personal use; any other use of the work is strictly prohibited. Your right to use the work may be terminated if you fail to comply with these terms.

THE WORK IS PROVIDED "AS IS." WF WALDRIP AND ITS LICENSORS MAKE NO GUARANTEES OR WARRANTIES AS TO THE ACCURACY, ADEQUACY OR COMPLETENESS OF OR RESULTS TO BE OBTAINED FROM USING THE WORK, INCLUDING ANY INFORMATION THAT CAN BE ACCESSED THROUGH THE WORK VIA HYPERLINK OR OTHERWISE, AND EXPRESSLY DISCLAIM ANY WARRANTY, EXPRESS OR IMPLIED,
INCLUDING BUT NOT LIMITED TO IMPLIED WARRANTIES OF MERCHANTABILITY OR FITNESS FOR A PARTICULAR PURPOSE.

WF Waldrip and his licensors do not warrant or guarantee that the functions contained in the work will meet your requirements or that its operation will be uninterrupted or error free. Neither WF Waldrip nor his licensors shall be liable to you or anyone else for any inaccuracy, error or omission, regardless of cause, in the work or for any damages resulting therefrom. WF Waldrip has no responsibility for the content of any information accessed through the work. Under no circumstances shall WF Waldrip and/or his licensors be liable for any indirect, incidental, special, punitive, consequential or similar damages that result from the use of or inability to use the work, even if any of them has been advised of the possibility of such damages. This limitation of liability shall apply to any claim or cause whatsoever whether such claim or cause arises in contract, tort or otherwise.

The author gratefully acknowledges the copyrighted or trademarked status and trademark owners of the following, mentioned in this work of fiction: A-1 Beer; Bakelite; Band Aid; Bonanza; Cinderella's Castle; Coke; Coke Zero; Colt Python; Craigslist: Dairy Queen; Diet Coke; Dilly Bar; Disneyland; Ford Mustang; Google; Google Earth; Gunsmoke; Have Gun, Will Travel; Hells Angels; Jeep; Kleenex; Kreskin's ESP; Lucky Strike; Milk Bone; Ouija; Oompa Loompa; Post-It Notes; Rolex; TEAC; Walther P22; Winchester; Wrangler; Zippo

Manuscript line edited, copy edited and prepared for publication by Maurice R. Azurdia.

Maps designed by Maurice Azurdia.

Cover design by WF Waldrip.

Also available from

WF Waldrip

⭐⭐⭐⭐⭐ **great novel!**

What a wonderful novel! The author drew very vivid pictures of the characters and events. What a riveting book! A fascinating read !

Published on June 3, 2014 by Vincent R. Mayr

Find more at www.amazon.com

Also available from

WF Waldrip

⭐⭐⭐⭐⭐ **An Excellant Sequel**

By michael caburis on October 12, 2014

Format: Kindle Edition   Verified Purchase

A riviting sequel to The Guards Themselves .
i hope another by the author is forthcoming
WF Waldrip is a must read author

Find more at www.amazon.com

ABOUT THE AUTHOR

WF Waldrip ——————

WF Waldrip is a widely traveled author, native of Arizona.

His writing style is true to life, bypassing the 'Politically Correct."

The Float is his third novel.